W9-BGR-658

1

I really loved Roxie's Angels. The book grabbed me from the very beginning and it was alternately funny, sad, charming and just a darn good read. My daughter and I read it together. We laughed at her exploits that got her into trouble, and we cried at the tragedies she endured. Read Roxie's story. You will never look at lemons again without seeing a great big, ice cold pitcher of lemonade on a lovely summer evening.

Angela Batts

Mrs. Lee, I really liked reading about the horses, Roxie's life and the ranch. Someday I want to be a writer just like you.

Kylie Burdette, age 9

Loved the book. Fell head over heels for Roxie.

I laughed when she got herself into trouble. I cried when she lost her beloved El Con.

I hope you are writing a second book. I want to read more of her exploits and experiences.

Morgan Henderson, age 16

Roxie is an inspiration for anybody. She makes me want to make the world a better place. I would love to have a friend just like Roxie. I ride too.

It was really interesting to me to see the differences in what life was like back in the fifties and see how much is still the same today.

El Con was just as real to me as my own cow pony. And his last days and his funeral were so vivid. I was there. Please write a whole book about this magnificent animal.

Bobby Gomez, age 18

ISBN: 978-0-557-48484-3

Roxie's Angels

This Book is dedicated to

the memory

of all   of MY ANGEL CREW

My Father, Harry Belk Worden,

My birth mother, Nanette Lee Hallman

My incredible, wonderful, beautiful real sister Maureen

My charming, funny, handsome brother, Wes

Those real people who are represented by fictional names

Past, Present and Future

My children

Grandchildren

and

Great-Grandchildren

And to all of the adopted children who must take that scary, arduous journey to find birth parents and the story of their past.

We all part and parcel of what came before, how we are nurtured and those who interact with us.

I am an avid proponent of adoption. I had three and adopted three.   They are all my children. Love is earned as well as being a birthright.

I am one of the lucky ones.   I had a birth mother who chose to give me a better life. I will be grateful to her for this sacrifice for the rest of my life.

I was also very fortunate in that I met my birthmother a ten and again at almost sixteen.

I have an incredible, wonderful, amazing relationship with my sister, Maureen, my mother's other daughter.   Together we have learned about our grandmother's life in Hollywood working for MGM and we have been able to research the family back generations.

I met my birth father at the age of eighteen.   Sadly I was not to get to know him very well, but I have a fantastic, rewarding relationship with my brother and all of the other relatives from that side of my heritage. Because of my brother, Wes, I was able to research the family back to the 1840s.

My father taught me two lessons about two old common adages. He showed me the truth in both of them.

1.   When Life gives you lemons, make the best lemonade anybody has ever tasted.

2.   What does not kill you, makes you strong.

Well, Dad, I learned my lessons.

A very special thanks to Mr. Fred Becchetti, my English teacher from high school who began my writing journey, and my passion for great literature.

His help putting the final polish on the book was invaluable. He is still correcting my spelling, my syntax and my grammar.

It was the best of times, it was the worst of times.

Charles Dickens

March 12

I know, I know, Dickens wrote that first that but it sure feels like my life. Great times, really crappy times. I want to be able to write about the good and the bad. I have been writing bits and pieces for a long time. Hang on, my Dear Diary, it is going to be a bumpy ride!

The best of times? I have a great life growing up on a ranch, great dad, good times. The worst of times? I have an adoptive mother who is legally insane who has "little episodes" that frequently land me in the hospital, but my Dad does not seem to get that she is never going to be normal or get better. I don't really know what legally insane means.

She never says crappy things to me when Dad is around and she never hurts me if anybody else is at home. So I know that she can control what she says and does. She never does anything bad around an adult. Just around Brenda or the maids. And they are so afraid of her that they never say anything.

Today was my thirteenth birthday and Dad gave me this incredibly beautiful, leather bound book, with lovely empty, pristine pages. My dad knows how much I like to write and he thought this would be a good place for me to put my private thoughts and feelings. I guess Dad thought it was time for me to put up or shut up. And anybody who knows me, knows I can't shut up. So here goes. Whatever I think, or feel or what happens, I am going to write about it.

I guess I could say it is the most fascinating of times, and it is the most boring of times. That is probably true of everybody's life. But because it is my life, I think it is fascinating. Dear Diary, at least you can't argue with me. So sit back and enjoy the ride. Because I am going to tell it, warts and all.

Dad kept a diary/journal all through his college years and he gave it to me to read last year. I loved reading about that time and how different his life was compared to mine. So I see that I will have to explain many things in case I ever decide to show this book of "me" to my future children. Who knows where I will be living or what kind of life I will have. Dad said that he would have never guessed that he would be living in Arizona and living on a ranch. He grew up in England, went to college there and did not move to America until he was in his twenties. So I can see that the future can be very different from what we plan. I know this will be more journal than diary but Dear Diary sounds better.

A journal sounds kind of formal and this is not going to be formal, not by a long shot. I also like "Dear Reader" but that is so "old writing" style back to the writers of the 1850s. And these are the 1950s. I am definitely a modern 50s girl. OK, so I am an old fashioned, modern girl. So, you be the judge!

Dear Diary,. I am a thirteen year old girl who is a ninth grader. The reason that I am only thirteen is because I skipped two grades. I skipped fourth grade when I was in private school in Tucson and then I skipped seventh grade here in Cochise. I don't have any brothers or sisters that I live with. I have a half-sister who lives in California but she is only six. I live in two different houses. I live on a ranch with my dad, our horses, scads of cattle, the people who work on our ranch, and my other animals.

Then sometimes I also have to live in our house in Cochise. Cochise is a really small town in Southern Arizona. We moved here from Tucson five years ago. The town has about 1500 people. Everybody knows everybody's business. Dad says that the main occupation in town is to mind other people's business and forget to take care of their own business.

I like the town, but I don't like to have to stay in the house in town. Dear Diary, why, you ask? Because my adoptive mother lives in the house in town because she hates the ranch. I call the house in Cochise "The House of Ida".   Ida hates cows, she hates horses, she hate cactus she hates every thing about the ranch, but mostly she hates me. She constantly says that she got stuck with me .

Dad says I have to go into town sometimes because he is convinced that if Ida and I spend time together we will begin to bond.   It has been eleven years and we have not bonded yet. Obviously Dad is a cockeyed optimist. He says that maybe someday we can get along. Fat chance! She just screams at me and she throws things at me. She also hits me when ever she feels like it. I try to tell Dad but he says that I just have to stay out of her way. Sometimes I think that he just convinces himself that he does not see her do it, somehow it is not real. Ergo, I get to go to the House of Ida every time the mood strikes her.   Lucky for me, she does not like to be around me any more than I like to be around her.

But at least most of my time is spent here on our wonderful TriangleR. It stands for Dad's nickname which is Red. His hair used to be very red but now it is a lighter red and he has a lot of silver at his temples and even through some of his hair. I also tease him because he has a nice little bald spot on the top of his head so he always wears his Stetson hat when he is outdoors. His real name is Harrison Rayburn. My name is Roxanna. Get it? The three Rs.   Red plus Rayburn plus Roxanna.   And here is a coincidence for you! The ranch was called TriangleR when Dad bought it. But I don't know what the three Rs stood for then. Joe, the ranch foreman, said that it had been called that as long as he could remember.

Most people call me Roxie but that is not the name I was born with. That name was Deirdre Maura Antoinette. A lotta name huh?. I do not know what last name I was born with. My dad changed it to Roxanna Rayburn when I was adopted at eighteen months old. I like the name Roxie. My middle name is Annalise which was my grandmother's name.

Dad and I went over to Fry's house because Cora gave a birthday party for Jack and me because my birthday was today and Jack's is tomorrow. I spend a lot of my time at the Fry's. Cora, the mom has worked for our family since we moved to Cochise. Jack, Cora's, husband does odd jobs for us too, as well as their sons. Buddy, who is twenty-two, Booth is nineteen, Brahm is fifteen and Brenda is Eight, all B names. I wonder why people do that?

Anyway, Cora is a nurse and she takes care of Ida, my adoptive mother. Ida's real name is IdaGladys. It is all one name. It is a German name and Ida is pure German. Cora helps take care of her when she is sick which she is a lot of the time. She has a heart condition, diabetes, arthritis and other ailments. She is in and out of our local hospital.

Cora also works at Harlan's hospital and then comes to the Cochise House when Ida needs her or helps take care of her when she is at Harlan's. Dad says it is because of how sick she is but I think it has more to do with the fact that the other nurses do not want to deal with Ida.

I know Ida is sick but she really takes advantage of it and uses it to get her way. Dad said one time that she has "mental issues" that are not her fault. That is a load of "you know what", Ida is just mean and hurtful. I know that everybody is afraid of her and they only deal with her because they really like and respect Dad.

The hospital is named Cochise Hospital but everybody calls it Harlan's for Doc Harlan. It is an eight bed hospital. Some have rooms two beds and some just have one bed. Ida is always in a one-bed room because she does not like to be with anybody else and I can't imagine anybody having to be in the same room with her. That person would just get sicker because she is not pleasant to be around. Hey, this is my diary so I can say what I want. Ida is just plain crazy and evil.

Doc Harlan is a paraplegic because he got hurt in an accident when he went to a wreck on Highway 87. A man had gone off a big drop-off and the car was way down at the bottom of a very steep ravine. As Doc came to the scene, somebody was trying to see the wreck and that man in that car ran into Doc Harlan's ambulance and he went over the side too. Doc still drives his own ambulance it is fixed up with special equipment so that he can. The really sad

13

part is that the first guy in the car that went over was already dead, and Doc wound up being paralyzed by the guy who was rubber necking to see the first wreck. He could use his arms but not his legs. That happened when I was about ten. I remember Dad getting real upset about it. He and Doc are very good friends. They play poker every week with the sheriff and the Justice of the Peace for Cochise and some other cronies.

I really like Doc. Some people don't. They say he changed after the wreck. Well, wouldn't anybody? I can't imagine what it would be like to be in a wheel chair for life. I had to be in one for a few months when I fell down the side of a rock bridge and broke both of my hips. I spent three months in the hospital.

Just like most of the things in my life it was both a good and bad experience. Seems funny to think that there was anything good about staying in a hospital for almost three months, but now when I look back on this experience, some of it was very good.

I think what helps make it good was that I like Doc and he seems to like me. He says that he likes the way I always want to know about everything and he thinks I am really funny. He was the first person to say I had a finely developed sense of the absurd. I had to ask him what that meant. He said it meant that somebody has the ability to see how people do really weird things and some people can see how funny this is.

It started out to be a great day. It was the last day of school and the day after I had graduated from eighth grade. We had already had a party out at the Tri-R but we all wanted to have a big all-out-fun picnic out at Texas Canyon. Texas Canyon is where a glacier finally melted and left giant rocks and boulders in the middle of a desert area. I have no idea why somebody named it Texas Canyon when it is in Arizona.

There is a big natural clearing that has a border of giant rocks that make a big circle. So over time, people have created areas to do different activities. The middle has a picnic area that has fire-pits and some of the barrel type barbeque pits. There is a big open area where guys can play baseball or horseshoes. And people can go hiking or rock climbing or just sit and do nothing in the picnic area. The whole school was invited, not just the kids who had graduated. So Brahm was there too with a bunch of his buddies. There were probably more than one hundred high school kids which would be about half of our high school plus thirty or so of the eighth graders.

Lots of food, lots of fun. After lunch Brahm said he and his buddies were going over to the Natural Bridge to go climbing. I asked him if I could go along but he said, "You can't go because you have on cowboy boots and you need climbing boots." I said, "Well, I could borrow some climbing boots." Brahm said with great exasperation, "Nobody wants you to come with us. You can't do what we are going to do." And the little band of merry men walked off leaving me standing in the middle of the clearing feeling like a fool in front of my friends .

The Natural Bridge is a big, huge rock formation that is made of two huge slabs of granite stone. One boulder that sits on top of another rock that is even bigger. There is a big gap under the top rock and it makes it look like a bridge. Dad said later that he thinks to the top rock which slants down at a sharp angle, is about a hundred feet across. You reach the top of the "bridge" part by climbing on the adjacent rocks that get to the top of this formation. There is a place to sit at the top but that is all you can do because there is nowhere to hold onto or places to put your feet. To get down, the climber has to go back the way the climber came up. I had never been to the top before so I thought I would try to find them or try it by myself. Here is a good place to say that I clearly had not thought my way though this situation. I did not plan to go down the wrong way.

After about fifteen minutes I was pretty mad at Brahm and I still had not found them. When I got to the Bridge Rock, nobody was there. I guess they had gone somewhere else. So I climbed up to the top of where the top rock begins to slant down and I managed to get myself on the very top of it. I wanted Brahm to see me at the top if he and his guys showed up. Then I heard voices and here they came.

Brahm started yelling at me to get down. He started up, I guess to get me. So I started to turn around to get down from there but I started slipping. Instead of getting down on the side that I came up on, I started going down the bridge part and I just kept going down. I tried to hold on but there was nothing to hold onto but just solid rock. It seemed to take forever. And then I hit the bottom, and I mean hit. It knocked my breath out. It was worse than any time I had been thrown from El Con or Lizzie.   I really was in pain and I knew it was bad.

I could hear Brahm yelling to see if I was OK but I couldn't even answer. I looked up and I could see him at the top and he was yelling that he would be there and "Just wait!"   I remember thinking, well, where does he think I am going to go? My second thought was that I did not know how he was going to get to where I was.

He was just sitting at the top. Then he yelled down, "Just hang in there, Roxie, the guys have gone for rope." I tried to yell an answer but it hurt too much to talk. I didn't know what good a rope would do because I knew I couldn't hold onto a rope to get out. A little while later I saw Brahm coming down the rock. He had a rope tied around him and he was kinda walking down the rock on the rope. The guys at the top were holding on to the other end of the rope.

Brahm finally got down and he said "Get up and the guys will pull you up." I tried to get up and the pain was so bad I screamed. Brahm yelled up and said. "This is not going to work. We are going to have to do something else." So Brahm stayed with me. In a little while. two firemen started coming down.

Cochise has a volunteer fire department. And there were more of them at the top. They had a bed-like carrier that was coming down by rope too. They got down, and one of. the guys began to check me out and said, "I think she has broken bones." He looked at my hands that were all bloody and he wrapped them up in some gauze stuff and then said. "We are going to have to get her flat to pick her up."

Somehow with me doing a lot of screaming and yelling, and I admit, a little name calling, they got me flat onto some boards that were inside the bed thing. They were working a space that was only a few feet wide and not very much longer. They had told Brahm to go on up to get out of the way.

There is a lot of that part I do not remember. I remember being about half way up in the bed thing with ropes tied all around it and guys pulling from the top.

When we got up there everybody was all gathered around and I remember crying because I was embarrassed that I had done something so stupid. Then they carried me to the clearing and I saw Doc's ambulance and he was behind the wheel. They put me in the back still in the bed thing and Brahm went too.

I don't remember anything else until I woke up in a hospital bed and I had this huge cast that went around my middle under my waist and just to the end of my back side.

Boy, did I hurt. My hands were all bandaged and one foot had a cast on it. It turned out that I had broken both of my hip bones, shattered my arch on my left foot and a branch of something had gone into the top of my ankle. All of the tips of my fingers were damaged. Doc said I "sanded" them off to the bone while I was trying to hold on to the rock.

So basically I was a mess. Doc said I was "Darn lucky to be alive." I told him that I could not sleep because of the cast and he said he would fix it. He called Cora and they got a bunch of pads and rigged it up so that the pads were above and below the cast. That helped because it kind of leveled me out.

16

For a couple days, I was a soggy, whinny mess. Then Doc came in and said to stop being Miss Weepy Willow. I asked "Why? And he said "Because you are getting on my nerves. You did something stupid and it could have ended a lot worse. So stop! When you get a little better you can help me with some things. You can also help Cora." I was so excited I couldn't stand it. Seemed like a really good deal to me.

Doc had them rig up a thing that looked like a trapeze over the top of the bed and I could use it to pull myself into a wheel chair so I could get around the hospital. He did not want me to walk for at least a couple of months and maybe more. He told me that he had the same thing rigged up for him to get in and out of his wheel chair. He even uses a rig that is similar to get in and out of the ambulance. So we became chair buddies.

During the time that I was in the hospital, Doc would either come by my room or call me and tell me to go to one of the rooms in the hospital. I saw babies be born (seven of them including one pair of twins), and I saw him do several operations. He would make me wash up and put on a mask and I would sit where I was not in the way and get to watch everything.

One day he came wheeling by my room and he yelled as he sailed past to go to the Dead Room. Yes, that is what he calls it! It is where dead people are cut up to see why the died. So I pulled and jerked and got my self dropped into my chair and wheeled myself down the hallway to the back of the hospital where he was. As I came through the door, I saw a man laid out on the long, silver, metal table. His top was naked and he had a sheet across his middle. Doc said, "OK, Roxie, I am going to fix it so that you will never smoke." I looked at Doc and said "I really had not planned on smoking and how is a dead guy going to fix that?" and Doc said, "You'll see." He told me pull my chair right next to him.

All of the operating tables and other stuff had been fixed so that it was the right height for Doc to be able to work.

He started cutting and then turned to me and said, "Are you OK?" I said, I was and he said, "I knew you would be fine, my Little Sidekick!". He cut the man's chest open and into the stomach area. Then he used a tool to make the ribs come apart. And he started taking out organs. When he got to the lungs, he took one out and he said, "Now watch." He sliced it open and then he started scraping black stuff off the skin part. He said "This is what your lungs look like if you smoke for years."

"Now go to my office and get a big book off the self that is called <u>Grey's Anatomy</u> and bring it back here." So I wheeled down to his office, found the book, a really big one, and brought it back. He opened it to a page that showed lungs. He said this is what your lungs look like when you do not smoke. I said, "That is what lungs look like when we butcher." Doc said, "Right, an animal has good lungs unless it has a disease." Then he asked me if I thought I would ever smoke. I said, "Well, not after that." Then I asked Doc if Dad's lungs look like the dead guy's. He said he thought they did and possibly worse because of how long Dad has smoked. I asked him if it can be fixed and he said that right now they can't. I asked him if Dad stopped smoking would it help and he said he did not know.

Later on during one of his visits to the hospital to see me, I talked to Dad and tried to get him to stop smoking. Dad said he could not stop because it was one of his pleasures in life. He did not drink or have other vices.

He really does have another vice, but it is a funny one. He cusses like a drunken trail driver on the Abilene Trail. He uses really bad words but he uses them in a hilarious way. He puts the words together that nobody else uses together. Most of the time he is a very dignified man but get him mad and he really gets going. It is funny as long as he is not mad at me.

One time I cut my finger with a cake knife when I was helping Marta clear the table, I was nine or ten. Dad rushed me over to Doc Harlan's and while he was sewing up my finger, I said a few words to Doc. Dad was shocked and said, "Where did you learn to talk like that?" Doc and I just looked at him. He still did not get it and Doc just laughed like crazy and said "Oh, Harrison, where do you think she gets it?"

Unfortunately, Dad smokes all the time. He smokes cigarettes, cigars and sometimes a pipe. I like the smell of the pipe but not the other stuff. The cigarettes and cigars give me a headache and make my eyes run. Especially when I am in the car with Dad. I always have to have the window down. I think I am allergic to everything.

The good part of my accident was that while I spent the time in the hospital with Doc and I learned a lot of things about my self. I know I never want to take care of sick people, and certainly not dead people!

My hips are fine now. Doc told me I have to be careful riding so I don't re-break anything but I am not worried about that. My foot hurts sometimes when I ride for a long time. I have a great big scar where the branch went in. And Doc says my fingerprints are not as clear and when my fingers healed they will have very faint scar tissue.

Dad came to visit all the time and we played cards and we read to each other and other stuff. I even got to play poker with

Dad and his cronies. And that was really fun. All of my friends came to visit and even some of my teachers. Doc let Lana stay overnight many times. She slept in the other bed and we had a lot of fun zipping all over the hospital and pretending we were doctors, nurses and patients.

The bad part was that I did not get to ride all summer and I really missed the ranch, Joe, El Con, and Lizzie.

The reason I was at Harlan's for the whole summer was because Ida did not want to take care of me. Lucky me. I guess you could say that was a good part. Dad was afraid that if I went back to the ranch I would try to ride too soon.

Ever since we moved here, Ida has been in and out of Doc Harlan's and two different hospitals in Tucson. Sometimes she is really sick and sometimes it seems like she just wants to go to the Center in Tucson.

They call it Saguaro Gardens Rehabilitation Center. But it is like a vacation place. Instead of rooms there are small individual "houses" with a bedroom, a sitting place, a tiny little kitchen and a bathroom. And the Center has everything. Tennis, a golf course, swimming pool and a rec room. When dad and I go over to visit her when she is there, he just tells me to go off and do something and I do. That is where I learned to play tennis. They have a guy whose job it is to just teach tennis.

When I was in the fifth grade she stayed there for a whole year until about halfway through the next year. And then she was there for a couple of months during my eighth grade. She was there for over half of the beginning of this year. But the really bad part is that Dad says it is really expensive for him when she is there.

I don't know how much it is but it must be a lot because he normally never complains about money most of the time. But one time he said that it was cheaper when she was in Harlan's than when she went to the Center. So then I feel guilty because life is so much easier for me when she is in Tucson. I do know that she has had to go into the center several times when she has hurt me physically. I just wish Dad knew that it is just as hurtful when she says the awful stuff when she gets into her rants.

When she is away I don't have to go into the House of Ida or have to listen to her do her "rant du jour". Don't you love that phrase? Means something that happens every day or "of the day". Mrs. Mason says that about our vocabulary lists. Here is the "list du Jour". I plan to take French in college because they don't have it in our school, only Spanish.

There is so much stuff in the news about the Soviet Union. Dad said that it is called a cold war because nobody has declared war but both sides are trying to out-do the other with weapons and armies. Joseph Stalin just died. Dad said it will be interesting how things will change and who will take over.

March 13

School was fun today. Mrs. Mason read a poem by Richard Wright. It is so good. I want to see if I can find more of his poems at the library. I never thought about what it must be like to be a negro but his poem makes you think about how people of all different cultures are treated.

Ida hates everyone who is not like people like her. Dad is not that way, I have never heard Dad make mean remarks about anybody unless they earned it. Ida uses all kinds of names about people that are really hateful.

When I was younger, kids used to tease me about being adopted. So I sort of understand what it is like to have a label stuck on you. People are what people are. One of the things that I really love about Dad is that he proves everyday that he judges people by what is on the inside. Well, with one exception, and we know whot that exception is, don't we, Dear Diary?

After school I did my chores. I did a super-duper grooming and I gave both a special message. I muck almost everyday. I have two horses, one is a beautiful palomino gelding who is part quarter horse and part Arabian. Joe says he has the quarter horse butt. His name is El Conquistador but I call him El Con for short. He is 15.2 hands.

I have a mare named Tin Lizzie. She is pure Arabian. Her coat is auburn bay with all black points. That means she has black ears, muzzle and has a black mane and tail. She is 14.5 hands. A hand is a measurement for horses. Each hand is four inches. I think it is tradition that horses are measured this way and it goes way back in time according to what Joe says.

El has a blaze face but Lizzie just has a snip of color on her face. Her muzzle has this small white marking. I love both of their faces and I love their muzzles because they feel just like velvet. And their lips are so soft and they tickle when they are doing that silly horse thing of nuzzling. They do a muzzle nuzzle! That would make a funny name for my next horse. HA!

Joe's horse, Topper, is a flaxen chestnut appaloosa. He is really gorgeous. He is a15.1 gelding, his mane and tail are a pale cream. His back in is speckled with the wonderful AP spots.

20

If I ever get another horse it is definitely going to be an AP. I saw a strawberry AP colt over at the Tucson arena that I almost asked Dad to look at but I think I probably have too much to do now.

By the way, Dear Diary, the reason that I explain everything is because Mrs. Mason says that when you write you have to assume that the reader may not know everything about the topic that you are writing about. I know that this is supposed to be a diary but I plan to have Mrs. Mason read it because she likes to read what I write and it helps me when she does read everything. I like to write for so many reasons. I think I understand a problem so much better after I have written about it.

Someday I might ask Dad to read this. It might help him understand some things that I have not been able to talk to him about. But right now I am not ready to have him or Mrs. Mason read anything.

The other good part about this being a diary "of thoughts and memories" is that I do not have to worry about the writing. It is just what comes out as I think about my day or have a memory about something. Mrs. Mason calls it "raw writing".

The other day in class she said in front of everybody that she loved a short story that I had turned in for an assignment. That I used words to create a picture. That was really wonderful. It was a story about Pudgy, my dog who just died a little while ago. Still pretty fresh so it still hurts.

Dad, Joe and I had a burial ceremony for him and we buried him by my favorite spot on the ranch. I go out and put a flower on his little spot every time El Con and I ride out. Just one flower. A white carnation that I get from our florist in town and I can keep a vase of them in the fridge. It is from Dad and me.

Joe is the head wrangler (foreman) on the TriR. He is a great guy who teaches me about riding and about horse anatomy and care and he is helping me to get better at barrel.

I love barrel racing and I hope I am getting better. But I can't spend all my time riding barrel because I have to do chores on the ranch. Dad says it is important that people earn what they get. So I ride fence and do other chores.

Oh, Dear Diary, Here is an explanation of what "riding fence" is. It is when a ranch worker rides next to all the fence that surrounds the ranch. You have to look for broken barbed wire or downed posts to make sure that the cattle do not get out. Dad says that the fence is there not only to keep cattle and horses in but also to keep

21

people from driving across the property but people still do it anyway. And there's a lotta fence that goes around the Tri-R.

I like to ride fence because it is a way to be by myself and spend the day with El Con and I know he likes it too. Sometimes I can even do the two things I love best, read and ride. I just prop my book up on the saddle horn and read. Joe says that would give him a headache. Unless it is too hot or too cold, I ride fence at least once a week, usually on the weekend or if I have a day off from school.

I have to muck, usually everyday, but I really don't mind doing it. I will explain what mucking is. It is when I shovel out all of the old hay and horse droppings and other yucky stuff, and then put in new hay. I need a shovel, a rake, a wheelbarrow and a broom. I usually do it before school but sometimes when it is really cold Joe does it for me and then I try to do a chore for him later. Anyway, I take out all the old hay and stack it in the wheelbarrow. It is done everyday to keep the horses clean and healthy.

I wish I had a nickel for every time I have spilled the wheelbarrow or fallen into it and that is not fun. Guess what is usually right on top? Yeah, right! Horse poop. I wear rubber boots because I learned very quickly that it was a great idea to wear something over my clothes. Dad got me a yellow, plastic raincoat that I put it on before I push the wheelbarrow to the garbage wagon. So now if I fall in I can just go get the hose and woosh! I get most of it is off! Joe says that walking in horse poop is lucky and that I must be very lucky because I am always walking in it. He says cow people just scrape off what they can and go about their business. But I have to get it all off so sometimes Joe calls me a dandy.

There is a ravine that is pretty deep that is where we dump garbage. We haul it in a small garbage wagon which is a 4X8 trailer bed that we pull behind a ranch truck. I have only jackknifed it once and it was not that bad a dent. We have been hauling everything to this dumping pit for years but it never seems to get any fuller. I guess it packs down and I think animals take some of it. It doesn't even smell that bad because the heat really seems to bake the heck out of everything.

You'd think I wouldn't like to muck, ride fence and haul garbage but I do. I just hate housework when it is somebody else's mess. By housework I mean washing clothes, ironing, doing dishes, cleaning bathrooms, scrubbing floors. I don't know how women do that if it is all they do. I know a lot of mothers who don't seem to do anything but take care of their family. And that part is good, but don't they want to do something out in the world? Create something or learn things or be really good at something? I have been thinking a lot about this lately.

I have been thinking that I have to have a plan for my life. I don't want to be just a ranch wife. I don't even know if I want to get married. So many of my friends don't even see this as a choice, they just see being a housewife as part of their future.

I was also thinking about feelings. Why do humans have to hide so much and pretend. Sometimes I think I would rather be with the horses. Even the people who work around horses seem to be more honest. When I turn El Con out he has a good time just running or he visits with Lizzie. I love to watch them nuzzle. I wish people were as genuine with their feelings as horses are. The best thing is that you always know how they feel, not an ounce of pretending.

Mrs. Mason talked one time about how people always wear masks. She said that much of great literature has as its theme the idea that humans do not communicate with one another. She says that humans are so busy putting on a false front that they never expose real feelings. But Horses and dogs don't hide how they feel. They always let you know. Maybe that is why I would rather be around horses and dogs.

After school, James gave me a ride home. He is a good friend. Not a boyfriend. Well, he is a boy and a friend but you know what I mean. James just turned sixteen. Dad says it is OK for me to go to the movies when we all go as a group or even when there are four of us. But I cannot just go with James as a "date". Well, I do not want to go as a "date" and I don't think James does either. A few of the girls have boyfriends but I don't want to get that way about boys for a long time.

Sometimes the kids I go to school with forget that I am younger than they are. I know that is a good thing because it helps me to not be treated like a "brainy freak" but I would really rather read or be out with El Con most of the time. I have a ton of homework to catch up and I have a new book. The Good Earth by Pearl Buck that is so good.

This book is a good example of people who are not really communicating with each other. Olan never talks and she takes all kind of abuse. She is so pure and loyal and yet Wang Lung does not really appreciate what she does. I love how Wang Lung is emotionally tied to his land. I can really understand that.

Mrs. Mason asked me to make a list of imagery in the book and we are going to talk about it after school next week. And I am finding such wonderful examples.

In the news, Dag Hammarskjold has just become the U.N. secretary General. Dad said that he thinks he is a very good leader and he may help with the cold war. He also said that each side thinks that the other side is out to get them.

I am trying to get more interested in world issues. Dad says that everybody needs to think about the world and not just a little part of it where they live. He believes that too many people only worry about small issues and not about what is necessary for the world. So, I am trying. I read the paper everyday and then Dad and I talk about it. I love it when he shares his ideas and opinions with me.

March 14

Yea! Today is Saturday. All day with El Con! I am so glad it is already getting warm. The mornings are glorious. And I love the desert and everything in it. It smells wonderful. It is so still and yet there are sounds if you really listen. There are so many creatures in the desert. And you never know which ones you will see or sometimes hear. Every day is a new chance to see something. On my past few rides I have seen two fat gila monsters, a horny toad, several coyotes and I often hear the erie sound of the rattler.

Dad says the coyotes are really getting cheeky. They used to run away when they saw humans but not now, they will even trail after a horse. And you can usually tell if something died. Because the buzzards will circle above. But sometimes these horrible birds will be feasting on something and then they get spooked by something and they fly up in a bunch. I really do hate buzzards. Sometimes you don't see them because they are so busy feasting on the carcass du jour.

I went out really early. Dad says I am a strange duck because I like to get up early. I think I developed the habit to get away from Ida when I had to be in the house with her all the time when we lived in the house in Tucson. She sleeps late. Very late. So sometimes when I am in town I can get up, get out and get away.

Started the day doing the feeding for El Con and Lizzie. Sometimes I feed Joe's horses too. I am not supposed to feed the other horses because some of the crew feed different things. The horses get fed three times a day.

Watering is done continually by everybody. Everybody checks water for all of the horses frequently. And there is a stable boy, Joaquin, whose job it is to make sure that the horses are watered and there are no wet areas that a horse could slip on. Joe had to put one of the mares down when she slipped on a puddle and had a very serious injury.

El Con, Lizzie and Topper get hay, molasses, silage, carrots, apples, a combo of oats, barley, corn, oil, and some pellets that Joe says are good, mineral feed and a salt lick, the one for horses. There is also a vitamin feed that has cod liver oil and brewer's yeast. I tasted it once and I don't know why the horses don't spit it out. It is vile.

I bring out apples and carrots and they check my pockets to see what I have. El blows at me when he wants what I have. The problem with that is that sometimes he blows flies and god-knows-what else at me. I won't mention the wet stuff! Ha! Lizzie is a little more polite and a lot dryer! But I really think it is funny when El blows at me or on me. Good thing, huh? Sometimes when I am walking him down he blows on the back of my neck. And then I get all the weird stuff going down the back of my shirt. Sometimes I have to take three showers a day.

Today was so pretty. People think the desert is quiet but it's not. You can hear so much when you just listen. I love to hear the sound E's hooves make. And sometimes we just stop and listen. El Con's ears tell me so much. When I see them turn I know he hears something and I try to hear too. One time, really early in the morning, it was a line of javalinas and believe me we turned and went the other way. Fast. They scare me silly and E is more scared than I am. It is one of the times he will be very skittish. I feel him tense before I see what has spooked him..

One of my favorite sounds is the sound of the desert doves. I think they sound just like flutes playing. One of our crew is mostly Indian and he plays a wooden flute and he can make it sound like the doves. I love how each imitates the other.

Today we had a lovely time talking about my life. That is what is great about E. He never gets tired of hearing all about my problems and my happy stuff. His ears just flick off and on and sometimes he even turns his head to look at me when I have said something particularly funny. HA! I am kidding but maybe only half kidding.

I think El likes to hear me talk. Today I told him all about school and who I like and who I do not like, of course, that part took longer. So many of the girls just want to talk about boys, and sports and girly stuff. And they love to talk about clothes. Ugh!. I have no idea what is so exciting about a skirt or a blouse or even shoes. Just give me my boots, Levis and a shirt with good pearl snaps and I am happy.

I went in early because Dad asked me if I would make cookies. I love to make oatmeal cookies because he likes them. You want to hear crazy? He eats them and jalapeños together! He eats a lot of weird things. I guess that is the another thing I like about him. He will try any food. He likes food from all different cultures. I don't know why somebody would like Mexican food and German food together but he does. I am not that brave about food.

Dad is English. He even went to college in England. His dad was a candy maker from England. There were three brothers. Dad's two uncles came to America and started candy making companies while Dad's father remained in England.

Dad can make really good caramels, chocolate caramels, divinity, taffy and all kinds of chocolate. I learned how to make some of the candy. I love all of it except the taffy and anything chocolate. Dad says that is another weird thing about me, I do not like chocolate.

I put El Con in his stall after I walked him down, did a good groom and went in. I needed a good groom too! Most of the time I think I smell just like E, but then that is a good smell. I swear, I will never wear perfume. It makes me gag every time I smell Ida's perfume, Chanel #5. One time one of the ranch hands said it smelled just like main-street-border-town and everybody laughed but I didn't get it.

In the news: Khrushchev Is First Secretary of the Soviet Union. Dad says that means he is like a president. It is hard to keep up with all of these names. And it is really scary when they talk about having an Atomic Bomb War. We do all these things in school about what have to do if there is an attack. I think it is kinda dumb to get under the desk. Dad said just look at Hiroshima and those people did not have time to hide anywhere. Dad said that not to worry. He thinks that nobody wants to start another war. He has been trying to explain The Korean war to me but he says it was not really a war.

Lana had a brother who went to Korea but he did not come back. I really feel sorry for her and her mother. She doesn't have a dad but I do not know what happened to him. She says her mother cries all the time and hardly ever goes out of her house.

March 15

Ida had a big fight with me about saying that I need to be in town more, and I said "Why?" Dad said "You have to do what your mother said." Of course he supported her. Well, they can't control what I think so I think: What Mother? She never does anything mother-like for me. Anyway it went on forever. I don't understand why she wants me to come into town when she just yells or talks about Sharon, my birth mother.

Ida hates Sharon so I don't think what she says about Sharon has much value. Ida goes on and on about how horrible Sharon is and that I am just like her.

I met Sharon, her husband, Ryan and baby Morgana three years ago. I remember most of that visit. I had been having huge problems with Ida and some with Dad at that time. I knew I wanted to meet Sharon because she had been telling me so many bad things about her. Ida said that Sharon lives in Long Beach, California. Dad told me about Sharon and I believe what he says. We had just moved to Cochise and I was in fifth grade. So I was nine. We went there for a week and it was wonderful to get to know Sharon and Morgana. Sharon told me a little about of her story and why I was adopted.

Sharon grew up in California. When she was ten years old her mother died. Sharon's mother was already divorced from her husband and he died a year after they got divorced. When her mother died Sharon had to go live with relatives and she got she was put into a boarding school in New Jersey. After she graduated from high school and she was eighteen she went out on her own.

When she was nineteen Sharon met a guy named Troy Ashford who was from Texas. They met on a farm that grew strawberries and other fruit. Troy was really a sheep rancher's son who was out in California just for visiting his aunt who owned the farm. Anyway, they had a relationship and they were supposed to get married and Sharon had a baby which turned out to be me. Troy was from a big sheep ranch in Brownsville, Texas. But I guess he did not want to be a father and he wanted to go back to Texas. He did not stay with Sharon. She did not say why they did not get married.

One time Dad said that I was the best thing that he ever knew that came from Strawberry Fields. I have always wanted to see a strawberry field.

It is too bad but it seems like when women have babies and they are not married, only the woman has to be responsible for taking care of the baby.

That makes me think about a book we just read for English. The Scarlet Letter. In it, Hester has a baby and a minister, Dimmsdale is the father. But she is the only one who gets punished. She loves the baby and takes care of her but she has to wear a symbol of her "badness", a letter she has to sew on her dress. All the people in the community have nothing to do with her.

I really wonder if that is why Sharon gave me away? Was it so that other people would not see her as being bad. And the other thing I wonder about all the time is who is my real father is. Is he sorry that he did not stick and be a father? Is he ever sorry that he did not marry Sharon. But the thing I wonder about the most is does my birth father ever wonder about me? I really want to know what he looks like and if I am anything like him. I plan to go find him after I finish college.

Somehow Sharon went from California to Tucson, Arizona. She began working for a business that Dad owned in Tucson. Somebody told him that she was thinking about putting her little girl, me, up for adoption because she could not keep me anymore. So Dad talked to her and asked if she would let him and Ida adopt me. Sharon said she would let them take me for a few weeks and she would think about it. I guess it must have gone OK because I got adopted, age eighteen months..

Dad says that Sharon is not a bad person. That she is a person who got into a situation that got beyond her and she had to make decisions. Someday I really want to talk to Sharon and find out more. There has to be a lot more to her story. I just can't understand why somebody would give up a baby if they really loved the baby even if they are ashamed and people are being mean.

But then I don't get why somebody adopts a baby if they really don't want it. I am not saying anything against adoption. I think it is great when somebody takes a child to love. Someday when I am grown up and married I am going to adopt a child, maybe two. I think about that a lot.

So, guess what, Dear Diary, I don't understand Ida or Sharon but Dad says I will someday. He does try to explain stuff but I think even he does not understand either. I know he tries to understand me but if he understands me at all, why doesn't he take my side with Ida when he knows Ida is doing something bad or she is hurting me?

OK, back to how I got in contact with Sharon. At that time I used to ride into town with Joe every day when he came in for all of the stuff he had to get for the ranch. He goes to the post office every day to pick up mail. It is my job to go in and get all of the stuff out of the big box that was on the bottom row. It is fun to do the combination and say "Hi" to all of the people at the counter.

One day when getting the mail I saw an envelope that said Sharon Moore on it. And the post mark said Long Beach! I didn't know her last name. But I did know where she lived. So who else could it be. I folded up the letter and I put it inside my Levi pocket. We went by the House of Ida and gave Ida her mail.

After Joe and I got back to the Tri-R, I went out to the stalls and tore open the letter and read it to El Con. Sharon had written a letter to Dad.   She was asking him all about me. She wanted to

28

know how big I was. What were my interests now? Did I ask him anything about her?

All I knew is that I needed to communicate with this woman who was my *REAL* mother. I went up to the house and got every thing to write a letter and went back to El Con's stall.

I wrote a letter and answered all of her questions. But I knew that I did not want any letter that she might write back to have a chance to get to Ida. So I waited to mail the letter that I wrote. I had a friend from school and I asked her if I could get her to use her post office box to receive letters for me. She asked her mother and her mother said OK as long as they were from Sharon. Gabby and I had explained the situation to her mother and lucky for me she seemed to understand. So I wrote Sharon how we could communicate with this new box number and mailed the letter to her.

This began a letter exchange which led to the trip only a few months later as soon as school was out. Ida was furious when she found out that we had been in contact. But Dad stood up for a change and even said that we could drive to California to see Sharon.

The visit was good and bad. Sharon was very different from what Ida had told me but then she was also very different from what I imagined. But I loved the baby, Morgana. She was an adorable little two-year-old happy, giggly butterball.

It was hard to think of having a sister. We looked so different. I am tall and skinny with jet black hair and blue eyes. Sharon says I am black Irish. And that means dark hair, very pale skin and dark blue eyes. Sharon said that I am three-fourths Irish and one-forth French. And Morgana is half Scandinavian so she is very blonde, very pale skin. But we both have the same big blue eyes. Dad even said so. It is still hard to think about having a sister. I think of my self as an only child until I remember about Morgana.

Sharon is medium tall, has very dark brown hair, with hazel eyes. So I guess I got my eyes from my birth father.

They also live a very different life in a big apartment place that had row after row of streets with the same apartments. Tiny little yards and the kids play in the streets and ride bicycles on the sidewalks. We went back to Arizona and I felt as if I had more questions than before we had gone. All the way back Ida said terrible, hurtful things about Sharon and I remember hating Ida completely. Later Dad said that I should be more understanding. That it is not her fault. What a load of horse hockey pucks. In fact horse poop is too good for what Ida is. She is what is at the bottom of the Fry's outhouse!

I just have to make Dad understand that it is not fair to make me stay in town. It means that Joe and the other guys have to do my work at the TriR. I know he understands but I also know that he does not always stand up to Ida. I don't get that either because she is always mean to him too. She never says anything nice and she just complains about money all the time.

Ida just wants to play bridge and go to the Tucson Women's Club or to her card parties.

Dad goes to the El Rio Golf Club to play poker and golf. He has told me so many stories about people he saw golf, Bebe Zaharias, Bing Crosby and Ben Hogan.

Sometimes Dad takes me with him to go to the Club to eat. One time one of the golf people tried to teach me how to "drive" the ball but I was not very good. I think it is a very boring game to watch and I know I would never want to play. But Dad seems to be pretty good at it. I wish he would spend more time doing something that he thinks is fun.

I think Dad would rather be at the ranch. He told me one time and the only place he ever really finds peace is here. He does not ride very well but he will go out sometimes. But he will work right alongside of Joe. I know all of the crew likes him. Joe said that he is the best man he has ever worked for.

This evening Brahm came out to the TriR and we did one of our favorite things to do. We took the chuck-truck out, loaded it with a bunch of horse blankets and the stuff we needed. We asked Dad, Joe and a couple of the other hands to have a desert supper with us. I gathered up chicken legs and steaks, and all the junk munch I could find. Cook made potato salad and I had made my cookies. So we went out to what Brahm and I have named Roxie's Desert Café.

It is a beautiful spot with large boulders, a full stand of mesquite trees and all the cactus anybody could want. Over time Brahm and I have cleared most of the chaparral out. We have lugged two wood tables all the benches that we have been able to scrounge up. Best of all we found a wonderful old wood chair that looks like the kind you see at beaches. And that is Dad special chair. There is a permanent fire pit. We have to bring out firewood. We all gather around and we each have a special thing to sit on. Mine is a chair I found in one of the storage sheds. It has three legs and a little short back. Makes me think of a Cinderella stool. Brahm likes to sit on the big logs because most of the crew does.

The hands play guitars, harmonicas, and desert flutes and we sing and just have a great time.

I love it when it gets really dark with a full, puffed, silver moon and the stars look as if a terrestrial giant has flung all the diamonds in the world just for us to look at and make up a story about them. The game that we play is that each person has to pick a constellation and make up a story about it. Brahm is not very good at making up stories. But Joe and Wade tell great stories. Sometimes mine are pretty good too.

My whole class came out here for eighth grade graduation. My dad donated a whole side of beef and Joe roasted it. And the kids brought everything else. And it was a great picnic. All of our teachers were here except Mr. Anderson.

I hope this is going to be something we do every year. The picnic part, not the part afterward when I had my accident out at Texas Canyon!

When the sky is all silvery and the light shimmers across the cactus making little dancing, light patters in the thorns and leaves of the cactus, it reminds me of the poem, The <u>Highwayman</u>. I love the way that Alfred Noyes described the road as a ribbon of moonlight. I love the way he repeats words and creates a story with so few words in a poem. I don't know what I like better, the story or the images he creates with words.

March 16.

I just got back from the Lions-Rotary basketball game. Dad belongs to both clubs but he says he is too old to play. He organizes everything. They tied the score. Earlier I had another fight with Ida. I had to go there to give her mail and she started in. I guess this is as good a time as any to say what she talks about. Ida says that why should she want me when my own mother did not want me. She even says that she talked to Sharon when we went to California and said that she would have left me there but Sharon said she did not want me and was very happy with Morgana. I did not believe this and I even wrote to her and she wrote back that she did not say that. Ida is just nuts.

She also says I am just like Sharon and I will do stuff with boys. I will have a baby and give it away just like Sharon did. I try to tell her that I don't do stuff. The most I do is go to the show and to the school stuff. I don't even like to hold hands and the only thing I want to kiss now is El Con or even Lizzie. But the idea of kissing a boy is just icky. Why can't she JUST LEAVE ME ALONE? I don't do anything to her and I never start anything. I just try to keep quiet and then she says stuff until I lose it and answer her and then I am in trouble, again!

March 17

Dad got really mad when he read the paper this morning. He said that there is no reason to be doing nuclear tests. I don't even get what that is about. He said it has to do with a bomb that is worse that what they did in Japan. Anyway he said that he is worried that it could cause a bigger war than there ever has been. He can get very upset over news.

Boy, was it a rainy day. After school I it rained so much that all I could do was muck and then I had to go inside. I read and listened to the radio. Dad had a meeting with a bunch of other ranchers so I never had a chance to talk to him. I just read, and did homework in my room.

March 18

The Tombstone HS Band was at Cochise High today. They played the best I have ever heard them. Lana came out to the ranch and we played some Canasta. Then we went to bed and had a giggle fest. Dad came in twice and told us to keep it down. But he really does not get mad about it. We snuck out to the kitchen and made tortillas with peanut butter and jelly. We were up almost all night so I know I will be very sleepy at school tomorrow.

March 19

Up early. Did my chores. Good day at school. Mr. Bertram read us The Raven. It is by Edgar Allan Poe. He is so much fun and so dramatic. The poem is incredible. I am not in Mr. Bertram's class but I am his teacher helper. I love to grade papers and I get to be in his class instead of study hall.

Hard to believe that Poe lived a hundred years ago. And he died really young. He really loved the young girl he married. Mr. Bertram said he would read the poem Annabelle Lee tomorrow. But I am going to see if I can find it in the library. Mrs. Mason has so many poetry books and she lends them to me. She says I read more than she does!

That's me! I read and ride and sing. Maybe I can be the reading, singing cowgirl! HA HA!

Lana and I are going to the show. She is hoping to run into Leslie. We have this crazy movie show theater. It is pretty small. The ones in Tucson are lots bigger and better but I don't think they are as much fun.

The Cochise Movie Theater is better for us though. Some goofy things happen. The movie stops and the booth guy has to fix it and everybody screams and yells. Sometimes everybody stomps their feet. Or the lights go out. Many times the booth guy put the wrong part on and we had had to wait while he fixes it.

Tonight we saw the <u>African Queen</u> with Humphrey Bogart and Kathryn Hepburn. What a great story. She was a church lady who winds up in an adventure with a free spirited guy. And on top of everything they fall in love. And they are way older. And best of all it had a great surprise ending.

I love Dish Night. They give away these green dishes that are pretty ugly but everybody seems to want them. You get a ticket every time you come to the show and you use the tickets to get dishes. I get them and give them to Cora. She said that she knows they are ugly, but her dishes get broken so much that she likes to have the extras. And then there are ice tea set nights. These are metal glasses that are different colors and you can get a pitcher too. Cora likes those because she says all of us break her glasses too. I guess it is better than jelly jars anyway. But because they are metal, they freeze your hands when you put a lot of ice into them.

Dad says The Picture Show is the best spent 25 cents there is. The movie costs 10 cents, popcorn is 5 cents, soda is 5 cents and candy is 5 cents. And the best deal is on Sat. because they have a double feature and then a little short movie that is called a serial. I love the musicals and Dean Martin and Jerry Lewis and so many more good movies. Another favorite pair is Abbot and Costello. But I hate the Three Stooges.

I really love the serials because when I see a serial chapter (that is what each part is called because I guess it is like a chapter in a book) I go home and I write what I think the next chapter will be. And sometimes I am right! But then I guess it is easy to figure out because you know the hero or the heroine is always going to win and not get killed or anything.

I have choir practice all this week after school. I have two solos for Easter Sunday. <u>In the Garden</u> plus a new song. Mrs. Johnson just drags practice out. I think her piano playing stinks. But I can't choose who I want to play for my solos. Samantha plays so much better but I guess when you are the Minister's wife you get to do whatever you want.

Dad and I went to Tucson after practice because he had a meeting at the Club and then we had dinner with a couple of people I had not met before, sort of boring. I wanted to look at some record players. but it was too late. I want one so bad because I could have music in my bedroom.

I also need some new tack for Lizzie. She needs a new saddle too. The one I am using for her now is just too big and too heavy. I slip in it all the time. And I don't like rigging plates. I want a five inch cantle. The problem is that you can't just buy this special kind of saddle. You have to get one from a custom saddle maker.

Joe knows a guy that is just starting to make saddles for barrel with the new changes. I rode one at the arena. Mary Jane had one and what a difference it makes especially when you are skinny and don't weigh enough to sit as well as I would like. I hardly slid in her saddle.

Dad said I could get one made but it would mean not getting some other stuff. That's OK. I hope Dad will take me over to the saddle maker so that he can start making the saddle because it will take at least two months. I want new boots too but I know that will have to wait.

This evening I went up to Cami's to watch a program on her TV. It was the awards show for movies. I have listened to it on the radio before but this was the first time on TV. What pretty dresses and so fun to see them as they got the little statues.

Some of the movies that got awards tonight were <u>FROM HERE TO ETERNITY,</u> <u>THE MOON IS BLUE,</u> <u>THE ROBE</u> <u>AND</u> <u>ROMAN HOLLIDAY.</u> I saw all of them at the show in Tucson with Dad. That is the only place where you can see the new picture shows.

March 20

Joe finished the barrel run that he has been making for me. It is wonderful. Now I do not have to go practice at the arena. El Con is getting used to it. It seems like the back barrel is too far away but Joe said it is exactly the same distance as the arena one. I plan to get more practice in, but it is hard to get somebody to time me. I tried to get Dad today but he was too busy and nobody from school wants to do it either. I wish I had a barrel buddy. Everybody who does barrel is from somewhere else.

I know a girl who lives in Tombstone but then either her horse or mine had to get trailered and that is a big deal too.

Lana came over this evening. She and Leslie got mad at each other. Leslie and Lana are both 15 and here I am the 13 year-old trying to patch things up. In what universe does this make sense? HA! She is trying to get me to talk to Leslie for her. I really don't want to be in the middle of this silly stuff. But we do have a lot of fun when she spends the night.

Booth came home from boot camp. Cora is making all of his favorite foods. I might even make my famous cookies! Dad says he is proud of what both of the Fry boys are doing.

Dad said he missed both wars, too young for the first one and too old for the second one. But he did some kind of work with the

34

government. He did something that helped with the ration books during WWII.

March 21

Rodeod at the arena, and boy, do I really need more practice. I did a 18.5 and a 18. I think I am going backward. I guess I am going to have to make time to do more practice. And that means some things have gotta go.

There is a girl, Mary Jane, from outside of Tucson who is really good. Their ranch is way out on the west side. She took the first. And her horse, Jackson, is really good too. He is pure quarter so he is a little bigger and heavier. I used to think faster was better but her horse really turns great. I looked at the sign sheet and Jackson's full name is Stonewall Jackson. Cool name.

I wish I knew a really good trainer. Joe is good but that is not his job and he can only spend so much time with me. Dad says I would spend all day with him and he is right, I would.

I am hoping to have a chance to talk to Mary Jane. She looks different from most of the girls who do barrel racing. She is bigger than I am. Not fat. Just sort of square. She has very broad shoulders. You can tell how strong she is. I would like to get more like that. I have never seen her with any friends, so I plan to try talk to her the next time I see her. I really admire her ability to ride like she does. I don't think she knows what a talent she has. I wonder if there is any way that we could practice together. It would really be nice to have a friend to practice with who likes to do barrel. I don't think I could ever be as good as she is but it would still be fun. I also saw on the sign sheet that she is sixteen.

March 22

After Church Dad and I went to Tucson to the Club for lunch. Ida stayed home because she did not feel well. She doesn't like the Golf Club. He played golf and I played tennis. There is a new tennis teacher there who showed me a couple of things that would help my backhand. He said I could have a strong backhand if I learn to control it better. He said I am strong for being so skinny.

I think that the same is true for the barrel, I really need to be heavier. Joe says the same thing. But the new saddle will help. Sometimes he says I ride like Olive Oil. I am so tired of skinny jokes, but I don't mind when Joe teases me because I know he is just kidding.

March 23

Buddy came for lunch. He goes back to the Army soon. And Leslie came out to the ranch for a while. He had some kid with him. Nice looking and had a nice car. Maybe Leslie will introduce him to boy-crazy Lana! HA! Maybe not!

El and I had a wonderful ride this morning. Our rides give me a lot of time to think about things.

I fell into the freezer today. Clumsy me. We have a big freezer at the ranch. It is like a huge chest, with two big lids, and it is really deep. Some times when you are looking for something on the bottom you have to lean way over and dig around. I was looking for frozen peaches because I was going to make a peach pie for Dad. Cook will make stuff if I ask her but I like to make special things for him. I leaned way in looking for the peaches that were in freezer boxes and I fell in. Nothing bad could have happened because my bottom was hanging over the side. Marta thought it was funny. I thought it was embarrassing and funny.

I told Dad, thinking he would think it was funny too. But he said that it could have been a problem and he had TC remove all the locks from both lids so that it will still close but it can't lock. Does he think I am three?

Cami and I went to the show. I love to go to the show, I love all kinds of picture shows. Usually go about three times a week. Our little picture show house does not get all of the new movies, we have to go to Tucson for those. Sometimes my dad likes to go to the shows in Tucson or he drops me and who ever else is going with me off at the Fox, then he does what he needs to do.

Usually we go to the show on Sunday, but if we don't then we go on Monday because it is the same show. Tonight we saw Doris Day in <u>Lullaby of Broadway</u>. Silly story but it had some great songs in it.

March 24

Busy day at school. Leslie called tonight about Lana. I sure wish they could work on their problems without me in the middle. Lana came out to the ranch we talked a bunch while I did my mucking. After she went home and I did my reading and homework. I like Lana but I think I would rather ride El Con or read and not spend so much time just gossiping and talking about stuff that is not really that interesting.

Joe says that El is getting so good that I don't need to practice every day. He says just ride the rest of the week and practice one day only. He says that El is a natural athlete.

Dad says I want to do too many things. I like to read and write, and do my singing and I want to be in all the school stuff and then spend time running the barrels and spend time with both El Con and Lizzie.

Dad told me that he offered to pay Joe for working with me on the barrels. And Joe said, no, that he really enjoyed it too and that he was proud of how hard I worked on it. So I told Dad maybe there was another way that he could do something nice for Joe.

March 25

Joe and I took El Con and Topper and ran the barrels. It was really fun to do that with him. TC timed. Joe had never done barrel before he started working with me. Topper is new at it too, but boy, does he move! Joe says that a cowpony has a lot of the same moves.

Dear Diary, I will tell you about how you do barrel riding. Joe told me that only women and girls do it, and I guess that is true because I have never seen guys do it. The rodeos at the arena do not always have a barrel event. Makes me mad that gets they don't.

Some people call it Barrel Racing. Joe calls it "ride barrels". It is when a horse and rider race around three barrels to see who can do it the fastest. If a rider knocks over a barrel the rider 5 seconds added to her total score. A rider can't win or even place if she knocks over a barrel because it would make her time too long even if she had a good run.

A rider can injure her horse if she hits a barrel or take a turn too low or lots of other problems. Joe says that the horse always comes first. I agree with him. I have spilled a couple of times but I learn each time what to do better the next time. I use both El Con and Lizzie. El Con turns better but Lizzie is faster. She is 100% Arabian which means she is smaller.

I really think I can control El better and he seems to know what I want him to do without as much from me. Lizzie has to be "directed" more from the saddle by my legs and my knees as well as how I am leaning. So I get a lot more tired when I use her. I watch Joe and he just seems to be a part of Topper.

Sometimes when I am with El, I feel like we are the same being. I even know what he is thinking just by his ears and the way he holds his body. And I think that he knows what I am thinking.

The barrels are 55-gallon oil drums. They are set up in a triangle. And the rider goes around them in what is called a clover leaf pattern.

I use a light spur when I am doing barrel (I never use spurs for just riding). El Con never seems to need spurring. I ride almost standing up and forward. Even with just regular riding I raise up when I am in a gallop or any gait that is going to flop me around. It hurts when you smack your bottom on the saddle or worse on the cantle. Once I even smacked the horn because I was way forward. Boy, that hurt for days.

Comparing El Con to Lizzie. Lizzie weighs just short of 800 lbs and El weighs 1020 lbs. Liz has a short back but Joe says she has really strong bones and a better center. The only problem she has had was with her cannon bone but she is OK now.

My best time so far is 17.5. And that was only in a practice run, but even that is not really very good but I am working on it. I would love to get under 16.0 The really good races are over at the Tucson Arena. Some of those girls have amazing times, especially Mary Jane.

Dad and went up to see Booth off. Everybody is worried that he might go overseas. He was supposed to leave earlier but his orders got changed.   Cora had a really nice dinner for him with all of his favorites, cheese enchiladas, tacos, and homemade ice cream. Dad brought some tortillas and tamales from the ranch and   made flan and Brenda was my little helper.

March 26

Well, I spent an evening at home for a change. Dad and I had a wonderful dinner, just the two of us. He has been having a bunch of meetings. Lately he has been very grumpy but tonight he was in a good mood and was telling stories about when he was young. He said that what I am doing is more of a journal than a diary. I said I only sort of know the difference. He said that a diary is just when you write down what you did and a journal tells more about what you think about things or to make a judgment about something.   I said that Mrs. Mason says the same things but I seem to write about what I do and what I think about that. He said that is exactly what I should be doing and that made it more "journalish".

So I think I am doing a bit of both, but I will still call you Dear Diary. But I like the idea about writing down what I think. I told Dad that that is what I have been doing. I even told him that Mrs. Mason says it is sometimes easier to write more than less and I guess I am one of the "more" people.

There are so many things I cannot tell anybody. I am trying to learn about the world and what is right and wrong. I see so many people who are hypocrites about how they live their lives. They say that they believe a certain way but their actions are exactly the opposite. I have a lot of questions that I ask in Sunday School but I don't think I always get an answer to what I am asking.

Dad said what is in the news is amazing. A doctor has invented a vaccine for polio. I know two people who have died from polio. Ida's best friend is Bertha Peterson and her eighteen-year-old son,

Norman, died a few months ago. I went with Ida to visit him in the hospital at Tucson. He was in an IRON LUNG thing. It was a big, long, green metal tube and Mrs. Peterson said it did the breathing for him. She said all parts of him were paralyzed even his lungs.

I have very mixed feelings about Norman. He always scared me because he was a very mean kid. One time in Tucson there was an incident that really got me into trouble with Ida but Norman was the one who did the bad thing.

Bertha and Norman had come over to our house and Norman asked me if I wanted to go get come comic books. Of course I did, being the little rabid, comic book collector that I was. So off we went to the comic book store. We brought back our booty of books and went back to the little porch that was Norman's room. It was like a rec room and bedroom all combined. Anyway, I hunkered down to read my new Wonder Woman, and suddenly Norman was trying to kiss me. I smacked him on the nose, ran out of the room and went to tell Bertha and Ida.

Indignantly I reported what had happened, Ida stood up and smacked me so hard I fell on my bottom. Bertha said, "Ida, don't hit her, what Norman did is not right and it scared her." Ida jerked me out of the house, stuffed me in the car and all the way home I knew what was coming. Another beating, and it was a doozy, all the while she is screaming that I embarrassed her and "What did I do to Norman that made him act that way?" I'm this little kid who has no did what he did, and certainly not why Ida is never a Mother who protects me or cares about me.

I avoided Norman from then on. But he was the one idea why any of this is happening. Not why Norman who found me and told his mother when it was the Peacock Pin Incident. So as I said, I had very mixed feelings and was truly sorry when he was so gravely ill. And when he died I was just one big turmoil of feelings. I did feel sorry for him and his mother. He had been her only child.

I don't know why he did not have a father. Bertha was never the same after that. I never saw her smile or be easy and jokey again.

I wondered if somebody could catch it. Dad said that they are not really sure how somebody gets polio.

The other person was a boy, Jasper, whose family rents one of the apartments that Dad owns in Tucson.

Nobody in Cochise has ever gotten polio. Dad says I will get a shot to keep from having polio and he is going to find out where to get the shot. Maybe it is like the TB thing that I got. It made a big scab but it keeps you from getting TB. They did this scratchy thing instead of a a shot and it got really sore. So I asked Doc it that was OK and he said yes, that was a normal reaction.

Went to the show with Cami to see <u>That's My Boy</u>. Gosh, I love Dean Martin and Jerry Lewis and they were really funny in this one. The Jerry character had a "football" father and the mother and the father want the Jerry character to be a football hero. So they hire the Dean guy to help him but Jerry just wants to take care of little animals. Lots more silly stuff and the usual happy ending. We ran into the rest of the gang so we had a ton of fun.

March 27

Mrs. Mason asked me to stay after school today so she could talk to me about writing.   She said I should write everyday and I said that is what Dad said, and she said he is right about the "thinking about something part".   I told her that I write every night before I go to sleep. Even when I am really tired I still want to write. She said that is what writers do. They have a need to write. She said that I had a very "analytical" mind. I had to look it up. I guess I do. I try to talk to people about stuff I think and they just look at me like I am nuts. So I guess writing it is best. At least I can talk to people like Dad, Mrs. Mason and Pug.

Even Cora told me one time. "You think too much!" I wondered how can anybody stop thinking? How do you think too much?

I never tell anybody from school about reading newspapers or about most of the books that I read. I have been called the "walking dictionary", "encyclopedia girl," "egg head" and other names. Well, I guess that is better than what Ida calls me.

I am just realizing lately that being really smart is a good thing. And I know that I am smart.   Not just because that is what everybody says to me. I know the teachers think it is a good thing. I used to think I was always "teacher's pet" because they felt sorry for me about Ida. But now I think it is because they know that I have this "bug" to learn.

I am so grateful they all get me books, books, and more books. Dad had a whole set of shelves put in my room. He says that I should give some away but I don't know anybody who wants them and I really want to keep them anyway. But back to the smart part. I really wonder if it is being conceited to know that you are good at something and to say it. I know what things I am good at. I made a list one time. And I made a list of the stuff I am not good at. But Ida says I am just one big fat blob of conceit. I don't think so. I think it is dumb when people say they are not something when somebody pays them a compliment or acknowledges that they are good at something.

I also know I am clumsy, impatient, judgmental, and a bunch of other stuff. And I do know that I can annoy people. I am always asking questions and I want to understand everything. I like some people and not others. I like to be alone a lot of the time. Cami likes everybody. Every time I say something about somebody she says "Oh, you shouldn't say that." Cami is my other friend besides Lana. She likes to be around people all the time.

I love to sing, I love to read, and I love to learn about everything. I also love my horses and Fala as well as a whole list of people. I am adding more people to my list all the time.

I have so many things I can do I am never going to worry about what I can't do, there is just no point wasting time on that. Of course, sometimes I have to remind myself to think this way. Joe says "The best a body can be is the best a body can be." I told him a long time ago that it did not make sense. Now I see that it does.

Cami's family moved to Cochise at the beginning of our Freshman year. We are starting to be better friends even though we are complete opposites. She is fifteen but does not care that I am younger. I do not spend as much time with Lana especially now that she and Leslie spend a lot more time together.

Cami does not read anything unless it is assigned for class. I read everything. I read books that are supposed to be to "old" for me, whatever that means. I love to "talk" books with Mrs. Mason and Mr. Bertram. They both say that they like the fact that I need to know everything, do everything and be everything.. They tell me I can be anything. And I say that I want to be a lawyer and then a judge. I want to help make better laws to protect children.

I love classics and new authors and I even love comic books. Reading helps me understand the world. Cami and I have almost totally opposite interests. But we do have a big thing in common. The picture show. We both love movies.

We go to the show a much as we can. I think it is as much for the show as it is to hang out with the other kids. I am a lot more into pictures and reading than I am into sports except for barrel racing. Most of the kids I go to school with do not see barrel racing as a sport. Joe says it is harder and takes more ability than most of the sports played in school. I will take his opinion any old day.

Speaking of books, that makes me think about the comic books that I used to have. I had hundreds, all stacked up in my bedroom in the house in Tucson. One weekend I came home from boarding school to find out that Ida had taken them out to the burn pit that is next to the culvert that rand behind the house. Every comic book I had all been burned along with a bunch of cigar boxes that I contained all my little collections. There were also so many things

I had written.   Some of the things had even been items that Dad's mother and his grandmother had given to me.

She had also burned all my clothes, everything I owned. I went out the burn pit and there was this huge pile of ashes that had bits and colored pieces sticking out that was a sad reminder of what had been. I know it is dopy but I think there were bits and pieces of me in the ashes.

Three different times she has either burned or torn up everything I have. And every time Dad just says to go out and get new stuff. He seems to think that this solves everything but it is not the same. He didn't even say anything about the things that had been his mother's or grandmother's. He just seems to accept what Ida does.

I wish I could put a lock on my room. Thank goodness she does not come out to the ranch at all or I would have to worry about that.

Played in band for the school play. I want to take drama for next year but I wonder if I will have enough time to add that into everything else.

Dad and I went to Tucson for pink heels, pink taffeta dress, pink hat and purse for Easter. The heels had to be dyed. I got a charming, white outfit for Palm Sunday.

March 28

Rode fence, and did my mucking plus helping Joe. He called it Stall Cleaning Day and everybody worked on taking everything out and scrubbing down all of the stalls. I think he had found some bugs and he gets crazy if he finds anything in the stalls. One of the hands put on a glove and got bit by a black widow. Joe told Reese that he should know to check his gloves, boots and everything. I hate all bugs but I hate widows and scorpions the most. Tarantulas are big and ugly but still not as dangerous as the other two. Joe made everybody scrub the watering containers and clean with something he got from the feed store. Boy did that cleaner stuff smell.

I even found some stall toys that I thought were lost and Joe even made me clean them.   All of the tack got cleaned and organized. Now the guys are replacing some of the boards and walls that have some rot.

Had a terrible headache but Dad wanted me to go to the show with him so I went. It wasn't a very good movie.

March 29

We went to Tucson to get Ida because she has been at the Center. Dad and I stayed for dinner in her little house that they call a bungalow. I spent the time reading until we went home and took her to the House of Ida. So far Ida is leaving me alone, but then she does not do any of the really bad stuff in front of Dad. I wish she would and he could hear what she says, even better what she does. I know she is able to control what she does, no matter what Dad says. I wish I knew why am I the one who has to understand her, I'm not the adult.

We went to the show, another really funny one, <u>Bedtime for Bonzo</u>.

Bonzo is a chimpanzee who does some crazy stuff. I think they are cute when they are little but I would be afraid of one if it were big. Ronald Reagan and Diana Lynn were in it. Dad wanted to see it but he had to go spend the evening with Ida.

March 30

Dad actually rode with me today to go over to Mr. Brown's for a lunch meeting. His Ranch, the DoubleB is next to our ranch and is almost as big as ours. Lizzie was bred on the DoubleB and she is from his prize stock. He raises Arabians besides running Hereford cattle. Dad rode Dandy a big sorrel that belongs to Joe. I wish Dad would get his own horse but he says he does not ride enough for it to be worth the extra work. I told him I would take care of his horse if he got one but he said I have too much to do now.

Mr. Brown's house has this really beautiful inner courtyard. The house is shaped like a big U and the inside of the U is all glass, you can see the living room, dining room, kitchen and one of the bedrooms from the courtyard. At the top of the U is a six foot tall wrought iron fence with beautiful double gates.

In the middle of the court yard, there is a little covered area that has a fish pond in it and it has big fish that look like giant goldfish. Most of them are gold but some are really weird colors. His cook says that these fish are his "passion"! She said the covered area is called a gazebo and the pond is called a wading pool but people do not wade in it. The courtyard is really beautiful with all kinds of greenery, flowering shrubs, cactus and short palm trees. The running water and the smells from the flowers make it a little oasis and I love reading out there.

His cook said one time she came out there and there were a couple of javalinas right there drinking out of the pond! That was when Mr. Brown had the wrought iron fence put at the end of the courtyard.

The gates are this incredible intricate pattern and it happens that they are in the direction where the sun sets. It make a "wow" of the light in that last little bit of daylight when everything is all soft and pretty. Mr. Brown has always said I could ride over anytime and just read in his courtyard.

I always watch out for javalinas. Dad said they are attracted by the smell of water when the desert is very dry.

I learned in science that javalinas are not pigs but are a peccary. This is a type of swine. They eat small animals and desert foliage. They travel in large herds and some of them can weigh up to 90 pounds. The main thing I have learned is that you do not mess with them because they are really mean creatures.

Went to the show with Cami and I took tickets for a while. Since our little movie theater is very small it only gets the older movies. But all the kids go all the time and we love it. We can't do stuff in the Tucson movies houses that we can here. We talk and yell and move from seat to seat and nobody cares. The picture show theater probably only holds about two hundred people.

Sunday and Monday have the newer movies. Not real new, you have to go to Tucson for that. There are two shows on Sunday. The afternoon movie is the kids go to and the evening movie is the show that the grownups go to.

Grownups go to the Monday movies too. Kids go if they missed the Sunday matinee. Tuesday has movies that are in Spanish and there is only one show.

Wednesday and Thursday are a different movie. One movie with a short is the one that that kids go to either on Wednesday or Thursday.

Friday is a different movie. One early show and one later show. Older kids go to the movie on Friday, usually with a date. The older kids don't like it when the younger kids go on Fridays.

Saturday is the best time for the show. There is an afternoon show and an evening show.

There are always two movies and a serial. I have always loved it there on Saturday . They show everything twice, it starts at 12:00 and sometimes we don't get out until 10:00 if we stay to see everything twice. During the show, somebody can go next door and get a bag of hamburgers and get back in . I used to go to the early show and stay more before I got so busy with everything. So now I usually just go to the later show. Sometimes I get to take tickets or sell tickets in the ticket booth. I really like to do that too.

Melvin owns the show. He is a nice guy and his sister works there too. She is very unusual, she wears men's trousers, not Levis, but men's pants with suspenders, and a white shirt and she has a man's hair cut. Her name is Bobbie. A lot of the kids don't like her but I do. She has always been very nice to me and talks to me about my horses. She lets me work anytime I want to take tickets and then she goes and works in the candy and popcorn part. Of course I don't get paid, I just do it for fun because I just like to take tickets.   They quit selling tickets a half an hour after the main picture starts and sometimes people who can't afford a ticket come in then.   Melvin and Bobbie do not care about that so that tells you what kind of good people they are. Bobbie said one time that some people just cannot afford the price of a ticket. I know a lot of kids from school who come in late.   I don't think anybody who can pay takes advantage of the "late entry trick".   I love living in a small town just for this reason.   It is so fun to go to the show and enjoy being with friends and the fact that it is almost like being in a giant living room with all the kids you know.   And don't forget the popcorn! HA!

Melvin does the film booth most of the time but there is a guy who also does that sometimes. This other guy, I don't even know his name, never talks. He is short and thin and has a little pointy beard. James said that he thought the guy slept in his truck behind the show in the alley part. And one time Ray Jones, the sheriff, arrested him and Dad said he was in the drunk tank.

March 31

Don't feel good today. I will write tomorrow.

April 1

Very quiet April Fools Day. Nobody did any April Fools. Daddy had gone to the track meet with Jack to watch Brahm but I stayed home to do my homework and reading. Mrs. Mason gave me a new book, Fahrenheit 451. It is about a future society that bans books. Boy, that would be a bad time to live. Then Dad and all the Frys came over after the track meet for coffee and dessert. Usually Jack or one of the boys do a really big "Fooled Ya" thing but not today. I think Dad was disappointed.

April 2

Guess what! Joe did a really good April Fool. It really was a surprise because who is expecting it on the next day? Anyway Joe came running into the house and said, "Hurry we have to go find all the horses, they are all gone. Somebody turned them all out and the gates are all open! And some of the cows got hit on the highway!" So Dad and I got in the Jeep and followed him out to the road and started looking all over. The gates were all closed and

45

then we saw Topper and then the rest of the horses and Joe started laughing like a loon and all the guys yelled "APRIL FOOL!" Dad and I both laughed like crazy too.

Since it was Thursday, I had to hurry up and get to school because I had early band practice. I am so tired of having to practice the stupid clarinet and do all the band stuff but Dad won't let me quit. Mr. Anderson is the only teacher who does not like me. And I have no idea why. I never did anything to him, but he really did a mean thing to me.

I came into the school in the middle of the fifth grade. I had been in a private Catholic boarding school in Tucson before we moved to Cochise.

Our school is so small that you start Band and Chorus here in the fifth grade. And he is the band and chorus teacher. The Elementary and Junior high combine for special holidays. It seems to work out to have the younger kids be able to play and sing with the high school groups for these special performances.

My dad told Mr. Anderson that I had done public singing all over Tucson for different events since the first grade. So immediately he had me doing solos for the school programs. And Mr. Anderson thought it would be a good idea for me to be in band playing the clarinet. I was not too happy with that because I had just finished two years of playing the violin and I did not like that either. I had been taking singing lessons in Tucson since first grade from a really old voice teacher, Mr. Schneider. And boy, was he a tough old bird. But I love singing and so the lessons were hard but I like doing them.

Now I take voice lessons from Pug. She is actually a classically trained musician in both violin and voice. A lot of people do not know that about her and only know that she is a great fiddle player.

One day toward the end of the fifth grade, I had gone to chorus practice. Earlier another kid had given me bubble gum. Chewing gum is rather unusual for me. I don't even chew gum now that I am in high school. But that day I was not only chewing gum I had a big wad that I was chomping away on during class. Right in the middle of a song, Mr. Anderson stopped everybody from singing and he said, "Miss Rayburn, What do you have in your mouth?" And he walked up to me and put out his hand. I spit the gum into his hand and he said, "Stand up."

And I did. He said "Hold up your hair."

My hair was very long, almost down to my waist. But I held it up and he proceeded to stretch out the gum and then wrap the gum around my neck. And I had to sit there that way until the end of chorus practice.   As soon as I could leave class I went to Miss Eagleton's office (the elementary principal) and called my dad. He drove into town to the school and picked me up. I told him what happened.

The next day I was sitting in chorus practice when my dad walked in, crossed over to Mr. Anderson's podium and got right up to Mr. Anderson's face and said, "Do not ever touch my daughter again." Then he turned on his boot and the room was silent except for the sound of my dad stomping out of the room.

I am still in chorus and band. I don't like being in either one and I don't like Mr. Anderson. I am hoping that Dad will let me quit for next year. After all I am in both of the choirs for church. Both the children's choir and the regular choir. Sometimes I feel like all I do is practice for a million things.

Six of us went to the show and sat with the rest of our little gang. The show was wonderful. I love Fred Astaire and Jane Powell. I try to sing like she does sometimes. The show was Royal Wedding. I wish I would have gone last night so I could have seen it again tonight. Great story, fantastic dancing and singing.

April 3

I rearranged my furniture in my room and gave it a really good cleaning. We were off school because of Good Friday. My dad tells the maids not to clean my room. He thinks that I should do stuff for myself. I even have to do my own ironing. Ugh!   Most of the time I do not mind, just when I am so busy doing other stuff, but I do get why he does that. I have stayed overnight with many of my friends and they do not have to do anything, because of that they do not know how to do anything. I think that would be pretty boring.

Then I went out with Joe for the rest of the day. I love Joe, he is one of my very favorite people. He is as close to a grandfather as I have ever had. He is very serious but he says very funny things. He thinks the world is a place where everybody is out for themselves. I don't think he likes very many people but he really does like my dad. He calls him Honcho or Boss. Joe has always been a cowboy except when he was in the Army during WWII. He grew up on a ranch near Wilcox but I think he has relatives in New Mexico. And he tells the most wonderful stories about cattle round-ups and cattle drives that I could listen to forever.

Joe is really good with a lariat and he teaches it to a lot of the other hands. He has tried to teach me but I have no ability. He used to do calf roping in both the Cochise rodeo and the Tucson rodeo and he won a lot of money that he says he is saving up for his own ranch.

If he ever had a ranch I would want to get a job on it. He has a cattle dog that is really old and it stays in the bunkhouse. He used to be out all the time running after everything but now he can't. Joe really takes good care of Johnny and he is always getting stuff from Cook to give to him. I asked him one time why the dog was named Johnny and he said he couldn't remember. I asked him how old the dog is and he said that he thought he was over fifteen and that was at least a year ago.

I have never had a dog that old. My dog, Pudgy had died at the age of three, when somebody fed him ground glass. That was one of the few times that I ever saw Dad get really crazy. He and the sheriff tried to find out who did it. Seven dogs in Cochise were fed ground glass. Whoever did it put it in hamburger and put it where the dogs could eat it. I am convinced that it was Ida. I tried to talk to Dad about it and he did not say that he did not think she did it but he shut me down about talking about Ida. That told me volumes. I even heard a snip of an argument between Dad and Joe and they never argue. But it had to do with Ida and Pudgy. So go figure. I try not to hate her but that is not really working out very well right now.

I only had this wonderful, funny, loyal little dog for a few years but he will always be "that special dog" for me. I have so many Pudgy stories, so I plan to write a Pudgy Story for you Dear Diary.

Joe said he used to have a family but he never talked any more about that. He has worked on this ranch for over fifteen years, that is way before Dad bought it. His job is to tell all the hands what to do and to make sure that the cattle are fed, healthy and safe.

It is also Joe's job to take care of every aspect of taking care of the herd, the horses and everything that keeps the ranch functioning. He makes sure a hand gets a horse ready to ride if one or more is needed. Of course, each hand is responsible for his own horse. Joe is responsible for working with the vet and the farrier. He hires and fires all of the hands and hires part time help when that is needed. He says he also is like a judge when any of the hands have a problem and he decides things and his decisions are final. Joe says he is responsible for every living creature on this big piece of property. He makes it look easy but I know how hard it is and how hard he works. I think that Joe and Dad have a lot of similar qualities.

He never says so but I think he is responsible for me too and that is fine with me. He is more like a grandfather that anybody I know but sometimes I tease him and tell him that he acts like a mother hen. I know he is older, but I don't know exactly how old he is. If I ask him he says, "Well, how old do you think I am?" He is also the best rider I know. He says he used to ride bull but he doesn't that anymore because he broke too many bones and he never made any money at it.

I love to watch bull riders. One time at the rodeo I was sitting on a chute wall pretty close to the bulls and Joe caught me and he jerked me off the wall and told me I had extra chores but he never told Dad. I didn't do that anymore.

April 4

Ida and I had another big row because she wants me to stay in town because the last maid quit and she doesn't like the new one. So I guess the new maid is going to either quit or get fired. That is crap. I can't believe that Dad will make me. Why is it my job to take care of her? When she is not sick she is perfectly able to do her own stuff. When dad is around she will say, "Oh, my heart really hurts."

I asked Doc one time, if a heart really hurts and he said only if somebody is having a heart attack.

I am not going to cook and clean for her. And even worse, I am supposed to do all the stuff for her card parties. I am not going to do it.

All she does is play bridge. She goes to The Tucson Woman's Club and plays cards or she has these women over to play at the house. Most of these women I don't even know. They are not from our town or the Dad's Club or even our church. Dad says that it is what makes her happy. I don't give a darn if she is happy. She sure does not care if I am! They bet on the card games, I don't know if she wins or loses but I know that they play for pretty high stakes and I really do not know why that is fun.

Went to see <u>Meet the Invisible Man</u>, Abbot and Costello. It was so silly.

April 5

Well, did I speak too soon! Dad dropped me off just after I did my chores and said I had to help her all day so what I was going to do just does not matter. Dad says to look at helping Ida the same as doing my chores on the ranch. It is not the same.

Ida was having a card party for two tables so I had to get the house ready. The house was a mess because she does NOT do anything. Not a cotton-pickin' thing. Her bathroom is disgusting. I had to wash all her clothes for the past week and do all the hand

49

washing for her stockings and underwear. Nobody should have to do that. I don't know why Dad can't hire another maid because there are women in town who will do house cleaning. And some of those older women would be able to deal with her. I know the young girls can't put up with her.

She is so mean about everything, I was cleaning the kitchen and she was standing right behind me and going on about Sharon and saying things like "Did I think that the illegitimate child of a _____ is too good to do scrubby work.. That is what she calls it!! Scrubby Work! I won't say what the word in the blank is. Because it is a terrible word and I don't ever want to say words like that.

Dad came back and picked me up to go to church because I had a solo. And then he took me back. I begged him to let me go home but he said sometimes people have to do what is necessary. This is such horse pucky. It is not necessary for her to make me do her stuff. She never, ever has been a mother to me. I can't remember one single time that she ever touched me or read to me or anything. She has never taken care of me. Dad said, "Well, she is a different kind of mother." If I hadn't thought I would get in trouble I would have laughed. Yeah, she is different!

Dad stands up to everybody else who is mean to me but not to her. It just gets worse. I do not know which is worse. The things she says to me or when she hurts me. She has put me in the hospital three times. And all three times, there have been people who have tried to have me taken away from the Rayburns. But I do not want to be taken away from Dad. I just don't want to be around Ida. What usually happens after an "episode" is that Ida goes to the Center in Tucson and has a long stay. Things are fine then until for reasons that I do not understand, Dad decides that she is "all better" and she comes back. And somehow he convinces himself that if we spend time together, we are going to become this perfect "mother and daughter" team. Nobody else believes that. I guess he just wants that to happen so much that he is able to fool himself into thinking it is possible.

I tried to turn around and move away and she grabbed my arm and with those horrible, long fingernails of hers, she dug in. I got as much done as I could before I went to church. I showed Dad the marks. He said we would talk later. Then when I went up to the choir benches Mrs. Johnson asked me what happened. I told her I got caught in some cactus. And that is the other thing. I am really tired of lying to cover up for what she does. She just does whatever she wants and everybody else has to take care of it.

The gang met at the show. We saw <u>Alice in Wonderland</u>. I read the book last year and I love all of the characters. Mrs. Mason said that if I read the book again in ten years the characters will have a

50

whole new meaning. I don't understand how the characters can change but even Mr. Bertram said so too.

Well, Dad did talk about "The Ida Problem". Here we go again. Dad says "You have to understand. She does not really mean what she does. Ida has problems that you do not understand."

I don't know one other mother who is like this. She is sure not like Cora or Mrs. Delgado and especially not like Pug. That is who I wish could be my mother, Pug. I have wanted that every since we moved to Cochise from Tucson and Pug started taking care of me.

Dad bought several houses that were on both sides of the street on Sedona Street. Three houses on one side, two houses on the other plus two duplexes. The duplex was right across the street from the house that Ida lives in. When we moved to Cochise, Dad, Ida and I lived in this house in town for half of my fifth grade year and then Dad and I moved out to the TriR. She would not have moved to the ranch anyway. She says the TriR is nothing but a big pile of dirt that has ugly animals that smell. She is the one who smells. But it was at the same time that she had put me in the hospital from a beating with the vacuum cleaner cord, and she went into the Center and we moved out to the ranch.

Pug lives in the front duplex (the duplex goes sideways, so the front was really the side). They are actually kind of pretty with adobe wall that has a Mexican design tile trim all around the doors and windows. The duplexes have red tile roofs. Her duplex is closest to the street.

She plays the fiddle and has won the Fiddle Player Title several times. I don't think that is the exact name of the title. But people from all over the country come to Tucson to compete. She is really good. Dad is always asking her to play the <u>Cannon Ball Express</u>.

April 6

Mrs. Mason gave us a writing assignment today and I have been working on it all evening. As soon as I got my chores done, I came in and started it. She wants us to write about a special person.

I even made a list of my special people. I am going to tell Mrs. Mason that I am going to write one for each person on my list. Dad, of course., Joe, Pug, Cora, Cami's mother Sarah, Mrs. Mason, Mr. Bertram, Doc Harlan, Mr. Garrison from fifth grade and both Sister Mary Margaret and Mother Superior. It just dawned on me that I have a very big list.

I wonder if animals can be on the list. Well, I guess if it is my list they can, but I will make that list later.

So I have decided to write about Johanna May Belkis. She was a lady who lived in Cochise. Her house was on my way home from school when I had to walk home to the Cochise house. I used to go by and visit with her. I have written the paper the way Mrs. Mason told us. And now I am copying it into you, Dear Diary.

Johanna May Beliks

Meeting Johanna was a happy accident. I was on my way home from school one wonderful, sparkly May day. I was having happy thoughts about the last day of school which was just around the corner.

I had seen and spoken to her on several occasions. She was always cheerful and would make a comment about the weather or come comment about my pretty braids or what I was wearing.

This particular day she asked me if I could do a chore for her. I said, "Of course,' and climbed the stairs to her porch. I entered a greenery shrouded, lusciously cool, fragrant little oasis with honeysuckle and climbing-rose-covered lattices. I felt as if I had stepped into a different world. And I had.

I said, "How are you doing, Mrs. Belkis?" And she said, "Oh, Roxanne, you can call me Johanna." I was surprised that she knew my name. But then it was Cochise and everybody knew everybody.

She asked me if I wanted to earn a quarter a week. I told her I would be happy to do whatever she needed. She said that she had a girl who did housework for her but she would not clean the cat box. It was getting difficult for her to do it herself. I told her that was easy and I would do it whenever she needed it. She said that twice a week would be better because it "could get pretty stinky". Just then a giant, orange, tabby cat slowly climbed onto the porch, made a great leap and landed in Johanna's lap where he stayed. Johanna said his name was Major.

Johanna, herself, was shabby and elegant at the same time. She was layered like an old artichoke. What I could not see I could imagine. She wore old, thick stockings with seams that pointed every direction except up and down. On top of the stockings, she wore droopy ankle socks that were shapeless from many washings.

She sported serviceable, old, clunky, brown shoes that laced up the front. A white slip peeped out from under a dark, crepe dress. She was never without a wool sweater about her frail shoulders. And she buttoned this sweater with one button right in the middle even on the hottest of days. All together she looked like a once elegant old mansion, which had been lived in, cherished, and still was much loved.

Her face was a treasure of angles and lines. I was always fascinated by her eyes. I knew that she had seen a world that I was only beginning to imagine.

What started out to be a twice weekly thing, quickly became an every day visit. She used to watch for me form the massive old rocker that her father had brought from Poland somewhere around 1800.

It turned out that Major's cat box was just a cardboard box filled with dirt from her back yard. I got my dad to get several bags of sand from the lumber yard and put them under the back porch. He got a short, galvanized tub that became his new cat box. He also got me a little garden rake to scrape the icky from the sand. I learned how to do a cat box cleaning.

Her house was always cool and dark. It was dingy with age and neglect, but it was a happy place. I loved being with this incredible person who so clearly loved me and loved being with me .

Johanna had been a nurse in World War I. Her exciting stories took me to the front lines and to the people of Italy and France.

After the war she had become a teacher. She said that she had had enough of death and dying and she wanted to work with young people who were the future of the world and because she wanted to be around youth and energy.

She and I would read from her books. We would read Twain, Dickens and especially from so many of the women authors, Mary Shelly's Frankenstein, Eliot's Silas Marner and all of the Bronte books. Because of her, I was reading the classics when my school mates were discovering Nancy Drew.

She introduced me to real tragedy. Her husband had been a mining engineer who had lost his life in a mining accident and her only child, a boy, had died from diphtheria.

Johanna has given me the gift of pride. She had a fierce, abiding confidence in herself, women in general and me in particular.

I know that because of Johanna I am better able to deal with my problems with Ida. She has helped me to understand that it is more about the problems that Ida has and not as much about me. She says that Ida has inner demons that are as much a problem for her as they are for me. She says I will understand a lot more when I am older. One of her favorite sayings was, "When a body has problems, this too shall pass."

She used to tell me I could do anything, be anything, I just needed to prepare myself with the fundamentals of education and determination.

And best of all she connected me to a world that had passed on by.

I had just begun a romance with the Civil War novels. Johanna told me that she had been born a few years before the surrender of Lee to Grant and I was enthralled.

Her stories were my first person guide and magic carpet to an era that I could only visit through her stories. She had been there, she had lived in this exciting time gone by.

She told me stories about Prohibition, flappers, presidents from Cleveland to Truman and stories of both World Wars.

She died last year at ninety-six. Major had died the year before.

When days are tough for me, I think of Johanna. She was a gentle, prideful, beautiful angel who sits on my shoulder. She will always be there.

She is for all time, my Johanna May Belkis. She is one of my Angel Crew.

April 6

Pretty normal Monday at school. Usual band, chorus, classes . But, Dear Diary, what was different, James asked me to the dance after the football game on Friday. I have always liked James and I think I will go. Lana is going with Leslie and we can double. James even said he will get his dad's car so we can double. Guess the truck would not be too good! HA! Can't imagine Lana and Leslie in the back in the truck bed!

I guess that will be different than going to the movies. We usually just kinda meet up there. Dad says that I can go as long as it is with our group.

By the way Dear Diary, I do know that "kinda" is not correct spelling. But I like it because Ida only knows a little about correct speaking and spelling and it irritates her when I do kinda because it is one of the few things she knows about. HA!

Leslie has a truck too. I wish it was OK for girls to drive on dates because I could use my dad's car but that is such a NO-NO. What a drag.

Lana and I met up with the "dangerous duo" at the show. We saw "Street Car Named Desire" and I was the only one who liked it. The boys liked the Marlon Brando part but I loved the Vivian Leigh part. I get that she was crazy and why. She was not mean crazy. The only person she hurt was herself. Other people really hurt her because she did not have any self esteem and she was so desperate for love.   But nobody wanted to talk about the movie.   So I am going to talk to Mr. Bertram about it on Monday.

April 7

OK, now comes the teasing part.   I did not realize I had such a reputation as a "cowgirl".   Somebody told James that he was lucky that I liked him better than El Con.   James works on his dad's ranch but I don't think he is really into it.

He never rides for fun and never goes to the rodeos.   I have asked him out to our ranch a bunch of times but he says "Let's do something in town."   And I think we are going to the show on Wednesday.   I do kinda like him.   But still as just a friend.

April 8

Mr. Bertram asked me to stay after school and meet with him and Mrs. Mason.   I thought I was in trouble but couldn't think why.   Turns out they wanted to know if I wanted to do a reading program.   That meant they would make up a list of things to read, I would read them and then they would discuss the reading with me and give me an assignment.   I asked what the assignments would be and they said to write a "response" or an analysis.   Mr. B said a response was when you read something and then you say what you liked and why.   I always do that in my head anyway.   And I like to write.   I write a lot.

I like the idea.   Mr. Bertram teaches an evening class over at the U of A and he said that most of the readings would be from the college list of readings.   I am all ready for that.   Sounds fun and I am glad they want to give me the extra time.   Mr. Bertram and Mrs. Mason said I could meet with them every Monday after school and that would give me the weekend to do the extra work.   Boy, do they know me.   I read a lot anyway, but I really love the idea of getting to discuss how I feel about what I read.   I can't get anybody else to "talk books".

April 9

Today was really horrible.   This is the third dead person I have seen who died from an accident.   Here is how it happened.   Early this morning Joe came into the house.   Dad was still eating breakfast and reading the paper.   And Joe said that Randy had not come in for chow yesterday and he still had not shown up this morning.   Joe told dad that the crew was getting ready to go out to look for him.   Joe told dad that Randy had been riding Geronimo and he had not come back yesterday or this morning.

Dad said "What do you need?" And Joe said, "We might have to go off the property and we might need some extra horses." He asked Dad if he could call Mr. Brown to get some more hands and horses. That is when I knew it was pretty serious.

Dad and Joe talked about where everybody would meet and what they would need. Dad told me to go to the bunk house and start filling saddle bags with water. Everybody would carry two instead of the regular one. So I ran quickly, got my Levis and boots on and went on out. Outside all of the horses that we had were tied to the post fence. Mr. Brown's hands came in and even Mr. Brown himself. Everybody was gathered outside. So I went on out and saddled up El. Then Dad came over and said to me, "You are not going". And I started arguing and Joe jumped in and said, "She can go with my group and I will take care of it." I guess I was "it".

So everybody split up into three groups. We rode out.

Stetson, everybody called him Stetson because he always wears one, was in the lead. I have never seen him without his hat on. It was always clean and in a uncurled shape and not curled like everybody else's was. Anyway, he had been doing a whistle with his fingers because he could do the loudest one. We all kept listening for any sounds from Randy or Geronimo.

It was almost sundown before Wade, who had ridden out ahead of Stetson, came trotting back and said "I just found him in the wash." Before Joe could stop me (because I knew he would) I kicked El to the front. I came over to the edge of the wash where several of the other hands had gathered.

There he was. Both Randy and Geronimo were at the bottom of the wash. It was really not very good to see. Both of them had been gutted just like when somebody slaughters a deer. All the insides were all over and everything was so bloody. One of the guys said it had to be javalinas and Joe said he thought so too. So several of the guys went over and built a fire and then started fanning smoke. About a half an hour later one of the other groups showed up and then just a little later the last group came. Somebody said they would go back and get one of the trucks and blankets and what else they needed.

But my dad said "No, somebody has to go get Ray and he will have to tell us what needs to be done. We can do anything until then."

Then dad came over and told me to go back with Reese and Joe. He asked me how I was. I said, "OK". I said, "Don't get mad at Joe, he told me not to look." Dad still looked mad. Dad asked the men if anybody knew if Randy had any family. And TC said he thought there was an aunt in Texas. But he did not know where. He knew that Randy had grown up in Texas somewhere south of Fort Worth. Then Dad said to Joe, "Better get her back'"

By now it was dark and after what I had just seen it was pretty creepy. I practically had El Con stepping on the back of Topper's hooves. I stayed as close to Joe as I could. And Joe kept saying "Are you OK?" I wasn't but I did not want to cry in front of anybody but not even half way back I started crying and I couldn't stop. And I kept telling Joe not to tell Dad I cried. He said "I think your father will figure it out."

When we got back I said I would put the horses away for everybody. Joe said OK. I walked all three horses down and then unsaddled and did a quick groom. It had been a really long day for the horses as well as for all of the people. Of course, I could not sleep. It was hours before I heard the crew and the truck come back, with them was the sheriff's truck.

I found out latter that they did not bring Randy back to the ranch but Doc's ambulance came out to the wash area and the fire truck with some of the guys from the fire department. They brought Randy out and put him into the ambulance. Doc is also the M.E. That was after the sheriff said it was OK. And everybody agreed that it had been javalinas and that it must have been a large group to take down Geronimo too. And besides they saw all the tracks.

Dad told Ray, the sheriff, that he would pay for everything and he told him about the aunt but nobody knew how to get ahold of her.

Everybody slowly filtered into the bunkhouse and sat on bunks, storage chests and what chairs there were in a big circle. Some were sitting on the floor and some on the bunks. Some other men came from Brownie's that I did not even know. Everybody started telling stories. Dad told me to go on up to the house and I asked if I could stay. He said "OK, as long as you do not get upset." I sat down between Dad and Joe and I rammed up as close as I could get to both of them.

The stories were amazing. I am hoping that I can remember some of them. Several of our own guys told about cattle drives. One of the guys, TC, had worked on a ranch in Montana with Randy and he told a bunch of funny things that had happened. Here is one of the stories.

One time they were driving cattle in Montana. It was their job to go all over the area and pick up strays and doggies (younger cattle that have been abandoned for some reason) and take them back to the rancher that they worked for. The rancher would contact the owners by the brand. Randy and TC got paid for each stray.

He told a story about one time when they had been out for over two months, they were camped out in the sleeping rolls. TC woke up during the night and started to get up for a nature call. But Randy went "Shhhhh'. TC whispered, "Why?" Randy whispered back, "Don't talk". So they both laid very still for hours. Finally the sun came up warming everything. A huge timber rattler slithered out from under Randy's trail blanket and went on its merry way.

Wade said, "That is a good story TC!" And all the guys laughed. I asked Dad why and he said he would tell me later.

TC had told me stories before when I was out mucking with him. He did not have any front teeth on top and he had told me that one time during a branding, a calf had taken a real "Mad to the branding iron" and had kicked him from here to Abilene. Another time he told me about a stampede when one of the point drivers had been in the direction of the spooked cows. There had been nothing to identify the drover except for his belt buckle.

I had always thought TC's stories were a lot exaggerated but now I was not so sure.

TC looked at me and said, "Roxie, do you want me to tell you a story that Randy told me about when he was a kid and went on his first round-up?"

I was tucked in tight to Dad's arm but I nodded as much as I could and he began his story.

"One day while Randy and his dad, the range boss for a big spread outside of Houston, the crew was eating out by the campfire after a branding. His dad said, "Boy, do you realize that we just branded over 60 of our little calves and 34 cows for old Jack (the owner of the ranch)? Now I think it is time that you took your place on a round-up. Randy's father was the range boss.

Randy was overjoyed to go on the round-up and to take this first step toward manhood. Randy would be turning nine a month after the drive. He knew his father was saying something very important. Randy spent many nights so excited he could hardly sleep.

Finally the big day came. This was the day that all the drovers began to get everything ready for the drive. Randy's dad told him that getting everything ready was as important as what they would do on the drive.

The two Oxen (castrated bulls who were used for draft) would be pulling the covered wagon used to carry food, cooking utensils, water, medicine, fire needs, hardtack starters, and any other needed supplies. This was called the cook's wagon. The hands carried most of their own needs in rolls on their saddles. They used the horse blankets to sleep on, saddles for pillows and they carried an extra blanket and one change of clothing. They wore their chaps and a few had a cowboy duster and long underwear for really cold weather.

Randy was told that he would ride next to his brother who was fourteen. he was to do what ever his brother told him to do. Exactly.

His dad said they should be able to cover fifteen miles a day. And they were going to go 136 miles to a railhead, a railroad stockyard. They were to go over land that was open and they would have to go onto dirt roads were land was fenced off.

Randy's job was to make sure that no cattle would stray on the part that he was responsible for. His part was a little section on the right side of the herd and toward the far back. This would be the safest place in case of a stampede. Usually in a stampede the cattle would be surging forward. Since it was in the early 1920s there would be a few cars passing when they had to go onto a road. And the cars were loud and would spook the cattle. This was when it was dangerous for the drivers. If an entire herd were to spook the men could be hurt or killed as well as endangering the horses.

It was Monday, April 23rd, 1923. Randy would always remember the exact day because it was a month away from his birthday. His dad woke him up he knew it was early because the moon was still so high in the sky.

All the drivers were around the fire drinking coffee from the big galvanized coffee pot. The smell of frying potatoes and boiling beans competed with the hard tack biscuits, so stomachs growled. The drovers drifted closer and closer to the fire.

Randy's dad said, "Hey, boys, this here is the newest little cowpoke on the trail.

He woulda come out sooner but we ain't had a trail for a while. But he has been on a couple 'a round-ups and he can already bust a mustang as well as his older brothers.

He shoots, and cuts and brands like a big'un. You just watch 'im. I'm real proud of all my boys. "Randy told me this story a million times." TC continued, "He always said that his dad's words was his proudest moment. And that cattle drive was the best time of his life."

Suddenly everyone in the bunkhouse was very quiet. The only sound was the gurgle of the coffeepot on the cook stove. Then TC continued.

"He used to tell more stories, and sometimes they changed, about the storms, the stampedes, the heat and how he kept his "responsibilities" just like a man. You know, Randy never married, never had kids. He was a wanderer just like a lot of us.

But let me tell you something, in case you never got to know him right well. He was an honest son-of-a-gun. I never knew anybody I could trust more. And I am going to miss having him as part of this crew. Him an' me have spent a lotta time on too many ranches and round-ups to count. He was as much a family as I ever had."

All of the guys were nodding and looking really sad, then Jake spoke up. "Mr. Rayburn, I gotta say this. You are the best boss I ever had, and one time me and Randy was talking about bosses, we says, you are the best and the most fair. I think alls us really do appreciate that you are taking care of Randy like you are."

And every body in the bunkhouse clapped and said the same thing.

Dad said, "Listen guys, don't give me any extra credit. I am just doing what is right. And I do know that Randy was a good man. He did an honest days work. And he never gave any of us any guff."

Several of the guy had wet eyes and were looking down at their boots. Just then Jake grabbed his guitar and started playing a beautiful ballad that I had heard him play before. I knew the words so I started singing and then all of the guys were singing too.

Then beat the drum slowly, play the fife lowly,

Play the dead march as you carry me along,

Take me to the green valley, lay the sod on me.

I'm a young cowboy and I know I've done wrong.

It was the most beautiful moment. I felt like I was in church. But even more so. I felt that everybody was connected and we were all thinking and feeling the same thing.

The song ended and the everything got very quiet.

Reese, who is usually very quiet, spoke up and said, "Could I tell about my grandpa and his brothers? He worked ramrod for several of the old roundups on the Chisholm Trail for thirty years until he got too old to sit a horse."

My dad said, "Hold up, Reese, I want Roxie to go on up to the house to get some sleep." I turned to Dad and said, "Please don't make me go now. I want to stay and I want to hear Reece's story."

Wade said, "Mr. Rayburn, I don't think any of us are going to be doin' any sleeping. Dad didn't say anything, but he didn't make me go.

60

One of the hands from Mr. Brown's place said, "Go on Reese, tell us."

Reece said, "The is the story I was hearing since I was knee high to a jackrabbit. My grampy had three brothers and they all rode together and always worked the same jobs. And they were named Matthew, Mark, Luke and John. But as the story goes, that's as close as they ever came to being connected to anything from the Bible. They were a fighting, drinking, hard riding crew, and the best old cowboys that ever rode a trail. Matthew, the oldest was the ramrod, Mark and Luke were cutters and John was the cook.

John had broken his back in a stampede and became a trail cook and a darned good one at that. He was also a pretty good trail "doctor" with all kinds of cures and fixes for anything that didn't already kill one of the hands. They rode the Chisholm Trail and I've listened to hunerts of stories about them but I'll just tell about one of the drives.

Somehow the four of them had wound up working on a spread outside of San Antonio. This drive started out about twenty-miles south of San Antonio and had seven thousand head of longhorns. The trail would go past San Antonio, Dallas, Red River Station, through Indian territory and up to Sedalia, Kansas to the rail head. This was some time around 1866. And ranchers were trying to get more cattle to where it needed to go.

I 'member him tellin' stories about Indian raids, stampedes, fights with ranchers, runnin' all night to get to water before the cattle done went down from thirst and the stories the crew told around the campfire."

Suddenly, Dad was gently shaking me and I realized that I had fallen asleep. Dad said, "Boys, I got to get this little filly up to the house. She is done in. I will talk to you in the morning and let you know what the plans are."

I tried to protest but Dad was gently pulling me to my feet and I realized how tired I was. I wanted to be in my quiet room.

Joe said, "I'll walk with you, Boss." We walked the short distance to the house and Dad asked me if I wanted anything. I said "It's OK, I'll get it." I went to the kitchen and got a couple of sodas and took them to my room. I did not want anything to eat. I was so exhausted I drank one of the sodas, took my boots off and just got into bed with all my clothes on.

April 12

Dear Diary it has taken me three nights of writing to tell about what happened to Randy. So I will go back to you tomorrow night. I am just all written out. Randy's funeral is going to be tomorrow.

I did not know Randy very well, but I am so sad about what has happened. I don't even know how old he was. Joe is trying to get in touch with any family. Maybe Joe will find out more about him. It is the first time I have thought about the kind of lives that some people lead. I wonder if he was lonely. The rest of the hands were his friends but I don't think they are the kind of friends that tell each other everything.

Dad did not know if he went to church or what kind of church if he did go. So the service for Randy will be at our church and be buried in the Cochise Cemetery.

April 13

Randy's funeral was very nice. If you can use the word nice about an event when someone has died. I was really glad to see how many people were there. Many of the men I did not know. But Rev. Johnson gave a nice, brief talk, then asked the others to speak. Joe told more things about Randy. And then several of the hands talked and even a couple of men who had worked with him on other ranches.

Dad spoke last. I had never heard him so serious and he said some wonderful things about the value of life and how important the choices were. And he said that Randy had made good choices and that he had left a mark because he cared about people and lived an honest and honorable life. I thought he made more sense than Rev. Anderson did. All the cars and trucks went out to the Cochise Cemetery.

When we got there, the first thing I saw was Old Smoky. Old Smoky was the grey gelding that Randy used to use as his second string horse. He was by the big hole that was there for the casket. He was saddled and had Randy's bedroll. He had a pair of Randy's boots hanging off the saddle horn. And his reins were ground-tied. I even think Smoky knew what was going on. He had his head down and looked as sad as the rest of us.

Rev. Johnson kept his words short and just TC spoke and said a poem about a cowboy's lot in life. I never thought of TC saying a poem. Then one of the hands took Smoky and loaded him and we all headed back to the TriR for a get together. Cook had made a big spread and some of the Ladies from our church had brought some of their special dishes.

Usually hands make food disappear like locusts on a field but today they hardly ate. Cook said for everybody to come back in for supper because she did not want to have to put away all that food. I also think it was to be nice to the hands so that everybody could get together one more time.

April 14

Dad has been on the phone all day trying to find any relatives that Randy had. He has been trying to find any relative for days. Finally he said that he could not find any and he would put information in several papers to see if any turned up. Otherwise he was going to give what there was to TC.

April 25

Dear Diary, I have not written anything for many days just because I have not been in the mood to write anything. I've been going to school, riding fence and hanging out with Cami. Joe told me to not even muck for a while just because everybody just needed time. I know what he means.

But the last couple of days, everybody seems to be a little better we were even smiling and making little jokes.

Well, I have to tell what happened today. It was hilarious. At least it was until I got majorly grounded.

But let me tell it from the beginning.

Dad said he was going to go to Tucson for a meeting and asked if I want to go. So I asked if Cami could go too. He said yes, so I called her and said get ready and we would come pick her up. Cami and I talked about what we would wear since we always dressed as much alike as possible because we were "in the mix". We decided on red, circle-skirts, white, sheer blouses, really "bomb" red leather, ballerina slippers. We were going all out capital COOL!

Dad has a big yellow Cadillac that he drives to Tucson and other places when he does not want to use one of the trucks. I love the crazy car. It has electric windows that I love to play with and other really cool stuff.

My slippers were all scuffed and we were going to the Fox Movie Theater. So I brought the red shoe polish with us. It was the liquid kind in a little bottle.

We were in the back seat and I was trying to be careful so that my dad would not see that I had a bottle of open liquid polish and was doing my shoes. I knew he couldn't smell the polish because he can't smell anything.

We were in downtown Tucson and on 6th Avenue. Everybody is on the street and it is very busy even for a Saturday. My dad stops all the sudden at a stop light and of course, the polish spills. All over the floor carpeting. There is red everywhere. I know that I am in mega trouble.

You know how when it is already as bad as it can be and you just go ahead and do something even more stupid? Well, I did. Cami is looking at me and I can tell she is about ready to freak out.

I reach down with my right hand and dip it in the polish and I roll the window down and now my hand is hanging out of the car and polish is dripping off my hand. I am flapping my hand at people who are walking by on the street and people are jumping back and kinda yelling.

Dad sees what I am doing. He pulls the car over to the side as soon as he can stop, gets out and comes back and jerks me out of the car. People are walking over to the car to find out what is wrong. My dad is yelling. I mean YELLING! He is telling people, "It is shoe polish!" "Just shoe polish!" "SHOE POLISH!"

Now I have it all over me. Dad it trying to find something in the trunk to clean with. Altogether it was a fine mess.

Dad went to a car cleaning place. Dad made us go inside and wait. He had them clean up as much as they could.

He kept telling Cami that it had nothing to do with her and she was not in trouble in anyway. Just me. I don't know what he is planning on doing but he said he will tell me tomorrow. He did not even go to his meeting. As soon as the cleaners did whatever they could (and believe me it is still bad) we headed back. That stuff just does not come out. It is on the seats, the floor, on me and even some got on Dad.

That was kinda the coup de grace as far as he was concerned. I know my clothes are ruined and probably his suit. Cami rode in the front all the way home. Dad talked to her and they just had a gay old time talking and nobody talked to me. But actually, no matter what happens to me, down deep I really think the whole thing is funny.

I loved the look on people's faces as they were jumping back as my hand was flapping and dripping all over the place. I was my own scary movie. Of course Cami was being a cube and I am in the backseat being my usual spaz self.

I guess I might not think it is so funny tomorrow after I get the royal shaft.

April 26

Well, it is not as funny today. Dad says I am so grounded. I can only ride fence. I can't go to any shows, or see any friends for a month. Boy, I had better never tell him I like to ride fence. Right now I would rather be with Joe. Cami can be a stick sometimes.

I guess I will get a lot of reading done. But I also have to help in the kitchen. When Gretchen comes to cook I have to help her. But I still think yesterday was funny. I crack myself up every time I think about my hand out the window.

April 27

Gretchen came today after school and it was not even her day. I smell a rat. And it gets worse! I go into the kitchen and tell Gretch that I will help her for a bit then I gotta go out and do my fence chore. That should take care of it. She says, "NO, Father says you learn to bake today." And I say again, "No, I have to ride fence, it is my JOB! She says "NO!". Now I am mad so I start to walk on out. She grabs me by the back of my belt and spins me around.

Remember, she is about three times my weight. And she plants me in front of the counter. She says, "We bake!. And bake we did. All day. I learned to make cinnamon yeast rolls. From scratch!. We made four batches. Do you know how long that takes? Each batch has to rise forever.

But I will admit the last batch was pretty good. We took all the extras out to the bunkhouse and the crew told me they were great. I just wonder what else Dad has in store for me. Maybe tomorrow I will learn how to make adobe!

April 28

Of course the story is all over school. Everybody thinks it a riot. James put some red crayon on his hand and walked down the hallway shaking at everybody. Cami said that everybody was being ridiculous. I thought they were too funny.

Everybody thought it was a drag that I could not go to anything over the weekend. No games, no dance or anything. Well, I guess I better grab a new book from Mrs. Mason. Maybe two. Don't know how long I am going to be in the dog house. So it is reading and getting a lot of homework and housework done. Oh Joy! Double Joy! NOT! Right now I would like to use some of Dad's words.

May 1

I did not feel like writing for a couple of days. Still don't. Have not done anything but reading and doing homework. I knew it! The good part is I am not doing it in town. Dad is being tough on this one. Usually he gives up and lets me off. Not this time. He has let me do a couple of things but I am not completely free.

I have so many feelings right now. They are all mixed up. I am sad when I think about Randy

Then I get mad when I think about how Ida treats me when I do not do anything bad to her. Then something funny happens and I get silly and then I feel guilty because I am too happy. I hope that very soon I will stop being all crazy and mixed up. I try to remember that "this too shall pass".

Cami wanted to go to the Friday Show so we did. Dad said it was OK. I think that helps. I know she is trying to help me get over being sad and she is a good friend.

May 2

Dad made me go in a help Ida. It has been a wonderful, long, while since we have had to be together. So I guess she had a good while to load up on mean things to say. She gave me both barrels. And she did not even know about the shoe polish escapade. She was just her usual vile, disagreeable self. Same old refrain about Sharon so why repeat it.

She made me do the sheets on that horrible old mangle. I get burned every time I use that stupid ironing machine. I think it is just easier to use an iron rather than that big ironing monstrosity. Who ever invented a machine that is just a wide hot surface that no matter how careful you are you still get burned?

Not everybody has one of these instruments of torture. So I will describe it. It is this big machine about three feet wide with two hot surfaces. The top part is a big round roller and it pulls the sheet or whatever you are ironing through it. The problem is that it can pull fingers too. Or your arm touches the hot part. It has a cabinet just like a giant sewing machine. Then after you use it you have to clean it. I don't get it. It is easier just to use a regular iron. But I guess Ida gets her jollies knowing I am stuck using this horrible thing. Long day. Dad did not pick me up until after nine so Ida had plenty of time to get into her rant.

I have learned how to get through some of her "episodes". I think about Strawberry Fields. How beautiful it must be to see the tender green plants in row after row as far as I can see. And the tiny jewel-like fruit bursting into their dark, ruby red glory. The heady aroma in the warm breeze. Fluffy clouds high in an azure sky.

As long as I can pretend that I am in the middle of this paradise I can tune out all of the hurtful things that Ida says to me.

May 3

Church. Had a solo that I really had not practiced enough and I was having a hard time remembering the words. Mrs. Johnson glared at me a bunch of times when I kinda improvised words. They sounded OK to me.

Went home and Dad said I could go out and ride. I did. Boy did I need that. I stayed out until dark. Then Dad and I went to the Fry's for a late dinner. They were waiting for Brahm anyway because he was over at Janelle's house with her family.

May 4

Mrs. Mason asked me if I was ready for the reading list or if I wanted to wait. I said it would be a good thing. I had even talked to Dad about it. He said he would read some of the stuff too and we could talk about it. That will be so fun. Dad has always been a great reader and he has given me a lot of books and he is always reading something.

I know we are not real "blood" but I think I get my love of ideas, and learning from Dad. Lately we have been talking about what is important about living. He says that one of his most important beliefs is that people make a contribution in life be making life better for other human beings.

He also said that people are "immortal as long as somebody remembers them". I love that idea. He said to think about how I feel about Johanna and that as long as I am alive and remember her she will be immortal. And that will be true of people all my life. He said he felt that way about his father, mother and his uncles. He called it the chain of life. And the best thing he said was that if we tell stories to our children that become part of the fabric of a family then we carry that person for generations.

May 5

I love school but this year I am really ready for it to be summer vacation. Something happened in school that was both funny and sad at the same time. Mr. Pendleton is our History teacher. He is really a stick. He knows a lot of history but I don't think he gets the students very excited about it.

I just happen to love to read about history. Always have. But anyway, Mr. Pendleton is really more strict and more rigid than any of the other teachers. He always wears grey suits, with grey ties, and a white shirt. Three different suits. He wears one for a week and then the next one and then the next one. the class counted one time. He has eight ties. And he wears them in a row. Exactly. We don't know how many white shirts he has. They look alike if there is more than one. We have never seen him in anything else. He comes to our church and he is in the same thing except he has different ties he wears to church. They are shiny. He wears black shoes, always with a high shine and black socks.

His classroom is different from all of our other classrooms. He can't stand it if one desk is out of line and they have to be exact distance front to back and side to side. The boys move the desks just to annoy him. Mr. Pendleton's desk is always very clean. The other teachers have books and papers stacked up but not him. Papers have to go in a certain place and they have to be neat. That is his favorite word. "NEAT!' "Students, you must be neat." He really goes overboard on how we do our papers, how we keep our desks and more. His desk is always shiny clean.

Today, Tiny, a boy in our class who is quite large, went up to Mr. Pendleton's desk and started to say he was sick. Well, he got as far as "Mr. Pendleton, I am...."

Then he proceeded to throw up all over Mr. Pendleton, his desk, his chair, and the floor. I have never seen anybody throw up that much. Ever. Poor Mr. Pendleton just froze and looked from Tiny to us and then back to Tiny. He did not move for a couple of minutes. Tiny just looked so surprised and sorry. He turned and ran out of the room. Two of the other boys got up and went after him. To help him, I guess.

Mr. Pendleton just kept sitting there like a rabbit when it is frozen in fear.

Mr. Pendleton finally stood up with what dignity he could muster considering that he was covered pretty much from his shoulders to the rest of the way down, with this runny, smelly, yellow, gooey stuff.

He walked to the door. Without turning around he said, "One of you, go get Mrs. Bennett. Tell her I will not be back until tomorrow." And then he walked out of the room. We all just sat there, nobody said anything for several minutes.

Then somebody in the classroom started laughing and soon we all were. Finally Jerry said, "Hey, we gotta go tell Mrs. Bennett."

James, ever the goof, said, "Why? We could just go outside." Benny said, "We have almost an hour before English. We could go to the gym. Greta said "Don't be stupid, we have to tell somebody." And in case you haven't noticed, the room really stinks!"

Everybody started laughing all over again. I don't think anybody was laughing at Tiny. We felt sorry for him. Everybody was laughing at Mr. Pendleton. Of all the teachers it could have happened to, it had to be Mr. Rigid.

James turned around to my desk and said, "Roxie, you go tell Mrs. Bennett." I said "Why me?" James said "Just because." Mrs. Bennett is the vice principal.

But I knew why, I was always the bigmouth. I'm usually teacher's pet. Except for Mr. Anderson. Even Mr. Pendleton likes me because I like history. He would always leave me in charge when he had to leave the classroom just like most of the other teachers did.

So I got up and went to the office. Mrs. Cantwell is the school secretary and I think she is about a hundred years old. She has white hair and she is really tiny. But boy is she tough. Everybody says she runs the school more than Mr. Langtry does. I stood at the counter until she finished what she was doing. She does not like to be interrupted. So we don't. She finished whatever she was doing, looked up at me and said, "What do you want, Roxie?"

I told her the whole thing. I was surprised that instead of getting mad, she had a sort of smile on her face. Then she went into Mrs. Bennett's office and I could hear the two of them laughing like loons. I had never seen Mrs. Cantwell smile or laugh before. They finally came out together and they were trying not to laugh but it was not working very well. Mrs. Bennett, said, "Come on, Roxie", and I followed her back to class.

When we got to the room, she stopped at the door and said, "Alright, class, please go outside by the flagpole. Stay there until I send for you." I noticed that Mrs. Bennett did not go all the way into the room. We went outside and Mrs. Cantwell came out and we were out there until time to go to English. The rest of Mr. Pendleton's classes went to the library and had study hall.

Tomorrow should be weird. Wonder what everybody will say. Especially Tiny and Mr. Pendleton.

May 6

Tiny did not come to school today. Mr. Pendleton just acted in class as if nothing had happened. I wonder if the "throw-up suit" will become a "thrown-away-suit?"

But the room stills smells like an old chicken coop. Mr. Pendleton opened all the windows and got George, the school handy man, to bring in two big black fans. I think it made the smell worse. But, boy, were we quiet all period.

James asked me if I wanted to go to the prom. He said he had not asked me sooner because so much had been going on and he was afraid that I would say no. Well, I do like him and we have fun together and the best part is that he seems to understand that I do not want to get serious like some of the other girls do. Even I know we are too young. So, yeah, I'm in.

At dinner tonight I told Dad that James asked me to the prom. Dad asked me if I was beginning to like boys instead of horses. Had to think about that one. Not really. I still would rather be with El Con, and do barrel racing and do my reading and writing. But I do like James. As long as we have fun just hanging out. spend so much time with. I said I do know that and I also know that I am not ready for the "real boyfriend" like Lana is with Leslie. I know that is years away.

Dad said, "Try to remember that you only get a few years to be a kid. And you get a lot of years to be a grownup with all that goes with being an adult. I just want you to have the fun of being silly and being carefree. Don't get old too soon."

Dad reminded me that I am younger than the kids that I go to school with. I asked Dad not to say anything to Ida because I don't want to hear her say the crappie things that she does. But then it is Cochise, so it won't be long before somebody says something and she will be on my case. Big Time.

We all met up at the Dairy Queen. He bought me a banana split. And he remembered that I do not like chocolate so he asked Melanie to put extra strawberries on it. How can you not like a guy who remembers what you like and what you don't like? So does this mean I have a boyfriend? I guess so as long as the friend part is the most important part.

May 7

Somehow everybody thinks James and I are an "item". Even James. I don't really mind but you would think I would have been consulted. I really do not want to date anybody else but I am also sure that I do not want to "go steady". I will have to talk with James about it. We have agreed to just be friends who go out as part of our group. We do not really date. I know I am too young and I like to spend time with James but we do not really do "kissy" stuff. There is so much time for that silly stuff in the future.

Great day at school. Told Mr. Bertram that I am going to Tucson to get some of the books on his list. He said he will lend me some of the books that he has.

But the big deal at school is that everybody is all gaga over the Prom. All the girls are talking about what they will wear and shoes and colors of corsages. Sometimes I really worry because I know I am different. I do not get that excited over the same things that they do. Even Cami is really going overboard on what she is wearing and all excited about the fact that it is her first prom and even more excited about Evan. Evan is James' cousin.

The Tucson schools are different and only juniors and Seniors can go to the prom. But our school is so small that all four grades in high school can go to the prom. But we are very tightly supervised at the prom and afterward. I think that is a good thing. I have heard so many stories about kids who have gone to the formal dances and then gone out drinking or getting into trouble in other ways. That seems so stupid to me because it should be a fun time and not a time to mess up your future. Dad, Pug and Mrs. Mason are some of the chaperones for the dance. So there is not much danger involved for me. Too many eyes everywhere!

When I got home after school, I told dad we needed to make a quick trip to Tucson and why. He said "Then hurry before the stores close." So we drove in to Levy's in downtown Tucson. We got there with just a little over an hour until closing time. So I had an hour to get what I needed. I didn't even need that.

A wonderful saleslady helped. After I told her what I wanted she brought out five white dresses. I saw the one I wanted right away. It had a shirred satin fitted, with a spaghetti strap top. And the skirt part was Cinderella beautiful with three layers of silk chiffon that floated like a cloud on a summer day. I was enchanted. The saleslady, Mrs. Soams, said it would need three crinolines, those poufy under slips. Everybody at school was wearing them under their circle-skirts but I didn't have any. They are so pretty they could make a prom dress by themselves!

Then we were off to find shoes. White satin pumps. Highest heel I have ever had. I will have to practice walking. Don't know how I will dance in them. So Mrs. Soams and I went into the dressing room. She started helping me take off my clothes.

OK, not so fast, I told her I could do that part my self. She stepped out of the room and I put it all on. It was a real struggle. I got everything on but I had to call her back in to zip up the back.

I did feel like a newly minted Cinderella. I looked completely different. One of the really great things about the dress was that the way the top was made it did not show how flat I am. One of the problems with being younger than every body else in my class. That was something I had never really thought about before. Well, not a lot I can do about it so I am just not going to worry about "what I don't have"!

Mrs. Soams held up my hair and said "With all this hair it would look charming up." Then she said "Let's go show your father." I asked her how much everything was and she said, "Your father has already taken care of it."

She walked me out and my dad just smiled and said, "Where has my little girl gone?".

"Roxie, I think you have picked very well. And fast!" He turned to Mrs. Soams and he asked her if anything needed alteration. She said, "No, she is very easy to fit. The top will fit perfectly with a special bra and the length is just right." Lucky for me that she knew what length it was supposed to be. I didn't even know what size I was for a formal. She left to go find the "special bra" and then came back with it. Ugh. But I guess I need it.

Mrs. Soams asked Dad if I needed jewelry. He said "No, I have that taken care of." I did not know that my dad knew about this stuff. Dad said, "We will take it all now." She was gone for a little while then came back with everything in one big box and two giant bags.

On the way home I asked him why he said that he had the jewelry taken care of. He told me not to worry about it. I didn't because I had a choker-necklace that was white beads on a white ribbon that tied in the back. And it had matching earrings and a bracelet. The Fry's had given me the set at Christmas.

Suddenly I was beginning to get some enthusiasm for the big dance! We were both quiet going home and just before our turnoff Dad said. "You know, you are growing up a lot faster than I am ready for. Yesterday all you wanted to wear was Levis and now you are in your first grownup formal." We both realized that this was true and a big change had occurred without either one of us noticing until we were at the department store.

Then Dad said, "Well, there is one good thing!" I said, "What?" He said, "When you are dancing, James will not be able to get closer than three feet from you with all those slips and that fluffy dress!" And we both busted out laughing and we laughed clear up our road to the house.

I called Cami as soon as I got to my room and told her what I had gotten. And we talked about a million things. I couldn't wait for it to be morning and to go to school and for once it had nothing to do with classes!

May 8

Our class has History first period. When I got to my desk, there was a note and a Big Hunk candy bar. James knows I love the crazy candy. The note said, What color is your dress? Would you rather have roses, orchids, or camellias? I wrote back, White Baby Orchids. Can't remember one thing that Mr. Pendleton said. So many firsts for me.

Got home, did my chores. Pug called and said to come early Sat morning so she can have extra time with my hair. She wants to take a picture so James and I will have to stop by her house before the dance. I love that she cares that much. Ida would not care, as a matter of fact I think it would just annoy her if we stopped by the House of Ida.

James called and asked if Cami and I were going to the show. I said yes, and he said they will see us there after football practice if they get finished in time.

Cami and I went and sat where we usually sit and we saved seats for the guys. The movie is called <u>The Thing</u>.

They guys did not show up so we figured that practice ran long. It got to the part where the Thing is trying to get into the door and the men are trying to keep it out. All the sudden something grabs my leg and Cami's leg and we jump up and scream bloody murder. James and Evan had sneaked in behind us and crawled under the seats and at the right time, they grabbed our legs. Everybody in the show is laughing. Turns out that James and Evan had planned this. I guess it was funny after I got finished being scared and then embarrassed.

The rest of the movie is pretty scary too. Toward the end James put his arm on the back of my seat. I am glad that he did not put his arm around me. Cami and Evan hold hands a lot and he puts his arm around her in the movie show. But I think James understands that I am just not as ready as Cami is. He is a very cool guy. I don't even need Dad to tell me that we need to take it slowly. That is what I want too.

May 9

I think today was a useless day at school. Everybody was all a-twitter. By now everybody knows who is going with whom and who is not going. Of course, everybody knows all about the story of the "leg grabbing" at the show. Even Mr. Bertram laughed about it.

Mr. Bertram said he had some books for me and to pick them up after school and I said I would. I went by after school and he gave me a burlap sack of books. I will look at them Sunday.

I went home, saddled up and El and we spent a nice peaceful hour by ourselves. I discussed many issues with him and he gave me his usual advice in his usual sensible horse language. He said go have a wonderful time tomorrow and he would spend his day with Lizzie.

May 9

It is the big day, my first prom, so let the preparations begin. Dad took me into Pug's. She took two hours to do my hair. It is in big, fat curls in an "up do". It actually looks great. She put little pearl Bobbie pins all over. They are pins with pearls on the ends. I don't know where she got them.

Pug did something so wonderful. When Dad and I went shopping I didn't even think about underwear or new stockings. But Pug gave me a beautiful set of pale, beige colored, undies and some wonderful new stockings, the new kind without seams.

Joe had already said he would do my mucking and my chores. So I went home and tried to keep from messing up my hair. I tried to read but for once I did not want to.

Dad asked if I wanted to take a ride over to Brownie's ride over to Mr. We would go in the car not ride over. It was very nice to sit out by Brownie's fish while he and Dad talked.

We went home and we had an early dinner. I thought I would not be hungry but I was.

Finally it was time to finish getting ready.   Pug had shown me how to put on the make up, even the rouge,   and she gave me lessons about the eye goop. Seemed like it took me forever to get it right, but it did look good.

Dad came in and said James was here. But before I went out to the living room he wanted to give me something. He handed me a black velvet box.   In it was a beautiful pearl necklace and pearl earrings. I was just stunned. That is the first time Dad ever gave me jewelry.   He said, "Don't cry, you will miss up your makeup." But he looked like he was more ready to cry than I was.

I went out and James was sitting stiffly on the couch and he looked great. He had on charcoal slacks and a pale cream dinner jacket. I have never seen him look like that. I was used to his Levis and cowboy shirts.   He had the little plastic container with a beautiful white orchid with white ribbon and some baby breath. It was a wrist corsage. James remembered that I do not like the ones you pin on. They look like a headlight on a dress. When I lifted up the corsage, underneath was a beautiful pearl bracelet. I guess he and Dad had it all planned.

James had his grandfather's car.   Evan was sitting in the car waiting for us. We all went to Cami's house and Evan went in to get her.   She looked beautiful in her pink lace and net dress. I think she had on three crinolines too. We were all laughing about how much space we took up. We looked like we were plopped in the middle of a sea of cotton candy. We barely fit in the seats. We stopped at Pug's so she could take the pictures of the four of us. Pug still makes me wish she was my mother.

Well, I am not going to tell about every dance, but every minute of the dance was magical. Half way through I had to take off my heels. So the rest of the time James called me Cindy for Cinderella. I have never had such a good time.

Dad and the rest of the chaperones sat off in the corner and I felt good knowing that they were there just to make sure that everybody was safe and happy. Dad had said that I could stay out one hour after the dance ended. I did not mind that Dad and the others were at the dance. They seemed to be having fun, themselves, sitting at a table talking and laughing. I so seldom see Dad laughing lately that I really liked seeing him enjoying himself.

After the prom we all went to the Milo and most of our gang was there. So there we sat in our beautiful clothes eating hamburgers and fries. The perfect ending. My very first prom. And I did not turn into a pumpkin! For one magical evening, I felt as old as the rest of my gang. Sometimes I feel older and sometimes I feel much younger. But tonight I think I got it just right. It was a Strawberry Fields night.

May 10

OK, the princess has had to turn back into the cowgirl. I have not been doing as many chores as I should and I have only done barrel once a week or not at all. So I told Joe, I would get up extra early and do two days this week. He is off today but I ran the barrel anyway. Did not need timing because I was so rusty. I am so out of practice.

El seemed very glad to be running. He really did well. I think he was directing me. We went back in and I did a great grooming including his special massage. And I even did extra brushing on his mane and forelock. He was a very happy horse.

Dad came out and said he had to go to Mr. Brown's and we could ride over. I wonder what is going on with the two of them.? I told him I would take Lizzie and he could use Dan. I saddled up both, went into the house got a book. Dad said James had called and I said I could call him back from Mr. Brown's. As we rode over Dad asked me how my dance was and if everybody liked my dress? I said he should know, and he answered that he had not really been paying that much attention. Fat chance! But I let him think that I believed that he had not been watching me like a hawk.

I told him I had the prettiest dress and the pearls were the hit of the dance. He said I was turning into a lovely young woman. I almost cried.

Called James from Mr. Brown's. We talked forever. He came to dinner at the ranch. Maybe I will be able to get him to start riding yet.

May 11

Well, good times are at an end. For the time being anyway. Have end of the year tests coming up. And there is a national test that our school is taking. Mrs. Mason told the English Class that it would be next week. It is called an Achievement test. And then Mrs. Mason told me that five students from our school were picked to take another test. I was one of the five. Oh joy, one more test!

So I am studying. Cami and I are going to alternate going to each other's house. Tonight I went to her house. We worked on English. I am better at English, writing, understanding, reading etc. She is better at math and science. Cami hates to write. She says she can't understand why I write so much when I don't have too. I tell her I need to and she tells me that it does not make sense. Nobody needs to write. And I said yes, and even Mrs. Mason says the same thing. And she said of course you would agree with her and all the other teachers. You are always teacher's pet. First time she ever said that. Kind of hurt my feelings but I did not say so. So we studied.

May 12

No reading for fun, no show, just studying. James is studying too so we have agreed not to hang out until after the tests.

May 13

No time for writing, as it is chores, choir practice, school work and studying. I will check back in, Dear Diary, after all of the tests are over. Even El Con is complaining that I have no time.

May 15

Got our annuals today. We spent the day running around to get everybody to sign them. Then we had a big slumber party at my house. All the girls in our gang, all seven girls. We had so much fun but I don't think Dad did. And I know that a couple of the hands were actually on 'guard" to keep the boys from crashing. I guess Dad thought that was necessary because I went to a slumber party out at the TriangeT and a couple of the boys crashed and Mr. Ellsworth, Penny's dad had to make them go home. They were not really doing anything, they were just outside playing guitar under her bedroom window and everybody was laughing like loons. But as far as coming out to our ranch, I don't think any of them would have the nerve anyway, knowing my dad. I think we all got to sleep after five. I know I have a lot of catch up work to do.

May 16

Everybody came to pick up the girls. Then Dad and I went to Tucson. I wanted to get a dress to wear for the CUHS Awards ceremony. Got a pretty white eyelet dress with spaghetti straps and a little bolero jacket. I will use my prom pumps. And the pearls of course.

James picked me up and we go get Cami and Evan who was at her house and we went to the show. It was Marilyn Monroe and Richard Widmark in <u>Don't Bother to Knock</u>. It was a very strange story with all kinds of twists and turns. I didn't like it that much. We almost got up and left and afterwards in the Milo everybody said we should have left.

May 17

Church solo, pot luck dinner. Ida was there. Which was unusual because she does not like Dad's church. She has a different religion. She is Catholic but I have never seen her go to church that much. Boy, could she use some of the lessons about being kind to your fellow people. I used to have to go to two churches and be in two choirs. But since Ida has been at the Center so much, Dad let me stop going to her church. And what was even weirder, she rarely went to her church herself. She just made me go.

I just realized how long it has been since I have seen her. I know Dad goes in a couple of evenings a week but I have escaped for a good while.

She hardly even speaks to me. I guess she would just rather say the garbage that she does when she has me alone.

Anyway I helped the church ladies clean up then went home and read. Friday, I told Mr. Bertram that I was not starting on the list until after school was out and he say he knows how busy I am. So I am just reading for fun. I was reading Henry V and I love the St. Cripians speech. "Once more into the Breech men..." "We few, we happy few, we band of brothers..."

May 18

Awards night. Fun. I got bars and my sweater in Drama, English, Chorus, Band and I got a special award for Chorus as soloist. Odd, since he is the teacher that I like the least. I am first chair clarinet band. James got Football and Basketball bars and his sweater. He is not all that crazy about any of his classes.

May 19

The farrier came and shod all of the horses that needed it. Joe wanted to do another super mucking and cleaning and we did. I was off school so I worked all day. Joe said I made up for some of my missed chores. And after school is out I will be doing more.

May 21

Sang in chorus for Senior Graduation. Then we went to Palmas for Mexican food.

May 22

Sang in chorus for 8th graduation then the four of us all went to the Milo and then to Cami's and watched television. Schools out!

May 23

Well, this is bad news. BAD! Dad said they were letting the town maid go and I would have to go into town to help Ida. I could be in town half the week and Home half the week. What a bummer. I know where this is headed. How can I do my chores, "help" Ida, which really means do everything for her and still do my summer reading and working with El Con and Lizzie? Dad said I don't have to do my chores at the ranch. But I WANT to do my chores at the ranch. As usual, the only reason she wants me to come into the town house is to do all of the housework and washing and ironing. Major bummer!

I even think Joe is ticked at Dad as well. But of course, he can't say anything. But Cora did. She said she could help Ida more but Dad said no, that would not work out. I think something is going on but I do not know what.

May 24

Dad and I made a deal. It is better than nothing. I have to go in and "help" Ida after I do my chores. Unless she has a card party or something I can leave after I have finished with lunch dishes. I don't know why but he is not going to hire another maid for the "House of Ida". So guess who is it. Ta Da! Little ol' me.

But most days I can get away and still be able to be back to the ranch and my real life. For once he stood up because she wanted me to be there all the time. Not because she wants my wonderful company but she wants somebody to wait on her hand and foot. So she only gets "half" of her way. Score one for my side. Or at least half of a one.

May 25

I don't know what I do that seems to get me on the wrong side of luck but after I got back to the ranch today, I was riding fence and El Con shied at something and he caught my left foot between him and a fence post. My fault really because I know better, I was riding too close. Turned the stirrup around and I have a lovely sprain. Doc taped it and I can barely walk. Doc says stay off for a few days. Now let's see if Ida leaves me alone until I can do her bidding. Dad will talk to her.

May 26

I told Joe I could still do fence even if I can't muck and he said no I could do more harm to the ankle. He said I could make it up to him in July because he is going to go to New Mexico for a week. I don't know why and he did not say. So I took a book and went out and sat with El. Jacinto is going to groom El for a week. Only Joe can ride him. He is not good with anybody but me and Joe. Dad tried to ride him one time and he said, " I don't know what you say to him but it must be good." Topper is that way with Joe too. I can ride Topper but he is still better with Joe. TC tried to ride Topper one time and he became a high roller. Joe said it was pretty funny.

May 27

Well, I have time. So I am reviewing the reading list Mr. Bertram gave me. Boy, that sure got put to the side, did it not? I am going to pick five books at a time, read those, write what I think and then pick out the next five. I wish I could get somebody to do it with me. Dad said he would read some "as time permits". I will lobe to discuss some with him. He is a great reader and certainly a great thinker.

He says one of the biggest problems with the world is that most people just take ideas and information without really thinking through and make decisions based on faulty or lacking information. He said that people use the same thinking when they elect leaders and then they get the government they deserve. He said that the country elected a war hero as a president which just proves his point. He said the qualifications for the two jobs are so very different but the general public cannot tell the difference. Dad talks a lot about politics and the economy. Some I understand and some I do not.

But I am trying to learn because if I want to be a judge someday, I need to understand the larger world. I sure don't want to be an Ida who is only interested in a little tiny piece of the world.

My five picks for reading. Kate Chopin, The Story of an Hour, The Awakening. Steven Crane, The Red Badge of Courage. Bret Harte, The Outcasts of Poker Flats. Nathaniel Hawthorne, The Scarlet Letter. Sherwood Anderson, Short Stories, Winesburg, Ohio

I picked these because Mr. Bertram already gave me the books. One story is just a couple of typed pages that he gave me. The Story of an Hour, Chopin. WOW! Double WOW! It is so good. Just this little short story. About a woman who finds out her husband has been killed. DD, I can't tell you more or I would give away the surprise. I asked Dad if he had read it and he said, no, but he would. And we could talk about it at dinner. And we did. We really had a great conversation about the writer and the story.

Dad talked about how society thinks that there are limits to what women can do and all kinds of things I have never heard him talk about. And he said that I can do what ever I want to do because I am born into a time when women are thinking more for themselves than they have before. He said his sisters never married because they chose not too and people thought they were strange but now it is not so strange. It was really a most wonderful evening. I had been planning to go to the show but I stayed home. Dad and I watched TV but we talked more than we watched.

May 28

I can stand on my foot especially if I put my weight on the other leg. So I went out and groomed El. Joe told me about some of the history about Cochise.

The town of Cochise is on the banks of the San Pedro River and is surrounded by mountains. There was actually an outlaw called Jack the Ripper who was killed in Fisher's Saloon. I guess somebody copied the Ripper from England. Joe did not know how the name came about.

The town is where the Butterfield Stage coaches crossed the San Pedro. It was the first railroad connection for this area and cattle were brought here to be shipped to stockyards. Early ranchers had to put up with Indian raids, bad weather, and during the Civil War, there were even solider encampments. Indian stories are about two different tribes. The Navajo and the Chiricahua Apaches.

The town began with a blacksmith, farrier, general store, feed store, other store fronts that supplied needed goods, but mostly it had saloons that served all of the cowboys and other travelers. The saloons catered to the cowboys, supplying crap games, "likker", other card games, all forms of gambling, and ladies of the night. There were singers and other theatrical acts that performed for the large crowds.

The Apache Chief, Vitorio, was headquartered in the Dragoon Mountains. He and his men were a constant threat to the cattle and sometimes to the ranchers themselves until his capture. Joe said that one of his uncles, his uncle's wife, and children were all killed in an Indian raid. Joe said that he could understand why though, because the soldiers and the settlers had killed as many of the Indians as possible and had broken every treaty made with the Indians.

I said to Joe, that Indian history was never mentioned in school and he said, that since the white men had actually come in and stolen the lands from the Indians, they had to make the Indians out to be the bad guys. Joe said that the Cochise was tricked into giving up but Geronimo was the smart one who knew the white men were lying about the treaties and he fought to the end. And he was tricked in the end as well.

Boy, did he give me something to think about. And all the cowboy shows that we go to always make the Indians out to be savages or not very smart.

May 29

James came out and picked me up and we went to Silver Lake to go swimming. The "lake" part is pretty funny as a name. It is an artesian well. There is water underground that is under pressure and if a pipe is put into the ground where the water is it comes up from the pressure. There are these artesian wells all over the area and it has created a little oasis with trees, a lot of greenery and wells that range in size from the size of a swimming pool to big ones that are the size of a couple of football fields.

Silver Lake is one of the big artesian wells. It is about ten miles from Cochise and it is the only swimming place we have. It is where we all go out to swim. But we have to be very careful. In the middle of the water are tall weeds that grow up from the bottom and a person can get tangled up in them and drown.

In the last few years, three people have drowned. Last year a bunch of us had just gotten to the Lake when somebody said that they were closing because they were looking for somebody who had gone in and not come up.

So we went to the pavilion which was not closed and waited to see what was happening. They spent hours trying to find the person and they finally said that they would have to drain the pond. They brought in big equipment and they pumped and opened some drain pipes that run out of the pond. It took clear into the evening before they got it drained enough to find the person. It was a man from Tucson who was visiting some relatives. Maybe he did not know about the weeds.

I am afraid of going in any farther than I can stand up. I am not much of a swimmer so I just paddle around the edges.

But today was a fun day at the lake. We stopped and picked up Evan and Cami. James said the others were already out there. We got there and immediately went to the pavilion. I have to admit that is my favorite part. They sell tamales, bean burritos, fry bread and snow cones besides other stuff.   I love the tamales. Mrs. Casillas makes them.   Dad gets a couple a dozen of them every week.

But back to Silver Lake. We all got the stuff to snack on and then Cami and I went to change to our suits. The guys had theirs under their Levis.   Then we got over to where everybody was parked on the blankets on the sandy part that goes around the lake.

While we were out at the Lake, Evan asked Cami if she would go steady. She has really been hoping that he would ask her and give her his sweater to wear. I am sure that she will get his sweater by next fall. The good thing is that they are not as serious as Lana and Leslie. Both Cami and Evan plan to go to college so they know they have a lot of time in front of them.

One of the things that makes me really happy about James is that he seems to be genuinely happy to be with me and likes me exactly the way I am. I know a lot of the boys expect a lot of the "other stuff" but that is just not me. I think there is lots of time for growing up.

May 30

Normal Friday stuff.   The gang went to the Milo for fries and milk shakes then we all went to the early show. The picture show was The Member of the Wedding.   It had Julie Harris playing Frankie the young girl. At first I thought she was a boy and she even had a boys name, Frankie.   Oh, my goodness, it was so fantastic and wonderful. We stayed for both the early show and the late show. I just had to see it again.

It is about being different and lonely and being rejected by family. I asked James if he liked it and he said he was glad I did and he enjoyed being at the show with me. I really like that he is honest that way.   Then we went to the Milo again and had hamburgers and a ton of fries because we were starving.

June 1

James came out and we rode fence. I had told him about Pudgy and how Pudgy died. He asked me if I was going to ever get another dog and I said I had wanted one but things had been so crazy and I did not know what kind I wanted. I love so many different kinds.

I told him more about Ida and some stuff about Sharon. And then he told me why he lives with his grandparents. His mother had died from an illness when he was eleven. And then his father just disappeared. And nobody had heard from him since. So his grandmother and grandfather took him. He had lived in Roswell, New Mexico until he came to his grandparent's ranch.

82

He had never ridden a horse or anything before that. That explained a lot. I could tell he did not really like to talk about it. Especially his mother.

I know his grandmother from church but his grandfather does not come to church. I have never been to their ranch. But dad has met his grandfather and likes him.

James is a very big guy. He is almost six feet. He weighs 170 and according to Coach he will be a great linebacker. But he is a gentle bear of a guy. And did I mention he is very good looking? He has a strong face with a square jaw, very, very blue eyes and dishwater blonde hair. Pug says we "will" make a "pretty" couple. She tells me that we are being very sensible to just be buddies for now. I know that she worries that I will get serious while I am too young, but I know I won't.

James said that he is going to have a surprise for me on Wednesday, and then he had to go work at his place.

Cami and I spent forever on the phone.

June 2

Did my chores then went to House of Ida and was working in the kitchen when Ida came in and started in about James. I knew that had to happen. She just kept on. I had decided that I was not going to let her get to me. I was doing a really good job considering my ankle. I asked her twice to just let me do what I needed to do. She started saying really bad stuff about what I was "doing" with James. I tried to tell her that we were just friends and she could even as Pug. She said she did not need Pug to tell her anything.

Then Ida said she wanted to talk to him to tell him that I was really "bad news" and she needed to warn him about me. I turned around and told her to just leave me alone. She said it was her house and she could do whatever she wanted to do.

She was constantly right behind me. She just kept going on about what kind of a person I was and always would be. She used some new words that I did not even know what they meant.

I started to walk away from her and I was trying to get to the bathroom because I was going lock my self in there until Dad came back to get me. She blocked me in front of the bathroom door.

She had on that big leather belt with the turquoise and silver buckle that she wears and she pulled it off and started hitting me with it. She was holding it by the middle and the heavy buckle connected with the back of my head and my back. And as I turned to try to get to another part of the room to get past her, she screamed at me that she would not be ignored, and she kicked me square on my right knee. I am not even over the ankle thing and now my knee is a mess. There was really no reason. I had not done anything. And I had tried so hard to not say anything to get her nuts. But she gets nuts anyway.

I knew I was bleeding from where the buckle had hit my head and the two places on my back felt sticky too. I couldn't put much weight on the knee where she had kicked me. But I got out of the house and across the street to Pug. Ida followed right behind me to Pug's and just stood there yelling, "See what she made me do?"

Pug called Dad and told him to meet us up at Harlan's She told Ida that whatever it took, she would see the she stopped hurting me. Ida said that I made her do it. Pug said that she and Doc are going to report this and she has to stop.

I wish Ida would listen to her. Then Pug told Ida to get out of her house. Ida really looked surprised and even more angry, it that is possible, but she left.

Pug put me in her car and took me to Doc's. Doc got madder than I have ever seen him. Pug told him that she had called Dad and he was on his way to the hospital.

Doc told Pug, "You know, I have gone along with a lot because Harrison is my friend, but this stops here. I am not going to help him cover up for that woman this time. He has got to finally figure out that the woman is a lunatic and a dangerous one. For a smart man he can really be stupid where that maniac is concerned. I told him something like this was going to happen."

He had to put stitches in the back of my head. What was worse was that he had to shave the hair around the cut. My shoulder had one cut that needed stitches but the other one didn't. Then he put a really tight bandage on my knee. By that time Cora was there too. He told Cora to go get the camera and take pictures of everything. That surprised me. I never knew somebody would take pictures of when somebody got hurt. After that was all done and he had taken care of everything, he told Cora to put me in a room until Dad came. Pug said she would be back to the room in a little while but she wanted to talk to Dad. Cora left too.

I saw Joe's truck come up in front. I don't know why Dad had Joe drive him in. I went up to the front where Doc's office is and went into the room next to it. I wanted to know what Doc and Pug was going to tell him. They really got into a shouting match. I never heard anybody talk to Dad that way before. Doc said that "Ida can't keep doing that to Roxie." And Dad said he knew but he didn't think it would happen this time because Ida had been so much better.

Doc said "That is bull......!" Dad said, "You don't know what it is like, I can't just lock her up for good." Doc said, "I don't care what you think it is like. You put that kid in that situation. I am going to make a report and this time I won't help you. You are going to have to take Ida back to Tucson and put her back into the facility. But this time you put her in the psyche ward in the main building. Not in one of those useless little facilities that don't monitor what she is doing." Dad said, "The bills are breaking me."

Pug said, "Then put her in a cheaper place. But keep the kid away from her until you put her somewhere. I don't blame Ida. I blame you. You know that she has problems. Harrison, You know you can't fix it. And yet you make the kid go into that hell hole. You know Ida is nuts. Harrison, you have to finally get it through that tough English skull of yours that you can't fix that woman. She needs to be committed. Permanently. And if you can't do it, we are going to have it done for you. What did you think was going to happen? "

Pug continued, "Roxie is a child. And you make her go with that woman? Now, I am keeping that kid with me or she can go to Cora's but she is not going back to that house. If you ever put her in danger again, I am going to have you committed or arrested. Because that makes you as nuts as Ida is. Harrison, Do you get what I am saying?", Pug was almost yelling.

Dad said, "I really don't know what to do." And Doc said, "Then listen, I am telling you what to do. If you do not get that kid out, Ida is going to kill her. Is that what you want?" Dad said, "You know that would not happen."

Doc said, "You have been kidding yourself for years. Time to get your head out of your butt." Dad said, "Doc, you do not know what problems I have." Doc said, "Yes, I hear the talk. I know what is going on. But you have to do something. Listen, I am going to call the sanitarium. I might be able to pull a couple of strings and get you some relief on the bills. But you are going to have to put her somewhere. Or you are going to have bigger problems than you have right now."

The room got quiet so I was afraid that they were coming out so I scampered back to the room that Cora had put me into. And I was pretty stunned at what Doc had said. I wondered what other problems that Dad had? And did people really think that Ida was so crazy that she should be locked up? I knew she was mean. Was that why she went away all the time? It that is true, then why does he bring her back? Can crazy people get fixed? She has hurt me so many times but this one of the worst. And now everybody would know about her. I didn't know if that would be good or bad. Because I was ashamed for her and for me. Part of me wanted everybody to know what she did. And the other part of me did not want anybody to know. My head hurt inside and outside.

Did what Doc said mean that Ida was being put in the Center because she had to go there? Maybe it was not even a resort. I thought a sanitarium was for really crazy people. Did Ida go there because she wanted to or because she had to? Had Dad tried to protect me by having two places? If that was true then why did he make me go there? It was a puzzle that I did not have any answers for. My head was spinning from thinking about all of the new things I had just heard.

Dad came into the room and asked me if I wanted to go to Pug's or back to the ranch. I said I would go home with him to the ranch. I did not even want to be across the street from where Ida was.

Pug came into the room with Cora. Both of them hugged me gently because of the bandages and my back. And Pug looked at Dad and said, in a voice that I had never heard her use before, "Harrison, This is never going to happen again." Dad just nodded. He looked terrible.

We went out and Joe was sitting in the truck. Everybody was very quiet on the way home. Joe tried to make a joke that I was just trying to get out of doing my chores but nobody laughed.

When we got home, I asked Dad if I could go out with El Con and Dad said no, to stay out of the barn for a few days. He said that there was a problem with infection. Dad said, "Roxie, I know none of this is your fault. You didn't do anything wrong. I did."

I burst out crying. I had not cried at all until then. And I couldn't stop. Dad started to follow me and I told him to just leave me alone. I knew Dad felt bad but right then I did not even want to talk to him. I knew he was in the middle between me and Ida. But I was not the one who kept doing stuff. I just hoped that now he would make the right choice.

I asked cook to make me a little dinner to take to my room. I just wanted to be alone. And just be with you, Dear Diary . I really wanted to be out in the barn. I was trying to understand what Pug, Doc and Dad had talked about. I really had a lot to think about so I am trying to sort it out by writing about what happened.

Pug called and wanted to know if I wanted her to come out to the ranch. I told her I was fine. I would talk to her tomorrow. But I am glad that she took me to Harlan's. There are a few people who do not put up with Ida. Pug and Doc and Mrs. Mason in her own way. Cora too. Then Cora called. She said that things were going to get better and that she did not think I would have to go be with Ida alone anymore.

That is the best news I have heard in a long time.

June 3

I forgot all about my surprise until I saw James' truck came pulled up in front. He got out carrying a big cardboard box. And what a surprise it turned out to be!

A little, fluffy, fur ball of a puppy. He is a cocker spaniel. Eleven weeks old. He is a little fat butterball. He makes little snorty sounds. James told me that he had asked Dad a week ago if it was OK if he gave me the puppy and lucky for me, Dad had said yes.

I have named him Fala after President Roosevelt's Scotty dog. He was solid black too. Dad said Fala was a really smart dog.

So my new best friend except for El Con has a new home and I have a new buddy. He snuggled in my arms all night long. And even with all that had been going on, I felt very happy with this little guy all warm and making his little "chuffie" noises

James and I did not talk about what happened. I really appreciated that. I didn't know how to explain it but I had the feeling that I didn't have to. And the puppy is the perfect "gift". Better than any medicine.

June 4

I tried to finish reading <u>The Awakening</u>. That is the book by Chopin. I guess I am not ready for this book. I just could not get into it. Maybe when I am older. I just did not care about any of the characters. Especially the main character. So I have started a new book. I will talk to Mrs. Mason about <u>The Awakening</u> after school starts. Not Mr. Bertram. Too much "woman" stuff.

So I started The <u>Red Badge of Courage</u> and so far it is wonderful. I love history stuff.

June 5

Dad took Ida back to the "Resort". But this time she had to go and she has been put in a different part, not one of the little bungalows. Cora told me that. Don't know for how long but my knees thank him. I wish I could care about her. She has just never let that happen.

Pug came out to the ranch, picked me up and took me to Doc's. I don't think Dad wanted to go in right now. But it gave me a little time to talk to Pug. She said that she and Doc were trying to fix it so that Ida would have to stay at the Center or in another facility.

The one thing I really can't talk to Dad about is Ida. He really loves her. I know that. I don't get why but I know he does. One time he said, "The heart wants, what the heart wants." I guess that is true, but I know that if James was a mean person, I would not care about him. I know I am not "in love". I don't even know what that is. But I know I am definitely "in like". HA! But I know I could not like anybody who hurt people either physically or by saying hurtful things.

Doc said I am healing nicely and should be about to do stuff if I take it easy. Then he said, "Who am I kidding, you don't know what "take it easy" means!", and he laughed. He put a tight black elastic band on my knee. It really helped. He said that he wanted me to go to a doctor in Tucson next week and get an x-ray on the knee cap. I started to tell him about Fala and he said he knew. That is Cochise. People know things almost before they happen.

Then he said, "OK, Pug and I need to talk to you about something." That really scared me.

He was talking so serious. "Then he said, "You know Judge Hunter." I said. "Of course, you and Dad play poker with him." Doc said, "Yes, but this time you are going to see him because he is a Judge." I said, "Why me? Doc answered, "Because this is about Ida and what she did to you."

I really did not know how to answer this. I knew this was going to be hard for Dad and I knew he did not want me to say anything. Doc seemed to understand why I was being quiet.

Doc continued, "Roxie, I know you are in a bad situation. But what she did this time, you dad can't fix anymore. She has to put her in the Center, or some other mental institution or she is going to have to go to jail.

I was stunned and did not know what to say at all. Pug was holding my hand and she pulled my face around to her and she said, "Rox, listen, we have to fix it so that she can't hurt you any more. And we have to fix it so that your dad can't let it happen either. She is dangerous. To you and even to other people. So you have to go see Judge Hunter and you have to tell him what happened.

I asked Doc why he couldn't just tell him. And Doc said that it did not work that way.

Then I asked if there would be people there like in a trial. Doc said that this was different, that is was a closed hearing. And then he said that it would not be my fault because I did not have a choice. I had to do it and I had to tell Judge Hunter the truth. That helped. Because now Dad would know I was not doing it to hurt him.

Pug took me home and asked me if I wanted to talk. I said I did, but could it wait for a few days. Stuff was just too much right now.

I am tired of being shut up inside, I just want to be able to go out with El Con. I would really like to be able to do my chores. Thank goodness for Fala. Or I would be crazy. There are just so many things to think about right now.

June 6

I went out to show Joe the puppy and he said he already knew about him. And he had a present for me! He had a kind of a saddle bag thing made from burlap. But it was for the puppy and instead of going on the horse, it went on me! It has a wide strap that goes around my neck and the bag part hangs in front and the puppy fits in the pouchy part. And Fala loves it.

Joe saddled El Con and Topper. Then we all headed out. The puppy just snuggled up and fell asleep and the five of us had a great ride. Two horses, one puppy, Joe and I. We happy few!

We just rode and did not talk. Some grown ups just know when to be there and be quiet. I know he knows what is going on and I know he would like to fix things for me.

We had plenty of water for Fala and stopped for potty breaks and everything. El wanted to see what he was and snorted and smelled and seemed to make his approval.

Now we are the five musketeers. A girl, an old wrangler, two horses and a dog. We rode for an hour and then came in. I told Joe I would do the walk-down and groom and he said that I had a few more days of "Vacation". He got real quiet and then he said, "Roxie, you know that I think you are a good kid, don't you?" I said yes I did and that was high praise coming from him. He laughed.

Then he started telling me how to take care of the puppy. Joe said to not take him out if it is too hot. So I will only ride early in the morning.

One of the wonderful things about southern Arizona is that it is always cool in the morning and late in the evening even on the hottest of days. I have been up to Phoenix and Scottsdale and it is horrible. It is even hot at night. I could not live there.

I have been thinking about what is going to happen about Ida. I want to talk to Dad about it but I am afraid to bring it up and I don't know what to ask him. I guess I will have to wait until he talks to me about it.

June 7

Today, got up early, took Fala in his little pouch, saddled El, and we had a glorious morning. Fantabulous! My made up word! Cool huh! I feel like "superwoman". I could jump tall cactus, or at least sort of tall. Or maybe I am just Mighty Mouse. I didn't hurt as much as I had and I seemed to have come to an understanding with my self about the "hearing".

Maybe this was a new beginning for me. It would be wonderful not to have to worry about being hurt by Ida any more. Not in any way.

This was a lush, heady day. My breakfast of two tortillas slathered with peanut butter and jelly were snug in my trusty saddle bag. Fala was curled up, dreaming puppy dreams and making his little chortling sounds.

Meandering drunkenly across the cracked desert floor is a hairy black tarantula searching for a quick breakfast before he darts back into his hidey hole.

Suddenly there is the bleep-bleep of the roadrunner and he runs full tilt in and around the chaparral.

For me the desert of our ranch is solitude at its best. I am never alone. Just the opposite. If I stop El Con's soothing clop-clop for a few minutes, I can begin to see and hear many of the real inhabitants of this land. I see the wiggle of Jack rabbit ears coming out from under bottle bush and if it is early and cool enough I will see the slither of a rattler. I will not hear him unless he thinks he is in danger. Then he will set off his warning rattles. That is one sound that El does not take in stride. So that is one sound and sight that I will avoid given a choice.

I am always grateful that I have this beautiful place to be a part of. I understand how the Indians believe that no one could actually "own" the land. That they were just the tenders of the land, and that they owed the land great care and reverence. That makes a lot of sense to me. The land does own me. And I think of the lines from Shakespeare's Richard II.

This earth of majesty, This seat of mars,

This other Eden, demi-Paridise,

This Fortress built by Nature, for herself.......

This is how anybody who loves a land must feel. I am so grateful to Mrs. Mason for helping me discover Shakespeare. So often as I read the plays, I find something he has said that is exactly how I feel about something and there are these wonderful words about feelings. Amazing how on target it is even after almost four hundred years.

June 8

At breakfast Dad asked if I wanted to go to the Canyon for a few days. Wow! Yes, and more yes. He said Joe had everything under control and he had a bunch of meetings coming up in a couple of weeks so why not get away now. The hearing about Ida is going to be in a two weeks on the 22nd.

So I thought it was a great idea. We are going to go with Colton and Mitzy Tate. Colton and Dad have been friends for over thirty years, even before he married Mitzy.

Mitzy is really nice and even fun for somebody her age. They do not have any kids and they are always fun to be around. They have always done stuff with Dad but they would never do stuff with Ida. I don't know why and I would never ask. One time a few years ago, Mitzy had even told me I could come live with them if I ever wanted to and I knew she meant because of Ida.

So Dad started getting stuff ready and Joe did too. We have a special truck that Dad outfitted like a old style chuck wagon. And we call it the chuck-truck. The truck bed has built up sides and has cabinets that hold all the camping and cooking stuff. And the middle of the truck bed has a mattress because I won't sleep on the ground. Heard to many snake stories. Not to mention scorpion and other creepy-crawlies. The chuck-truck it has everything. And the Tates have their own truck with more stuff.

I love Grand Canyon. We go up and camp at least once a year. Have every since I can remember. And usually with the Tates and sometimes some of the hands. Joe has gone too. But not this time.

Got my clothes ready. Since it can be cold up there even this time of the year, I take my "cold clothes". I even have a pair of long underwear with the funny trap door. Joe calls them "Johnnys" I put them on under my jammies to sleep in. And we go up to the north rim. We hike and we play and eat. Pretty much it. And it is the best time. I asked Cami one time but she did not want to go. I think we are an odd pair. We are best friends who like to do different things. That might be true of James too. Some things we like the same but mostly we are different.

I had asked Dad if Fala could go. He said yes, but I was responsible. He was not going to carry him or take care of him.

Well, things are all ready and we will be up and off by five in the morning. I takes six hours to drive to the Canyon. It is a fun drive

91

except for Dad's cigarettes. He even had a couple of cigars with him. Bummer. But we had some good conversations. He said that he could not go visit Ida because she had to be in tests for a week. So that made it a good time to get away.

He said he was sorry that things had happened the way they had. He and Ida had talked and she had promised that she was not going to talk about Sharon or do the hitting and other things. But he said he should know better that she can not always control what she does. He even had tears in his eyes.

Dad said not to be afraid of the hearing and just go in and tell the truth. That was the best thing he could have said to me. He said when I am older he is going to tell me some things that will help me understand better. But he never wanted me to be hurt again in any way.

I know he really gets caught in the middle. And I know he loves me. And I really love him. That is all I need to know.

Dad has this crazy way of going somewhere. He has to see how many miles he can go in the shortest time. I am lucky he stops for nature calls. I don't like to eat on long drives but I drink a lot of soda. We have a galvanized bucket with a lid in back with ice and Nehi grape and orange sodas. So that means I want to stop, a lot. And we had to make puppy stops which also worked for me too. Fala slept most of the way and I did too. I try to stay awake to keep dad company but riding in a car makes me so sleepy.

But we do make good time. Dad knows that I drive. I drive our garbage truck to our ravine and I drive the ranch Jeep. But he will not let me drive on the highway yet. Maybe next year.

We got to Parker and we all stopped and had a big breakfast at this big truck stop that Colton and Dad like. I bought an Indian blanket that was just beautiful and will be nice and warm for my truck bed. I want to get some turquoise jewelry before we go home. Several of the roadside stands sell silver pieces for horse tack too, and I want some button covers too.

We got to the Canyon camping place. We have a cabin at Pine Top but it is too far from where Dad likes to camp.

The men got all set up. Dad and Colton had their jillion cups of coffee and then we went hiking the rim. We went all the way to the end of North Kaibab Trail . Fala was in his little bag. Everybody offered to help carry him but he really is not that heavy. I just move the pouch around when one way gets too much. I think I am lucky because I am skinny but strong and I don't stay still much. But in a couple of months I don't think I will be able to carry him.

Dad always picks a different point to go to each day. We hiked back and then we made a great dinner over the fire pit. Made trail potatoes and steaks. Cook had packed tamales, tortillas and some Mexican pastries. Yum.

We spent the evening around the campfire until I was too sleepy to stay awake. So I went to my little truck bedroom and Fala and I slept like logs.

June 9 to June 11

Three more days of hiking, eating, camp fire stories, and sleeping. Three mornings of biscuits and homemade preserves. Ham, bacon, eggs. Hot coffee for them, hot chocolate for me. Mitzi and I went to a little store just outside of the Canyon that had fruit and some other fresh stuff.

They even had some pig ears for Fala. He was in puppy heaven. I bought a ton because he is chewing on everything including me. And we got a whole bunch of candy bars, and Big Hunks of course. And beef jerky for the men. We had brought some with us but Dad likes to try different kinds and up at the Canyon you can get the homemade kind.

June 12

Got home late this evening. Dad said he is going to Tucson to see Ida. I said I will stay home and get some chores done and do some reading.

June 13

We had the Fry's to dinner. Buddy came home on leave and we all found out that he had married a Japanese girl. She seems nice, very quiet. No wonder, she does not speak any English, none. And of course we can't talk to her. It was really a surprise but Cora seems OK with it.

Anyway Dad had Cook make a nice celebration dinner and then he gave the new couple a check. I think that after he gets out of the Army they are going to live in Tucson. He asked Dad about one of the houses that Dad rents out in Tucson. Dad said it would be available after Nov. and he said that would work out for them. James, Evan and Cami were at dinner too.

After dinner all of us went to the late show. We saw <u>Superman and the Molemen</u>. It was so stupid that it was funny. Everybody kept saying stuff and throwing things at the screen. I have seen serials of Superman before but this was the first time it was a whole picture show. We just laughed ourselves silly about everything. Dad said he would puppy-sit. I think he is getting quite fond of Fala.

93

June 14

Dad said that Ida was going to be at the facility for a long time. I was hoping for forever but for a long time will have to do for now. I asked him if we still had to do the hearing and he said yes because it was a legal thing. He told me that there would be a lawyer there who represented Ida but Ida would probably not be there. She is not allowed out of the Center right now.

I don't really understand a lot of it. I wish I could ask more questions but I can tell that he is only willing to talk about part of the issue. But he has shut up the house in Cochise.

I have some time to do what I need to do and what I want to do. My barrel time is not getting better. But I have gotten in touch with Mary Jane. She is going to trailer over once a week and I will go there once a week so that gives us two days. I am really getting to like her. She does not babble on like I do but what she says is very interesting. She has good views about a lot of things.

Boy, can she ride! She is good at everything. She moves just like silk. She is as good as Joe is. I could never ride like that. She calls me Spider Butt. That's funny.

I got the barrel saddle. Wow, does it make a difference.

So I am trying to do it all. The barrel, my chores, time with James, and with Cami. I am catching up on my reading as well as having fun going swimming, to the show and hanging out at the Milo. And let's not forget that Dad has me baking and cooking with Gretchen. I am actually getting to like it, it really is a creative thing to do.

June 15

Well. I should have known that things were just going too good. I really did it this time and I can't blame it on anybody else. Boy, did I do this one! I am so grounded, majorly, and I knew better! Here is another instance of not thinking any of what happened through. Dear Diary. this I is why I will not be going anywhere or doing anything fun for a while.

The day started pretty normal. I did my chores. Cami was in Douglas with relatives, James had to do work on his ranch. I hardly see Lana anymore because she is with Leslie all the time. So I called Brahm and said let's do something because we have not spent any time together. And he did not have anything going on so he came over. I had not seen the "Green Hornet" since he fixed it. The name is wrong now. All the green is gone. He took the chassis off his old Chevy and put in roll bars. And it has sand tires. So he said let's go take a ride and go "washing". That is when you drive down the middle of a wash.

94

I didn't want to go anywhere near where Randy had died so we went the other direction a good ways off. We were thoroughly enjoying ourselves and all the sudden, we got stuck. One of the tires just got sucked right into a big sand hole and there we were. We are not all that close to the house. So we trek all the way back. Took a while. And we got boards and what we needed and took one of the ranch trucks to go back.

I forgot to mention that my dad was in a big meet in his office with about ten men. And no way was I going to go in and interrupt that. So we just sorta borrowed the truck. We would get unstuck, bring the truck and the Green Hornet back and everything would be Hunky Dunky. Right? Wrong!

We go back to the stuck little Hornet and we try to get it out with the boards but that did not work. So now we will use the chain and pull out with the truck. I know, clearly I did not think this through. And yes, we sink the truck.

Good grief, now we have to go back again and get something to get TWO vehicles out. So we go all the way back and I am hoping my dad's meeting is over. It is not. So we go get the big cattle truck that I can barely drive and Brahm is not much better. But we take it thinking it will pull anything out. We get all the way back to the wash, the two sunk junks. But now I am going to be very smart. We will not take the big cattle truck into the wash.

We will leave it up on the top of the bank and pull the truck out first but at a long angle. We have a very long chain and this is going to the trick. OK. Not thinking this through again. It is all set up. Chain on. Truck hooked up. Big truck pulling. And then the bank slowly, but surely gives way and I watch while the big truck starts a slow slide down into the wash. Brahm jumps out just as it slips all the way down. Fortunately right side up. But sunk.

Now I know that life is over as I know it. And I have a choice. I can run away or I can go back to the ranch, get my dad, confess all and throw myself upon his wrath.

We trek all the way back. Now all of this has taken up the entire day and we are rapidly descending into evening. We get back, tired, dirty, and mostly scared.

As we go into the house the men are gathered around in the living room having a final drink before they all depart for where ever they are from. I ask my Dad if I can talk to him and he says wait. I say, "I really need to tell you something now." So he says, "What?" I tell him. He says to the men, "I seem to have a crisis on my hands" and then he tells them. They think it is hilarious. I can tell that my dear father does not think it is funny.

Several of the men, my dad and I all go out in a couple of the trucks back to our wonderful sea of stuck scrap metal. And it is completely dark and we have to use the portable lights plus the truck lights. It is quickly determined that nothing can be done this late. And we go back.

The men from the meeting go home. Brahm goes home. My dad says, "Go to bed. We will talk in the morning." And I know that morning is not going to be great. Tough times ahead.

Morning arrives. I am up early. I have done my chores and some of Joe's. I would have built a room on the house if that get my dad not to be mad. He said he had a cat coming to get the trucks out. A cat! Wow! How did he do that? I guess he called in a favor. In a little while, here comes the giant, yellow, machine chugging up our ranch road.

My dad goes out and tells the driver to follow. Then he waves me over and says I can go out too. I hop in with Dad and Joe. On the way, Joe asks, "Roxie, how did you manage to outdo your self? What was your plan?" And Dad and Joe give each other the look that says everything.

Well, the final chapter to this story is that the big Cat stays way back on solid ground and slowly pulls all three vehicles out. Everything will run. Dad takes the truck back, I take the smaller truck and Brahm who was already there, takes his now stingless hornet back to his house.

I go to my dad's office to find out what my sentence will be. And it is a doozy. I am not to ride for pleasure, not to go to the show or on a date or see Cami. I am in solitaire. Now all I can hope for is time off for good behavior. The whole world thinks this entire thing is funny except for my dad. At least there is no school so I don't have to hear about it from all of the gang.

Now I will start my sentence of three weeks. One for each vehicle. And I can't even call Brahm to find out what happened to him. THREE WEEKS! I hope James understands. Maybe he can bring me a cake with a file in it. At least I have El Con and Fala. I can't ride except for fence but I can groom and muck. Oh, Joy!

June 16 to June 21

I am in prison. I read, do chores and then do more chores. Dad made me work in the kitchen. Dishes, pots and pans. Not a heap to write about. Actually it felt good to be busy. Dad has hardly been around because he has been going back and forth to Tucson.

Church on Sunday. No solo. I would have loved to have had the excuse to go to practice. I'm guessing that Dad engineered that!

I have had a ton of time to think about things. One is that I think he was a little harsh about what Braham and I did for a reason. He wanted me to have time to think about things. We have had several talks during my incarceration.   I think I do understand some things.   He wants me to make good decisions when I become an adult.

Dad says that just being smart is not enough. That I have to be able to understand actions and consequences if I am going to be successful at whatever I choose to do. He said that raising a child was the hardest job in the world. that The responsibility was scary in many ways. He said that he felt responsible for Ida and for me. That he had let his judgment slip. And that he meant what he said on the way to the canyon. I should tell the truth. About the last thing and about whatever else I would be asked.

He said just like when I thought we could fix the problem of the sunk trucks, he thought that if Ida and I spent time together we would learn to get along. He had been wrong But he needed me to understand that she might not always be in the Center or some other place. She might get better.

 I know deep in my gut that she will never be better. But I also know something else. I know that he needs to think that she will get better.   I am glad I read so much. Because I think that I am beginning to understand that there are some kinds of love that just do not make sense to anybody else. And Dad and Ida have one of those.

Too bad Shakespeare did not write about somebody like them. But then again, maybe he did because I have not read all of his plays.

June 22

The hearing was today, and it was not anything that I expected. It was not nearly as scary as I thought it would be. Judge Hunter just asked me questions that I answered. He asked me what happened and I told it. And he already knew about two of the other occasions.   He knew about the time she hit me with the vacuum cleaner cord and when my fifth grade teacher, had reported it and Doc had been involved in getting Dad to put her in the Center after that episode.

Judge Hunter knew about several of the incidents that had happened in Tucson. He knew about the time when we lived on Alameda Street and she had hit me with a tree switch and I had to have stitches to close up the long gashes that the switch laid open. A teacher had discovered it when I was bleeding all over the desk seat.

He said to tell him what the worst one I could remember. I told him about he time that Ida thought I had taken a pin of hers. It is a pin called a chatelaine. It was a peacock with one big peacock and then two little ones that were connected by a chain. I always liked the pin but I did not take it.

Ida took me to the door to my bedroom and she tied my hands with rope and put the rope over the top of the door. This pulled my hands up and I was there, hands high in the air, tethered to the door for hours. I do not know how long she would have left me there, but Norman and his mother came in sometime in the afternoon and Mrs. Peterson made her undo the rope and let me down.

That was the incident that caused my dad to put me into private school in Tucson.

I tried to turn and look at Dad but Judge Hunter said not to turn around. This was just another thing I tried to talk to him about. His solution was to separate us for a while. Judge Hunter asked me what I thought about that. I said I liked it when I did not have to be around Ida because I was afraid of her.

There were many more questions but I just answered everything. Dad was in the back with the other man who I guess was the lawyer. The other man did not say anything until Judge Hunter was finished asking me questions. All he said was that his client was not responsible because of mental illness.

Then I was told to go out into the hallway.

I wondered what the outcome would be this time. Every time she had done one of these things and somebody found out, she would go away for a while and then she would be back.

There is always this sword hanging over my head. It is good while she is gone but I always know it can change. I never know when. But I just have to remember that some 'away' is better than none. Doc and Pug have said they are going to try to fix it so that she never comes back. I will just have to wait and see.

June 23

Let's see, what have I learned. Well, Dear Diary, I have learned to think things through and try to figure out what the result will be. I need to think things through and understand the consequences of an action or decision. Dad said that I should have come to him as soon as we sunk the Hornet. He would have sent one of the hands out to get it out and all would have been over. Well, I get that NOW!

Dad said it is a good lesson to learn while I am young. He says that he knows so many adults who do not think things through. I kept my mouth shut and did not mention that sometimes he does the same thing when it comes to Ida. I did not think it was a good time to bring that to his attention.

I know something is going on with him. He has never been this upset and worried. I do not know if this is about Ida or if there is more going on. We had a really good talk last night at dinner. He told me that the Center that Ida has been going to for all this time is really a mental sanitarium. He said Ida never goes there by her choice, but she goes there because there is a reason. The only option is a different place that is not private and is a pretty bad place to go to. It is a state institution that is up in Phoenix.

Dad said that is only part of his problems. He said that ranching is changing all over the southwest and the big corporations are moving in and the small ranches cannot compete.

I said that we had a large ranch. He said yes, it terms of land. But it was a pretty complicated business. He said that all of the ranchers in his association were drowning in debt and there was really no solution except that the ranchers would have to adjust or go out of business.

Dad said that it had ranching would have to become more efficient. The past few years had been under drought conditions and that cattle prices were very low. He said that is what all of the meetings had been about.

Dad said there was a meeting in Bisbee for a very large group of ranchers from all over the area this coming Saturday. He wanted to know if I wanted to go to Bisbee. I said, that would be great because I had been wanting to go back to the Copper Queen Hotel. We had stayed there last year when he went to another meeting. Dad said that would be possible because the meeting would go late and it was better than driving back. I love that hotel. It goes back to the old cowboy days. It is supposed to have ghosts and everything. I asked if Cami could go and he said sure.

We were on the phone forever talking about what we would take to wear and what we planned to do. And I told her all about the hearing.

June 24

I asked Dad if I could go into Cochise and go to Mrs. Mason's. He said yes because it had to do with school. So Joe took me in.

Mrs. Mason had said come in anytime so I did. She seemed very glad to see me. Sitting her little living room, it just dawned on me that teachers are probably tired of seeing students and teaching as much as the kids are tired of school.

She has this wonderful collection of Kachina Dolls. They are not really dolls. They are little statues made out of wood with feathers, clothing, masks and more. They represent Kachina dancers from the Hopi and Zuni tribes. I really love them and I want to start collecting them someday. She must have over fifty. They are all over her house. She has a guest room that has a high shelf that goes all around the room and all four sides of this high shelf are covered. And she said that there are not two alike. I will take her word for that! They are just beautiful and she says that the people who make them are true artists.

She and I talked about what I have been reading. She asked me if I would like to stay for dinner which surprised me. So I called Dad and he said OK.

She made lasagna. She had to tell me how to spell it. I had never even heard of it. It is Italian. It has layers of this funny flat stuff that is like a giant flat noodle. In strips. Then it has tomato sauce with meat and cheese. But the cheese is white! She said she has to get the cheese stuff in Tucson at a special store. It was really good. I wonder if Cook would make it. It has some of the same stuff as Mexican food. Anyway, I ate until I was so stuffed.

After dinner she asked me about Ida. I told her that she had gone back to the Center in Tucson. She said she knew that, she just wanted to know if she was going to be coming back to the town house. I told her that I did not know.

And then she said something that has made me think about for the rest of the night until now while I am writing. She said, "Roxie, do you know that you are being raised by committee?" I said, "What do you mean?" She said, "I just want you to know that you have an entire group of people who really care for you and want the best for you." "I said I know that." She said "You are always making lists. Make a list of all the people that help take care of you. You may surprise yourself." I said I would. She continued, "Sometimes when bad things happen, it is easy to make that the most important thing. You need to make sure that you focus on what is good. You have so fortunate things in your life. So always be grateful for what you do have. I know you have had a tough time with Ida. You are getting old enough to realize that most of it is not her fault. She has an illness that makes her behave the way she does. And it may take a long time, but someday you will forgive her." I thought this was a strange conversation but the more I have thought about it the more I see why she was saying this to me. And I have made a list of the positive people in my life. And yes, it did surprise me.

Before I left she said she had an assignment for me. I said good and she said, "You know, you are the only person I know who would think that doing school work is a good thing in the month of June." And she laughed. Then she said, "I want you to write about MEMORIES." I asked her what memories? She said, just start writing about little events or happenings that you can remember. I asked her if they should be good or bad memories and she said that they should be both. She said that writing has such a power to help people let go of the bad and cherish the good. And that I should have fun with it but she knew I would. She said that in twenty-six years of teaching, I was the one who liked writing and reading the most.

Then she said another thing that was really interesting. She said "You are never lonely when you are writing are you?" I said, "Not really." And she said, "That is because writing is your constant companion and always will be." And Dear Diary, she is right. I never feel alone when I am alone. When I am writing or out riding by myself. That does not mean I do not like to be with people. It is just that I don't want to be with people just for the heck of it. I would rather be alone that be with some people. I guess I am still trying to sort out what I mean.

So my plan is that I will try to write one memory a day. It has begun to sound like a really fun idea.

June 25

Cami and I were on the phone in one of our marathon talks. I told her what Mrs. Mason said about writing memories. Cami said, "We are not old enough to have a bunch of memories." I said, "Everybody has all kinds of memories." She said "But why would you want to write about them?" I guess that is the difference in the way we think. I think it is fun and she sees it as boring.

Later James called and asked if I was out of prison yet. He wanted to go to the show. So I went and found Dad. Dad said, "Yes, I had been very good and I had some "Good points in the bank" whatever that meant. But I was FREE! So I called James back and he is calling Evan and Evan will call Cami. Fun times ahead!

And I told James about the Memories and he asked if he could read some. I said maybe. Not out of my diary! So I will put a few on regular paper if I want him to read them.

So we all went to see <u>We're Not Married</u>. Ginger Rogers and Marilyn Monroe. It was pretty silly. And fun. A whole bunch of couples find out that the Judge that married them was not really a judge yet and it was not legal. So the couple can get remarried or not be married anymore. Silly. We had a great time and laughing

101

our heads off at the show and then at the Milo. We were all saying what if that happened after we were married a long time.

James said, "Stay married, of course, or why else get married." Cami said, "Well, if you get married in the church you have to stay married." I didn't know what I would do. Sometimes I don't think I ever want to get married but I don't ever tell anybody that.

Dad Fala-sat. I think he is as crazy about my little fat fuzzball as I am. When I got home Dad was asleep with Fala in bed with him. I just left him there.

June 26

We had so much fun last night at the show that we went again. The movie was not so good but we had a lot of laughs making fun of it. It was a space picture show that the costumes and the sets were so fake. And the actors were so silly and the words were like, WE COME IN PEACE. WE WILL NOT HURT YOU. Silly.

Then I came home to work on Memory #1.

I will start with a school story. Mrs. Mason said they should be little, short vignettes. One idea, one setting, one or two main characters.

We moved to Cochise in the middle of my fifth grade year. I always got along with the teachers but I did not always get along with some of the other kids. There were two girls in particular that I did not like and I think the feeling was more than mutual. One day, out on the playground at recess, both of them were saying wonderful little fifth grade girl insults toward me and I got a little testy.

Well, a lot testy. So the playground teacher sent me inside to the office. Mrs. Brockhurst told me to sit at the outer desk and read. And then she went back into her office.

OK, me alone in the office, with a phone and I am very mad at the two who got me into trouble. So what could go wrong? Everything! I called the mother of one of the girls who lived on a ranch on the other side of Cochise that was about fifteen miles away. Mrs. Allen. Janice Allen's mother. And I said, very sweetly, "Mrs. Allen, is Janice alright? She did not come to school today." And Mrs. Allen, said, "Oh, My God!" and the phone went dead. Suddenly I knew that what I had hoped would happen had taken a whole different direction. What I thought would happen was that Janice would go home and get into trouble for not going to school. But now I knew I was going to be the one in trouble. Mrs. Brockhurst came out and told me to go back to my room. I did, but I really wanted to just leave and go home. Of course it was not long before Mrs. Brocihurst came to the classroom and called me back to the office. Not Janice, of course not. Just dumb old me.

I followed her and walked into her office and there was Mrs. Allen. One look at her face and I knew I had really gone too far. Way too far. Suddenly the door opened again and in walked my dad. I just wanted to shrivel up and disappear.

Dad said, "Roxie, what did you do? Do you know you made Janice's mother drive to school all upset? What if she had an accident? Do you know how much trouble you have caused?"

Well, if I hadn't I did by then. I was truly ashamed.

Mrs. Allen said, "Roxie, why did you call me and tell me that? Did Janice do something to you. I know that she and Carson have not been very nice. And she walked over to me and put her arms around me. And that brought on the waterworks. I had done something so mean to this woman and she was feeling sorry for me. Mrs. Allen said to Mrs. Brockhurst, "I think that Roxie understands what she did. And I don't think we need to talk about this any more." I said, "You mean you are not going to tell anybody?" She said not if you are sorry and it will never happen again. Oh, was I sorry. And no, this would not happen again. Ever.

Then she said to my dad, "I think it is over, don't you?" Dad very quietly said, "Thank you."

Nobody ever mentioned it again. But every time I think about it, I am ashamed all over again.

That was over five years ago. Janice and I have never been good friends but she and Carson have not said hateful things to me either. When it happened I would have thought it was a bad memory. Now I think it is a good memory thanks to the kindness that Mrs. Allen showed me. The little "odd girl out" on the playground.

June 28

Dad said that Cami could come with us to Bisbee. We had a wonderful time. I love the Copper Queen. It is such an old building and it is so easy to imagine about all of the people who have been here. And the stories of the ghosts. So Cami and I played GHOST! We acted like ten year olds.

Oh, my gosh, we had so much fun going on the different floors and pretending to hear sounds and ghostly images. One ghost is supposed to be a young woman who was in love with a man who stayed at the hotel but he did not love her and she killed her self for love. And supposedly she is still around trying to find love.

I love the beautiful staircase. The hotel has an elevator but the staircase is much more glamorous and fun. And I don't think the elevator is very safe. I have a fear of getting stuck between floors. Then I would probably become a ghost who is trying to find my way out!

The design is all very Victorian. I love every thing about that period of history. The art, the design, the style of picture frames, the furniture. It is all so elegant.

The fifties have lost so much in the way of graceful lines and interesting anything.

Dad had a dinner meeting so Cami and I got to eat by ourselves. That was really great.

We just kept pretending everything. We had lobster and steak. And this wonderful dessert that was called a baked Alaska. I never knew you could bake ice cream. And the waiter was so nice too. He figured out what we were doing and he played right along. My name was Mrs. Samantha MacGillicuddy. Cami was Mrs. Duella MacPhearson. We were Irish princesses descended from King Duncan. And we were in America to find a descendant of Macbeth because we want to bring him to trial. Yes, I know the Macbeth in the Shakespeare play does not have any children, but since we are pretending we can make it be whatever we want.

After we finished one of the women who works for the hotel came and asked if we would like a tour so that we could see some of the rooms. How wonderful! She took us on all the floors and we got to see that the rooms have all different furniture and they are decorated differently. And there are paintings and pictures on the walls that are really fun to see.

I know that Cami and I were really hoping that we might see or hear something that could be a ghost but maybe that requires that you believe in ghosts.

We explored every nook and cranny and finally went to our room. Of course, Dad has his own room and we had the room next door. I don't know if we kept him up but we giggled and laughed and told each other stories until much later than what Dad calls the witching hour.

In the morning he still had some meeting, so Cami and I walked around Bisbee. It is really easy to see that it was based on mining. One of the plaques that we saw said that at one time there were over 20,000 people living there and most of them were connected to the mining industry in some way.

The thing I really do not like about Bisbee is the ugly open pit that has been dug into the earth and I guess there is no way to fill it back up and it is just the horrible hole in the world.

June 29

Joe is sick. That is very unusual for him. So I am helping out as much as I can. Dad came out and mucked with me and helped feed. And then he went out with the crew to do some of what Joe usually does.

Memory #2

While we lived in Tucson and while I was at the boarding school, I used to be a child singer who would sing at events, mostly on weekends. My dad would take me to these events. I had several little long gowns and pretty patient-leather shoes and a gold locket and bracelet that was kind of my "uniform" for these little productions. I enjoyed it immensely. No shrinking violet, I.

One May 5th, I was scheduled to sing at a Fiesta and Randolph Park. We got there and immediately I spied a little girl even younger than I was who was dressed in a beautiful flamenco dress (at the time I did not know what the style was, just that it was more beautiful than what I had on). She had black shoes with heels that had steel taps and castanets that she clearly knew how to use.

I asked my dad who she was and he said that she was a dancer who would be dancing next and I was after her. I told my dad that if she danced I would not sing. He said, "Fine!" He picked me up, stuck me under his arm like a football and carried me back to our car with me yelling all the way.

For all of my future singing events, I never had a tantrum again. Lesson learned.

Here is a teeny-tiny vignette: Memory #3

One time I got into an argument on the playground (where else?). This time it was with Tommy Thompson. He called me "Little Rich Girl". So when I got home that night, I asked dad, "Are we rich?" He got really quiet and did not answer right away. Finally he said, "I am." And I got exactly what I was supposed to. I had not earned anything yet. He was the one with money. He was the one who was responsible for the "rich".

He was telling me not to act "rich" and to take advantage of having more than others. I not only have not earned it, I don't know what the responsibilities are. Dad has always said that those who have more, have more responsibilities to those who have less.

105

He does not just talk the talk. He does much to help others. He has started so many programs in Cochise that have provided housing and health care for those in need. He started programs for delivering food baskets for all of the holidays and even during the year when it is not holiday time. He started a program with Cami's father. Cami's dad owns several grocery stores. So they have this room that used to be a storage room that is next to the grocery store in Cochise and poor people can go get what they need for basics. And Dad even pays for the lady who runs the program. So I hope that I will be able to do the same kind of good someday that he does now.

So no, I am not rich. But my father is. Rich in humanity, rich in character and rich in love for his fellow man and woman.

June 30

Memory #4

Things we are ashamed of seem to be a large part of memory. This is certainly one that I think I will never forget.

Cami and I were in her dad's store. Often when we are together we start playing just like little kids. This day we were chasing each other around the grocery aisles. As she can come behind me she pinched me and then ran around the aisle with me right after her. And I yelled loudly, "Stop, Little Miss Retarded!" I have no idea what possessed me to say something so truly hateful. Even in fun.

Just as I said it, a woman I know from church came around the corner toward me. And she had the most shocked and sad look on her face. She is the mother of a very severely retarded little boy. He is about nine or ten but can't speak or do anything for himself. Of course I apologized but as I was saying the words I realized that nothing I could say could make up for being so unfeeling. And now Mrs. Snow and I were both crying. Cami came up and said, "Mrs. Snow, she didn't mean anything bad." Mrs. Snow put her arms around both of us and said that she knew I did not mean anything. She said people just use the word in the wrong way.

Every time I see her at church I feel bad. Two times on a Sunday when I have not had a solo I have gone to the pew that her family sits in and I have sat by the little boy, Bobby. He is really very sweet. I offered to babysit for Mrs. Snow. She said that they do not go anywhere without Bobby. She said that the good thing was that now I had an awareness of how words hurt. That is for sure. I am sorry I said it but I am glad to get to know Bobby a little bit.

Candy is growing and getting a cute little personality. He is very bullheaded and knows what he wants and what he does not want. He thinks he should go everywhere that I do. And I am amazed that

El Con is very careful not to step on him. I also try to keep him out of harms way as well. He still likes to be in his little pouch when I ride. And I have to keep him in the house in my room when I run the barrels.

James came out the ranch and had dinner with Dad and I. They got into a great discussion on the value of sports for getting into college.

Dad had cook make an early dinner because we told him we would watch TV with him. We usually eat at 7 but we ate at 6 tonight. And Cook made some snacks for our evening.

Dad and I are both news hounds so we watched the news at 7. Then Douglas Edwards. Then we watched the Jane Froman program because Dad thinks that I sound like she does. He says I am a cross between Jane Froman and Deanna Durbin.

Dad loves the Milton Berle Show. It was as much fun to watch him laughing as it was to watch the show. There were two drama shows on at 9 but none of us were paying much attention. We got into a discussion where to go to college. James said he thought he would not be able to go to college and Dad was telling him about athletic scholarships. All together it was a really nice evening.

I can only watch TV about one night a week. So much of it is just silly. I would rather be at the movies. But I try to watch with Dad because otherwise he is alone for the evening.

He is only going into Tucson one evening a week. He used to go more often but he said that now Ida can only have a visitor once a week.

He has some favorite shows so I am going to make an effort to watch them with him when I can.

He likes Dragnet on Thursdays, Meet Millie on Sunday and The Jackie Gleason Show.

We both like Our Miss Brooks on Friday, but that is usually a night that I am out.

We have only had the TV for a little over a year. I like to watch sometimes but I would still rather read and most of the shows that are on are not anywhere near real life. Maybe that is what people like about them.

But we do not get a very good picture because we are so far about from the TV station that is in Tucson. If it is bad weather the picture just goes totally fuzzy. And I can't count how many times it will be right in the middle of a program and the TV just starts rolling or going in crazy patterns.

Thank goodness he plays poker or goes into Tucson to the club more than he watches TV.

I don't know who said it, but somebody said in the paper that Americans were getting fried brains from being glued to the BOOB TUBE. I agree.

It is halfway through summer and I am already wanting school to start.

School year 1953-1954

Sept 8

Wow! I am getting excited about the Cheer tryouts for tomorrow. Lana and I have been working very hard. I really appreciate what she has been doing to help me. I know the two cheers and all the moves for the "big day" tomorrow. I talked to Joe and Dad about doing more activities at school this year. Dad said, "All things considered, it is a great idea" which surprised me. Since I have

Sept 9

I thought the tryouts went well. Seventeen girls tried out for the two places on the squad. The two who get it will be part of the team of five. The three already on the team are Lana, a junior and the two seniors Janet and Char (her name is Charity). I tried to get Cami to try out but she wants to do Pom-Pom. In some ways that is good because we spend so much time together and I think we need some of our own things to do. Can't wait to find out who get chosen.

Mrs. Gladmore chooses the ones who are voted on. Then the whole high school votes in Mr. Pendleton's class. He is very careful with the votes.

James has been busy at football practice on the JV team but he got put on the Varsity team for this year. Only a few sophomores have made Varsity and James did for this year. Dad says that James is a natural athlete.

Sept. 10

I MADE IT! I MADE IT! Dad said that he was glad that I am doing group activities because I can be such a loner. Mrs. Mason had already told me that I am in the drama club. So that is two things besides the chorus and band. Dad said that being active is what I need right now. I guess. All I know is that this is going to be very good school year.

Practice for Cheer starts tomorrow. James and Leslie have football practice.

James has to go to his place and do his chores. He does a lot because it is only he and his grandfather who work his ranch. It is small but they have a pretty decent herd of cattle. Their ranch is the RockingChar. They brand RocC but it looks like a C with a rocker line underneath.

I have gone with James a few times to his ranch. I helped him feed yesterday. It was fun to work together.

His grandfather also breeds Charolais cattle. I love this breed almost as much as Dad's Black Angus. The Charolais is really an interesting breed. They are huge. They can go 2.000 pounds or over. They are white and do not have a very heavy coat. More like the Hereford that way. They are very calm. One of the bulls, called Neptune, is really cool. He seems to like people.

I am going to get Dad to come out to the RocC to meet Mr. Walker. He already knows Mrs. Walker from church. But I know he will enjoy seeing the Charolais.

Some of the ranchers who have this breed have inter-bred them with Herefords and other breeds but I think they should just breed them pure. Mr. Walker says for their size they do well in the open range and in Arizona heat.

Lana, Leslie, James and I went to the drive in. It was _Bend of the River_ with Jimmy Stewart.

Sept 11

There was a practice scrimmage tonight. It was a good practice for the cheerleaders too. I can see where we need to get a lot better. But it was fun. I had to use a skirt that was way too big. Thank goodness for safety pins! Janet is head Cheerleader and she wants us to practice this Sat. from 10 until 2. In between we are going to go to the Milo for lunch. We are going to get our uniforms on Monday. Tinker is the other new cheerleader. She is Junior. And yes, that is her name. Too bad her last name is not Bell! Ha Ha!

Sept 12

Dad has gone up to Scottsdale on business. He is going to be gone tomorrow too. It is unusual for Dad to miss church. I could have gone but since I had the cheer practice and I have a solo part for Sunday. I didn't go with him. I felt bad that I didn't go because that is such a long trip for him. He seems so sad lately. I guess he misses Ida.

I also think he is worried about the ranch. He is selling some of the equipment and he said that he might have to sell the horse trailer. That was a surprise. But he said that he was selling it to

109

Brownie so I will still be able to use it. But I will do whatever I can to help. I told Joe to give me extra chores.

Practice was really fun and the lunch at the Milo was crazy. Everything was funny, I even enjoyed talking about guys, clothes and other gossipy stuff.

When I got home and was doing chores with Joe, I was talking about some of it and Joe said I was turning into a girly-girl.

Two more of the crew have gone to work on a different ranch and Joquin, who was doing the watering and his dad have gone too.

So, here is my problem. Dad is telling me to be in the activities that I want to be in at school but I know that I need to do more on the ranch. There is just so much time in a day. Joe said it will work out but I don't see how.

Sept 13

Church, solo and then I went over to James's for Sunday dinner. It was really very nice. Mrs. Walker is a very good cook. She made macaroni and Cheese and fried chicken. All kinds of other stuff . She made an orange chiffon cake. I told her that I wanted to learn how to make the macaroni and cheese and the cake. Mr. Walker told James he had "a keeper" if I knew how to cook. I told him that I was still learning but I was lucky because so many people were teaching me.

Then we went to the Sunday movie. _Angel Face_. It was really a stupid story. I think Robert Mitchum is kind of a creepy actor.

Sept 14

Already there is a lot of school work and practice for everything. Mrs. Mason said that tryouts for the new fall play is in two weeks. We are going to do _Little Women_. Then right after that we will have tryouts for _A Christmas Carol._

She gave out the script sheets for the tryouts. I will decide by tomorrow what, or should I say, who. I want to tryout for. But really for me there is really no doubt. I want to play Josephine. I just hope that Mrs. Mason does not want me to play one of the other wimpy sisters. Evan is in drama too, so we will catch up with the other two, Cami and James after practice. Altogether we have three different practices.

Sept 15

I have really been thinking about my classes, and the other things that I am doing. I am going to organize my time in order to get it all in. Mrs. Mason told me today that she will help me after school to make a plan.

I think it will be good for all four of us to have a plan. We all have very full school obligations and then we have the home stuff. Cami does not do much at home but she spends more time studying than I do. So it kind of evens out.

Sept. 16

Dad said that he wants me to have dinner with him tomorrow night and not plan anything for after dinner. I asked him why and he said he will tell me then. I am wondering if it has something to do with Ida.

Dad does not talk about her. Mrs. Mason said she is in the Center in the part where she has to stay there. Mrs. Mason said that she would have been charged with a crime for hurting me, but her doctors said that her actions were due to her mental state. I still think people can control what they do.

So I asked her if she can ever get out of the Center and Mrs. Mason said that she did not know.

Sept 17

I will never forget this dinner. The way everything looked is burned into my memory. How the crisp white tablecloth looked, laid with our white and silver china. I will always remember the way the silver service and our beautiful crystal reflecting the candle flickers while the chandelier that had belonged to Dad's mother, cast a soft glow over everything. The table was set the way is always set. To enjoy a meal and wonderful conversation.

Dad and I both love Mexican food. So Cook had made all of our favorites. An enchilada dinner with a three-bean salad. She had made her special rice and beans and of course her home made tortillas.

I was so happy to enjoying a quiet dinner with Dad because we have both been so busy that dinners have together had been very spotty. Or dinners have just been quick hurry up and eat and out the door for an activity. I was so very happy at the beginning our meal.

I was not happy for very long. And neither of us ate anything.

Dad finally told me what has been going on with all of his meetings and business trips.

The ranch has been sold to a corporation. They have bought three of the ranches on the east side of Cochise and they have bought seven of the smaller ranches on the west side.

I do not think that Dad could have told me anything that would have devastated me more. He said he knew that it was a big change and that our lives would never be the same.

Well, that is an understatement. I asked about Joe and the rest of the crew. He said that Mr. Brown is not going to sell his ranch and that Joe and some of the rest of the crew would go over to Brown's ranch.

I asked what would happen about El Con and Lizzie. Dad said that that was one of his big concerns. He and Mr. Brown had worked out many issues and that was the one of them. He said the other problem that he had worked out was the horse trailer. He said that it was over at Mr. Brown's and that it was really mine but the paperwork was in Mr. Brown's name. The same thing would be true for both of my horses.

I do not understand most of what he was saying about the reasons for selling and how things were being transferred and all of the other arrangements. All I understand is that we have to move out of our real home and go into the house in town. We have to be completely off of the ranch by October first.

How am I going to be able to be with El Con and Lizzie? What is going to happen to my life? My life is here. Riding, working on the ranch. This is who I am. I am not a town girl.

I do not know who was more upset, Dad or me. I just kept thinking about where the people on the ranch would go. Would we see them anymore?

Dad says that several of the crew are going over to a ranch in Wilcox. And Cook and Ponchita are going to the same ranch. Dad said he had been working on getting everyone situated. Everyone will have a job to go to. But I know that nobody will ever be the same. I think that the people who worked on our ranch did not just see it as a job. They are part of our family.

I am reeling. I finally told Dad that I could not talk about anything anymore. And I went to my room. But not to sleep.

I can't write anymore tonight because my mind is just a jumbled mass of questions with no answers.

Oct 3

As you can see here, Dear Diary, I have not written anything for many days. This has been for a ton of reasons. I have been very upset and confused. Dad and I had to decide what to take, what to sell and what to leave. So we have both been very busy.

The sale of the ranch was final on the first. The sale included rest of the herd that had not already been sold as well as all of the buildings and the equipment. Fortunately none of the horses went with the sale. El Con and Lizzie belong to me and the rest of the horses belong to the crew.

Dad said our house on the ranch is not going to be a house anymore. The house is going to be the office for the company that bought the ranch. The only people who will live on the ranch will be the crew that they bring in. They will all be in the bunkhouse. So I guess the people who will run the ranch will not actually live there. That is really weird to think about.

They offered Joe a job but he said that he would not do that kind of ranching. He said that he would not even know how.

I am so glad Joe is going over to Mr. Brown's to work. I just can't think about losing one more person who I care about.

Even Mr. Brown is changing the kind of ranching that he is doing. He is going to use most of his horses to make a stable where people can come and ride for a day.

I really hope that he is going to keep breeding and training his Arabians

Joe is going to be a trail guide. I think he actually likes that idea. And Joe said that Mr. Brown is going to start boarding and training horses for other people. Well, not Mr. Brown himself, the guys who work there.

El Con and Lizzie are the first two boarders. Joe will take care of them and I will help as much as I can. Just one more thing added to what I have to do. And at least I will be able to trailer them when I need to. Joe says he will use his truck when I need to trailer. I know it is costing Dad money to keep my horses at Brownies.

Dad sold everything except his yellow Caddie and my little Jeep. Yes, I drive even without a license. I just don't drive out of the area.

I really do not know what is the worst thing. Leaving my own house and my own room. Having to move into the House of Ida. Dad says I have to stop calling it that. Not being able to go out to be with El whenever I want to. Not having Joe as a big part of my life. Not being able to ride on our own property.

I know this is really petty, but I am so very embarrassed about what has happened. I did not go to school for the rest of the week after Dad told me. Thank goodness, school excused me. But I had to finally go back and it feels very weird. Some of the kids are very nice about it and I can tell they are being genuine. But I also know that some of them are glad about what has happened.

I had never thought about people being glad when something bad happens. But I see where that is true. Cami said that when bad things happen you can always tell who your friends are. Mrs. Mason and Cami's mother said the same thing.

Speaking of Mrs. Trent, and the rest of my angels, I think they must have had a meeting. One at a time they have been checking on me and spending time with me. Pug took me to Palmas for dinner on Wednesday.

She wanted to know how I am doing. She said we still needed to go to Tucson and get the rest of my clothes for school. I told her I had what I needed. She said we could talk about it later. I said that I was going to have to save money for keeping my horses. I asked Pug what the group called itself. The "See how Roxie is Doing Club? She laughed, I told her I call of them my angels. And that I know they all care. She said, "That we do".

Last night Dad and I went up to the Fry's for dinner. Dad tried to pay Brahm for helping move us into Cochise. Brahm said he would not take it because Dad does so much for their family but Dad said it was a two-way street.

I went over to Doc's yesterday because I had really bad cramps. He gave me the medicine he does, when the pain gets really bad. When I woke up, Doc and Dad were sitting by my bed. I said, "Am I dying?" and that was the first time I have heard Dad laugh since this whole mess began. Then Doc said, "Roxie, we are going to go over to my house and play poker with Evelyn," (that is Doc's wife) "and you can come play with us or you can get your beauty sleep." Of course I wanted to go play poker.

I was surprised that we spent the rest of the evening laughing and playing cards. So maybe this is the start of things getting to be almost normal. Different but still good.

Oct 4

Church but I did not sing in the choir because I have not gone to any practices. I will try to attend this week. After church, James came over. I really have not seen him much because of all that is going on. I know he feels bad about all of it. He asked me if I wanted to talk about "it", I told him that there really was not much to talk about. Things change, just like Dad said. James said, he knew how things change because of his mom dying and his dad going away.

I felt really awful, because my troubles were not anything compared to that. It was the first time in a couple of weeks that it occurred to me that other people have problems too and many problems are a lot worse than mine.

Mrs. Mason had said the same thing but in a different way. She said, among other things, that I was lucky in my own way because I have a "bounce back" personality. I guess I do.

She said that all of my problems are fixable. That there are so many problems that people have that cannot be fixed.   So I am going to try to stop feeling sorry for myself and figure out what I need to do to fix what I can.

Then Mrs. Mason said something that really makes me think about it. She said that Ida has problems that cannot be fixed. Boy, I have never thought that, but now I guess I have to think about it. If she really has mental problems that she cannot control, then I have to try to understand her. But I don't know if I can do that. Mrs. Mason said, "Roxie, it may take a while but you will see that I am right" I think it will take quite a while.

So I made one of my lists. Everybody laughs about my lists but they work for me. I draw a line down the paper. Then I put what is good on the right side and what is bad on the left side. Right for good, get it?

So here is some of what is good and on the right side.

Dad

I get to fix up the house now that we are living in it.

I still have El Con, Lizzie and Fala

I still have Joe in my life

Ida is not hurting me or saying bad things to me

My Angel Crew

James, Cami and all my other fiends

My Books, My reading, My music,

School

For now I am just not going to worry about what is on the left side.

Dad said I can do what ever I want to do to the house. Now it is the <u>House of the Rayburns</u>. So Dad and I are going to Tucson to Old Santa Fe Furniture. I love western style and Dad does too. It is crazy but so many people in Cochise have decorated their houses in this new Danish furniture. It is so ugly and plain. Light wood and just square or whatever. The wood looks like plastic to me.

Dad hired Brahm and Jack to paint inside and out. He had told Ida she could fix up the house but she never wanted to. I think it is going to be so fun.

The outside is going to be a very warm beige. With a warm terra cotta trim for the windows and doors. The front door is mesquite wood with the stained glass middle. So it just needs to be sanded and re-stained. Inside, I picked all beige with terra cotta trim for the baseboards and doorways.

The kitchen is really not in good shape. So Jack is going to put in new cabinets. We are getting a new stove. It is an RCA Estate. It has a griddle in the middle of the top, two ovens, and two drawers underneath. It is gas, of course.

And new refrigerator. It is an Admiral Dual Temp. The freezer part is on the top with its own door. The big chest freezer that we already have is fine. It will fit on the back porch. Dad is having the back porch closed in so that it makes a room for kitchen storage, a pantry and a place for the washer. That is new too. It is a Thor and it washes the cloths and spins them. They have dryers but we are not going to get one. I don't mind hanging the clothes up and now there is just the two of us.

Dad said that we could have kept one maid but I think it will be just fine with just us. That way we still have an extra bedroom and I don't mind cooking or cleaning. I don't mind work. I just hated it with Ida because of what she would be doing or saying to me.

Dad wants Gretchen to come once week and cook and bake. I know he like German food a lot better when she makes it.

But I am getting a lot better at making many things and I am beginning to like to bake.

I can't wait to go pick out a living room set and dining room set. I have all of our antiques in my room. The bed and everything was Dad's mother's. I have all of the antique furniture in my room. Everybody thinks that I am totally nuts but I love the old stuff. Especially Early American. I have a huge four poster bed, a six foot mirror over a six-sided carved marble-topped table, a six-drawer chest, a hope chest, a grandmother clock(a wonderful half version of a grandfather clock), and a beautiful roll-top desk. It is all golden oak. Dad says he is glad that I can appreciate good wood.

Ida got rid of his mother's living room set. It was so beautiful. It was Queen Anne, black and white stripped satin upholstery on a couch and loveseat and many tables, several were marble topped. I wish I could get them back. Dad is going to cut through the wall in my bedroom and make a sitting room out of the room that is next to my bedroom and that furniture would have been perfect in there. But I will find something for that room. I think Dad is pretty smart, because then I will have a place to have friends over and it will not be so noisey for Dad.

Oct. 5

School is kind of back to normal. I have cheer practice after school everyday. James has football. Cami has her Pom Pom. Now add in play practice three nights a week, seven to nine and it makes for some really full days.

Dad said that after cheer practice tomorrow, we need to drive out to Mr. Brown's. I am glad. I need to see El Con and Liz.

Oct 6

We drove out to Mr. Brown's. He reminded me to call him Brownie. That is what almost everybody calls him. I think Brownie is in his eighties. But he is really sharp and he rides and everything.

So while Dad and Brownie talked, I went out to see Joe and the horses. We saddled up and rode for over an hour. We talked and made a plan for how I would come out to help take care of the horses and to be able to ride.

Joe said that Brownie told him that he could make me a barrel run but I said wait because my time was so crazy now and I don't think it would be worth it.

When I went back inside, I told Brownie how wonderful it was that he offered about the barrel run. Dad said the same thing. *I told* dad and Brownie that Joe and I had worked out a weekend work plan. I am going to do Joe's chores on Sunday so that he can be off and then we will work together on Saturday mornings. I guess I am lucky that I like to get up early. So many of my friends waste half the day on the week- ends but getting up early will help me do what I need to do. Brownie said that I am "a little go-getter-busy-bee". Very funny. Really. I am getting very fond of Brownie. Odd how life works. We have one set back but we get a good thing from it. I am very glad to know him.

Oct. 7

The guys have been painting for days. Dad told Jack that Joe would sent a couple of guys in to do the outside. Jack thought that was a good idea.

Mrs. Mason told me to come by her house after Cheer practice today. When I got there she said she wanted to talk about the play. She said she would give me the part of Josephine. Since I have read the book I already knew that was the part I wanted.

Mrs. Mason said, "Roxie, I know that you are really busy right now and I don't want to put more on you unless that is what you really want." I said, "Yes, that is what I really want." She told me that I could come by her house and she would work with me when I wanted to. And then she laughed and said, I could do that during my "Free time!"

One of Dad's sayings is "Time is a thief". I just now get what that means. And another thing he says is "Some people use time and other people waste time." In order to be in drama and have this big part, I have to use my time wisely.

Mrs. Mason is giving the part of Laurie Laurence to Evan. If I had not read the book I would have thought that was a girl. Mrs. Mason said that in England that is a guy's name. Laurie is the rich boy who lives next door to the March Family.

I know it is acting, but I think I would have hard time playing any of the other sisters. They are all so nicey-nicey.

So I have my script and now I start learning lines. Brownie is right, busy-bee me!

Oct. 9

Let's see. Game, cheer, Milo. Buzz-buzz! Using my time!

Oct 10

Got up at 5. Went out to Brownie's. I love working along side of Joe. My body just hums with the barn smells, the horse sounds. I feel as if the day is just wrapping its arms around me.

Joe had even brought my own wheel barrow. The better to fall into! Anyway, we mucked and talked and laughed. The day was sparkly bright, and cool. This is what passes for fall in Arizona.

I was thinking, I know what a family is. A family is the people who love you when you need them. And you love them. Joe is family. He said I should have brought Fala and I said I would next time.

Fala has to adjust too. He has to stay inside the fence at his new digs. He is used to running free. I guess I can say that about me too! I don't feel as free as I did. But now I feel like I have more purpose. Dad says that everything in life is a trade-off.

This is one of things that I really like about reading and writing. It helps me to think things through. I want to understand everything. Reading lets be understand a new time or a new place or how other people thought and acted. Cami says I think too much and she says I bug her with so many questions about everything. Well, sometimes she bugs me too because she is just a "doer".

There is nothing wrong with being a doer but why can't she see that my way is OK too.

Joe and I worked until noon and then Dad and I went into Tucson to the furniture store. We got the most beautiful furniture sets.

The living room set is brown leather. A really large couch that has what they called hobnails all around it. And we got dad a brown leather La-Z-Boy. Really comfy. Four Rosewood end tables. Two for the couch and one for the La-Z-Boy. The fourth table is a coffee table. We got two really beautiful lamps. They are alabaster with dark brown shades. The ones that were in the house were two of the ugliest lamps in history. They were ballerinas. Ugh!

I hate things that are made into other things. Things should be what they are.

Then we picked out a dining room set. It is Spanish Colonial Style and is made of Rosewood also. It is really beautiful. It has this huge china cabinet and the table has six chairs.

When we were picking everything out, the woman saleslady kept talking to Dad. He kept telling her that I was picking everything out. I would ask a question and she would answer but talk to Dad.

I really think she was more interested in finding out if Dad was married. I finally turned to Dad and said, "Gee, I'll bet Mom and the twins are really going to like what we pick out for them." And then the sales lady quit talking to Dad and we got on with the business of picking furniture.

She said we will get everything in two weeks. Dad said that was perfect. And then the woman said very icky, sweetly, "I hope your wife is going to like everything that you let your little girl pick out." Dad shot me a look that said, "Keep quiet". But I guess I just had to be me and I said, "Who knows, but I like it, but if she doesn't then we will just have to send it all back won't we!" Dad hurried me out of the store but he laughed all the way home.

Oct. 29

Oh, Dear Diary, do I need to tell you that I have been too busy to write? Dad says I am burning three candles at both ends. But he says that I am managing so far.

Just to catch you up on Ida. She has been moved into a different part of the Center. I did not even know that there were different parts. Dad explained that there is a part where people are actually locked up and that is the big building that is on the property. The two top floors have rooms that are really just very nice cells. The are fixed up very nicely, but the person is locked in. Of course, there is only one person in a room. And Ida has been in one of the rooms. She has had some special treatments that are supposed to help.

Dad said she has been diagnosed as a schizophrenic. He said it used to be called dementia praecox. But they don't know what causes it and they are not sure how to fix it. The doctors (she has three of them) think that she has a split personality. I asked Dad how come she can control what she does. He said she can't control it. I said yes, she does because she does not do the same things in front of him that she does when he is not around.

Ida is even different when Cora is around or if it is somebody else. Cora sees some of the stuff that she does not show other people. I told dad that Ida is different around different people. She put on more for some people and less for others. I asked him if that did not prove that she had the ability to be responsible for what she does. Dad said he could not answer that. I think he is just trying to find excuses for her just like he always does. So we quit talking about her.

Oct 30

There is going to be a Halloween dance on Saturday. We have been making costumes. I am going as Dorothy from the Wizard of Oz and James is the Scarecrow. It was pretty easy to make his. Just Levis, an old shirt of Dad's that I could rip up to make all raggedy and a bunch of straw. I hand sewed the straw on the cuffs and pants cuffs. One piece at a time! And then more at the neck and under a hat. Joe had an old straw cowboy hat he gave me. Dad got a picture of Dorothy from somebody in Tucson so that I could copy her dress. Pug helped me make the pattern and it came out quite good. I am really looking forward to the dance.

Dad is letting us use the Caddy because there will be six of us. Lana and Leslie are going too. This is hilarious. Lana is going to be Tweety Bird and Leslie is Sylvester. Evan is wearing a toga and Cami is Cleopatra. Her mom made her outfit. The dance should be so much fun.

Oct 31

Everybody met at our house and then we went Trick or Treating before we went to the dance. It was "the bomb"! We even tried to get Dad to go with us to the Milo before we went Trick or Treating.. He does not go out so much now. And he still can only see Ida once a week. I wish he would do more with his friends.

The dance was one of the best dances I have gone to. Except for the prom, of course! James and I danced almost every dance, except for when we traded with the other two couples. Then we all went to the Milo. Dad was still up when I came home so I told him all about my super, groovy evening.

Nov 1

Did my work at Brownie's and then took El out for a nice long ride. It was wonderful. I guess it is very selfish of me to want it all. I want to be able to ride every day and get back to doing barrel. But I want to keep up with my school work and be in all of the school stuff and be able to go out and do things with James and Cami and everyone else.

Everybody is telling me prioritize. Boy, do I know what that word means now. I used to think I had too much to do when I had to do all Ida's stuff, but I hardly have any time to even read now.

Mr. Bertram asked me an interesting question after class. He asked me, What was the most long term goal that I could think of. I said that I want to be a state judge. And I want to work to make better laws that protect children.

Then I was talking about it to Dad and he said that his most basic belief was that people need goals but they need a plan for the goal. I think that is true. I hear kids saying they want to be something but they don't do anything that is going to help them be what ever that is.

Nov 16

I have been doing my chores at Brownie's, my school work, choir practice, cheer practice, play practice and taking care of our house. I have hardly seen James. He is just as busy. Maybe things won't be so busy after the play.

Dad said that he wants me to go with him to see Ida for Thanksgiving. He said he won't make me but he wants me to go. Well, of course I cannot say no. But this really changes what I thought would be a wonderful Thanksgiving. Bummer! But, Thanks a Lot!

I wonder if there is a holiday for "I really am not thankful for anything I have to do on this day!"

So I asked Dad if we could celebrate our own Thanksgiving on the 29th. I want to try to roast a turkey. He said yes.

Nov 17 to Nov 24

I am a busy little bee.....

Nov 25

121

Now I have to go to the "Place Where I Hope They Keep Ida for Ever" for Thanksgiving. I am not looking forward to this. I wonder if I could say "looking backward" no, that does not work!

I wonder if there is a special dining room for these "celebrations"? I know I do not want to be in her room. But Dad says that he never goes to her room either.

Dad popped a new wrinkle on me! Now he says that I am supposed to see one of her doctors so that he can explain her illness. I know what her illness is. I have lived it. I don't need to have somebody tell me what they see because I know that she is just showing them what she wants them to see. I know she has a lot of people fooled. Not me. And not Pug or Doc or Cora. And many of the other people in Cochise that she had fooled are not fooled any more.

I really do try to understand her. I know that she does have some kind of mental illness. But I guess I have a long way to go because I just want her to stay where she is and I never want to have to live with her again.

I would like to tell them what my diagnosis is. She is a rabid rabbit. I have seen her when her eyes are bugged out and she is almost foaming at the mouth. Oh, joy, I just can't wait for this day to come so that I can be ever so thankful!

Nov 26

I got up and made a special breakfast for Dad. He loves steak for breakfast. So I made a T-bone. He eats the big part and I eat the little part on the inside of the bone. And I fried grits in a ton of butter.

And I made my special extra big and extra fluffy biscuits with pepper gravy. Dad says I eat like a truck driver so he can't understand why I stay so skinny. I wonder too. If I could get a little heavier I would ride better.

So off we go to see the wizard. Maybe I should be wearing my Dorothy costume. Am I the only one who knows that there is no wise wizard behind the curtain?

I haven't been to the Center for a while. I forget how pretty the grounds are. And how expensive it has to be for Dad. I wish he could put her where Doc says she should be. Up in the place in Phoenix. Maybe next year.

We had a great talk all the way to Tucson and then it seemed as if even the air changed as soon as we drove into the gates. I never thought about it before but entire property has a very tall wall, and it has gates that they close at night. I had always thought it was to keep people out, but now I think that it is probably to keep the people in.

That is one of the more interesting things about how our perceptions change. Things seem one way until we get more information and then we realize that it is different and what we believed before was wrong. Now I have to wonder how many other things have another meaning and I just do not know it yet.

We went into the main building. I had not been there before. There is a large dining room. Just like at Dad's golf club. And there were twelve (I counted) round tables. They were all set with linen, crystal, good silver and wonderful china. I was amazed. There were flowers on each table. But I noticed that there were no candle sticks or candles. I guess that would just be asking for trouble. The tables had ten places so we wound up eating with a family that had a young boy who was on the same floor with Ida.

I am sorry, but it was not a pleasant meal. The food was very good. That was not the problem. The boy, his name was Jason, just kept making noises. Loud noises. Scary noises. I was sitting in between Dad and Marc's mother. I really felt sorry for his family. They had two other boys who were there and they were just regular kids. Nobody seemed to pay any attention to his outbursts except me.

Once he stood up and screamed as loud as he could. Dad reached over and put his hand on my shoulder or I would have gone four feet in the air. I just wanted this meal to be over. It just got weirder. Ida never spoke one word to me. I might as well as not been there. She just kept telling Dad that she was better and he needed to bring her home. She seemed really different. I could tell that she had some kind of medication. But she just kept talking about "going home".

Well, there is a scary thought.

I know this is not kind, but I hope she never goes anywhere but right where she is unless it is to Phoenix. If she ever gets to come home I am going to have Dad get me a suit of armor. Or boxing lessons.

On the way home I was thinking about how other things do change. Like having a ranch and never worrying about money and then we don't and I worry about money all the time. I asked Dad if we were poor now and he said something I really like. He said rich and poor was nothing more than a state of mind and it is really about how a person thinks about things. And he said that most people do not understand that the rich have as many problems as the poor do. They are just different problems. He said that most people do not know this because they have only had the problems they have, and not the problems that the "other people" have. I really had to think about this for a while and I beginning to see what he means.

Stop worrying about what you don't have and enjoy what you do have. I see that is how he has always lived his life.

Nov 27

The house really looks nice now. Everything is done, the back porch has become a combination laundry room, pantry, storage room and a place for things we don't know what else to do with them.

The kitchen is perfect with the new fridge and stove. And I love making stuff on the "griddle in the middle". Dad laughs every time I say that. The living room and dining room are lovely. Even James thought the house went from just plain to really "in the mix"!

Dad has done something wonderful. He says I am too busy and he wants me to stay in school activities. So he has hired Gretchen's daughter, Beth Ann, to come in to do cleaning and laundry two days a week. Boy, will that help! And Gretchen is going to cook three days a week and do the kitchen on those days.

That way I will have days that I can do what I need to do without worrying about the house and taking care of Dad.

Dress rehearsal for the play. Everything went wrong. Mrs. Mason said that is supposed to happen. That it means we will have a good play. I hope she is right.

Nov 28

The play was wonderful if I do say so myself. Both the matinee and the evening performance. Dad and James both gave me flowers. I had made my own dress, (all the girls did) and once everyone was in costume and on stage, it really felt like we were really the people we were playing. I really love Josephine. She is smart and sassy. But I would not have wanted to live in that time period. Women had so few choices.

I told Mrs. Mason that I am just too loaded up to be in the Christmas play. She said it was OK and she understands. I am going to be in the Music Program that is during the holidays but that is easy to practice for. I am singing Oh, Holy Night in both English and French. So I am working hard on the French part.

Thanks to Beth Ann and the play being over I can get out to Brownie's more and back to more time with my hay burners. Joe just spent his own money getting him shod and for his eats for the next month. But I really want to try to do my part. El Con and Lizzie are my responsibility.

Nov 29

This was my real Thanksgiving. We invited the Fry's and Joe. All of the Fry boys are at home so it was a wonderful time for everyone. It was the first meal where we were all together in some time. Gretchen and her daughter helped me. Well, to be really honest, I think they did more than I did. But I really enjoyed what I did. Gretchen showed me how to stuff the turkey after making the special stuffing. Then we made yeast rolls. Cora brought her famous sweet potato pie and Gretchen and I make pumpkin pies and Dad's favorite, lemon meringue pie. Lots of other food, lots of good cheer and we had one of the best holidays I have had in a long time. Cora said it even felt like Thanksgiving to all of them too because we had much to be thankful for.

Nov 30

Dear Diary, did I tell you the very best thing of all? No? Well, I will tell you now. Dad has set up a lunch date with Ted DeGrazia. He is a friend of Dad's and he is an artist who has a studio in Tucson. He has this huge piece of property that has beautiful areas with cactus and all kinds of desert foliage. He does paintings of Indians. Both Dad and I love his work. We have three of them already. Thank goodness we brought them in from the ranch.

I went with Dad last year to his place in Tucson on Swan Road. Dad said Ted has only been there a little while and before that he had a different place. But Ted said that Tucson was moving in on him and he moved to be further away and have more space. I told Dad he was very strange and Dad said yes, but in a very good, creative way.

Dad said that I met him many years ago at a charity event. I do not remember that meeting. Ted had some of his paintings of children that either do not have eyes or just have dots for eyes. Dad said I told Mr. DeGrazia that "I could do that", and Dad said that Ted just laughed like crazy. Well, of course, now I can see why. I am lucky that he thought it was funny. Dad said that most artists who are as accomplished (Dad's word) as Ted would not have thought it was funny. I just remember going there last year. We already had two of his paintings and we got the third one.

Dad said that we can get two new paintings. One for my bedroom and one for over the new couch. He said he already talked to Ted and that he has several that he thinks will work for what we want.

Dec 1

Mrs. Mason asked how my memories were coming and I said I had not put any in for quite a while. She reminded me that I had written some for her about when I was in boarding school in Tucson. I said that was a good idea and I will add some of those in here during Dec. So instead the same old daily things, these will be Memory Bits for those school years.

But first I will tell you what is a little different about this holiday season.

Dad is talking about seeing Ida for Christmas. Well that is not a bad thing. What could be bad is he wants to bring her "home" for the holidays. If that happens, there goes any chance I would have for Happy Holidays. I talked to Doc and the Judge and they both said the same thing. It is legal if her doctors say she is "better" and is not dangerous anymore.

All of my Angel crew is pretty upset with Dad right now and especially Doc. Cora told me that they had a big, loud argument and Doc told Dad that if he brought her back to Cochise, Doc and he were not going to be friends anymore. I really hope that does not happen because Dad needs people like Doc. And Pug just went nuts when she heard and said she is going to talk to Dad too.

I am working with Mrs. Johnson on my Christmas solo. I am singing <u>Oh, Holy Night</u> in both the church choir and for the school Christmas Holiday Program. I have been singing this piece for several years. It is really a favorite of mine. It really fits my voice range. This year I am going to do it in French and English by altering each section. This is a song that was created from a French poem and I have studied it in English, French, and Italian. I am also doing *Ave Maria*.

Mrs. Johnson wants to do an Easter Hymn in Gaelic. I had studied two pieces in Gaelic with my voice coach, Mr. Schneider. He was my coach in Tucson.

Pug does not teach in any other language. She kids that she is barely functional in English. I love her voice and I have learned so much from her on phrasing and delivery. She has helped me put more emotion in. Before I was singing to come as close as possible to how a piece is written and she has taught me that a good singer puts their own stamp on what ever they are doing.

Dec 3

Dear Diary, The story of how I went to boarding school for five years starts with an incident with Ida.

126

Back in the late forties, Dad owned a business that had branches in California, Arizona, New Mexico and Texas. I am not really sure what these places did. But it did mean that he was out of town a lot. It had to do with some kind of manufacture of something that had to do with WWII. The business did quite well until a few years after the war and then his business began going south. So he began to be out of town even more.

That meant that I was with Ida for longer periods of time without him. I am not going to detail each of the instances of things she did. If I did, this diary would just turn into one giant, blubbering mess.

I have been trying to be more positive. But there was an instance that caused the chain of events that got me to The Immaculate Heart Academy. This was the infamous "Chatelaine Pin" disaster.

I know, Dear Diary, that I have told you this before, briefly. But this is part of how I got to Immaculate Heart, so I will re-tell it in a little more detail.

Not to rehash too much, but Ida thought that I had taken her favorite pin. The pin was rather beautiful. It was a peacock that was connected by little gold chains to two smaller peacocks. It had semi precious jewels as well as diamonds. (I learned later about the diamonds and jewels) Then I just liked it because it was shiny and pretty. I was six, and had just started first grade.

I had not taken the pin. I admired it very much and used to beg to hold it. Of course, I was a kid and it was shiny with a beautiful bird and baby birds.. Ida kept asking where I had hidden the pin. This was typical Ida. She would begin to fixate on something and then it would become a huge issue. Sometimes it was a long verbal harangue and sometimes it turned into a violent act on her part.

Having a parent such as Ida, I would never have taken anything from her. I cannot remember a time when I had not been afraid of her and her rages. I learned very early to try to avoid any conflict. But sadly, most of her rages did not have anything to do with what I had done. She would just find something to vent about and then an assault would begin.

She was off and running and convinced that I had done this deed. She had spent the day telling me to go get the pin. Well, I could not produce what I did not have. I did not know what had happened to it. This continued all day. Some time in the afternoon she took rope and tied my wrists and hung the top of the rope over the top of the door to my bedroom.

And there I stood, arms high in the air, no possible escape and all the time she is screaming that she will let me go when I tell her

127

"The Truth" The truth was that I did not know the whereabouts of the lost peacocks.

I do know that I was tethered to this door for a very long time. It had been dark for a quite a while, when I heard Ida's friend Bertha come into the house. And lucky for me, her son wandered back to the part of the house I was in.   I heard him go back and tell his mother. She came rushing in, found me, untied me, and as Ida came into the hallway, Bertha said, "Ida, what have you done this time?" Ida began with the story of her missing pin. Bertha told Ida that she was taking me home with her.

We went back to Bertha's house where she had me take a very necessary bath, put on clean pajamas and robe and then put me into their guest room.

The next morning, as I was eating the pancakes that Bertha had made, Dad came to collect me. Dad told me to go put on the clothes that he had brought for me. He handed me a bag of new clothes. He said "Go get dressed while I talk to Bertha." I dressed, and we left.

We took a ride to Randolph Park. While we sat at a bench in the park, Dad asked me what had happened. I explained. He asked me what I would think about going to a school where I would stay there during the week and even weekends if he was not going to be home. I asked him if I could go with him and he said that just would not work out. Dad said, "Look, I know this is doing this really fast but I have talked to many people and they know that this is a really good school and the Sisters there will take good care of you. I asked him what a Sister was. He said they were women who were very good people who were either teachers or nurses. He also said that some people call them nuns. Dad continued, "They are very good with children and make sure they are safe. I think you would like it there.

I said, "If Ida is not there I think I could like it." Dad said, "We can try this and if you do not like it we will try something else."   I said, "What if the Sisters do not like me? " He said, "Roxie, my Baby, everybody loves you. They will like you."   I said, "Ida doesn't."   He said "I know you can't understand, but we can't worry about that now."

Dad said, "Well, let's just take care of this right now." Dad drove over to the Academy which   is in downtown Tucson on 6th Avenue. The school was housed in a very pretty building, four stories tall and very square. When you enter the double doors in the front of the building, there is a curving staircase with a gleaming cherry wood banister that rises gracefully up to the next floor   I could imagine a great lady in a beautiful gossamer dress floating down to greet her prince charming.

But the very best part of the school? Ida was not there. I would not have to be at the Tucson house with her unless Dad was there. I was sold. Sign me up.

I went to school there until I was almost nine and we moved to Cochise.

This is the part of the story that turns "happy". Almost "happy ever after". But as least happy while I was in school there.

I think that it says a great deal about how wise and fair Dad is. He is not Catholic. Ida is. But he put me into this school because he knew that it was the best place for me out of all of the boarding schools in Tucson. He chose what was best for the circumstances not what was best to further his own religious beliefs.

Just recently we were talking about different religions and I said that I did not understand how each one thought they were the only way to think when each had such different views. Dad said that he thought each one had merit and he saw them as all different roads to get to the same place. Everybody had the right to choose the road that was best for them.

This is my first Immaculate Heart memory:

Dad and I were ushered into a very large office. Big furniture, big desk, and a very big woman with a very big voice. She had on clothing I had never seen before. It was a nun's habit and she was Mother Superior, the Catholic equivalent of a principal. She was most imposing but for some reason, I was not afraid or intimidated by this person. I think we took an immediate assessment of each other, liked what we saw and it did not change over the next four years.

I had several encounters with Mother Superior. But it was always because I had made a bad choice, as will become clear in the memories, and she always treated me fairly.

I remember Mother Superior as being a giant lady. She wore the traditional nun garb. One of my escapades was trying to see what was under all of the layers, the coif, wimple, veil , the Holy Habit, and more. I will describe that later.

Dad had me sit in the outer office while he talked to Mother Superior. I am sure that he gave her a heads up about Ida. After they were finished, she took me to the dorm that I would be staying in.

We went up the beautiful staircase that curved on the first floor to rise to the second floor and then up one more flight. I was fascinated with the stairs because nothing I had ever lived in had stairs. These were polished wood with graceful curving lines. All the time that I lived at the school, I loved to go up and down these elegant steps.

We entered a large room with four beds, two on each side, and at the end of the room, a fireplace that had large windows on either side. The windows overlooked a courtyard with desert palms, flowering bushes, carved benches, and meandering stone walkways.

Over the next four years I would spend much of my time sitting in the window seat reading and looking out over this little oasis. The courtyard provided for sitting quietly in the moonlight or meandering around the pathways. It was a cozy place to hide out and read. These were two incredible places for the little reading fanatic that I was. I loved every nook and cranny of the this sanctuary both inside and out.

On this first day of my boarding school adventure, Mother Superior brought me into this dorm room, showed me which bed was mine, and introduced me to the two girls who were in the room, Rhonda and Penny. They were in the second grade. She said the other girl, June, would be there soon. And she said that Sister would be there to help me get "settled".

I started unpacking the two suitcases that contained my belongings. Oddly, I did not feel afraid. It just seemed to be a new adventure. Dad had said this way I would be away from Ida except when he was there. I really did not want to be with Ida when he was not around and I understood that he could not always be there. This new arrangement seemed OK to me.

While I was unpacking, the other girl, June, came in. June was eight and in the third grade. The other two were Rhonda and Penelope (Penny) who were both in second grade.

And even though it has been almost eight years ago I remember everything about Immaculate Heart very clearly. That first day was to let me know that it was going to be a good experience.

I was putting my things rather haphazardly into the little dresser that was part of my space when Sister came into the dorm. She immediately began to help me fold and organized my clothes. Then she showed me where I would hang things up. She explained that I would be wearing a uniform and she had brought it in with her. I tried it on and thought I looked rather snappy. I looked just like the other three.

It made me feel like I was one of them and the other girls seemed to accept me. It was a good beginning.

Sister (her name was Sister Mary Margaret) asked June if she would take me down to the dining room and show me around and help me meet other students. We went to dinner.

June showed me where to get a plate and silverware, and how to go through the line. The plates were heavy and they were colored all different, vibrant shades. You got the color that went with your grade. First grade was a pretty persimmon color. June's color was sky blue.

We got into line, and she told me different names of some of the other girls. I only remember a few. Then we went to tables that had places for ten students. Our table had seven girls including me.

June introduced me to everyone. And soon everyone was chatting and laughing. They asked me questions about where I was from and why I was in this school now. Each girl had a story about why she was at Immaculate Heart.

I did not feel out of place at all.

After dinner we went to a big room with sofas, big comfy chairs, card tables and chairs, some with games and some with puzzles, and a big radio in the corner. June said this was the rec room. The room slowly filled up with girls as they finished dinner and then with the rest of the girls after they finished the dining room duty. June had explained that too.

One of the girls asked me what I would like to do and I said I usually read a book. She asked me if I knew how to play Parcheesi and I said I did not even know what that was. She said, "OK, I will teach you." And she did. Turned out I liked the game.

This began a time period where I interacted with kids of my own age. I had not had friends to play with before. I had always been alone and had to do things on my own. This was new. This was fun.

But I will have to admit that I did not always play well with others. And the Sisters had to run a lot of interference where I was concerned. Being a loner who had a very indulgent father had created a little bit of the monster in me. Well, OK, maybe a big monster lurking inside.

Boarding school was one of the best things to happen to me at that time. I had to learn to get along.

Looking back on it now, I think the girls at the school were very tolerant and good to me. I imagine that they had to put up with a lot from this strange little waif.

At the end of that first evening, Mother Superior came in to the Rec Room and said, "Girls, it is 9 o'clock. It is time to retire." She did not even raise her voice. And everybody began to put everything away, and straighten up the room. Everybody seemed to have a task.

I followed June up the stairs to my new digs and June explained how we got ready for bed. Each girl had a certain amount of time in the bathroom that the four of us shared. On one side there was a shower and a tub. We could take a bath or a shower. The bathroom had a cabinet that had four shelves. One for each girl. I put the few things I had on the shelf. I took a shower, but I could not wash my hair. I had never washed my own hair. It was long and thick and took forever to dry. I tried to hurry knowing somebody else was waiting.

When I got back to my bed, the room was warming in the glow of the fireplace. I was glad that my bed was so near the fire.

Here is one of my very embarrassing facts. I was a bed wetter. I had wet the bed for as long as I could remember. And I had been severely punished for it for as long as I could remember if I did it when I was alone with Ida.

I used to try to stay awake as long as I could so that I would be awake and get to the bathroom in time. This never worked. When Dad was at home, there was no punishment. But this transgression on my part could send Ida into a true junk-yard-dog frenzy and too many violent episodes to ever recount.

True to form, on my first night in the dorm room, I woke up and I had wet my new little bed. I got up as quietly as I could, stripped off the offending sheet and went and sat down on the little rug by the fire trying to dry it.

Suddenly, I heard footsteps behind me on the hardwood floor. I braced for the beating that I knew was coming. Sister Mary Margaret sat down on the floor with me, and took one side of the sheet. We sat without talking until the sheet was dry, she helped me remake the bed, tucked me in, said goodnight and I went back to sleep. That was the last time that I ever wet the bed.

Sister Mary Margaret was incredible. Lucky for me, she taught first grade. Of course, I did not know it at the time, but she was to teach me a lot more than reading, writing, and arithmetic. She taught me that there were caring individuals in the world and that I

132

could trust grown-ups.   She was my mentor for the rest of the time that I boarded there.

I have gone to visit with Sister Mary Margaret many times when we go to Tucson. She told me recently that I had reminded her of herself when she was growing up. She said that sometime she will tell me some of the stories from her childhood.

My Angel Crew has so many members. I need to remember that. And Sister Mary Margaret and Mother Superior are two of the first ones that I am aware of. I know there are others before them.

Dad said that his mother was a great grandmother to me.   I remember bits and pieces. I have put them on my list of "Memory Bits".

Dec 5

Dad asked me today what I want for Christmas this year. I told him about my Angel Crew. I had never told him before that I feel this way about these people.   He said that he was so happy that I have this group of people to be there when I need them.

I told him that I want a charm bracelet that will somehow represent these people. He said to make a list of the people that I think are in my Angel Crew. He asked if I wanted silver or gold and I said, "Hey, Dad, you know I am a silver girl. Just like Lizzie!" And he laughed and said that I was the only one who would compare myself to a horse and think it was a good thing.

Every year I try to get him to tell me something that he wants but he just says, that I am enough for him and he loves the holidays and the church programs and my solos.

So I am racking my brain for something special for him. If I had a magic wand, I would wave it and have Ida be the perfect person and the perfect mother and never cause anybody but especially him any more problems. I used to think that somehow things could change and suddenly everything everybody wants just happens.

This past year has taught me that life is what it is. And a person can make the best of what they have or they can sit around an whine, or they can believe that other people cause their problems. I have figured out a big thing. True happiness come from what you do about what you have.

Well, I only sorta figured that out. It is what everybody has said to me in one way or another. Doc has said it. Pug has said it. All of my teachers say it. I used to think something would happen and Ida would change. She can't change.

So I just have to make the best of 'what is'. I know Dad wants me to "forgive" her. I have not been able to go that far yet. The best I can do for now is just try to understand that she can't help what she does. And I am trying. But I am really not there yet. I seem to go back and forth. One time I say well, maybe it is not her fault. Then I think that may be true but I do not ever want to have to live with her again. I am tired of being afraid. When she is not around I am not afraid.

I did not ask him what the plans were for Ida because I did not want to ruin our wonderful evening. But I know that the plans are coming. Darn it.

Dec 15

Been working like crazy. The Christmas Show is Friday. And I have been trying to work as much at Brownies as possible. Dad and I need to go to Tucson and get presents for so many people. I know what I want to get everybody but there just has not been time.

Well, here is my good news. I even consider it a Christmas present to me. Dad told me he had been trying to get permission to have Ida be able to come for Christmas Day. But they (whoever makes these decisions) will not let her. For this, I thank them. I don't even think it is good for Dad. He just seems to get upset when he is around her too. I will never understand why he does this to himself.

So we are going there Christmas afternoon. For two hours. I can manage that. No worries. She will not speak to me anyway.

And Dear Diary, wait until I tell you the plans that Cami, Evan, James and I have for New Years. It is one of my early presents from Dad. Bet you can't guess. But you will have to wait to find out. Too much to do!

I can't believe that it is almost 1954.

Mr. Bertram just gave me several books to read over the holidays. The authors are James Joyce and George Orwell.

Since it is so near the beginning of a new year, I am going to start with George Orwell's _1984._

Mr. Bertram said that it is about a future society that is not allowed to read or write. I just can't imagine living in a time like that. Mr. Bertram said that Orwell is predicting what it would be like in a society where the population was controlled in what they think because by not reading and sharing information, people just go along with everything like sheep.

134

I was telling Dad that. He said he has already read the book and we will talk about it after I read it. Dad also said that he thinks that our society is closer to it than most people believe because too many people to not get enough information about a subject before they make up their minds about it.

Well, even as young as I am, I believe that. Too many people just believe what their families or their groups believe. Nobody wants to hear the other side of an issue.

Cami and her family are Catholic. And I go to the Presbyterian Church. We have tried to have conversations about what we believe but sometimes we do not agree and we both get pretty insistent about the other believing what we believe. So I guess I am guilty of narrow thinking too.

Can't wait to get time to read _1984._ Wish I could get Cami to read it too.

Dec 18

The Christmas Show went quite well. Both of my solos. Oh Holy Night, and the aria in Ave Maria. And It also helps that I am also doing "Night" for the church service on Sunday.

We all went to the Milo after the Christmas Program finished. Everybody was talking about what they were doing for Christmas Day which is next Friday.

Dad, Cami and I are going to Tucson tomorrow. He is going to the Club, she and I are going shopping for last minute presents. My list is really big this year. And I tried to put a lot of thought into what I was getting for the people on my list. And the two horses and one dog! Then Cam and I will meet Dad at the club for dinner.

Dad and I got Joe a new, custom saddle. His was on it's last legs. He had repaired the fenders and the structure was pretty shot. I knew what kind he liked and we had the saddle maker make it. Can't wait for him to see it.

We got Brownie a set of leather bound books. Dad had a list that he and Brownie had talked about. What Dad does not know is that I got him some of the books that he wanted too. I found some first editions of several of the old authors that he reads.

Dad had a great idea. I know he is getting me the charm bracelet. So he said why not get bracelet for all of my special people (females, of course!) and that is what we did. The jeweler is making bracelets with several charms on each. I spent almost a whole afternoon at the jeweler's picking out the charms for each person.

Pug's has a fiddle , a car (her husband, Mac, owns a repair shop), a musical note, a four-leaf clover (Pug's Irish), a heart, a Scottie dog, and an angel.

I tried to pick charms for each person that had special meaning for their lives.

All of the bracelets had an angel, including, Cami's Mom, Mrs. Delgado's. We got bracelets for Pug, Cora, Sarah, Mrs. Mason, Cami, and Lana. Cami's and Lana's had a girl in a cheer outfit. Close as we could come for Cami's because they don't make Pom girls.

Dad and I had Ted DeGrazia make a special statue for Doc for his waiting room. It is an angel (what else) in Ted's wonderful style. It is almost two feet high. And it is so beautiful.

Dad got gold earrings for Gretchen and Beth Ann. He even sent presents to Cook and the maids who used to work for us.

But the present that is the most important for me is the one I am getting for Dad. He never wants things. Especially now, so, I have done two things. I called the Center and talked to one of Ida's doctors, Dr. Weiner. I asked him if he would help me arrange for a special dinner for Christmas Eve. for just the two of them. He said he could work that out. So I am having a caterer from Dad's Club take care of the dinner at the Center (of course). Doc Weiner said there was a room that could be used and they could have two hours but I would have to pay for one of the attendants who was off to work the extra hours. I said that was not a problem.

The other thing I did for Dad for Christmas is that I wrote a special story to Dad about how I feel about him. Sorry, Dear Diary, but that is too personal and emotional for here. Maybe someday I will include it. Maybe when I am older.

Onetime Dad said that people do not tell people how they really feel, especially those we really care about. So I am trying to make that a life habit for me. The more I read the more I realize that it seems to be a human condition. We just do not know how to communicate with those we cherish. Or worse, we fail to realize what people do for us. I just read King Lear again, and I see where parents and children do not communicate because each has a different view of a problem. It is so hard to get out of ourselves to see the other side. Yeah, mea culpa, too!

Dec 25

Dad and I had a lovely morning. We had a yummy breakfast by the fireplace. I had set a very pretty table on our coffee table with our usual favorite stuff. Then we opened our presents. He gave me too much.

The charm bracelet is beautiful, two heavy ropes of silver with charms hanging from both. It has seven angels. Dear Diary, You already know my list of angels, and there is one for each. Plus there is a jeep charm, a spaniel charm, a girl reading a book charm, three horse charms, a cheerleader charm, and a special angel that was made by Ted. It is so beautiful.

The other big gift is an Angel that Dad had Ted make for my room. It is a free standing statue. Dad had a special carved bench made for it. The angel is three feet tall and she is so incredibly beautiful. And it is the only one. I love that nobody else will have one like it.

My Angel is carved wood but the real clothing is all white. White dress with a white Indian blanket around her shoulders. The blanket has silver threads running all through it. She is barefoot. The dress is tied with a silver rope. She has long black hair. The angel is carved from a beautiful piece of wood. The hair, and the DeGrazia features are painted on to the wood. But the clothes are of real cloth. What a perfect combination. Around her head is a silver, sparkly halo. She is seated on her haunches and she is holding a very young faun. The faun is actually a separate piece.

She is the most perfect thing I have ever seen. Dad says I need to remember that I am being watched over by human angels and by those who have already passed away and it is their happy task to watch over me.

This really puts together what I have been thinking about for a long time.

Another gift for me was the fact that Dad was absolutely thrilled with the dinner he had with Ida. The doctor called him and said he could come for dinner and he was looking forward to that. But Dad did not know about the surprise until he got there. I guess it turned out to be very nice. He said that she was like the person he married. Well, I have never met that person, but I am really happy for him. And I guess he has some hope for the future.

The doctors and everybody else do not think that she will get better but I know that he needs to believe that.

Then came the part that I did not like but I think that I am learning that there are some things that we do even when we do not want to. We do them because it is the right thing to do. It is a step toward being a good human. I know that sounds all nicey-nicey, but it is the way I feel. And I can't say that I am the only one. I know that James does very nice things for his grandparents, for me and for others. He is a really good guy.

My angels do many wonderful things for me.

Well, I digress. I must get back to the rest of my day. Some good parts. some bad.

Dad and I drove into Tucson to the Center. This is the big Christmas Day celebration for families and the "clients", Dad does not allow me to call Ida an inmate.

Our table was over by the wall where Molly stood a few feet behind Ida's chair. It must be a very difficult job to have to care for these patients.

For these occasions, certain patients have to have a caretaker with them. Ida is one of the ones who has to have one. Her name is Molly. She seems very competent at what she does. I never see her smile. She is very athletic looking. She reminds me of the gym teacher at our school.

For this dinner, only the people from Ida's floor are in the dinning room. Dad said they have a dinner scheduled for each floor today. So dinner only lasted an hour, thank goodness.

Anyway this time we were seated with just two other people. A man and his wife.

There are only women on Ida's floor and this was one of the other "clients" and her husband. Dad and he already knew each other.

Dinner started off OK if you call it good when I speak to Ida and she looks at me as if she would love to get me alone for a while. So I just kept quiet and stayed out of the conversation. Ida and the other woman, Jennifer, do not seem to like each other either. So the two men were talking. They were talking about Vice President Nixon's visit to Iran and the riots that the visit caused. They were also talking about President Eisenhower and what they thought about what he had done or had not done. Dad said that he had been pleasantly surprised that the President had done more toward peace than he had expected.

Just then Ida jumped up and screamed loudly, "Do I have to sit here with this white trash and this little tramp. Harrison, why do you bring her here? You know she put me here. GET HER OUT! GET HER OUT! And I won't sit here with that woman."

I didn't know if Ida was talking about Jennifer or me. Didn't care. I just wanted to get away.

The other man was up and taking his wife away. Ida was now screaming and making sounds I had never heard. It almost sounded like an animal. Molly was pushing Dad away, and trying to get between Ida and him. Ida was trying to scratch everybody with her nails. Fortunately, her nails are now cut short, I assume

138

by the Center's rules. Anyway, Molly was able to get her turned and two men orderlies came up and all three began putting Ida in a white jacket with straps. I had heard about a strait jacket, but I had never seen one and never expected to be where somebody was put in one.

Another orderly had pulled me back and was standing between me and what was going on. As soon as Ida was taken away, he moved at let me go to Dad. I started to say something to Dad and then really looked at him. He looked broken. Really shattered. I think he had seen such a positive Ida the night before and now he had seen the worst. Just out of nowhere, just like I have always seen it, so I guess Ida can no longer control it.

Dad and I walked out to the hallway, past all of the other people. Some of the people looked at us with great empathy. They had their own "situations".

Dad sat down in a chair in the big foyer. He looked so tired and older than I had ever seen him look. I think for the first time he no longer had hope for a future for him with Ida.

What a horrible Christmas present. I had wanted so much for him to be happy. I had wanted him to be able to have a chance to be with her. I had thought it would carry over to today and so it would be a good day too, so much for that.

I know I am only a kid. But I have known for a good while that Ida is exactly what she is. She has no ability to have feelings for others. She only can think about what she wants. Ever. I really do not know why Dad has not seen that she hurts people. I don't know how to explain this but I don't even think she hurts people on purpose, I just thinks she acts without any thinking about others at all.

One of Ida's doctors, not Dr. Weiner, came out to where we were and sat down next to Dad. I started to get up to walk away, Dad said, "It's OK, Roxie, you can stay." In five minutes, Dad had aged ten years.

The Doctor, Doctor Markowitz, said, "Mr. Rayburn, we talked about this, we have to go to the next level of restriction. She cannot be allowed this kind of interaction any longer. You and I will talk more next week and I will let you know then what we have decided. But you know what we have talked about, this may be the time to make this change."

Dad just kept looking at him and not saying anything. Finally, I said, "Dr. Markowitz, when can Dad come back to see her?" The doctor turned to me, "Your father will need to come back next week and we will make some decisions, right now, he needs to go home.

139

Take care of him. Your mother will get the treatment that she needs, but visits will be very restricted for a while." He patted me on the shoulder and then walked down the hallway to his office.

I told Dad, "Let's go home." He looked up as if he was surprised to be seeing me. We went out to the Caddy and Dad handed me the keys and said, "Roxie, you drive." He did not talk all the way home and I just let him alone.

I was really wondering what the doctor had meant about a "change" and I wondered what Dad was going to do if there was no possibility of Ida getting "better".

Just as we got to the edge of Cochise and began to drop down into the valley from the mesas, Dad finally spoke. "Roxie, I am so sorry that you are having to grow up so fast, sometimes I think you are the adult, and I sorry that you have not been able to be a kid anymore. The worst part is that for so long I thought I could fix this and all I did was put you in harm's way."

I said, "OK, it is still Christmas Day. Let's leave the sad stuff for another day. I am a kid and I am happy to be a kid. So I'm a tough kid. Pug is always telling me I am a survivor and I am tougher than a junk yard dog. So next week you will go see what you have to do, whatever that is. How about we get some of Mrs. Casillas' tortillas out of the freezer and some of the other stuff and have a Mexican feast tonight. Could I invite James and his grandparents over? Or do you want to be alone?"

Dad said "Ask them over, that would be nice."

James was supposed to be coming over anyway and I just hoped that his grandparents would come too.

I called him after we got home and he said sure, he thought that he could get Mr. and Mrs. Walker to come too. They did and we all wound up having a wonderful evening. Dad was even able to talk about what happened. Mrs. Hunter asked what he thought would happen to Ida now, and Dad told her that it was possible that she would have to go to the other hospital in Tucson. That really surprised me because I did not think that Dad would let that happen but then I wondered if he might not have a choice now that she had had her latest episode.

Sometimes when I am singing, some of the words have entirely new meanings. I guess that is what happens when you get older and begin to know about the world. Everyday something seems to happen that causes me to change my mind about some issue.

James and I talked about our plans for New Years. I can't believe it is going to be 1954 already, this year has just flown by, so

140

much has happened. I really feel like a different person than I did at the beginning of the year.

I was thinking about Eugene O'Neill's <u>Long Day's Journey into Night.</u> Mrs. Mason said it is really an autobiography. How sad. The father just could not do what he needed to do for his wife and his children because of all the bad things that had happened to him when he was a child.

The mother in that story had gone crazy after the second son was born. She uses opium so she can sleep. But did she go crazy because something happened or someone do something to her? Or did she go crazy because it just happened? These are things I really want to know. Dad had one opinion and Mr. Bertram had another opinion. So I guess each person just has to decide what they think when they read O'Neill's play. Life is like that. When we observe what happens to a person we know we have to guess about the reasons, even if people tell us something the truth may be something entirely different.

I wonder if Mr. O'Neill was ever happy? I wonder if his father was ever happy? Mr. O'Neill died in November and Dad said that he was one of the great playwrights because his plays caused people to think about their own lives.

Dear Diary, the next time I write it will be 1954. I hope it will be a wonderful new year.

The New Year 1954

January 1

What a wonderful New Year. The six of us, Cami, Evan, Lana, Leslie, James and I went in to the Santa Rita for their New Years Eve Gala. It was so wonderful. The theme was Silver Bells.

This time Pug and her husband were the chaperones. That was fine with me. We went in Dad's Caddie and Pug and Mac drove in his truck. Thank goodness that the rest of my merry band likes both of them. What's not to like? Anyway, they were going to sit at their own table and James, being the really good guy that he is, asked them to sit with us. We had a great time.

I wore my prom dress. Dad asked me if I wanted to go get a new dress. There was no reason to because the one I have is so beautiful. I would wear it all the time if I could just find a reason. It is like wearing an enchanted cloud of moonbeams. Corny, I know, but that is the way I feel.

We went back to Levy's and we even got the same saleslady. She helped me find a little silver bolero jacket that was just perfect. I had my prom shoes dyed silver. Then Dad took me over to our

141

jewelers and I got a truly beautiful Indian silver necklace that looks like an elegant collar piece.

Cami got a new white dress and her mother made her silver peplum jacket. She also got new silver ballet slippers. Lana had a black dress with silver trim. She wore black satin heels. It is all so sophisticated, not my usual levis and boots.

It was just like a fairy tale. The guys went to a rental place for jackets. So we all matched and felt very grown up and magical.

It was my first News Year's Eve on a sort of "date". We still do not go anywhere alone. Dad says I can't until I am sixteen which is still OK with me and James says fine with him.   I think it takes some of the pressure off of him as well because he knows that if he wants to be a college football coach, he has as much education in front of him as I do. Neither of us feel any pressure to change the way we are now. Good buddies who happen to care about each other. It is sort of as if we are going to be a steady item in the future. We are to busy taking care of our lives as they are now.

I know it bothers him sometimes that he is older but Dad told him that he has an advantage for getting a sports scholarship. I hope so. We have both talked about going to the U of A.

I felt bad that Dad was going to be home alone. Cora asked him to go up to their house but I don't know if that is what he was going to do that or not.

But I am off of the wonderful story of our fabulous, luscious, memorable evening.   We danced and danced and danced. Midnight was magical. The dance was both inside and out in the courtyard that was all lit up with lighted paper lanterns and little lights all over the trees and palms. We danced mostly outside so it was lucky that even for January it is just very cool, not cold at all.

The outside dancing part was on a huge veranda filled with fragrant flowering bushes, desert palms and potted plants. The filigreed, masonry wall opened to a winding pathway lined on each side with tall palms and old fashioned streetlights. That led down to a large pond that rippled and shimmered with reflected stars. The moon struck a river of light that illuminated the swans from above as they glided gracefully as if they were keeping time to the same music that we were dancing to.

I felt as if I had been swept into a fairy tale. I kept expecting the fairy band from Midsummer Night's Dream to appear in their gossamer garb and dance beside us. I did not want this night to be over. We ended the midnight dance with a very sweet and tender kiss. My first and it was so sweet and gentle.

I wore James' jacket all the way home and it was a beautiful start for the New Year.

The fairy princess and her prince had to go home and turn back in to their real selves because tomorrow is a work day.

Somehow it seems perfectly normal that I should go from high heels and gossamer into levis and a shovel full of horse poop. As far as I am concerned, that is not a bad thing, it is just the way my life is. One day I'm a princess and the next day I am on poop patrol!

Jan 8

Wow! A everybody has had a busy start to the new year too. Dad has gotten back involved with his business in Tucson. Especially his rentals and he has invested with a group of men who are building houses for the growing number of military men who are coming into Tucson.

He is really gone a lot and gets home late but he is always home at night for which I am very glad. I would not be very brave about being alone in the house.

I have been very busy working at Brownies doing chores, riding, mucking and spending time with both hay burners. I am finally getting back to practicing barrel. I am going to try to get Mary Jane to practice with me.

I have also been doing a great deal of reading. I am going to write some critiques over the next few entries. Mr. Bertram has been teaching how to critique literature and some of what I have been reading just takes the top of my head off and some of it leaves me cold, bored, or irritated.

Dear Diary, I will catch you up on Ida's condition and whereabouts. She got worse after the Christmas Day Episode. Hard to believe that she could get worse but she did, and it is all aimed at me. She has become more convinced, if that is possible, that I am responsible for putting her into the situation that she is in.

It has taken me a while, but I do now get that she is truly insane and cannot control her behavior. That makes it really much worse. The doctors told dad that she is not responding to medicine as well as they thought that she would and she has to be restrained often. So they told Dad that they could no longer keep her at the center because they were not equipped for her kind of illness plus the fact that she has all of the other physical illness as well.

Dad is really upset over it but she has been taken to a mental hospital. The good part for Dad is that it is still in Tucson. Dad says it is about a third of the cost of the Center and has better security and good medical services. It is the Desert Dove Hospital.

The name sounds nice doesn't it? I have only seen the outside. Her new doctors do not want me to visit her and Dad can only come once a month for a one hour visit. She is going to have some kind of new treatments and medicine as well as getting treated for whatever medical problems she has.

Dad says that this hospital is part of the system in Tucson that is where people are put who have committed a violent crime but cannot be convicted because they have a mental defect. All very mumbo jumbo to me but the good part is that she cannot get out on her own, and Dad could not take her out even if he wanted to.

I do not really understand all of it. I know that the hospital does have something to do with the legal system that is requiring Ida to be put into a facility. She could have been put into a state hospital in Phoenix. But because Dad is able to pay to keep her in this new hospital she does not have to go to the other one.

He finally explained to me that it was because there were three events on record and there was no choice but to put her into a facility. I did not know that the other two counted. Judge Hunter had to report the other two instances as part of the record for what she has done. That did not even count the "Peacock Incident" but it was added in because I reported it at the hearing.

I am beginning to piece a lot of this together. My fifth grade teacher, Mr. Garrison, reported the time that I came to school with legs that were shredded from the vacuum cleaner cord. Dad had been away on business and it was a pretty bad situation. She sent me to school on the morning that she did it and I was still bleeding. Mr. Garrison told Mrs. Brockhurst, she reported it to Judge Hunter. That was the first time she was sent to Tucson.

I thought she just went over to the Center because she wanted to. Now I realize that she had been committed there or she would have been prosecuted. The second time was when she took all of my stuff out of the Cochise house and burned it in the back yard. She had already done that before but I guess in Tucson it was easier for Dad to cover it up. In Cochise, nothing is secret.

There were many other instances but those were the ones that had gone into a record. The last one had caused Dad to have to put her at the Center. Her deterioration at the Center had her moved to Desert Dove.

Dad said that she would have had to move there anyway because of his finances.

144

Dad said that he just wanted me to understand that I would not have to worry about ever being alone with her again. He said that she would be at Desert Dove for at least a couple of years even if she got better. And If she did not improve it could be longer, much longer.

I really had to do a lot of thinking about that and I have figured out that I am not happy or unhappy about it. I am glad I do not have to be afraid anymore but I do not like that Dad has to be alone and the possibility that he will be alone after I am older and out on my own.

Jan 25

Mr. Bertram told me today that they got the results of the test that I took last semester. I had a very high score and he has proposed me for a special program that is being conducted at the University of Arizona.

The program is some kind of advanced learning plan. Students who are selected will take classes at the U at the same time that they go to High School. The classes are both High School and College credit. Confusing! Anyway, if I get accepted and if Dad and I decide that I should do it, I could graduate one year early. I think that is a good idea in many ways. But the bad part would be that I am already pretty loaded up with stuff to do and this would just add on more.

Well, no point worrying about that now. I have enough on my plate.

Feb 1

I am sorry that I have been so neglectful Dear Diary, but I have been busy with the normal stuff. I have been spending most of my free time out at Brownies and I have really been enjoying time with both El Con and Lizzie. I love working with Joe, sometimes I feel as if we are buddies in spite of the age gap. He is so wise that often I don't get something he is saying until I go home and start to think about it. And Wham! I get what he means and it helps me think about other things.

Joe does something that most of the hands do not do, he reads everything. He reads book, newspapers, history books and probably things I don't even know about. He and Dad talk about a lot of the same things and it comes from stuff they both read. Dad gets him all kinds of information about ranch things. The are always going to Tucson to learn more about what is going on. Now that Joe works for Brownie I hope that they can still do that.

I have a new project going. I want Joe and Dad to spend at least one evening or one day a week doing something. Already they have gone in to an auction and another time Joe played poker with Dad's group.

I am also busy with school. Mr. Bertram told me that I have been accepted into the program at the U of A. Dad thinks that it is wonderful. I hope so.

With cheer, homework, my part of keeping up the house and cooking and more, there has been very little time to spend with James and with Cami.

The wind of heaven is that which blows through a horse's ears

Arabian Proverb

March 1

Wow! Diary, I have really not had time for you. So sorry! But things have really been busy. Remember Busy Bee Buzz-Buzz-Buzz.....

I really have been flitting all over the place. Ridiculous, you say? I agree.

As much as I like to write, I have had to put my diary on a back burner. I am still writing for a great deal of my time but it has been for school, especially for the U of A program.

I have so many responsibilities now. At the house and out at Brownie's. Since the first of the year I have been very focused on school work, ranch work, house work and trying to spend time with my friends. So I have spent the last few weeks trying to determine what things I really want to do and what I need to let go.

Cami and I were talking yesterday about the "do nothings". The kids in school who really do not do anything, they do just enough school work to get by, they do not belong to any clubs or athletics and they are not very involved with their churches. I can't even imagine what they do to fill up time. Mr. Bertram had a group of us try to work with some of the Freshmen and get them involved. Only one girl joined the Pom-Pom squad. She replaced a girl who moved. But the rest just do not want to do anything. I even offered to teach a couple of the kids who are town kids, how to ride. You would think I offered to have them do extra homework. So it is not working to get some of these kids involved. Fortunately, some of them can be motivated. Mrs. Mason said that was what kept her going as a teacher. I have just about decided that people are somewhat "cooked" by the time they get to high school and the teachers or anybody else cannot motivate them.

146

I see all of the teachers work so hard to try to get students excited about a subject. And, hey, I am guilty of it too. I do not like math. I have no interest in it. I do not see what it has to do with what I want to do in life.

Brahm is a math whiz and he hates reading and history. His real passion is football. He talks it, does it and that is what he wants to do. He wants a college football scholarship and then he wants to go pro. Dad tried to tell him what the odds were. And Dad and Doc tried to tell him what the physical problems were. He has already had a serious knee injury. But they also tell me that too about the riding and barrel racing.

So I am fascinated about how people develop what they are interested in as well as what people are not interested in.

In some ways I am looking forward to my 14th birthday and in some ways I am not.

James is planning something special. I do not what could be more special than New Year's. I still think about it. How do you top a perfect date?

March 4

Dad said that they are doing a new treatment for Ida and he seems hopeful about it. I do not know what that means for her future or mine. Can she be released if she is better? I am very confused about what the real situation is so I am going to go talk to Judge Hunter about this. Is she legally locked up or is it voluntary and who the heck is going to make that decision, Dad? Is Ida agreeing so that she does not get prosecuted? I need to know what is going on so I will take the bull by the horns and find out if I need to worry or not.

March 5

Dad just told me that for my birthday, he is taking me to have lunch with Ted. How great is that! I love being in his studio as much as I love his art. He is such a fascinating man, Dad could not have chosen any better. We are finally going to get the paintings that we should have gotten when we moved back into town but so much went on that we just put it off.

March 6

I have just finished <u>Don Quixote</u> so now I have two more favorite characters, Don Quixote and Sancho Panza. I told Mrs. Mason that it worried me that sometimes I feel as if characters from a book have become friends and that most of the time I understand them better than I do some of the real flesh and blood people I know. She said that people who love literature feel that

147

way.   Thank goodness for Mrs. Mason, she says things to me that let me feel so much better about myself. Sometimes, I just think I am the only one who thinks a certain way.

Back to the character of Don Quixote.   I can't figure out if Cervantes was creating a dreamer or a man who was insane and fixated on his "cause". Maybe both. I am going to read it again. There is so much to it I don't think I can take it all in with just one reading. I just started reading about Cervantes himself. I guess he put some of his own story into the book, his life was its own drama. Dad said it has always been one of his own favorite books because Cervantes was so good at making fun of all the hypocrites.

Until I read this book I have always seen the Age of Chivalry as such an ideal but I guess it wasn't.   I am beginning to think that history is pretty much dependent on who is telling the story as well as the problem of who is telling the story and how the stories get changed and embellished over time.   The character of Sancho Panza demonstrates what a friendship should be.   Quixote is so idealistic that he cannot see the real world and poor Sancho keeps trying to help him see the world as it really is, all the while trying to take care of Quixote.

James and I have been going to the show or the drive-in once a week. Usually with Cami and Evan. Then we go to the Milo. Fun. But I have to admit, Dear Diary, that sometimes I get a little frustrated because I cannot always talk about what I want to talk about. Our little foursome is all about school, who is going with whom, the last game and griping about teachers. I care so much about all of them but I wanted to talk about Quixote but I know they would be bored out of their minds.

March 8

Busy Bee Buzz-Buzz

March 11

I received a letter and a birthday card from Sharon today.   Dad knows that I get letters from her now. I have had a few since I have been able to get them at our own post office box. She sent me some really cute pictures of Morgana. Morgana is almost eight now. She also sent a really funny picture of a cat sleeping in an empty fish bowl.

I have tried to get a complete sense of Sharon as a person but I do not seem to be able to. Dad and I have talked about my going to visit her. I have had so much conflicting information about her that I really want to sit down with her and ask her all kinds of questions.   She tells me bits and pieces in the letters but it is so fragmented that I really wind up with more questions.

March 12

Dad and I went to Tucson and had our lunch with Ted.   We picked out two paintings. The one for the living room is of a group of wild horses running into a wind.   Ted said that he is still thinking about a title for it. The other one is a group of angels in a circle, that went into   my bedroom. Could anything be any more perfect? Ted uses a palette knife for applying paint, I had never seen that before and it is incredible. It makes these images come alive.   They have texture and it causes the light to be different depending on the time of day as well as where the viewer is standing.

I don't know how it is possible, but the figures that he does are more real than when painters paint exactly.   I asked him about that, he replied that is the way the mind works, where there is less, the mind fills in.   He also said that this style is called. minimalism. I sort of get it but I think I have to do a lot more thinking about it.

Ted is not very tall, he is about an inch taller than I am, so that would make him about 5'7". He has black, curly hair with some silver in it and it is longer than I have ever seen on a man, but it looks normal for him. I don't think he tries to look a certain way. He just "is". He moves very quickly. He will say a lot and then he gets very quiet and he just seems to be watching but when he does talk he has a little bit of an accent.

I wish I could ask to be in his studio for a whole day and just listen and watch him.   But I get the idea that he is so focused on what he does that he needs to create without what I think would be a intrusion. I don't know how I know this but I have a feeling it is this way for most people who do a creative thing. I know that I do not want to write when other people are right there. When I write, as Greta Garbo said, "I want to be alone".

I love to be around Cami and James as well as my other people, but when I write, I have to be alone. I wanted to ask him about that and if he wants to be alone when he creates a painting, but I did not think it was OK to ask.

He and Dad were talking about Tucson and how it has changed. They were agreeing that so many people from other parts of the country, especially from back east have moved in and are changing the way Tucson looks as well as how the city is being run.

I asked if I could just walk around and look at things and he said, "Of, course, go where you want."   I had a wonderful time just wandering and taking my time to look at his work, some he is still working on and the ones that were done.

On the way home Dad and I had a wonderful talk about how people contribute to the world in so many ways. We talked about how some people contribute in ways that other people never see or recognize. Then he said that he has always thought about the things that never happened.

I asked him what that meant. He said that he thinks about the great artists that never got to paint, write a book, become a violinist, or any other creative person, or a profession that required years of education. He said that historically, there have been so many people who had a talent or a desire to be a certain thing, but they never did because they had to support a family or just never got the opportunity because of circumstances.

He said that he thought that was especially true of women. For most of history, women have not been able to be artists or writers or be in fields such as law, medicine and other professions that are considered a "Man's" job.

I had never thought about this before. This is one of those "WOW! moments for me. I saw exactly what he was talking about. I want to be a lawyer and eventually a judge. But all of the lawyers and judges I know are men. I just never thought about it before. How many women did not paint a picture that is in a museum because she was put into the "place" where she has to be a wife and mother who spends her days washing, cleaning, and taking care of other people.

It made me think about all of the teachers at school. None of them are married. Mrs. Mason is a widow. Others are widowed or never married but every one of the men teachers are married.

WOW! This gives me a whole new thing to think about. How will I be able to do what I want to do? I asked Dad what he thought about that. He said that he wants me to realize that I will have to work much harder to get to be whatever it is that I want.

He said that he wanted me to take typing class in school but after I graduate, I was never to tell people that I could type.

That idea took me by surprise. " What in the world does that mean?"

Dad continued, "Well, what happens is that women get trapped into what other people think that they should be. A woman who types, and is a great secretary, gets placed there and has no opportunity to move up because she is too valuable where she is to the person above her. That is in addition to what society has decided that women should be or should not be. Because woman have the babies, society had decided that they are the ones who are the nurturers. Women take care of the home and children and men go out and earn the money to provide for everything. "

"But the world is changing. Women have been coming out of the roles that have been there since the beginning and they are proving that they can do what men can do. The big problem is that men do not want this change. I see women having problems right now. Look at Pug. She has had to give up a lot to be where she is with the fiddle playing and the competitions.   People have said very hurtful things about her."

I asked, "But what about Cami's mother, Mrs. Delgado, she is a teacher and she is married?"   Dad said, "Yes, that is true, but it is just beginning to be true. It is only in the last few years that teachers in the lower grades are both teachers and married.   I think it will be a few more years before that happens in the upper grades, but it will happen. Since the war, women have not been as accepting of the roles that society has thought of collectively as appropriate."   Dad continued thoughtfully, "But don't get me wrong.   I think that being a mother is the most valuable contribution a woman can make. If she chooses to stay home or go to work that should be her choice. Somebody else should not make the choice for her any more that somebody should make choices for men in terms of what profession they choose."

So now I have a really big issue to think about. Can I be a wife, mother and have a career of what I want to be or will I be one of the women who has to make a choice?

The one thing that I know for sure is that I am so glad that I have a father who believes I can be anything that I want to be.

Mar 20

I have really been doing a lot of thinking about what Dad said. It is interesting, but now I am looking at things with a new filter.   I have watched a few TV shows with Dad. He had commented that TV is good in some ways but it reinforces so many stereotypes, especially for women.

He started talking about Ida.   He said that she is really smart and that many things had happened in her past that made her think in certain ways. He said that he accepts that she has mental issues but that she had other issues as well. He said that she was abused as a child by her father. Her mother was also beaten by her father and was powerless to help Ida. Dad had thought that with enough love from him she could overcome these issues but he has had realize that he couldn't.   He said that he has a much better understanding of her illness after dealing with her doctors with whom he has met with them for hours and hours.

151

Then he go to the "shocking" part. He said that the doctors at her new hospital are trying a new treatment for Ida. It is called shock therapy. It has to do with electricity. The doctors send a shock of electricity to the person's brain. This is supposed to make the person calm. I asked Dad three questions. How long does it last? Is it working for Ida? If it works will that mean he is going to bring her home?

I just do not know why Dad can be so smart about everything else in the world and so absolutely stupid about her. I know, I am angry, I don't care, Ida comes home and everything changes.

April 1

Dear Diary, I have just been too angry to write anything. I am not even going to talk about it right now either. SHE may be coming home by June. Oh, Joy! I have two months to be happy! SO I am going to concentrate on school and being with El Con, Lizzie, Joe and Fala. Right now I don't talk much to Dad, he knows how unhappy I am.

I know it is selfish of me. I know that in just two years and with this program it could be one year, I will be off to school in Tucson. I will not live here if she is here. But I know he is looking at the rest of his life and he wants her in it. I wish she knew how lucky she is, there is not one other human that thinks she has any value. None!

But just like he can't change her, I can't change him. I know he is caught in the middle between a child he loves and the love of his life. Here we go again. The heart wants, what the heart wants. Too bad Ida does not have a heart. I know what she wants.

In Sharon's letters over the last year she has been saying that she hopes I will come for a visit.

Dad and I talked last night and I said that this might be a good time to go to New York and visit her.

That way if he does bring her home we can see how that goes. He has said that if he brings her home she is going to have somebody here to be with her at all times. He will take a "shift" when he is home, which will be from the time he gets home until he goes to work. If he has to leave, Cora will come in. Beth Ann will be here during the day. I don't know if Beth Ann is tough enough for dealing with Ida.

"Wow!" I said to Dad, "You really have given this some thought and it sounds like a done deal!" He had the good grace to look away and said nothing.

So much for the good life. By the way, I kept waiting for him to say "April Fool! Well the joke is on me, there was no April Fool.

152

April 27

Dear Diary, last time I said I did not want to write and yet I wrote. Today I mean it. I have been writing letters to Sharon and we have been talking on the phone. Stay tuned, I will tell you about my plans when they are all complete.

May 20

Studying for finals, working, stepping up barrel practice and my world is just spinning by. Can't wait for school to be out just so that I can slow down on some things and do more out at Brownies and read more. Want to spend time with Fala, El Con, Lizzie, Mary Ann, Joe and Brownie.

May 26

It is Cami's birthday so our little band of merry people, went to Tucson to the Pago Pago. It is such a fun place and we had a wonderful happy and somewhat loud dinner with much laughing and jokes.

I told the group that I am going to spend the summer in New York with Sharon.

I told them a little more about Sharon, that she had moved to New York last year because her husband's company, Waldenbooks, moved his job to New York City. Sharon works at Macy's in the city too. She is a bookkeeper. His job is for a company that is starting to expand and they are making more stores around the country. They are like a library but it is a private company and you pay to rent the books.

They do not live in New York City. They live in the suburbs. They live in a town called Nyack. It is about thirty miles out of New York City.

So anyway, the gang was surprised and asked me about what I would do about the horses and everything I am doing? Joe is going to take care of my wonderful hay burners and Brownie is giving me more to do when I come back. Dad will take care of Fala. He has promised that if Ida is there he will keep her away from him.

James said, "Well, what if I took Fala out to our ranch if Ida comes home? I know your dad will have enough to deal with anyway. And my grandmother would love to have Fala until you get back." I told James that it was a great idea because it was one of the things that worried me. I still think even with everything that has happened in the last year, that Dad has no real understanding of what Ida is capable of.

Dear Diary, let me tell you about my very first dog. I was eight, in the fifth grade and we had only lived in Cochise for a few months. On the other side of where Pug lives, in the duplex, there was an older woman who was bedridden. Pug used to take me with her to visit. After I while I would even go to Mrs. Murphy's home on my own. Mrs. Murphy's first name was Fiona. But of course I did not call her that. Even Pug didn't. I think she had to be ninety or more. Much later, Pug told me that she was bedridden because she had cancer and she had no relative to take care of her. Her husband had died a long time ago and her children never came and never helped. Sad.

I would go to Pug first and she would give me a pie, pudding cups, a cake, cookies or some other goody to take with me. Pug made sure that Mrs. Murphy had three meals a day and I was the "Snack Girl" in the early afternoon. It made all of us very happy. Pug even took care of Lady, Mrs. Murphy's cocker spaniel. Lady was white and apricot colored. Pug told me that was name of the color, I would have called it kind of tanish. Lady spent most of her day lying right next to Mrs. Murphy.

Dear Diary, let me say right now that when I am completely grown up and on my own, I want to live my life just like Pug. I want to make a difference just like she does. The same is true for the rest of my Angel Band of caregivers. Dad makes a difference too. With the exception of his relationship with Ida, his life is very much about making the world a better place. I know I whine a lot because of Ida, but if I am being truly honest, I know that I am really lucky to have what I do have.

OK, back to the dog story. I know, I know, I just said how lucky I am and I am telling a story that is a "bad" Ida story. Well, that is life, isn't it? Cook would have said, "Asi es la vida!" Did I spell that right. Guess I better take more Spanish! I can say it, I can't always spell it.

One day when I went over to Mrs. Murphy's she told me that Lady had had a little adventure and was going to have puppies. I asked her who the father was. She said I would have to ask Lady but Lady was not telling. Having never been around a dog that was having puppies, I was rather surprised that it did not seem to take very long.

I arrived at Mrs. Murphy's house one day to be greeted by a large, wicker basket full of little tiny funny looking creatures that did not look anything like a cocker spaniel. Lady looked very pleased with herself. Pug had followed me over to tell me how to handle the puppies, well, actually to tell me what not to do. Pug said that the puppies could not be handled for at least a week maybe more depending on how Lady felt about it. Pug also said that Lady did not seem to have lived up to her name and the puppies were of very questionable parentage. I thought they were the cutest things I had seen but I also thought they looked more like baby pigs than they looked like puppies.

I watched them change every day. Everybody who saw them said they were the weirdest looking dogs they had ever seen. I loved them almost as much as Lady did but I had to admit that everybody was right. Even Dad came to see them and he laughed himself silly. "Lady, what did you do!" He said if he did not know better he would have thought she had gone out of her species.

Finally, one day, I asked Mrs. Murphy what she was going to do with the puppies. She said that Pug was looking for families to adopt them. I asked her how much they were. She starting laughing until she was coughing. I had not seen her laugh that hard before. She finally said that I could have one if it was OK with my parents. Well, of course, I thought immediately, Dad would be OK with it but the hard part was going to be Ida. For years she has said no pets. And we were still living in the town house. Ida's house. And I mean IDA"S HOUSE.

So I bounced my little self home and waited for dinner so that Dad would be there. Then I threw my bombshell into the dinner conversation. Talk stopped cold. Dad thought for a minutes, and then said, "Yes, Roxie I think that would be fine. Just so long as you know that the puppy you choose is not going to be a really good looking dog." Before I could answer Dad, Ida stood straight up and announced to both of us, or maybe it was to the world in general, "There will be no dog in this house, not as long as I am in it!." Well, I thought, but was not brave enough to say, 'Well, maybe you could not be in it.' But what I really said was a whiny "Why not?" And Surprise of the Century, Dad said "Ida, the kid is getting a puppy from Mrs. Murphy. Ida seemed truly shocked and she stomped out of the room. I was more shocked than Ida.

"Roxie, let's go get a puppy."

But first Dad went to the bakery in town and got a big bag of stuff and then he stopped at the drugstore and got a box of Chocolates. Then we went over to Pug's. He asked Pug if she thought Mrs. Murphy felt like visitors. I had never realized that Mrs. Murphy might not want a visitor because of being very sick. But she had been ill a few times and Pug did not let me go over to her house. This time she said, "Yes, let's all go over".

Mrs. Murphy really did not look very well. Pug told her why we were there and told her what Dad had brought. She sat with Mrs. Murphy while we went to the puppy pen. They had outgrown the wicker box and Pug's hubby had made a wooden dog box that was high enough for the puppies to stay contained. We called it the Puppy Pen.

There were two puppies that looked like twins. I really liked both of them. Dad saw me playing with both and read my mind. "Roxie, I think one is going to be the most that your mother can handle." I really did not like it when he called Ida my mother, but I was wise enough not to point this out right then.

I took the new puppy from his little home with his brothers and sisters, told him to say Goodbye to Lady and we were on our way. Pug had told us that Mrs. Murphy was getting too ill to see anyone anymore. She told dad she was taking the puppy box and Lady to her house. That was the last time that I ever saw Mrs. Murphy. Pug told me that Mrs. Murphy was very happy to know that this puppy was going to have such a wonderful little girl who loved him.

Then we went to the Cochise Feed Store on Patagonia Street and we got him a collar, leash, dog dishes and dog food. When we got back to the house and Dad found a box and blanket for him. He said he would get a dog bed when we went to Tucson. Dad told me that I could only hold him for a few minutes at a time but I had to leave him alone to sleep. As soon as Dad left my room, I laid down on the floor on the dog blanket and put the puppy next to me, he curled up and went right to sleep.

Every two hours I took him outside and he did what he was supposed to do. Of course he had done the same thing in the house a couple times and I had quickly cleaned up because I did not want Ida to have anything else to get mad about.

Bedtime arrived and everyone slept, Puppy, who still had no name, me, Dad and Ida, or so I thought. In the morning, I bounced up to get the puppy up and outside for his first tinkle of the day. I was horrified to discover that the puppy was stiff. I knew immediately that the puppy had died sometime during the night from right next to me where we had both been sleeping.

I went into Dad's room, crying hysterically. It took a few minutes for him to understand what I was screaming about. Finally he followed me back to my room. He saw the puppy, pulled me back to his den where the phone was. He called Pug and told her to take me back to where the puppies were and I was to get the other one that I had liked.

I was only eight, but I knew what had happened. I told Dad, while we were waiting for Pug, that Ida would just do it again. Dad said in a voice I had never heard before, "No, she won't." Pug arrived just then and Dad took her outside and I guess told her what happened. Then Dad came in, told me to get another puppy and not to worry for one minute.

We went back to Pug's got the new puppy and I stayed with Pug for the rest of the day.   I wanted to go see Mrs. Murphy but she said she was too sick and she did not need to know about the first puppy.   I had dinner with Pug and her husband, then Dad came and got me and Pudgy, the now named puppy.

I was truly scared.   I went to my room, and there was a new wooden dog bed with a pad and new blanket in it. And Dad had put a pad with a blanket beside the dog bed for me to lay on.   I was determined to stay awake. I think I did for a long time.   But I had taken what precautions I could I had pushed the chest that was next to my bedroom door in front of the door.   And I had put the trash can on the top of the dresser so if the dresser moved, the trash can would fall down and it would make a loud noise.

I will never know what Dad said to Ida.   It took me a while to believe that nothing would happen. Dad kept saying not to worry about it.   But I have spent my entire life worrying about what she will do next.   It is five years later and I am still worrying about what she will do next.

The good ending, at least for five years, is that he was a wonderful puppy who grew into a phenomenal dog.   He was incredibly smart and was a very happy, funny dog. I wish he had lived a very long dog life. But I try to be grateful that I had this phenomenal dog for the time that I did.

Dad and I moved to the ranch not too long after I got Pudgy, so at least I did not have to worry about him and he was safe. Pudgy died last year right before Christmas.   I still believe that Ida had something to do with it.

Pudgy used to ride in Dad's truck when he came to town and would sit in the back bed or he would run around town depending on what part of town dad was in while Dad did his chores.   On the Monday before Christmas of 1952, Pudgy became very ill.   The vet determined that he as well as six other dogs around Cochise had been fed ground glass.   It was a horrible way for an animal to die. I still think that Ida got her revenge but it just took her a while.   I know that Dad is aware that I think this but he just can't ever bring himself to believe it. I can.

But Dear Diary, let me tell a wonderful Pudgy story.   Dad owned a small building that housed a little deli type store. The man who ran the store lived in a nearby motel with his invalid wife. Somehow Pudgy learned that this old man would give him the ends off of the prepared lunch meats. So Pudgy always wanted to ride into town with Dad in the Morning when he came in. Pudgy would hop out by the motel, go sit on the front door step of the couple's room and wait for Mr. Schmidt to come out and Pudgy would walk

157

Mr. Schmidt to his little deli. Mr. Schmidt would prepare his store, and get the lunch meats ready. Pudgy would wait patiently by the door until he received his daily share of the ends off of the rolls of meats. I am sure that the old man gave him more than just the ends. Then Pudgy would go make his daily rounds which included going back to the motel where Pudgy would find, Rosa, the motel maid, who would let him into the Schmidt's room where Pudgy would spend time with Mrs. Schmidt. Pudgy had an actual routine that he would follow so Dad was always able to find him. Then they would make their way back to the ranch.

I still believe that Pudgy would be unhappy if he did not get to visit all the people on his list before Dad came to find him and bring him home. On weekends he would seem content to be with me unless I was going into town and then he thought that he should go everywhere I did. And he actually did. He was allowed to go to the movie house and to the drive in. He was not allowed into the Milo or into church so he would wait outside until I came out. He also used to howl during my solos and other songs that caused him to want to join into his own version of singing. I think many people in the congregation enjoyed Pudgy's singing much more than mine!

Now that I am in my teens I see that this may have not been business as usual. Pudgy will always be that special dog for me. I love Fala and he is a wonderful dog. But of course, he is not allowed or encouraged to do the things Pudgy did. He was very much a town dog. Townspeople still tell stories about The Late Great Pudgy. Maybe Pudgy is another of my special angels looking out for me.

Note: Mrs. Murphy died just a few weeks after I got Pudgy. She had told Pug that she was grateful for my visits. I have often wondered why her children left her alone while she was dying from cancer. Thank goodness there are people like Pug who was willing to be so good to her in her last years of life.

May 30

Sharon and I have made all of the arrangements for me to go visit her with Dad's approval. And I think that he thinks it is a good idea on many levels. He wants me to have a chance to know Sharon's story and by extension I will learn about Troy, my birth father.

This is going to give him a chance to bring Ida home if it is possible. When I get back Dad and I will have to sit down and make some decisions and have a plan but for now I am just going to go see Sharon and then worry about that when I return.

Boy, talk about playing everything by ear!

I have just begun to realize how stressed Dad is. And I am beginning to worry about his health. He looks so much more tired and old than he did just a year ago. I don't think he can take much more of this ping-pong with Ida.

I just wish I could say to him what I think and what everybody else thinks. Not even the doctors think she should be out. She is a burden for everyone but him the most. If this plan he wants works it is going to cost a fortune. Because between Beth Ann and Cora it will be an eight hour day, seven days a week. I can't do it even if I wanted to and we know how much I want to take care of Ida! HA, NOT NOT NOT! But her doctors say that she cannot interact with me, because I am the target of her "fixation". Well, yeah! Lucky me.

Dad tells me, well even if she is here I have you taken care of. I don't know who he is kidding, But it is not me. I will never be taken care of if we are in the same house. I wonder if I would be allowed to use one of the guns that Brahm and I use when we go target shooting. Brahm taught me to shoot a long time ago. I am not too bad a shot. I can use a 22 all the way to a 30-06 but I don't think that a gun is an option. I know this is a really bad joke but right now all I know to do is make jokes. Ha Ha! The reality scares me too much.

June 1

I leave tomorrow for New York. I am scared, anxious, hopeful and completely excited. What an adventure! To really get to know my birth mother and find out more about my birth father. I have so many questions about everything.

I have always wanted to see New York. Mrs. Mason asked me to dinner yesterday, and I went and when I went inside, and there was Dad, Joe, Brownie, Pug, Mac, Cami, Mrs. Delgado and Sarah, Mr. Bertram and Doc. It was wonderful, lovely dinner. It really made me realize what and who I have here. Lots for me to think about.

Mrs. Mason was saying that she has always wanted to go to NYC and see the Algonquin Hotel. Mr. Bertram and Mrs. Mason had made a list for me. This is where Dorothy Parker, Robert Benchley, Heywood Brown, Marc Connelly, Gane Grant, Ruth Hale, George S, Kaufman, Neysa McMein, Harold Ross, Robert E. Sherwood, Alexander Woollcott, Edna Ferber and Noel Coward all gathered almost daily. Mrs. Mason and Mr. Bertram said that so much changed , was collaborated on, or was created because the people all came together for over ten years.

So they gave me the challenge of finding out who these people were and what contribution they made. I recognize several of the names because Dad talks about them. Dorothy is one of Dad's favorite writers. He says she has one of the sharpest wits in the business. So this is one of the things I plan to do.

Every person gave me a charm for my bracelet and each person said that I was to go, take care of what I needed to and to come back ready to go on to the rest of High School and the U of A in the duel program. I think I really needed this dinner and these people.

Sometimes the right thing happens and the right time.

Tomorrow is all new, strange and a part of my growing toward knowing who I am. I guess I did not realize that I needed that either until the plans were made and it was a done deal.

Well, Dear Diary, I am off to see the Wizard. I just hope somebody is behind the curtain who does have all the answers.

Toto (Fala) is already at the Walkers. I think James was glad to have him too. I wonder if Fala remembers that Mrs. Walker's Molly is his mother. Maybe not. But they play and curl up together to sleep.

I have said goodbye to Cami and James and the rest of the Gang. They all have different opinions about my going.

Dear Diary, did I tell you this is my first plane ride? Not much of a surprise! I don't know of any other person I go to school with that has flown on a plane. I told Dad that I would go by bus or train and he said that, surprisingly, that the tickets were about the same price and it would be better for me because it would be safer for me. I get what he means. I am a kid traveling and I am not very knowledgeable about the real world. So I am glad I am flying too. It should be quite an adventure.

Dad picked TWA because he says they have a good safety record. I am really not afraid of the flying part. I am just afraid of crowds.

OK Diary, I said it. I am afraid of big crowds. I don't really like to be where there are too many people in an area and they get very close to you. I also do not like elevators.

One time when I was six, we were at the hospital in Tucson, and it was very late and Dad was visiting Ida. I wandered down the hallway and I decided for what ever stupid reason, I would take my self for an elevator ride. Of course I pushed the wrong buttons and I got the elevator stuck between floors. A maintenance man had to come down from the trap door in the top to get me out. So, you can get the picture. Scared kid stuck between floors and a stranger comes scooting down from the top. I started screaming and Dad said they heard me all over several floors. So if I can avoid it, I don't do elevators.   But I love escalators.   At least you can't get stuck on them.

Too bad Fala, El Con, and Lizzie could not go with me. I wonder how much their tickets would be?   HA!   I just had the funniest image of El Con on a plane. Have to be a pretty big seat!

I really do not know how well I am going to do without Dad, all of my angel crew and my animal angels.

I have never gone more than a few days without my horses so I guess I need to get used to it.   I am already thinking about how I am going to get the horses over to Tucson when I am going to the U of A and how I will get time for them.   But that is a worry for another day. Now I just need to worry about getting to the airport on time and getting to NYC and spending the summer getting to know an entirely new family. Or is it my old family?

June 1

I have been up all night thinking about the changes in my life. I don't usually write poetry, but some lines kept running through my head.   I remembered what Mr. Bertram said about free verse. Well, I think this is as free as it gets.

I am the throw-away-girl.

I wonder why?

I hear a baby crying, crying.

I see a silent toddler sitting alone

I want someone to want the child

I am the throw-away-girl.

I pretend that I have a mother who loves me

I feel a silent longing

I reach for elusive, loving arms

I worry that the fault is mine

I cry myself to sleep

I am the throw-away-girl

I understand the love of others

161

I say that they are enough

I dream that I will understand

I want this to be enough

I go to find the answers

I am the throw-away-girl

Thinking, thinking, thinking.   I am so hoping that I am doing the right thing by going to see Sharon. I hope that I am going to get answers that make things better and not worse.

Got up at 5 A.M. with almost no sleep. My first thought was that Tuesday seems like an odd day to start on this strange journey. And I wonder if I am tilting at windmills? Don Quixote would be proud of me! I am on a quest for truth.   Now if I just had a Sancho to try to keep me grounded.

High Flight

by John Gillespie Magee, Jr.

Oh, I have slipped the surly bonds of earth

And danced the skies on laughter-silvered wings;

Sunward I've climbed, and joined the tumbling mirth

Of sun-split clouds – and done a hundred things

You have not dreamed of- wheeled and soared and

   swung

High in the sunlit silence. Hov'ring there,

I've chased the shouting wind along, and flung

My eager craft through footless halls of air

Up, up the long, delirious, burning blue

I've topped the windswept heights with easy grace

Where never lark, or even eagle flew.

And, while with silent, lifting mind I've trod

The high untrespassed sanctity of space

Put out my hand, and touched the face of God.

June 1, 1954

My First Plane Ride

My bags were packed, my ticket was bought, Fala is at Jim's, Joe will care for my precious equine friends, and I think I was ready for whatever this trip would bring.

Dad loaded the car and we stopped to get Cami and James who were going to the airport in Tucson with us, I was so happy that they wanted to see me off.

We all chatted in the car about unimportant things and we finally arrived at the airport where everybody came inside. James and Cami had never been inside a terminal before.

James was very excited about the planes and was running from window to window to see the behemoths of the air. Cami kept saying, "But you are planning to come back aren't you?" And Dad kept saying that I was and even seemed to be getting irritated that she kept asking.

The time came for boarding, and after many hugs and more assurances, I boarded. I found my seat and suddenly I could hear all of the engine sounds, then the stewardess told everybody about the plane and emergency procedures. The plane is a DC-6. I did not know that the stewardesses are actually nurses, but that is what she said.

She said that she is there to help people if they get sick or to help make people more comfortable. I think she was also there to help people who were afraid of flying. There were two stewardesses, the other one came by my seat and asked if I was OK. I guess she was checking because I am so young, flying by myself. I said I was fine and I was, I was really enjoying myself about everything. James had given me a bunch of Big Hunks and I had some other stuff but I could not eat anything. I was so excited my body was humming. I am glad nobody took a picture because I think I would have looked like Sylvester the Cat just after the dog has taken a chomp.

Also amazing was that the flight only took a few short hours. I was so anxious about what was coming, time just seemed to fly by. A man was sitting next to me but I was very grateful when he did not talk very much. The only scary part of the trip was when the plane landed. It landed with a very big thump and seemed to skip several times until it began to travel on the runway by its wheels. It really traveled fast and I thought it was going to run right into the building for the La Guardia Air Port. It finally did stop, and we all went down the stairs from the plane and then we walked into the building.

The first thing I noticed was how hot and muggy it was. I felt like I was breathing water. Just walking the few hundred feet into the building, my clothes were all sticky. This was different for me because I am so used to dry weather.

As soon as I went inside, I saw Sharon, her husband Ryan and Morgana standing in the waiting area. Sharon came up to me and gave me a big hug, Morgana shyly let me hug her. Ryan shook my hand. Then we got my luggage from the place where they put it off the plane and we all walked out to the parking lot. They have a 1950 Chevy Deluxe 4-door Sedan that is grey with a dark blue top and grey cloth seats inside.

Ryan is a really good driver but it was still scary coming out of the airport and all the way the around the city on really busy highways and out to where they live. We went most of the way that was around the city by the Hudson River, and across the river I could see the tall buildings. That was "The City". Ryan said that real New Yorkers call it that and not "New York City". New Yorkers say, going to The City.

We crossed the George Washington Bridge and we crossed into New Jersey. First you could see big buildings across the Hudson River. Ryan said those building were in Westchester County.

Now here is the really crazy part. We left New York, passed through New Jersey and then we went back into New York to go to where they live in Nyack. He said he would show me on a map why that is. It is because you have to travel through a little triangle of New Jersey.

Sharon said that we would be going into The City next week. I am really looking forward to that because I have dreamed about New York City for as long as I can remember.

The drive to their house took almost two hours and that was really a surprise, I have never taken so long to go that distance. Less than fifty Miles! The traffic was really different for me. The roads have many main lanes and the cars drive very close to each other. But we did finally get to their house.

The house is nice. The rooms are small compared to the houses in Arizona, Sharon said it is called a Ranch House. This is funny to me because it has nothing to do with a ranch. But it has three bedrooms, a living room that has an area for a dining room table, a kitchen that has the washer and dryer in it, two bathrooms but one is just a toilet and sink, a basement and a garage.

The bedroom I am in is really small. I think it is 10 by 10. It has a twin bed, a dresser and a bedside table. I don't think anything else could fit, but it is very pleasant. It has wall paper with pink flowers growing on a trellis. I have never been in a house with wall paper and   all three of the bedrooms have wall paper.   I like pictures and paintings on walls. The wall paper is just too much design for me. The living room has something called paneling. But you can tell it is not real wood. Sharon really likes it. The house is a modern style and the furniture is all of the new simple, square style. The living room has a set that takes up the whole room.

You have to kind of move in between things to get around. They have a television, a Curtis-Mathis, that has a big container frame with a tiny little screen. But the picture is a lot better than our picture in Arizona.   They get programs all day and evening and that is very different.

Morgana watches several programs that I have never seen before. Morgana is growing into a very pretty, shy little girl. Right now, my biggest regret is that I have not lived with her and had her as part of my life as a sister.   That is the real tragedy of this situation, as far as I can see. I wonder if Sharon every thinks about that and wishes that she had been able to raise me too and that we would have all been a family. But I guess I am jumping the gun on that too, because I am still getting answers for everything.

Sharon works at Macy's in downtown New York City. She says it is a great job. We went out to dinner for the first evening to a place that Sharon called an Italian-deli-style. It had mostly sandwiches and many foods I have never eaten or even heard of. But it was really good. I had an "egg cream". It is a drink! And it was really good.   I love new things!   Another new thing was a pastrami sandwich that I was not that crazy about. Ryan said that while I was here he was going to show me all kinds of different foods and things.   I also had a piece of cheese cake and it was so wonderful that I have a new favorite dessert.

July 29

I am going to fly home tomorrow.   It has been a bitter sweet experience. Some good, some not so good. Well, that really fits my life doesn't it.   But if I am being very honest and just possibly I am growing up a bit, that must be true of all life and what would make the difference is to what degree is the ration of good to bad. So with my newfound glimmer of maturity, I have to acknowledge that my life has much more positive than negative.

I couldn't wait to try all of the new foods and there were many new things I had never tasted or heard of and many new places that we went to.   We went to Coney Island and so many other places that I had heard about before. Some of the places were better than I imagined and some were no better than some of the same things in Arizona.

Over the next two months, we went to many interesting places, and I had many new experiences. I will talk about these later in my little vignettes.

Several times while I was there, Ryan took Morgana over to a friend's house and left Sharon and I to talk. I could tell that it was hard for her to talk about many of the parts of her childhood. She even told me one time that there were many of the things that she talked about that she had not thought about for years and there were many things that she had taken a fresh look at from her perspective as an adult.

One of the things that surprised me was that she had had such a difficult childhood. Horrible. She lost her father when she was eight, her mother died when she was ten and her grandmother when she was fourteen. But she had not lived with her grandmother since her mother had died so she had really lost her then too. I had not imagined that Sharon would have had a worse life than I have had.

But to go along with what I said earlier, hers was really bad and mine has just had some bad episodes.

I really want to tell Sharon's story exactly as she told me. At the end of each evening, I would go to my room and write what she had said. I had even asked her if I could jot notes as she told me things so I would not forget and Sharon thought that was a good idea. I think it will take a while because I want to get it right. I will include it, Dear Diary as soon as I get it written. I also want to write more about the experiences that I had in New York .

Aug. 3

Dear Diary, I flew home Saturday, July 30th. I have many feelings about my two months in New York. I loved the area. I got to go into the City several times. I even got to see three different matinees on Broadway. Fanny with Florence Henderson was really good. Tea House of the August Moon was great, but the best was The Pajama Game with Janice Paige. Can't wait to get the records when I go to Tucson. Dad got me one of the new portable record players while I was gone. I hope they have the albums at the music store so I can sing and dance to them.

We went to Coney Island and did all the rides and ate all of the crazy foods. We had New York pizza and all of the other foods that are very special in New York. I will say that there was no good Mexican food anywhere in New York that I went to.

We went window shopping at Macy's and Bergdorf's, Lord and Taylor, and many other big department stores. It was fun to look at the clothes, but most of the things would never be worn in Arizona.

Ryan was really wonderful about taking me places. He took Morgana and me to the zoo and to Central Park. What I liked the very best was that Sharon and I spent several days with just the two of us going to the museums in NYC and out to lunch. There were so many places that I really loved. The department store, Altman's had a restaurant on the top floor. It as called the Charleston Gardens. It is a lovely place and I liked it because you would sit at tables with other people and have little talks with them, and I loved to listen to the accents.

I loved the Metropolitan Museum, the Metropolitan Museum of Modern art, The Guggenheim, The Museum of Natural History, The Frick and the Whitney. Most of the museums actually have cafés or restaurants in them.

I could have just spent days and days in each museum. One of the places that was really unusual but fabulous was the Cloisters. It is actually part of the Metropolitan Museum Group. It is in Fort Tryon New York, which is really at the edge of the city but very high up in a hilly area. It has artifacts from the fifteenth century with stained glass from churches from all over Europe and other really fascinating things. I did not know how short people were from that time period. Most of the suits of armor were shorter than I am. And the locations seems like it should be in Europe.

One of the wonderful facts to learn about Sharon was that she loves museums, history and other things that I am interested in too.

Those were the special days, as well as when she talked about her mother and other family members. Sharon talked about the time that she spent as a child in New York when her mother died.

These talks were very bitter sweet. With each passing day, I became more aware that Sharon had her life now and I had my life now. And that that we could get to know each other but there was just something missing and we would not ever be able to be a "real mother and daughter". I think both of us have developed a protective shell that keeps both of us from getting too close. And I don't think either of us could ever crack that shell. For the first time I realize that being "family" has as much to do with being there on a day by day basis as it does with being blood.

I just read a book where a person he referred to his history as an accident of birth. Now I get that too. People get born because of all sorts of reasons. Actually I don't think it really matters as much as how a person lives the life they get.

Oddly, when I told Sharon that I really had to get back to Arizona, I think that she was as relieved as I was. We will continue to have a relationship. I hope that I will be able to get to know

Morgana as she gets older and that we will be able to become real sisters.

Sharon is my real mother. But she really belongs to her life with her "real" family. And that is Morgana and Ryan. I really feel like an intruder, its nobody's fault, it is just the way it is.

For now I am very glad to be back in Arizona. But I came home to find that things are not really resolved about Ida. Dad has been trying to see if the shock treatments that she has been having are working. He hopes that they are working enough for her to be able to visit. I guess I will have to cross that bridge when it is necessary.

So the only fly in my ointment right now is the possibility of "The Return of Ida". Stay tuned, the ride may go from a little bumpy to a roller coaster on a down hill run.

The day after I got home, I dashed out to Brownies and to my very much missed horses. El Con and Lizzie both were as overjoyed as I was.

Brownie told me that Mary Jane had called him and left a message for me. I was to call her as soon as I got back.

August 25

I called Mary Jane and we are starting to practice together at least one day a week. I trailer there every other week and the other weeks she comes here so that works out great. She is really teaching me so very many things. And the more that I get to know her the better that I like her. She is a very genuine person, she does not put on about anything, she only says what she means. What a great friend that is because you can believe in anything she says. She does not talk mean about anyone else, she just does not talk about people she does not like or respect. If somebody does or says something mean she just ignores it. I asked her about that and she said that she does not want to spend any effort on people who are not kind or do mean or spiteful things. That is really the only way to be. I am trying to get more like that. I need to learn not to waste time on people who are not good for me. She is very sympathetic about Ida, but she also feels sorry for her. I am beginning trying to be able to see the value in what she says especially about Ida.

Aug 27

I have been so busy barreling with MJ and working at Brownies. Joe took a week off and I did many of his chores. I worked with Jake, who is Joe's best wrangler. I have been doing all of the mucking and done fence daily. Wow! I am brown as a berry. I try to cover up but I have really been out in the sun a lot. I am going to wear my riding gloves and keep a scarf on for the rest of the summer.   I might even use one of Dad's Stetsons because his brims are wider than mine. Won't he be overjoyed!   He is already complaining because I wear his boots to ride in. Guess what? It saves mine! Ha! But he lets me and I know he really thinks I'm a hoot!

Along with everything else, I have gone out to Silver Lake, our swimming hole, with Cami and James and the rest of the gang. The best part have been the dances.   I love the dances under the stars at the pavilion.

Fala was very glad to see me too, and he has been glued to my side.   I am spending as much time as possible with all of my creatures before school starts and that day is rushing up soon.

Speaking of school, Dad and I went up to school because Principal Lantry called and asked us to meet with him. He and Dad agreed to a special program where I will be taking all Senior classes except for Math. I will just do the regular Junior math.

Then I will be going to the U of A   as a real Freshman the following year. Dad asked me if I wanted to do it. I could see both sides, the good and the bad but I really see more good. The good is that I will be out of the house in one year in case Dad is able to bring Ida home.   I am also ready to go to classes that are a lot more challenging that what I am in now

The bad part is that I will not be in any classes with the kids I have gone to school with especially Cami and James. In some ways, that may be good too.

I am also going to go to the U of A on Fridays for a special "dual" class in American Literature and two other classes, history and art appreciation.   It means they are trying something out to see if it works. So I guess I am a guinea pig!

Dad said he and I are going to Tucson to get me a car for me that is better than the Jeep. He wants me to drive something more dependable.   I want to drive something more snazzy! So that should be a very interesting shopping trip!   Dad said he spoke to Ray and he thought I could get my license early because of "special need".   Probably be a good idea if I will be driving to Tucson.   I know several of the boys who work on family ranches have gotten early licenses.

Aug 28

Cami and I went to Tucson for school clothes. She had already gotten most of hers but I just have not had time. I don't need very much anyway.   I have gained about five pounds since last year so most of what I have still fits. I needed new Levis. And I got Dad to let me get new boots made. Two pair!   Black and some really beautiful dark red ones. I also needed a new Stetson. I got a great black hat and had the hat maker put silver and turquoise tack on it. Mary Jane is going to tell me that I am over the top!

I got several new blouses, three new circle skirts and two new church outfits. One is really wonderful. It is white embroidered pique dress with a fitted jacket. And the other is a wonderful black cotton with a great neckline that has a dropped short sleeve. Just love both. Then I got five new western shirts for riding, three chambrays and two cottons.

Mary Jane and I are doing the Tucson Rodeo tomorrow. I hope I do not embarrass her or myself! I have been working very hard and I think I am doing better. El Con is as ready as ever so we will see.

Aug 29

The best rodeo ever! I did a 17.0 Of course Mary Jane was so much better. She did a second with a 15.5. But we had such a great day. She introduced me to several of the other girls that do the Tucson. They are all going to college this year. Three of them go to the U of A, two are going to ASU and one is going up to Flagstaff to NAU. I like the way Jenna talks about the school but I don't think I would like the weather. She says it snows much of the winter. I guess I am just a hot house flower! Ha! They are a great group.

One of the girls, Heather Anne, said that she wants to be a judge someday too! We were talking about going to school and all of them said that they can't imagine getting married before they have a chance to do something with their lives. This is really very different from most of the girls that I go to school with now. Only Cami wants to go to school and then be a nurse. The rest think marriage is the prize. Yeah, the booby prize if that is all a person does. Then I remember what Dad says and I have to remember that just because I want to do something, it does not make somebody else's choice wrong. Everybody has to choose what is right for them.

I know if I have a major fault it is that I think I am always right. Everybody says the same thing to me so I guess I had better start believing it and try to accept other peoples opinions and choices. I try. Honestly, I do try. I guess I should tie a string around my nose to remind me not to be so judgmental. Hey, that is good! I want to be a judge, so maybe I have to be judgmental! HA!

I am really excited for the new school year. It is going to be different for me in so many ways.

170

I know that I am going to be really busy. I don't want everything to change too much. I hope that James and I will still be the same. I do not want to lose him but I do not want to get any more serious than we are.

I also have so many concerns about what is going to happen with Ida.

One of my other big worries is that I have to find enough time to take care of what I need to do out at Brownies. Joe and Dad both say not to worry about it and that things will work out.

But I know some things about myself now. There are things that I need. I need to write. I need to be with Dad, my Angel Crew, Cami James and I need to be with El Con. I really need that time alone, just thinking and putting all of the pieces together.

So, as I sit, alone in my room, a few days before the new school year, I wonder, wonder wonder. Where is the wizard and his crystal ball when I need him?

OK, life, bring it on!

Sept 6

It is Monday and the first day of school. It is really weird to be in all senior classes, except math, remember? I am the math dummy! Anyway, I am taking Eng. IV, History IV, Sci 4, Spanish III, Art, and I am still doing Library instead of a study hall.

I don't think that having two Eng and two historys will not be a problem because I can handle the reading. The only possible problem with be the papers and the research. Since the only library I can use is in Tucson at the U, that will involve extra hours. It just occurred to me that this could be a good thing in case Ida comes "home". It will keep me away longer. See, everything has a silver lining if you look for it.

I am going to be Mrs. Mason's teacher's aide this year. Works great. Looking forward to the Fridays at the U of A. I am in Band and Chorus but I am not doing cheer or twirling this year. I really do have enough to do as it is. I am not even going to do Drama this year and I really do love drama. Too much to do. Dad says I do more than any three people he knows. He even complains that I do not have time to spend evenings with him. So I am going to try to do at least one evening a week that I just do what he wants to do. I suggested that after church on Sunday, we could go over to his club and do lunch and then he could play golf while I did some research at the library. I am so glad they have Sunday hours.

171

Sept 30

I have been doing much more reading than writing for the month. I have started the Friday classes at the U. Got the reading list. The assignments just take the top of my head off. They are so much fun to do. Doesn't even seem like work.

The professor, for English Lit is Mr. Fanning, who is incredible. He has so much energy and passion for what he does. And the class is huge. He does half the time as a lecture and the second half he puts the class into study analysis and the groups have to develop an idea to present to the class for the next class session. There are twelve groups and the presentations are five minutes long.

That does not seem like very long but when it is in a presentation it is amazing how long it can be. The first book that we were assigned was The Sound and The Fury. We had a week to read it and get prepared to work with our group. Mr. Fanning compared Faulkner to Poe, Melville and Hawthorne. He says it was pure genius that Faulkner uses the device of telling a story through the eyes and perspective of four different people especially the retarded boy. I have already read it once and I am going to read it again. I get so involved with the story in a good book that I have to go back the second time to be able to see how the story is told. At first I thought the main character was Caddy Compson but as I got more into it I began to see that it depends on who is telling the story.

The next few books on the list are The Red Badge of Courage, A Farewell to Arms, and The Catcher in the Rye.

Oct15

Mary Jane's aunt called me to tell me that Mary Jane's father had a heart attack and died Wednesday. I am so sorry for her. She is such a good person. I wish I could understand why such bad things happen to good people. I stopped over at her house after class today. I am going to go to the funeral tomorrow. Dad is going to go with me.

I have really been thinking about how lucky I am. This makes my problems seem so puny. Her dad was a wonderful person. I always envied her because she seemed to have such a fairy tale life with her loving mom and her perfect father. So life just has to prove that nobody is immune to having serious catastrophes that slam you to the ground. I know that Mary Jane will be changed forever. I don't even know what to say. When I got to her house we all just hugged and hugged, her mom too. Her mother has always been a ranch wife. I have also been envious when I have been there just seeing how her mom and dad were together. This is when I really question the workings of the world. Why would this happen to such a wonderful family? What kind of life will Mrs. Edwards have now? I want to fix things, to make them better but there is no fixing this.

Dad says that this is all part of life. There is great happiness, great sorrow and everything else in between. I am really having a hard time with this. I can't even fathom what it must be like for Mary Jane.

We did <u>The Catcher in the Rye</u> in class today. I had read it of course, but I was having such a hard time concentrating. I finally told the group why and they did most of the work without me. I have been very fortunate to get into a group that does not treat me like a cowgirl hayseed. Sometimes some of the students treat the kids from the smaller schools and the kids from small towns as if they are hayseeds, hicks. They use the term cowboy in a very negative way. I have never thought that anybody would think that cowboys or ranchers would be thought of as being something to make fun of or put down. I am beginning to realize that humans have a tendency to put down what is different to them.

Some of the students act like there is something very different or backward just because the kids are from a rural area, especially the ones from Wilcox and Fry. It is really not fair. One of the students in our group said that it was how life is. That people make judgments that are general instead of specific. I am just beginning to see how that is true.

Because of what has just happened to Mary Jane and her mother, I really am questioning why people create problems. There seem to be enough of the bad stuff in the world with out humans being mean to each other for no real reason.

Oct 22

I just finished <u>The Grapes of Wrath</u>. What an eye opener that is. This is hardship not just for one family but for a whole group of people. The more I read the more I realize that life is a real struggle for most of mankind. I had seen people come through Cochise with trucks and cars that were completely full inside and outside with a families belongings and had heard people make jokes about them. After reading this book and learning about what caused the problems and what misery and heartache these people endured, I am ashamed of all of the people who made fun of these unfortunate souls who were trying to survive such deprivation and abject poverty.

I love to read, but the larger issue about reading is that it helps us understand about another culture, another time, another experience. I have never been hungry, or been homeless, or had major hardships. In Steinbeck's book, the reader is able to for a

173

brief moment, experience what it is to be hungry, cold, homeless, and endure death of loved one and be hopeless to make anything better. How horrible it would be to watch a child slowly starve to death.

This book makes me determined to grow up to try to help the world be a better place. I was thinking about all of my angels and how they do such good for others. All of the teachers in my life starting with a kindergarten teacher who gave me a book I still have. It is about a Skye Terrier. Sister Mary Margaret who taught me dignity. Mrs. Mason who turned me onto literature and drama. Pug, who taught me so much and has had my back for years. The list is quite long. I love my merry band of angels.   Yeah, I am back on my soapbox.

Dad and I talked about <u>The Grapes of Wrath</u> last night and he said that part of the problem with society today is that some church members and some politicians say they want to help fellowman but the reality is that many of the "haves" take advantage of the poor and do nothing to help them. It is as if certain people in society are expendable and others are allowed to take advantage and then move on to take advantage of the next group.

Oct 29

I read <u>A Farewell to Arms</u>.   I think my concentration is a little off now so I am going to have to reread it.   I liked parts of it and was totally confused by other parts of it. Maybe I just do not know enough about the world and about war to get all of it.   But I really do not like or care about the characters.   I keep thinking that they cause all of their own problems and do not do what they could do to make things better.   So maybe I will reread the book when I am older and see if I feel any differently about Henry and Catherine. Maybe.

Oct 30

The Red Badge of Courage is a knockout book.   Crane's "blue-clothed men and grey bewhiskered hordes" cause the reader to see and feel what it might be like to be a young soldier going into battle. A scared youth who begins to wonder how he got to this place and wonder about his bravery and about the idea of war.   What thoughts would we have under the same circumstances.   In the history of mankind, how many young lives have been wasted and lost to the battlefield. What accomplishments might have theses lost souls have achieved. That is what a great book does.   It makes me think about a subject in a whole new way.   It makes me want to write.   I want to be able to create a character who sings to the reader.

Oct 31

Poor Mary Jane. When it rains, it pours. Her horse, Jackson, took a bad fall during a practice and he had such a bad break, he had to be put down. I know she was using practice to help her with her grief about her dad and now this. I just wish there was more that I could do to help her. I am going to go over to her place tomorrow. But I will not take El Con. I am just going to go over to spend time with her. She goes to the U but I never see her there and I am only there on Fridays. It is such a large school, sometimes it really overwhelms me with how many students are there. A couple of times, I have tried to plan a lunch with her at the Student Union, but our schedules are so busy we have not been able to get together during school.

Evan, Cami, James and I had our costumes for Halloween and we went to the school dance but James and I left early and went back to my house and watched TV with Dad. I guess I was just not in a party mood. We talked about how you can never predict how your life is going to go. Dad said that he thought that each person had to just live life by taking what ever happens and making the best of it. James said that his grandfather says the same thing. I am trying but I am still having a hard time trying not to be angry about the bad things that happen.

Nov 6

Boy, Mary Jane is one tough cookie, she handles things so much better than I do. I just do not know how she does it, she never seems to get angry.

I have been doing a lot of thinking about many things. I see where I have too much to do and have needed help especially with my horses. So I told Mary Jane, if she wanted Lizzie, I would sell Lizzie to her. She has ridden her and she does really well with her. It is not fair for me to keep Lizzie.

It is costing Dad money. I do not ride her enough and there are days that I cannot do what is needed and that gives Joe too much extra work. This is a win-win for everybody. By selling her, I can pay for El Con's keep for more than a year. Mary Jane gets a good horse, Joe has less work and Dad does not have to pay for her keep.

Mary Jane is very happy and is going to trailer her back to her place on Sunday. I know she really loves Lizzie and I love how she takes care of her horses. She has two other horses, but neither of them can be used for barrel racing. I think Mary Jane has had enough heartache. I really feel so much for both Mary Jane and her mother.

Her mother has only been a ranch wife, I don't know if she ever went to college, and now with Mary Jane in school at Tucson she is by herself. Mary Jane offered to move home, but her mother said no. Joe suggested that she might want to hire Jake and I think that is going to happen. Mary Jane's dad did a lot of his own ranch work and there is just too much to keep up with.

Sometimes I just think life changes way too rapidly. I have been thinking about how many things have changed in just one year.

Nov 12

James and I have been spending more time together. He is really a good person. He is not so much into school but he is much more committed to sports than I am. I guess if I had his dedication to barrel racing like he does for football, I would be a lot better at it. Like Dad says, I try to do too many things. I just hope that he gets a collage scholarship so that he can go on to school.

I was afraid that he might have a problem with the fact that I have essentially skipped my junior year. But he has been great about it. He even hopes that he can get a football scholarship to the U so that some of our college years will overlap. He does worry about his grandparents. He thinks that his grandfather works way too hard for his age and James worries about what his grandfather will do once he in not there to help him.

Dec 1

I have been working on my solos for the new Christmas programs. This year the school program is going to be "An Old Fashioned Christmas" so we are doing songs from the years. I am doing a sort of Jane Froman review. We are just starting to choose the music for the church program. I can't believe that the semester is almost over. This year is really going way to fast.

Dec 13

Well, the other shoe has dropped. Dad said that the doctors think that Ida can come home for the holidays as a trial. They think that she will be OK if she takes the medicine and she can go back in to the hospital if needed. I know that Dad is very worried about money and that this will take some of the burden off of him. But there will still be the expense of having to have full time help. One of the main conditions is that she cannot be alone with me. I wish they would say that she cannot be even in the house with me.

Dad just wants so much to believe that some magic fairy is going to drop out of the sky and make Ida be this perfect mother type person. Darn it to all heck and back again. Horse feathers. Horse poop! I am so very, very tired of this back and forth crap. Yeah, I said crap. Actually I would like to use some of Dad's own

176

words.   He keeps telling me every time that it will never happen again. Well, how is he going to guarantee that if she comes back yet again.

I don't hate her. I hate what she does. I hate being afraid of her. I had that Dad becomes a basket case trying to walk this tightrope between the two of us.

I have been trying so hard to forgive her and understand her illness, but that is very difficult to do when I have to wonder when she will go off again and do something to me or to something connected with me.

I am even concerned about Fala. I am going to ask Mrs. Walker if she can take him back down to their ranch because I would have to worry about him while I was at school. Poor little guy, he does not know where he lives anymore.

Ida the Pretending will come home Sunday if all goes the way Dad thinks. He keeps trying to assure me that the treatments and the medicine has made a huge change. I just don't believe that just medicine can make that big a difference.

I am so concerned that it is affecting my reading, I am having a hard time concentrating. I don't even feel like doing the Christmas programs.   I am so glad that I have James, he has been a rock for me.   He has even gone riding with me to try to get me to think about something besides Ida coming home.   Great Christmas present, NOT! Ida all wrapped up in pretty, holiday paper.

Mary Jane did a really considerate thing. She and I were talking before we started our barrel practice and she said that she and her mother had talked about it and she said her mother suggested that if I wanted to I could move in with her mother for the rest of this school year. What a thoughtful thing to offer.   I am really not going to say no just in case that what I need to do. Pug has made the same offer. I think every one on my angel list thinks that Ida coming home is a bad idea. Guess we will see how it plays out.

Dec 20

She's back....let the games begin!

Dec 21

I am going to take Mary Jane's advice and try to make the best of things. But it is really hard for me to stay in the house. Dad let me put another lock on my bedroom door and I pull the dresser in front of the door when I go into my room. So that is two locks and the dresser. I still do not think that Dad has any idea how afraid of her I am.   I will always make sure that there is another person there if I am at home.

One of the reasons that I want to be a lawyer is because I want to change laws so that children are more protected. I am still trying to understand why there are different laws when a person is judged to be insane than if they commit a crime and they are supposed to be sane.

I wonder what she would have to do before they would lock her up for good? So far, she just acts like I am not there. And I am trying to do the same. Dad wants us to all eat dinner together. I have tried but she seems to get very agitated so Dad is not pressing so hard.

I am out of the house as much as possible. I have not even slept at home for over a week.

Mary Jane has invited me to spend the Christmas Holiday with her and her mother. I asked Dad and told him that is what I really wanted. I think he thought it is a good idea too. This will give him some time with Ida and I can get away from the pressure. At least I can keep my room locked.

Mary Jane even suggested that I bring El Con and Fala. Another win-win for everybody. Brownie said I can use the trailer and even keep it at MJ's while I am there.

I am still doing the Christmas programs. Staying at MJ's will really help me concentrate for all of my finals especially the ones for the U. I still need to finish my papers for the classes.

I am doing a paper on Faulkner and his use of the title from Shakespeare's speech from Macbeth when he finds out that Lady Macbeth has committed suicide. "...full of sound and fury, signifying nothing." I love seeing how Faulkner uses a fictional county for most of his stories. Yoknapatawpha County. His great use of the county and a family as the metaphoric symbol of the dissolution of the south as it changes into something different. The civil war that destroyed a way of life, full of sound and fury, signifying nothing.

For history, I am doing a paper on the Holocaust. The more research I do, the more I am horrified by what some humans can do to others for the stupidest of reasons. How can anybody believe that they have the right to do even the least little tiny bits of these things? The history teacher, Professor Shay said that Americans cannot be too smug about it because we have done the same to Negroes and Indians. Boy Howdy, did that start me thinking. I raised my hand and said that some of the same things have been done to Mexicans and he said, right, that was very true. Then there was this really lively, highly debated and sometimes heated discussion. At the end of class, Prof. Shay said that he was very happy with the students and that it was what school and learning was all about.

I see so many themes about life with literature, as well as in Shakespeare's plays and they all relate to life at least as I see it. I can take the themes and apply them to so many situations in the town that I live in. So I am sure that would be true anywhere.

Shakespeare said that there is nothing new under the sun. The more that I read, the more I see that this is true.

Dec 26

It has turned out to be a good Christmas. Mary Jane has been seeing a guy from one of her classes. He is really a keeper. His name is Travis Huntington from a ranch over by Marana. But he does not want to be "only" a rancher. He is in the Law Program at the U. So we have been able to double with them. We went to the Arizona Inn for Christmas Eve dinner. We had Mary Jane's mother and her aunt go with us too. What a lovely evening.

James gave me a promise ring. We have sort of agreed that it is a promise for a promise ring. We both know we have many years ahead. But right now I can't imagine my life without James in it. I know so many of the couples our age are getting very serious. And James is so low key and he does not pressure me for anything. We are two good buddies having a great time and enjoying each other's company without any extra obligations. I sure do not want a husband or a family for a long time.

I had the bootmaker make a special pair of boots for Dad. He wears his regular boots to church, so the boot maker made them look just a little more dressy. They are a glossy black leather with pearl grey stitching. They look great. I gave Ida a silk blouse. And she surprised me by seeming to like it. She even thanked me.

Dad gave me a car. Thank goodness, Sheriff Ray says I can get my license very soon, next week, in fact. Dad brought it out to Mary Jane's Christmas afternoon. It is rather unspoken between us, but I will not tell Ida that is where the car came from. Don't know what I will say if she asks but I just know that Dad does not want to deal with that problem with her now.

The car is a 55 Thunderbird. It is white with a black top. It is a new type of Ford car. It looks like a sports car but it is really not. It has a smaller engine than a sports car. Dad has a friend from his golf club who has a Ford dealership in Tucson and he had told him about his new model Ford. He was able to get a special price for the car. It sells for over $2,700. but he got it for Dad for $2200. This car is the most gorgeous thing I have ever seen. It just has a front seat, so does not work if there are over two people. But it is so great, it moves like the wind.

January 29

I told Dad that I know he is trying to make up for Ida but he said that was not true and he had been working on getting the car before he knew she was getting out of the hospital. He had ordered the car over four months ago right after I started at the U.

As I said the car is white with a black convertible top. The car has a black and white leather seat and it has a custom leather steering wheel. And my initials are on the glove box. The trunk is ity-bity. Fala loves to ride in the car. I think he thinks it is just his size! It is funny to see his ears flapping in the wind.

It is even too small to carry any of my tack or any other equipment. But I love it. I only use it for school and what I have been doing is parking it behind Pug's house. Mac has been wonderful and lets me park in his spot in the carport. I really do not want to take a chance on anything happening to it. James said I look like Elizabeth Taylor when I drive it. Why, I don't know. I guess he thinks it is a "movie star car". He adores the car and loves to drive it when we go to the drive in or to Tucson. And I can't drive to Tucson until I get my license next week. Thank goodness, nobody bothers me in Cochise.

The new semester is starting off very well. This semester is British Lit. We have our new reading list. Mr. Prichard does class differently. He has assigned our novels. Some are one a week and some are two. The "two" are by the same author. He has assigned each person an author and we have to do a full presentation on our author. I have James Joyce and I am thrilled. I am doing The Portrait of the Author as a Young Man and Finnegan's Wake. James Joyce had a fascinating life. I talked to Mrs. Mason and we thought it would be a good idea to use as my thesis, how Joyce's religious life shaped his views and made him the kind of writer that he was.

Feb 14

This was supposed to be a great day. James and I were going to go to a Valentine's dance at school. Things have been getting back to normal and I was really looking forward to this party. We had invited Mary Jane and Travis and we were going with Cami and Evan. Then we were going to go out to James for a Midnight supper that Mrs. Walker was making.

I was in the gym putting up decorations for the dance when Pug came in. As soon as I saw her I knew that something was wrong. She came up, pulled me toward her and said that I needed

180

to go home.   She said that Ida had had an episode and they had already taken her back to Tucson and Dad was at home.

I guess Pug thought Dad needed me. I told James to stay because he had to drive everybody home and I left with Pug. I got there and I don't know what was more of a mess. Dad or the house. Thankfully, it was true that Ida was already gone. But I have never seen anything like this, not even when Ida has burned or torn up my stuff.

It truly did look like what I imagined a house would look like if a tornado blew through. Total destruction everywhere I could see from the front door including the door.   The glass was smashed and little shards were twinkling light as if it was some kind of mad tea party. It was hard to see any of the tile floor or any of the throw rugs.   Unrecognizable pieces of everything were everywhere. And then I saw the blood and I was suddenly cold with fear.   Whose blood was it?

It was Beth Ann's blood.   Beth Ann had been on duty, and up until now she had been fine with Ida. Dad said that Ida seemed to like Beth Ann because she was so easy going and would do what ever Ida needed so there had been no problems. Dad had gone to Tucson on business and did not know there had been a problem until he came home and saw Ray's truck and the other vehicles around the house.

Nobody seems to know what started the problem. Since I know Ida so well, I know that there did not have to be a problem for Ida to go off. She just does.

Beth Ann said that Ida had asked her something and she did not understand so she asked Ida to repeat the question. Beth Ann said suddenly Ida was hitting her and she tried to get away but could not. Beth Ann has a broken arm, broken nose, her eyes are turning black and she has scratches from Ida's nails all over her arms.

Dear Diary, remember our wonderful new couches and tables? Well, they are in shreds and splinters now. Two of the tables are smashed. Lamps shattered, shades in tatters. Glass is everywhere. Two of the six dining room chars are broken. There is a long, deep gash in the top of the dining room table and every dish from the china hutch is now in little shards all over the room. I don't think a tornado would have done more damage. Or a hurricane. Just typhoon Ida.

And the very worst piece of destruction, almost symbolic,   the beautiful, painting of the Horses in the Wind is now in thin slivers of color. Smashed splinters of carved wood. I suddenly realized that Beth Ann had been lucky. She could have been the one in shreds.

The worst part is that Dad is shattered, completely, this was his last hope. I think this has finally driven home that she is not fixable. Everything was riding on the treatments and the medicine. I don't know if she was taking the medicine or not but this is the final "fit".

Ray told Dad that he will file charges that will prevent Dad from ever being able to get her released. And this time she has been taken to a state facility. Dad knows that this is the end. He does not have the money to fight the legal system and he does not have the money to put her anywhere else even if he could. So many times it was supposed to be the last time. So I just hope that this is the "real" last time.

So much for the dance. Boy, does Ida have a knack for ruining holidays! Christmas, Halloween and now Valentine's day. I remember so many holidays that were ruined since I was very young.

Everyone finally left. I started to try to clean up and Dad said, "Stop". He said he had already talked to Cora and he was going to pay they boys to come in and clean up and carry off what needed to be taken away, which was going to be quite a bit.

Dad asked me if I would go back to the furniture store and get what we needed. He did not want to go and I can really understand why he is so down about it.

He looked so sad, I said, "Well, maybe they can give her more treatments." And it really scared me when he just said so quietly that I almost couldn't hear him, "No this is it. I don't want her to come back. I believe it now. She is truly mad." He looked defeated. I have never seen him look like that. His skin looked grey and his face had a sunken look. But it was the eyes that were the worst. There was just no life there.

"Roxie, go get your car. I am going to get us two rooms at the Paladin Hotel. We will stay there until the house is fixed."

March 1

We have been at the Paladin for a couple of weeks. Things are so strange. I am really tired of people feeling sorry for me. I just want things to get back to normal.

Dad paid all of Beth Ann's bills and he is giving her what is called a "settlement". Gretchen said that she is going to get Beth Ann to use the money to go to beauty school to be a beautician. So in the long run, I hope some good can come out of Ida's Last Debacle.

But here is more money that has to be put out because of Ida. Dad said that the money situation is not as bad as it could be because he does not have the bill for the other Tucson Hospital any more. How ironic. Now that she is in the state hospital he does not have to pay any of her bills.

March 7

So James has said that something "fantazimal" is going to happen for my 15th big day.

But I have been very concerned with Dad. He just has not bounced back. Not even a little skip back. He is quiet and very turned inward. He knows now that Ida will never be out again, this time it is complete. He no longer has the false hope that has driven him for years.

He just told me yesterday, that he cannot even visit her in the same room. Her room has bars and she is not allowed to have a visitor except in a very controlled area. Dad will not talk about what the visits are like.

She is now considered dangerous and is fully committed. Poor dad. He is in a prison of his own, he will never get out either.

March 12

The big surprise! And ay, carumba, did it turn out to be a really a good one. Dad was in on it too. James told me to get ready and wear my prom dress. My white Cinderella dress. And my silver slippers. Pug did my hair up and put my "jewels" in. Pug gave me a beautiful necklace with a silver rose on a silver choker with a matching ring.

James came and picked me up and we drove out to Silver Lake. The pavilion had been all decorated with Japanese lanterns and the posts had lights wound all around. Everybody was there. My angel crew and all our gang from school. There was a small band from Tombstone and Mrs. Casillas and Cook had made mountains of food. Mary Jane and her mother were there. I looked over saw Joe who had brought out El Con and Fala! Jake had made a special "birthday cake" for El Con and birthday beef jerky for Fala.

This was such a great birthday. Silver Lake is really a pretty place at night and it was an evening filled with laughter and happiness. I am 15. It finally occurred to me that the Ida situation was resolved. She would not hurt anyone any more. Not even Dad. Now that the these decisions were out of his hands, he would be able to rebuild a life. I know it will take a while but at least this is a beginning.

And a really special present was that Dad looked more like himself than he had since our last "Ida event". It gives me hope that things for him can get better.

Dad told me that he had another surprise for me that I would see in the morning. The party did not break up until after 2 A.M. I don't think I will ever have a better birthday surprise.

March 12

Dad came and knocked on my door at 8 A.M. He said, get your car, we are taking a ride. And we drove up to the new area in Cochise. It is called The Heights because it is higher than the rest of the surrounding area. It is the newest area and houses have been being built for the last couple of years. The houses all have a minimum of two acres. Dad directed me to Pear Blossom Dr. At the top of the hill was a charming, white, Spanish-Mediterranean style house.

Dad said, "Well, you have a job to do. You have to get the furniture and get the house ready for us. I asked him why change houses, and he said he needed a new beginning. He was just going to rent the old house.

I told Dad that I did not want to do it alone and he said that was fine, and we would go next week to get what we needed. There was no hurry.

But I wondered if he was going to tell Ted what happened to the last painting!

The house is really beautiful. I wonder if I am going to want to live in Tucson or just commute. And the view is stunning. We can see a 180 degree view of the entire valley.

April 4

Went back to the furniture store. And as luck would have it, we got the same sales lady. She seemed very surprised that we were ordering new furniture. She asked if something happened and I said yes some pipes broke and the furniture got water damaged. Dad said, "Yeah, we had a bull in a china shop". I was surprised myself. It was the first time I had ever heard him make even a tiny joke about the situation. I almost burst out laughing.

This time I ordered two large couches because the living room is large enough to carry the two. But I ordered a huge, square coffee table for in between. Spanish Mediterranean in a warm, lighter wood. I found two really interesting statues that will work perfectly. I am also going to see if Ted has something that we can afford that will be the main focus for the room.

Luckily Ida had not been able to get into my room and she had only destroyed the living room and dining room so we did not have to replace anything else.   She also did not do anything in the kitchen. But then Ida usually forgets that houses have a kitchen so we were safe! HA!

Dad is making an appointment for us to go back to Ted's studio.

April 20

At lunch, Ted was very sympathetic with Dad about the situation. He gave me a painting that is so beautiful!   Horses of course. We have invited him to our house warming which is going to be May 1st after church.

Gretchen, Beth Ann, Cook, Marta and two other girls will cook, serve and clean.   By the way, Beth Ann is in beauty school in Tucson, she is living with her older sister and she is happy as a clam.   So, some good has come out of this.   She will be doing something she likes instead of cleaning houses.   To be honest, she wasn't very good at cleaning.   But she loves to do hair.   She even offered to do mine for free.   But I told her Pug never lets anyone do my hair but Pug.

Fala loves his new house and his new yard.   Dad had a really fab wrought iron fence put around part of the back yard in a Spanish design. Hopefully this will keep him in and most of the critters out. Some of the houses up in the Heights are building pools but I don't like swimming enough to want Dad to spend the money.   Plus I like the look of the yard the way it is.

Dad said something interesting last night at dinner.   He said that the worst thing about all of the events of the past few years was that he thought I had skipped childhood and had to become an adult long before I should have.

I told him that I thought I was just born old. I have never missed being silly. I like having the ability to think the way I do. I do not feel deprived in any way.

I think everybody has problems, just different ones.   Look at Mary Jane.   She had a mother and a father and a perfectly normal childhood and then lost her father before she was eighteen.

So many people are so much worse off. I have a great dad, great friends, a super boyfriend, my angels and I still have El Con and Fala.   I have learned to be appreciative of what I do have.   Too many people waste so much time whining about what they do not have.

May 1

We had a terrific house warming. Everybody came. Even people I do not know. Some were Dad's friends from the club in Tucson and many of his business friends. Pug had organized the gift giving for some of the Cochise people and they gave us a set of china that came from Zuni House in Tucson. It is hand painted in earth colors and with Dad's favorite flower the Sunflower, with a outer Band of chocolate brown. The set is really gorgeous enough to eat on! So we will!

Some were friends of friends. Even Ted came and I guess he does not go to very many parties that are outside of Tucson. He liked what we have done with the house and where we have his art. I have several of his plates on either side of the fireplace on stone shelves. They look so right there.

This house has a happy, light airy feel that the other house never had. The House of Ida was dark for so many reasons. Yes, that house is still the House of Ida no matter what else we called it. I hope I never cross the threshold on that House of Horrors ever again.

Even Pug remarked how much better Dad looked and sounded. He is playing golf and poker again and best of all he has his sense of humor back.

Beth Ann used the party to drum up business. She was at the buffet table serving and as everybody came through the line, she was offering her services for hairdos. Some people even said that they would try her out. Dad thought is was a good, positive sign. I told him to wait to see how she does. Her hair may not be her best advertisement. She has that new poodle cut, very short, close to the head and truly poodle type hair. Scary. Gretchen has long, fat braids that she wraps around her head into a kind of coronet so I doubt if she will be a customer. But you never know, Beth Ann could turn out to be the next Mr. Teasy Weasy.

Speaking of hair, I still wear mine long while evry-body else is getting the poodle cut. I asked Pug what she thought and she said that was exactly what I would look like. A poodle!

I am getting ready for the end of this school year, finals and papers are due. My paper on Joyce has progressed very well. I am reading Ulysses. This is the first book that I have read that is taking so much time. I have to keep re-reading and looking things up.

May 20

Awards night. I am still trying to believe that I am finished with High School. I got a full scholarship to the U of A. Four years and everything paid. Including the dorm fees if I decide to live there.

186

Jim got MVA, Most Valuable Athlete. Dad said he is pretty much guaranteed to get a scholarship next year for the U of A and maybe offers from other schools as well.

June 1

I am going to work at Brownies six days a week for the summer. That will build up some "credit". Both Joe and Brownie said that I did not have to do that but I want to. It may be the last summer that I can do it because I think I want to take summer classes by next year. I want to spend as much time as I can with El Con.

Mary Jane and I talked about doing the barrel competitions all summer since she and I are both getting to where the time may not be there next year for the same reason.

So we are calling it The Summer of Barrel Racing. I am hoping to get some time to spend with Cami too.

James really likes Travis so we go out with Mary Jane and Travis quite a bit. We have a favorite Mexican place here. Palma's. We always try to get Dad to go with us. He does most of the time because he knows that we really want him to. He likes to talk sports with the guys. MJ and I are not into any sport except the racing, Everything else makes our eyes roll back in our heads. The only thing I like about football is that it makes James happy.

June 8

Dad got a call from Principal Lantry. He said the "Duel Credit Program" students had been invited to view a film at the U of A The film is "Helen Keller in Her Story" The other student is from Wilcox. I am really excited about going to see this film. Keller is one of the great heroines of our century, overcoming being blind and deaf and yet she became someone who has changed the way people perceive these handicaps.

June 17

We went to Tucson to see the Helen Keller movie, The Unconquered. The movie was so incredible. I am so amazed and impressed with her story. Imagine overcoming two handicaps that left her in a dark, silent world. How her first teacher Anne Sullivan unlocked that world and gave her communication with the world. And Polly Thompson who was her second teacher. What Keller has accomplished is beyond what most people do who do not have any handicaps.

I will never think that I have a difficult life again. When I hear, see or read stories like Miss Keller's I am more and more aware of how lucky I really am to have what I do.

I had a long talk tonight with Dad.   I told him that I am determined to go to school and get the education that I need so that I can help children.   I want to be a lawyer who helps children who are abused or hurt.   I want to help make laws that protect children. Dad said that he is going to set up a meeting with Judge Hunter so that I can get some information from him.   I want to know everything now.   I have so many questions about everything I will need to do to become a lawyer.   I want to know how laws are created or how they are changed.   So many of the rules and laws about how children are treated do not make sense to me.

Dad said that we will make a plan that will make my goals come true.   So I know how lucky I am that I have a father who is there for me.   Dad said to remember that my Angel Crew was there for me.

These few, these happy few, my Angel Crew

June 20

Dad and I had Pug and Mac to dinner at our house.   We have had dinner so many times with them but this was the first time that we had them at our house.   Pug thinks our new house is scrumptious. Her word!   During dinner I was saying that I wish there was something I could do to help people like she does.   Pug said there was.   She is part of a group of women who help the elderly people in Cochise.   I did not know she did that or that there is a group.   Anyway she said that I can be a part of it and I can help her.

What a great idea and Dad said he would like to be able to help too. Then Mac said well, why not have two men in the group so he is going to be a part of it.   She said they were called "The Ladies who Lunch" but now they would have to get a new name.   I said well, I call all of you my "Angel Crew" so maybe that could be a new name. Pug said exclaimed "That's a great name!"

June 22

I am working an eight hour day at Brownie's.   It is smelly, allergy causing, dirty, arduous work and I love it.   Joe said that I might grow up to be a rancher yet.   But I said no, I really have a goal but I might own a ranch to live on so that I can always have horses.

Joe, Dad and I had lunch with Brownie. Dad told them about the "Angel Crew" and both Joe and Brownie said they want to be a part of it too.   Brownie laughed and said that he did not know if he would be a helper of if he would be one of the people the crew helped!   I think Brownie has a long way to go before he needs help.

Then Brownie said that he wanted to show me something.   He took us into the hallway.   And he said, "Rox, what do you think about my desk?"   I wondered why Brownie had brought me out to the hallway to show me a piece of furniture.   But I told him that I had always liked it and I have even done my homework using it when the weather has be cold or rainy and I have come inside.

I love this desk. It is an adult size desk but still small. It is made of beautiful golden oak and has a drop leaf front with little cubbies and drawers.   I have always wondered if it has a secret compartment.

Brownie continued, "Yes, I know that you have, I have seen you there.   Now I want to tell you a story about this little, wonderful desk."

"My father on my mother's side used to live in Wiesbaden, Germany. It was 1922, and he was sixteen.   The family was starving and there were seven children. My father and two of his brothers were working in a plant that made pots and pans. The factory used huge, fire spewing furnaces in this pot making process that consumed more than just fuel on many occasions.   One of these occasions took the life of Conrad's older brother, Wuerz.

Conrad's father decided then that he had to get the other two brothers out of the factory and even out of Germany.   So it was decided that Conrad would be the first to go and somehow the family came up with the price of a steerage ticket one of the Packet Ships that sailed between German and the United States.   The Ticket was $22.67. A very large amount then especially for a destitute family. The father brought home all of the information for the trip along with the "priceless ticket" to this new promised land.

Conrad was told that he could only bring one item to the ship containing what ever clothing and possessions he had.   Conrad's great grandfather had made a desk that had been passed down and given to the brother who had died in the recent accident and Conrad asked if it could be taken with him to his new life. His father told him that that the ship people would never, allow it to be taken on the ship but Conrad was insistent and the family arrived at the dock, desk in tow filled with the few belongings he had.

When Conrad got to the front of the line and presented his ticket, he was told loudly and somewhat angrily, "You can't take this with you. Well, after a little discussion, and some possible money exchange, it was agreed that the desk would be his suitcase and he would have only the tiny space for him and the desk which would mean that he would not be able to occupy one of the wooden births that contained three or four people. He would have to sleep on the hard floor. He agreed.

189

The voyage took over six weeks. The ship was huge, dirty and the steerage level was dark, smelly, disease riddled, dangerous, reeking of fetid air, water was a contaminated cesspool, and slop was everywhere.

The bunks, three tiers deep, held people stacked like human cordwood. Meals were cooked in a common kitchen. The price of the ticket included a weekly ration of food which included five pounds of oatmeal, two and a half pounds of biscuit mix, one pound of flour, two pounds of rice, three ounces of tea, and half a pound of molasses. There were fights, births, and deaths. Many of those who started the voyage did not arrive in the Brave New Land.

Brownie's father arrived in New York by way of Ellis Island. Somehow he migrated to Arizona and somehow this young man who had never seen a horse up close before managed to become a cowboy and a good one. He had started the DoubleB Ranch and had passed it on to Brownie when he died.

Brownie asked me again what I thought about the desk. I told him that I already loved it including the cigarette burn in the top, Brownie said it was a cigar burn that was made by his dad who was a prodigious cigar smoker.

"Well, I already love the desk, but I love it more because of how it came into being."

"Do you know that there is not a nail in it? It is all made with a tongue and grove method for joining the wood. That means that it is put together with pieces that fit together. OK Roxie, the desk is yours, and your dad will have it taken over to your house today."

"Why, you must still want it because it was your father's." I protested.

"Of course I love it, but it is time for me to pass it on and I do not have any children, so I want somebody to have it that will love it and then pass it on to someone else who will love it so that it continues to be a part of my father's history. The only thing that I ask is that you pass on the story of the desk and my father."

Well, of course I burst into tears and after much hugging and thank-you, thank you and more hugs, Dad and I went home. Joe is going to bring it to our house later this evening. I am just overwhelmed with the fact that he wanted me to have it and to pass it on.

June 23

Joe brought the desk over. It looks as if it has always been a part of my room. It is strange but I feel a connection with it as if it is real. Maybe because I know something about the person who

190

made it and the people who have cherished it for all of these years. Brownie said that he thought that the desk was at least 100 years old. WOW! Double WOW!

Years ago Dad gave me a gold Ladies Pocket watch that is on a long heavy gold chain. Luckily, it has always been kept in a safety deposit box in the bank so Ida was never able to get to it to do her special smashing trick on it. It along with many other really significant things will be with me forever. Pug says that one of my really quirky traits is that I love old things. Yeah, I do.

So, if there is ever an Olympic Game for somebody who can run the fastest "Odd Duck Mile" I will be a gold winner! I even like to collect odd things. Over the years, Ida has been the Destroyer Machine so most of my collections are gone now. I used to have a collection of demitasse cups and saucers. Gone. An Angel collection of all types of angels. Gone. A collection of turtles. Gone. And the one that I liked the best, I had a collection of horses that were all glass from Stueben Glass, to just regular glass. Gone, smashed, shattered.

For the first time, I believe that I can have things now. Dad has offered to replace things over the years and I have always said what is the point, but now I would like to replace some of the horses. But with just the ones that are really pretty and have an "artsy" quality. I want to get one from Ted and I want to replace a couple of the crystal horses. I don't want anymore glass ones.

June 28

I made a report for Mrs. Mason and Mr. Bertram on the Algonquin Writers Group. I really learned some interesting things about all of them. What a fascinating time it must have been. One of the things I read was that it was the largest group of writers to have an ongoing social meeting place since the 1850s when many of the English writers had gathered and socialized and exchanged ideas.

I have just started reading Sherwood Anderson's Winesburg Ohio and I can't wait to read more Dorothy Parker.

Mrs. Mason has invited Dad and me to dinner tomorrow and I hope Mr. Bertram is coming too and we will be able to have a discussion about all of this writers group.

July 2

Diary, I have been putting what Sharon told me on paper and I have tried to be as accurate as possible. She told it to me first person so that is what I am going to use for her story.

Sharon's Story

My story actually begins with my grandmother. She was generous, beautiful, unpredictable and definitely charming and gregarious. Her name was Colleen Alexandria Fitzgerald Quinn. She was a Fitzgerald from County Cork. She had come to the United States from Ireland when she was sixteen as the bride of Griffin Lee Sullivan.

My mother said that she always felt that Grandmother Colleen never really "left" Ireland and the largest part of her was still back in the "Old Country". She spoke with a lovely Irish lilt and had a beautiful singing voice. My mother used to talk about listening to Grandmother Colleen sing all of the old Irish lullabies as she did her housework and gardening. She was known for her cooking and her incredible flower garden.

The Sullivans settled in Elmsford, New York. This was in Westchester County, not far out of New York City. Grandfather Griffin was a silversmith who made a very good living and owned his own shop with several employees. Griffin and Colleen had two children, Georgia Alexandria and Liam Gill.

My mother, Georgia, had a warm, loving Irish upbringing. Both of the children attended New York Colleges. Gill became a professor of English Literature at Fordham University. Georgia went to Barnard College and earned a Liberal Arts Degree.

After graduating, Georgia went to work in NYC for a publishing house as a reader where she met her soon to be husband, Finnegan O'Shea, a photographer. They married a few months after they met and moved to Culver City, California.

Finnegan started a photography studio and Georgia went to work for MGM in the Script Reading Department.

In five years, Georgia had risen to Head of the Dept. and then she had been promoted to the writing department. She was the first woman to be promoted to that position for MGM. At the same time, the photo studio that Finnegan had started began to fail and finally closed. The inevitable happened and Georgia and Finnegan divorced.

Two years after the divorce, Finnegan was killed in an automobile accident. A year after that, Grandmother Colleen's husband Griffin had a heart attack and died.

So Grandmother moved to California to move in with us.

I do not remember much about my Grandfather Griffin. But my grandmother became a very important person in my life. Sometimes I think she was the one person who loved me without any reservations. She and my mother were the center of my universe.

Grandmother was the stay at home, loving care taker. Mother was the flamboyant, beautiful, outgoing, larger than life creature who came and went in my life.

During my first ten years of life, I only remember being unhappy a few times. It was as if there were two worlds. The quiet, calm, happy, normal world with my grandmother. A warm, happy, beautiful house on the beach. Pleasant meals. Days spent with sun and sand. Then there was my mother's world, tempestuous, exciting, filled with zany characters, life lived at lightning speed.

I did not like school but I did not hate it either. It just was. I was a very quiet child and I only had one friend, Virginia. But that was enough. She and I would go to each other houses and play the normal games, and days of pretend and dress-up.

I loved to go sit in my mother's room and watch her get dressed for the fabulous places that she would go. She wore shimmering, slinky, long, incredible gowns with elegant jewels and bangles. Her glossy, black hair was fashionably cut into the sleek bob of the time. She applied her make-up expertly and her beauty took my breath away.

I was in total awe of the magical creature who just happened to be my mother.

I remember bits and pieces of life from that time. I do remember one dinner party vividly. This particular night my mother told me I could stay up and join her guests for dinner. There were twelve people at the table. I remember that because that is how many people could sit at the table and it was full. I was seated next to a very charming man who told me funny stories and treated me very kindly. He made a mouse out of the linen napkin and then to amuse me, I think, he ran the mouse up his dinner companion's arm. She was startled and let out a little yelp that in turn scared me and I knocked over the man's very full wine glass. Turmoil ensued. I was promptly escorted off to bed.

Another time that I caused a problem at a party was while the guests were talking and milling about, I took a cigarette from the crystal container on the coffee table. My intention was to light the cigarette and take it to my mother. Not a good plan. I tried to light the horrible item in the fireplace. I don't know what I was thinking. Instead, I almost lit myself on fire. Again, I was ushered off to bed.

Not long after that little fiasco, we moved to a new address. The new house was on Vista del Mar, a street with a steep hill. I loved to skate down the hill toward Franklin Avenue. Sometimes I was going so fast I would have to roll off into somebody's lawn to stop myself. This was fine until the day that I smashed my horned rimmed glasses and had to go home and try to explain why it was not my fault. Not believed, of course.

Days were fun with Virginia. We were both six. We would play dress-up, use tons of make-up, wear my mother's old dresses, go stomping around on dangerously high heels, and we would look like we had fallen into a painter's paint pallet head first.

We were only allowed to play at her house or mine which were side by side. One day, an organ grinder came around with his exotic and fabulous trained monkey. Well, the temptation was just too great and we followed him for an entire day from street to street. My grandmother had spent hours looking for me and had finally reported me missing. A policeman found us and with a stern voice, ordered us into his police car and returned us to a very angry grandmother, an even angrier mother and Virginia's mother all waiting on my porch. We secretly loved the ride in the police car, we were not so thrilled with the paddling that we both received and the restriction for a week.

Our next move was to the Palisades del Ray which overlooked the Pacific Ocean. It was a beautiful house. A floor to ceiling fireplace with native stone, and the front wall was entirely of glass and afforded a magnificent view of the water. My grandmother and I would spend every day on the water with a few exceptions for bad weather. I became a fish in the water. My grandmother sat under her umbrella and read her books. I would dash in from school, don one of my three bathing suits and we would head for our favorite spot.

I think that this was a wonderful, happy, innocent time. I was blissfully unaware of how little time I would have before my world would crash and burn.

There was an incident at this house that was very traumatic for me. On night my mother came into my room, woke me up and said she had a surprise for me.   She had on a beautiful fox cape, she reached inside the cape and out came an incredible, soft long haired kitten with huge blue eyes.   It was love at first sight.   I named him Sailor.

Sailor was a little over a year old when we were down at the beach, I was in the water, Grandmother in her chair. Suddenly we saw and heard a pack of dogs in pursuit. And they were pursuing my precious Sailor. Before we could do anything, one of the dogs had captured him and another of the pack was trying to tear him away.   Grandmother was furious and she used the umbrella to chase the dogs and make them release their prize.

Of course it was too late and I was introduced to the death of something I dearly loved. Mother, Grandmother and I held a beautiful ceremony at the edge of the sand by the dunes. Sailor was wrapped in one of Mother's silk scarves in an elegant hat box. This was the only pet I ever had during my childhood.

One of my very favorite memories is that of long rides on Sunday mornings in Mother's new, shiny Buick into Hollywood to go to church. The car was blue with black fenders. I was permitted to sit alone in the rumble seat. I would watch the trees go by upside down in the glistening fenders and I would sing all the songs that I knew at the top of my lungs.

We went to church every Sunday but there was one flaw in the church going. My mother would roll up to the front steps, let Grandmother and me out and then vanish until time to pick us up after services.

One Sunday, my mother rolled up in that wonderful car, parked across the street and without a care in the world I dashed across the street. Almost there, a car came to a screeching halt and I was knocked down flat. Fortunately, the only thing damaged was one of my lovely "go-to-church dresses. From then on, my mother parked on the church side of the street.

Another vivid memory was about a Halloween costume. We were having a holiday affair at school and I begged Grandmother to go get me a costume. After much whining and cajoling we went to the costumer. I found the most incredible outfit that was a red satin Chinese Pajama set, slippers and all. It was $2.00. Grandmother thought that it was the price to buy. When the owner of the shop said no, this was just to rent for three days, Grandmother grabbed my hand and she stomped out of the store.

Somewhere, she found a pair of wooden shoes and she made me a beautiful gingham Dutch-Girl outfit with a crisp apron and cap. It was much better than the first costume.

When I was nine, my mother bought me a set of gold plated play dishes. I thought I had died and gone to heaven. It was one of my favorite possessions for many years.

For the first ten years of my life, I had the perfect existence. I was a nurtured, spoiled, privileged child living in Hollywood around all of the fabulous people that my mother worked with and knew.

Because my mother was a writer for the studio, I was sometimes allowed to go with her to this exciting, vibrant place filled with creative, fun, and sometimes zany people. It was not until I was much older that I realized who most of these people were. I had watched a movie being made at Charlie Chaplin's studio once when my mother had stopped by for some business reason.

I had been read to by Lon Chaney, sang to by Douglas Fairbanks and played ping-pong with John Gilbert.

My mother had a large, beautiful office with her name in gold on the glass door. Mrs. Georgia O'Shea. The office had a pair of Chintz covered love seats in front of a bank of floor to ceiling windows that overlooked the lot. It was really fun to curl up in one to watch the costumed people flowing in and out of the huge warehouse looking buildings. A few time, Mom even snuck me into one of the buildings to watch production. One, I remember because of the fantastic costumes, was <u>Ben Hur</u>. Of course, it was years later when I realized that I was having a very unique experience.

So many of the people whose names I recognize now were at dinner parties at our house. It is odd how when you are living a life, you do not realize how special it will become. Then later when you look back and wish you had been more aware of all of the details.

One day, during that last year, I was sitting in Mother's office, and a beautiful, young woman came in looking for her. She smiled at me and said, "Are you taking care of things?" Feeling very important, I stammered out, "Why, Yes, I am."

"Could you tell her that Joan Crawford stopped by, and I would like to talk with her? At least that is my new name, I have to keep telling myself that is my name." And she laughed a lovely, throaty laugh as she floated out the door. I didn't know at the time that I was talking to somebody who would be a big star. But I knew that she had something that made me want to just want to hear her, talk to her, and be around her.

My mother's best friend was Norma Shearer. She was the biggest star on the lot at that time but of course I had no understanding of that. She was called the First Lady of MGM. I did not know what that meant but it sounded important. I just knew they were friends and she worked at the same place Mother did. Norma was married to Irving Thalberg who was the head of MGM.

One time when Mother and I were at their house, Norma asked me if I wanted to play dress up. She brought out a bunch of dresses, shoes, hats and jewelry. I was in heaven. While Mother and she were out by the pool, I would put on a concocted outfit and then I would parade in front of them while they ooed and awed. These were among my happiest memories. What a joy filled afternoons!

Another time when I was allowed to go to work with her, we were eating in the movie lot cafeteria. She introduced me to several people who stopped by our table. They were John Gilbert and Lon Chaney Sr. who were both working on Ben Hur and Douglas Fairbanks. Of course I did not realize that they were huge stars. I was not aware that my life was so dramatically wonderful. I was happy but I just thought I was like everybody else. Too bad we never know what we have until we do not have it anymore.

I remember going out on their sail boat many times. I remember many of the different people who would be on the boat or at the many parties.

When the parties were at our house, I was allowed to "help" by keeping ash trays emptied and taking the dirty glasses to the kitchen. Then I would be bundled off to bed, where I would wait a reasonable amount of time and then get up and go into a little hidey place where I could watch all of the grown up fun.

Mother had gone to NYC many times on business. Each time I had begged to go with her. She kept promising that she would take me along on one of these trips.

One day at breakfast, she said that I was going to be able to go on a trip with her to New York. I was ecstatic.

We went shopping and I got several new outfits for this dream trip. A white organdy dress with a pink satin sash, two sailor dresses, one white and on navy blue a polka dotted middy, a blue plaid shirt-waist-dress, a wide brimmed straw hat, white with a navy blue satin ribbon. New undies, socks and shoes. And to top it all off, a large leather traveling case that was all my own.

The day arrived, we boarded the train that had Pullman compartments. It was just like a little playhouse. A tiny bathroom attached to a tiny living space. During the day this miniscule space had a couch that looked out at the beautiful panorama of country side and cityscapes though a huge window. I was enchanted.

Mom said, let's get ready to go to dinner. We dressed to the nines. I remember what she was wearing. A beautiful, silk taffeta black and white, long dress with a black satin wrap. The skirt swirled, and shimmered the reflected light of the candle on the linen draped table in the dining car.

We were joined by an older couple who were equally attired, he in a natty suit and she in a bronze satin gown. I was in pink organdy. A little grand for the plain child that I was but it was a dinner hour filled with fun, laughter, and best of all, many compliments on my dizzyingly gorgeous dress, and my impeccable

197

manners. This is one of those memories that I take out every so often, dust it off, and use it to remember those good times.

We sat in the smoker car for hours and talked to many different people. Everyone was enthralled with my mother's enchanting stories of the stars, the movie industry and her role as a writer.

It was to my great regret when she sent me back to our Pullman room to go to bed. When I got there, I discovered that the porter had magically transformed the little space from a living room to a bedroom. A bed had been made from the couch and another bed had dropped down from the wall. Now there were two beds. I , of course, scrambled to the top bunk to appropriate it for myself. And I could still see out of the window.

I remember as if it were yesterday. The moonlight lighting grasslands, the houses with warm glowing windows telling silent stories of the people inside, the bright lights of cities and towns as our train ate up the miles. I don't know how long I stayed awake that night or the rest of the nights that it took to go from the Pacific Coast to the Atlantic Shores.

Every night we dressed for dinner, every night the silver service reflected the candlelight, the dinner conversation sparkled, and five days rushed by with one happy little girl, a newly rested mother and memories that were going to have to last a lifetime.

We arrived in New York at Grand Central Station. We were picked up by the chauffer for the MGM Studio New York Office and taken to the Waldorf Hotel. It was as grand as I had always imagined it would be. We stayed there for a week. I had full run of the hotel, room service and all. I have a feeling that the polite little girl from the train turned into a deceptively dressed little monster. I did everything, went everywhere, tasted everything and just plain bedeviled everybody I encountered.

I suddenly became aware that the reason that my mother was not monitoring my behavior more closely was because she was not feeling well. She had been going to her meetings, then coming back to the hotel and spending her time "resting". Her health very rapidly deteriorated and she moved us from the hotel to the Park Crescent on Riverside Drive where the hotel "apartment" overlooked the Hudson River. She hired a nanny for me and told me that she was going to go into the hospital for some tests. She told me not to worry, but worry I did. I had never known my mother to be sick, ever. I had never even know her to go to a doctor. She was one of those robust, high energy, enthusiastic, vibrant people. She could not be ill. Not my mother.

And this was the beginning of the collapse of my world. I would ask the nanny, an older, very stern, emotionless woman, how my mother was.   She would say, "Your mother is fine, now go do something. Do not bother me."   I visited My Mother every day. The nanny and I would take a cab and go to the hospital.   I was allowed to sit with her for an hour and every day I would see her getting weaker and less able to talk. After a week, she was no longer smiling or joking. And she would just answer anything I said with just a word or two.

One day the nanny said that we could not go to the hospital because my mother was having an operation and we could go after she got better from the operation.

Several days later, she called me to come sit down on the couch. She sat across from me, and she calmly told me that my mother had died. Just like that. "Your mother has died." She did not get up and come to me. No hug. No, "I am sorry", nothing. She said she would stay with me until my grandmother could come get me. Her only concern was that she did not know who would pay her.

A few days later Irving Thalberg and Norma Shearer arrived at the hotel. Norma told me that my grandmother was too distraught and was having health issues of her own. They had arranged for nursing for her and told her they would take care of everything here. They dismissed the nanny after I told them how she had been. They settled the hotel bill and what ever else there was. Of course at the age of ten and just going through the death of my mother, much of it is a blur.

The funeral and the burial were in New York. Georgia had been born in New York, so it seemed only fitting to the Thalbergs that she should be buried there since the only relative in California was Grandmother and I was going to stay in New York. The service was held at Saint Luke's. Sadly, nobody ever told me where she was buried and I have never been able to find out.   Someday I am hoping that I will have enough time and money to try to find out where she was laid to rest.   I have gone to so many cemeteries to try to find her but so far, no luck.

Mr. and Mrs. Thalberg took me to a boarding school.   It was the Rose Haven School for Girls.   We started this future altering journey by taking a taxi that actually went onto a boat.   I was stunned, a car that rode on a boat. During the trip, I stood by the railing and watched the skyline of the City getting smaller and smaller.

I was not even grieving yet because I was still in such shock. I did not believe that my mother was gone. Since I had not attended the funeral or seen her after that last visit to the hospital, I could not believe what I was being told. I just kept thinking that it was a nasty, horrible dream and that I would wake up. This surreal boat ride just contributed to this feeling of being trance like bubble just waiting for some grown up to say, "OK, now let's go back to your real life."

Sadly that life faded further and further away as we chugged down the Hudson River to our destination and my new life. The taxi reclaimed its sad little trio of people and we motored off the boat and traveled up to the school.

We arrived at a magnificent and charming old style building with a large circular drive. A small, dignified sign proclaimed it to be The Rose Haven School.

Suddenly I was terrified and I was aware that it was real. I was being deposited in an entirely different world from any that I had ever known. All new people, not one person that I knew, or anyone who loved me. Deposited in a new state and a new environment that I knew nothing about. From warm sunny California to cold, cold New Jersey. People moved too fast, and they talked too fast, the accent grated on my ears.

We went into the office where two women stood in front of a huge desk that looked more like a table, with desk chairs on each side. I did not know who or what they were. Teachers? Principal? Vice Principal?

I was introduced to Miss Ruth Van Strum and Miss Mary Birchard. They appeared to be in awe of meeting Irving Thalberg and Norma Shearer. That was to have a great impact on my stay at this school. The only respect that I ever got at the school the entire time I was there was because of my association with the Thalbergs.

Mr. Thalberg paid for the entire year ($7,500.) based on the discussion that I overheard and he said that a check would be sent every year. Every year! I was being left for years? Until then I was just doing what I was told and was trying to take in all that had happened in such a short space of time.

I am ten years old, I have lost my mother, I am put into a new situation that I know nothing about and do not want and now I hear that it will be years. I felt a giant, heavy door slam. No Alice every walked into a stranger Wonderland. This was to be a cross between Never, Never Land and Lonely-ville. I do not mean to be so melodramatic but the reality was that I was just committed to the most lonely time of my life.

I was the girl who studied, read, sat in the corner and had no friends. The only time that I left the grounds was when there was an activity where all of the students went. Even then I was alone. No best friend chattering away. Just me, sitting by myself. I had become a ghost.

200

I did not talk or socialize.   I was never invited to spend a week end or even invited on a social activity.   In the beginning, some of the girls tried to befriend me but I had gone into such an inward depression that very quickly, people left me alone. I know that the teachers tried. But I developed a hard impassive shell. I did not let anybody in.

During my junior and senior years, I would walk to town to go window shopping, to a solitary movie and to the library.

That one time that I left school for a weekend was oddly lacking in reality for me. I felt as if it were happening to somebody else. Late one Friday one of my dorm mates came to my door (I was one of the few singles, most of the others had room-mates) and told me to dress and come downstairs   So I dressed in the only street outfit I had, the rest of the time I wore the school uniform, and I went downstairs.

In the waiting room was a middle aged couple with four children. I was introduced and told that the man was my father's brother. This was my Uncle Hadley. This was my Aunt Jasmine. And these were my cousins, all four of them!   I was going for a weekend visit.

We all piled into a rather large Buick and off we went to New Rochelle. The drive took over an hour.   A very long hour.   The four kids were smelly, sticky, loud and moving like whirling dervishes.

It was an even longer weekend. I was actually glad to return to the school.   I think it was a test to see if I would fit into the family. Obviously, I did not pass the test because that turned out to be the only visit. I never saw them again. I was not sorry at the time, but lately, I have been sorry that I did not have a chance to ask the uncle about my father.   And even more strange, I cannot remember one name of that any of the children in that family who did not want me. But at least this was one time the rejection was mutual.

The Thalbergs also made arrangements for my grandmother. She was put into a home for the aged. They paid a total of $5,000. and that paid her expenses there for as long as she lived. Well, that turned out to be only four years.   She died when I was fourteen and by the time I was told about it, she had already been buried.

Very sadly, this wonderful woman who had nurtured me and been as much mother as she was grandmother, was to live her life out at this home. I don't know is she were happy or not. She sent me a few letters but she was not the type to complain so I have always wondered what those last years were like.   I wrote to her and of course I did not complain to her either. There we stayed on opposite coasts, two people who loved each other, two people who nobody else loved, and we were denied those last few years. Fate is a cruel, cruel master.

There is really very little to tell about the eight years I spent at the school. Nobody was mean. No one was overly friendly. I just existed there. I did my studies, I was given small jobs in the office that earned me money. Since I did not go out most of the money was put away. The only thing I spent money on was to walk into town and go to a movie by myself. Summers I worked at the school. And I put all of that money away. My obsession was about going back to California and possibly going to the UCLA. But one thing was for sure, as soon as I graduated, I would be going back to California.

And that is exactly what I did. I did not want to use up what money I had saved because I knew I would need money to live on and I knew I wanted to find an apartment that I would be able to afford. I had such plans. Eighteen, on my own, going back I thought of as home. Now I knew how that baby bird in the nest felt with mama bird nudging her out of her little save home. Scared with anticipation but still ready to see what is out there. I was on my way. I tried to imagine that Mama was somewhere nudging me to fly back to this promised land of milk and honey. I think it was where she had always been the happiest.

It made me sad to know that neither Grandmother or Mother was there. But it was still the last place I had been happy and had a family. I did not know the names or the whereabouts of any of the other relatives. Of course with my mother dying so young and so unexpectedly, it had never occurred to her to make a will or write down information that I would have needed to stay in contact with any other family members.

So I was on my own. But I was headed where I wanted to be. And because I did not want to use any more money than I had to, I advertised in a local paper to be a helper for a trip to California. Another girl at school had done that to go to Las Vegas for a free trip. It worked.

The Wyatt family had two children and a mother who appeared to have very little interest in the two adorable little girls. It turned out that they needed a "helper" because they lived with the wife's mother who had flown ahead to get their summer house in California ready for the family. The reason they were driving was because Amy, the wife, would not fly. They had a large Buick sedan and I was in the back between Bridget, 2 and Hannah, 5. The were sweet, cuddly, rambunctious and surprisingly happy. The grandmother must be doing a wonderful job with them because

202

their mother did not interact with them the entire five days it took to drive from Cloister, New Jersey to Los Angeles.

I really enjoyed the kids but the mother irritated me to no end. She never shut up. She was not talking to me but to Ralph. Hair, clothing, they needed a bigger house, how much she hated her neighbors, how much she hated Closter. He worked in the City and she wanted to move there. And so much more. So much boring more.

Five days on the road. Five nights in motels. Five breakfasts, five lunches, five dinners. The only time I escaped Amy's constant barrage of twaddle was when I took the kids to the pool, for a walk and mercifully when I was in the separate room with the lovely little girls.

We arrived in Los Angles and I was within minutes of escaping and Ralph asked me if I would like to spend the rest of the summer at their California house because he felt that the girls were getting to be a bit much for the grandmother.

I felt as if I had nothing to lose, so I said I would if I could look for a job, stay with them and that way the grandmother would only have to take care of them during the day. Ralph said that was probably a good idea because the grandmother might feel better if she were not replaced entirely. So it was an arrangement that worked for everyone.

Sadly for the children, but good for me, I never saw much of Amy after we arrived at their house. And what a house it was! Ralph owned some kind of manufacturing plant that made parts for the automotive industry. I found out that he also had several other plants that were around the country and one here in LA. They must have been flourishing because this house was huge and quite beautiful. Typically California hacienda with stucco, rounded arched doorways and window, tile roof and the landscaping was luscious and tended by a team of gardeners.

Even the room they assigned to me was nicer than any room I had ever had. Just down the hallway from the girls two rooms. And these bedrooms were in a separate wing from where the parents were ensconced. The wing that the girls had was as big as a normal house, no, bigger. They had two huge bedrooms with enough toys for a battalion of kids and each had her own bathroom. They had a playroom outfitted with child sized furniture and appliances that were sectioned into rooms, its own little "house". Each little area had actually been designed by an architect and decorated by the decorator who had decorated the main house. I had stumbled into a California version of Wonderland.

Since I had my days free, I went looking for a job. I made a beeline to MGM and put in my application for three different departments. I got a call back about four days later and I went in for an interview. Mr. Higgins informed me that the accounting department was looking for a comptroller's assistant. I told him that I did not even know what that was. He said that it was just a name for bookkeeping. I told him that I had no experience but he said that my school transcript showed that I had great math skills and that I could be trained for the rest on the job. To my great surprise he offered me the job and the salary was so much more than I had expected. Again, with nothing to lose, and the possibility of learning a marketable skill I accepted. He told me to report a 8:30 sharp on Monday morning.

I only owned two outfits that would be acceptable for this job. So my next business of the day was to go to a clothing store that was within my budget. Let me tell you, that took some doing. I went into at least five stores and was shocked by the prices. I finally went into a store called Lerner's. It was still more than I wanted to pay but at least I could get enough to start out.

I chose carefully and got mix-n-match pieces that could make several changes for me. Blouses, white, black, cream, and rose. A black skirt, a grey pleated skirt and a black silk polka dotted dress with a wide, white belt. This took a large chunk of my money but since I had a place to stay with a tiny salary there and a new job, I thought I would be OK.

This was how it went for the following year. I stayed with the Wyatt family for two reasons. Partly because it allowed me to put money in the bank. But I think I stayed because I had gotten so attached to the two girls and they let me know every evening that I was an important part of their lives.

The job at MGM was interesting. I discovered that I had a real knack for numbers and this kind of accounting. I liked the people that I worked with and I was learning daily. The actual head of the department was Mr. Barshofsky. But it was really Sandy Wallace who ran the department. I was never sure how Mr. Barshofsky spent his days. When he was at work he was in his office behind a closed door. He was rarely seen by anyone except to arrive at 9 AM sharp, go to lunch at twelve on the dot, and not return for the rest of the day.

Sandy was a tough cookie but very fair and I much admired her. She was short and round with the reddest hair I have ever seen. She wore layers of gold jewelry that clinked and clattered as she made her rounds from cubicle to cubicle to make sure that each worker was on task. We each had several accounts that related to a studio project.

I was amazed how many different things went into making a picture. How many different items were required to be made, remade, altered, found, painted, and often changed after everything had been done. I was also amazed how many people it took to make a picture. Some on permanent salary to the studio and some just worked on one project. So many people that came and went and were involved with several projects at one time. Part of the job was to keep all of that information and make sure that everybody was paid, things were ordered and much, much more.

I was fascinated, busy, learning and that year just flew by. I had made a friend who did pretty much the same thing I did. Noel was in the next cubicle. All day long we would pop up and see how the other was doing and we would say things to keep us giggling as long as Sandy was not in earshot. But we both knew that Sandy liked us because we did our work and often helped out when others got behind or there was a special rush on something. I learned so much about the entire process of picture making and how it is funded.

Noel and I became such good buddies. She was from LA so she knew the city quite well. We spent most of our time going to the pictures shows. We went window shopping, we borrowed each other's clothes, we spent hours just talking about life. I was in heaven, I had never had a good friend before. Mr. Wyatt was wonderful about letting me have Noel come to the house. He joked that two nannies were better than one. He said that he could tell by what the girls told him that they were never neglected by us and that we "enhanced" their world. Noel had her own car, and Mr. Wyatt even let us take the girls to the studio to see a children's movie being made.

It appeared to me that Mrs. Wyatt was becoming more and more distant from her children and that he was grateful that the girls had the grandmother, me and even Noel.

Noel and I became inseparable. She was there so much that Mr. Wyatt even offered to pay her and she laughed and said, "No, just give Sharon a raise". And he did. So we used that money to fund what ever activities we did on my days off.

One beautiful, bright sparkly day in June I realized that the first anniversary of my living in LA had come and gone. I felt like a real inhabitant of the city. I had even gotten a raise at MGM.

Noel and I talked about getting an apartment together but we both knew that it was too important to stay with the little girls. Oddly they were still bubbly happy children. Hannah would be starting first grade in the fall. I had surprised myself that I cared so much for these almost orphans.   I just could not understand why Mrs. Wyatt did not take any more interest in them than she did. They were just like the clothes she wore or the car she drove. Something for her to show the world, her perfect children as if she had anything to do with it!

One day Noel said, "You know we have vacation time coming up. Let's talk to Sandy and see if we can get the same week off." Her idea was to go up to El Monte.   She had an aunt who owned a strawberry farm. It was beautiful country and it would get us out into a part of California that I had never seen and while we stayed with her aunt, we could take little jaunts up the coast line and have little day adventures. And the best part was that it would only cost the price of car gas. So I agreed if Sandy would agree to our time off idea. She did. We would leave July 17th. Now I had to get Mr. Wyatt to give me the week off as well. He did. He even thought it was a great idea.   The little munchkins were sad but after reassuring them that it was just for a little while and that we would both be back and we would bring surprises, they tearfully thought it would be OK.

The day for our coastline adventure arrived, we were packed, excited and ready for the open road. Noel's little black Ford roadster was very dependable and fun to drive. Noel had taught me to drive so we took turns driving the 335 miles. The drive took almost eight hours because we stopped so many times to eat and even look at shops and scenery along the way.

We arrived in El Monte and found Middle Country Road then to Chestnut Pond. The farm was named Strawberry Pickin's. Corny I know, but still cute. Mrs. Lawson greeted us from a shady, plant filled front porch. Actually it was way more than a porch. The farm house was more like something out of the book, _Gone with the Wind_.   Columns and all.   She stood on the wide veranda literally with open arms and after hugging and kissing Noel she did the same to me. The house was surrounded and shaded by huge oak trees that wore Spanish Moss shawls.   I had never seen a property as beautiful and lush as this.

Wicker furniture in all shades from white to dark brown graced the full veranda that wrapped around two sides of the three story house.   She shooed us inside to put our things away.   We were ushered to two rooms.   Mine was right out of every Southern movie I had ever seen.   Chintz covered loveseat under a window that overlooked an orchard and pond.   The white, antique, iron bed was covered in the same material, pink roses on a white background and pillows, pillow, pillows in all in shades of pink. White carpeting that felt as if it went up to my ankles.   The furniture had to go back to the Civil War.   Had we made a wrong turn and driven to Atlanta by mistake?

We both showered, put on fresh clothes and went back downstairs. Mrs. Lawson was sitting in her "pallor" and had prepared tea and cookies. The idea that we had somehow slipped into an antebellum world was becoming increasingly more possible by the minute. Mrs. Lawson looked at me and in a voice that might have been Melanie's, with molasses dripping by the pound, "Oh, Sharon my Dear, you must call me Miss Honey. Everybody does. Noel has told me so much about you, you poor, poor girl. We are your family now." I did not know whether to smile or glare at Noel.

We chatted while we had our tea and cookies. Just as Noel was telling Miss Honey, Aunt Honey to her, the door to the parlor burst open and a Greek god thundered into the room. He was in cowboy garb, boots and all. I never seen a man that incredibly handsome. And that is saying a lot since I worked on a movie lot and spent much of my time seeing the young hopefuls coming and going as well as those who were already on their way to being "stars".

That he was the real thing became obvious very quickly. He was not a want-to-be anything. He just was. Noel jumped up and the two hugged and did the kissy things and Noel squealed out, "Troy, what are you doing here?" In the space of less than two hours, Noel suddenly sounded more southern than her aunt. I had forgotten that she had been raised in Charleston, South Carolina.

Well, now I had a name to go with this heavenly creature who towered over all of us with his well filled out, six-foot-plus frame. Troy answered in an accent that was southern but not the same as Noel and Miss Honey's syrup laden syllables. "Well, dear Cousin Nosey Pants, if you must know, I am working for Aunt Honey. I am the head Pu Bah for the whole shootn' match for this summer's crop. And may I ask how did we get so lucky to get one ugly cousin and one ravishing creature as stands before me." Noel swatted him playfully and picked her up and swung her in a big circle almost knocking into a little rose wood table with all kinds of fragile knick-knack do-dads on it.

"Now you two children, you just settle your selves down and don't be cuttin' up in Miss Honey's parlor." Yes, she talked about herself in third person. It took me a while to get used to it.

Finally, Noel remember that I was there. "Oh, this tall drink of water is my cousin Troy from Texas. We try not to talk about him too much. He already thinks that the sun rises and sets on what ever spot he is standin' on. And he prides himself on his heart breakin' abilities. So, don't you be lettin' him sweep you off your pretty little tootsies."

In the space of seconds I knew her joking admonition had come too late. I was swept. I did not know how or why, I just knew that I had to know this rarified specimen of a man much better. I had never had a boyfriend. Not even a boy friend. I had never really known how to talk to boys. I had not even had any interest. Now I was interested. Very interested.

We all sat down again. Troy's hand shot out and quickly scooped all of the rest of the cookies of the silver dish and he ate them ravenously. Miss Honey dispatched herself to the kitchen to replenish the much needed supply.

Noel began telling Troy about me, the job, LA and more. I barely listened. I was acutely aware that Troy was looking at me with the most beautiful blue eyes I have ever seen on anyone much less on a man. Troy seemed to have been graced with more of the gods blessings than any one living specimen should have been entitled to.

Noel took a breath in her litany of the last year and Troy jumped in. "Sharon, I am glad you came up to spend time at the farm and with our version of family. I just graduated from UT and I am here to spend a summer before I go look for gainful employment or decide if I want to take over my duties at my father's ranch."

I was surprised to hear my own voice, sounding somewhat normal, ask him, "What kind of ranch?

"Sheep. Lots and lots of sheep. Dirty, smelly, stubborn lumps of wool. That's why I'm here. Not a sheep on the place. Cows, horses, rows and rows of strawberries but not one darn sheep. Not even a lamb. I got some big decision to make and I thought gettin' away might do the trick. The other thing that is not here is Daddy. Can't tell you what a good thing that is! And he grinned and that turned into a gut deep, throaty laugh that turned me into one big pile of molten lava.

"What might you two girls be up to? What are your plans? Are you here for the rest of the summer?" Before Noel could answer, I jumped in, again surprising myself, "No, we are just here for a week because that is all the vacation we have. What do you think we should be doing?"

Noel and I both did not recognize the voice that was coming out of my awestruck mouth. Noel was looking at me as if she had never seen me before. Well, she had never seen this side of me. I hadn't either. I was not sure who was more appalled. Was I Sharon the flirty? Sharon the vamp? I started to say something but I clamped my teeth shut so hard I bit the inside of my cheek. Both Troy and Noel were looking at me. I felt my entire body flush and my cheeks burned, I was sure I was the color of an overcooked lobster.

Troy broke the tension. "Well, girls, you are in luck, there is a shindig at the local roadhouse and I am going to take you to it. So after dinner, I want the two of you to get all gussied up and lookin' sharp and we will just go have us a smashin' good time. Now I gotta go back out to the fields and see who is workin' and who is taking a little little time off." Suddenly as an after thought, he turned to me, "Sharon, I'll bet you ain't never seen strawberries in the field before, have ya?" I shook my head no.

"Well, then, my little city slicker, put on some pants 'cause ya can't ride in that pretty lil' sundress and then we'll l saddle up."

Suddenly I was grateful for the riding lessons I had had to take at school. Without looking at a stunned Noel, I turned and ran upstairs. I changed and was down in a flash. Noel and Troy had been talking and Noel looked at me intently, "Sharon my good friend, just be careful." She gave me a long look, touched my arm and left to go find Miss Honey.

That is how it began. For the rest of that week, Troy and I spent every possible minute together. Noel and I had long talks about him. She told me the family history. Way back generations, Troy's family had split off from the other side and had gone to Abilene to become ranchers instead of tobacco farmers who stayed in South Carolina. Troy was the first born of two sons who were expected to continue the ranching tradition. Troy had gone to UT (University of Texas, I learned) and was on his way to becoming an architect. He was 23. He and his dad were battling over his career choice. His dad was a stubborn powerhouse who always got his way. No son of his was going to walk away from one of the biggest sheep ranches in South Texas.

Miss Honey kept telling me to enjoy the week but to not think that there would be any more to it. She knew that Troy had a longtime girlfriend who might even be a fiancé by now in Brownsville. They went back to grammar school as a couple. Vienna came from another powerful ranch family and it was as certain that they would marry as if it had been set in stone.

Noel told me the same thing. I kept telling Noel that I understood all that and I was just enjoying his company. She looked doubtful. I knew that in my heart, I was a lot more doubtful. I had feelings that I never knew were possible for me to have. Every time I saw even a glimpse of him, my heart fluttered, my skin grew icy, and I had to keep from running to him and flinging myself at his feet. Oh, this was not calm, reserved, Sharon who always evaluated every action before she took it.   This was new, emotional and if I were honest with myself, in-love Sharon.

I had always believed that people could control emotions and was scornful of the girls from my school dorm who had allowed themselves to get out of control over some handsome face or football hero and go around all Moonie-pied with that ridiculous goofy look of the newly in love.   I avoided mirrors because I could not bear to see that look on my face.   But it was not hard to tell that anybody else could tell at a glance that I had lost all my senses. Noel would look at me and just sigh.   Even Miss Honey took me aside and gave me a little "Beware of the birds and Bees" talk.

Troy told me that now he had two decisions to make. He told me about Vienna.   He said that they were very comfortable together but he was not in love with her.   He said that yes, he loved her but not kind of love that makes your heart flipity-flop.   He said that he had never thought about marrying anybody else, it was just expected of him.   Troy said bitterly that his whole life had been planned out for him.   At UT he had begun to have doubts about ranching and being tied to his father for so many more years.   He said his father was a tyrant who never allowed anyone to have an idea or new thought. And if you crossed Daddy, you paid dearly.

I saw two sides to Troy. The happy, funny, witty, engaging man with emotions he did not hide well. The other side was troubled, confused, angry and fearful of making a wrong choice for his future.

Sadly, the week flew by and it was time for Noel and I to go back to LA and our normal lives. I felt as if it was one more time that something I cared about (loved if I was being honest) was being taken away from me.

Troy and I had a long talk on that last evening. We walked in the moonlight in the strawberry field and both made promises that I was pretty sure that I would keep but doubted that he would. One last night at a brief, fierce, passionate, fling and I was back to normal.   But not so normal because I had had a glimpse of what might have been.   I knew my life was changed. I was changed.   I had spent the last eight years of my life guarding against any emotional attachment. But I could not guard against what had just happened here.   Fate had just played a very dirty trick on me. This odd chance meeting was to change the direction of my life.

We got up early, loaded our things in the little roadster, made our goodbyes, and Troy and I walked off for a final goodbye.   He said he would come to LA as much as he could.   I pretended that I believed him and he walked me back to Noel and my journey back to what I now called home.

Noel prattled all the way home and tried to make me join the conversation. She sang and acted silly and tried to get me out of the funk I was in. I was not very good company on the long journey back to my sane, secure life.

Monday was a long difficult day at work. I had to keep reminding myself to pay attention to my work and try to stop thinking about "him".

I arrived at the Wyatt's after work, and Mrs. Wyatt told me I had a call. I could tell she was curious. I told her that I was sorry that she had to take a call for me and she told me that she was so grateful for my help that it was no problem at all.

I was so happy that she said that because sometimes I was afraid that she resented me. There are two phone lines at the Wyatt's. One for them and one line that is just for the help. The only person who has ever called me there was Noel and she always knows when I am there. I went to my room and saw that there was a message for me. The paper said the number was from the strawberry farm. My heart jumped into my throat. Could it be Troy? I did not think that Miss Honey would be calling me. I dialed the number and crossed all of my fingers. Troy picked up on the first ring. We talked about everything and nothing. Then he asked if he could come to LA for the weekend, I said "Of course". It was agreed that he would stay with Noel.

I walked around on a cloud for the rest of the week. Saturday I woke up and just paced until Noel called me and said Troy had called her from a diner and said he would be there in less than an hour.

Normally my frugal sense would have prevailed and I would have taken the bus and the three block walk to her apartment building but I did the unthinkable for me and took a cab. The outrageous expense of it barely registered as I paid the cabbie and scooted into her building, ran up the two flights and pressed her buzzer. It seemed as if it took her ages to open the door.

My eyes swept the room, "he" was not there.

Noel said, "Calm down, you look like you just ran all the way here." She gave me an appraising look that surprised me.

"Sharon, you gotta get some reality back in that pretty Irish head of yours. Troy is not available. Not in any way. He likes you, I can tell, but that means nothing. He is going to have his "vacation" from his real life and then he is going to go back and do just what "Daddy" wants him to do. He is going to eventually take over all the little "sheeps" and that big ol' buncha land, but first he will marry Vienna and have a whole passel of little kiddie monsters.

211

That is the way it has been in that family for generations. Not the poor members like me.   Just the filthy rich, male ones.   Oh, Sweetie Pie, I don't want to see you get hurt."

I guess she read the look on my face and finished sadly, "Well, I guess that little tug-boat already sailed."

Just then the buzzer rang downstairs. Noel sighed, "Sharon, go on, go down and let him in, that'l give ya a coupla minutes. Looks like nothin' I say is going to change a cotton pickin' thing."

I was downstairs in a shot. I had never been so glad to see anybody in my life. This began one of the most glorious summers of my life. He came every weekend.

We did everything. We went everywhere. We were truly happy in each others company.

Sadly, it is the same story told by thousands of young, innocent, starry-eyed girls who fall in love and believe what they want to believe.

Troy told me he loved me. And the last week that he was to be in California, he proposed.   I still believe he meant it at the time. And I made the age old mistake. I truly believed that we were getting married. We talked about going to New Mexico to a very romantic city in the fall. This would give Troy enough time to go back to Brownsville to take care of what he had to do. It would let him tell his family and they could join us for the wedding if they wanted to.   We spent the last night together before he had to return home.

Well, the inevitable happened. He went back to Texas. The phone never rang. He did not call me at the Wyatt's. He never called me at Noel's. Sadly he never called my at my job. Total silence. One month turned into three. By then I knew I was going to have a baby.

I begged Noel to call him at his family's home. She said let's just give it another month. I agreed because I didn't have any other option.

By the time Noel agreed to call, Troy had been gone for over four months with no communication at all. I had come to terms with the idea that there was no future with him. What we had was all we were ever going to have. Yet this little tiny part of me hoped beyond all reason, that as soon as he knew about the precious life I was nurturing, it would make him want to keep all the promises that he had made.

I remember these few minutes as if they are a little movie playing in my head. Noel sat at her pretty, little Queen Anne desk with lemon colored light coming in the stained glass window behind her. She asked for Troy. And then she was very quiet for several long minutes. Her face became serious, then sad. She thanked her Aunt and said she would see them for Christmas when she went to visit her cousins.

I was afraid to have her tell me what was said. I knew that what ever it was, it was going to put a final stamp on what I already knew.

Noel spoke so quietly I had to lean in to hear her. "Sharon, Troy is on his honeymoon. He and Vienna were married two weeks ago. The wedding plans began as soon as he returned home. The reason nobody called me or invited me was because Troy told them I was going to go out of the country at the time of the wedding. Oh, Sweetie, I am so sorry. I know I tried to tell you but I should have tried harder. I know him. He always does what he wants and he always gets what he wants."

Noel looked close to tears. I tried to tell her that I would manage. She said firmly, "We will manage." We have to start making plans. At some point you are not going to be able to continue working at the Wyatts. And I don't know what will happen with your job. I think you need to tell the office manager that you got married over the weekend so that you can keep working as long as possible. Before the baby is born you can move in here.

She continued talking but my head was spinning and I was no longer hearing what she was saying. I stood up and said I needed to get back to the Wyatts. They were going away for the weekend. That was good for two reasons. The girls would keep me very busy and I would not have to talk to anybody else.

I was not showing yet but I would be very soon. I knew Mrs. Wyatt would figure out that I had a situation.

Well, I am going to tell the next part very quickly. The Wyatts were wonderful. I worked for them, both before you were born and afterward. They not only let me bring you to work with me, Amy's mother watched you during the day while I was at the studio. She actually said that she was grateful to have the opportunity to have a baby in the house.

This arrangement worked out until you were almost a year old. Mrs. Wyatt discovered that she was pregnant. She quit her job and I was no longer needed plus two babies in the house would have been too much for everyone.

You and I moved in with Noel. It was a one bedroom apartment. So it was a strain on everyone.

You had been a very healthy baby.   Actually a little butterball with chipmunk cheeks.   Suddenly you were having all kinds of problems. I started missing work. More and more I had to stay home. The inevitable happened and I was let go.

I also realized that I could no longer impose on Noel. She had given up her life to help us out.   By this time you were sixteen months old and you really needed more room. You needed so much of everything that I could not provide for you.

I discovered that it was virtually impossible for a poor, single woman to keep a child.   There was nobody I could turn to.   No relative, no help.   I spent several months finding a mother who would keep you during the day and I could work.   I could only get jobs that paid so little that I could not pay for your care, pay for a room and pay for food.   Even working, I could never afford more than a tiny room in the poorer sections of town.

I was drowning and you were not thriving.   I worried that you were not gaining weight as you should. You had gone from a plump baby into a thin toddler.

On one of my jobs, Helene, a young woman I met, said her cousin, from Tucson, had just written to her that she had a good job as a motel manager and it also gave her own place. That was the really interesting part for me. Helene's cousin had two kids that she was able to keep with her. This sounded wonderful to me.

I was on fire to figure out how I could earn enough to get us both to Tucson. I asked Helene if her cousin had a phone and could I call her.   Helene said sure. She said her cousin's name was Patsy Benton and she gave me her phone number. I used part of my bus money and I called her.

She gave me information about how to get this kind of job.   And she even knew about a new situation coming up because she knew somebody else who was asking if anybody was interested in managing some rentals over by A Mountain.   Wow!   Was I interested.   She said she would call Helene back in a few days and let me know.

It took three long days, while I thought of nothing else. By now you had croup.   I needed medicine I could not buy, I was barely able to buy milk and food you would eat. You only wanted milk and some mashed fruits and vegetables.   I owed money on the room we were in and the landlady said she was sympathetic to my problem, but I still could not stay there for free.

Patsy called and said her boss had talked to the man with the rentals and he would not only hire me but he would send me a bus ticket to a Tucson. I said, yes, yes, yes!   Within a week we were on our way to Tucson.

Patsy met me at the bus station. It did not take long to figure out that August in Arizona was different than any climate I had ever been in. But I could deal with anything if I was going to have a place to live with you and a salary. Patsy chattered on showing me different landmarks as we drove toward north Tucson. We drove down a wide avenue called Speedway. She pointed out the University of Arizona, as we went further north, the houses and businesses became fewer. But much of the area reminded me of California. Same palm trees, many of the same flowering plants, same cactus, just a lot more of it. Much of the architure looked the same, especially the small business. But for some reason the sort of fake Spanish Mission style houses had a different look and feel. I could not have said why but the houses seemed smaller and less substantial.

We drove into an area that had houses that all looked the same. They were not Spanish style, they were square and boxy, stucco walls, red tile roofs and all painted the same pale cream. But it was all very clean and pleasant. Little grassed front yards, tiny little hedges under big picture windows and carports filled with cars, trucks and kid's toys. We went to the end one which turned out to be the office.

The man sitting behind the desk was 40ish, pleasant looking, and immediately I felt this was a man who cared about people. Warm hazel eyes set in a face with a firm jaw, with dark auburn hair. "And who might this little charmer be?", and he reached out for you, and you, who never went to strangers, put out your arms and dove for him.

He held you though the entire interview, if that is what it was. He told me about his business and what would be expected of me. He said that he had several business, some of which were not in Arizona that required him to travel. He needed someone in the office full time to meet the needs of all of the renters. Somebody had to be able to call a plumber in an emergency or deal with any other problem. He gave me a list of people that I would need to know about and then he said, "I am going to show the rest of your place, then you can freshen up a little..

The office was one of the houses, but the living room had been made into the office. But there were two bedrooms, a kitchen and a bathroom and it was clean. Best of all there was a little back yard and a small patio with a wooden table and benches. I was in heaven. This was the first place that was mine. We would be snug as two bugs in a rug.

215

Mr. Rayburn put on his Stetson, and as he sailed out the door, said, "Sharon, I will be back in couple of hours, I have some chores to do, then we will take our little walk and meet the renters."

He left and I walked around what was now our place. Suddenly I realized how tired I was. I pushed the bed against the wall, put you between me and the wall and we both fell asleep.

The door bell rang. I had a doorbell! I went to the door and Mr. Rayburn and another man started bringing in some bags and boxes. He had bought a crib, a little metal stroller and a high chair. And the bags had clothes for you and groceries for both of us.

I was so stunned but I squeaked out, "Mr. Rayburn, why are you doing this? You just met me and Deirdre.

"Well, Sharon, first of all, call me Harrison. Then you need to know that I am a very selfish man. I have a goal to help those who need my help because it pleases me to do so. That is how I leave my mark on the world. I heard about your situation and I thought, here are two people that need that "Harrison Help". Someday you will do the same for somebody else. You came in with two little ol' suitcases and it was clear you needed this. It is not much but it is a start. The baby is too big to make a bed in a drawer and I was afraid she might take off on you because it is very clear this is an amblin' little one. After she outgrows everything, just pass it on. That'l make me happy too."

"George, here, is our handyman, he fixes what he can, and he takes care of the outside. He is going to help you until you understand everything. I will be back in every few days and you let me know what you need." With that he started to leave and you wanted to go with him.

Over the next several months, he came to the office and it was clear he was not there to see me or give me any further instructions. It was to see you. The two of you bonded completely and you cried every time he left. I did not know whether to be happy or jealous of your feelings for this very good man.

One day, he asked me if I would like to take any classes for anything. I said, "Classes for what?" He continued, "Classes for something you think you might like to do that could get you a real job that could help you for the future. You have that bookkeeping experience from your job in California, now you need to learn more so that you can get a better job than you have here." I had really never thought about that. I told him that I would think about it and tell him what I wanted to do the next time I saw him.

When he came back, I was ready.   I told him that I knew I was very good with math and figures for bookkeeping and I would like to learn how to do more with that.   He said "Fine, I will work on it."

"But, what about Deidre?"

Harrison looked thoughtful, "What about letting me and my wife take care of her during the week? I will bring her back on the weekends.

I don't think that he had an ulterior motive about taking you then.   I think he just thought it was good for everybody.   I also do not think he ever foresaw what Ida would be like with you.   He was so crazy about you that he thought she would be too.

The rest of the story is pretty simple if you do not count all the heartache it caused.

I went to school. The Rayburns kept you more and more. When you were with me you cried and by now you were calling him Dada and you would cry yourself to sleep saying, "Dada" over and over. I felt that I was depriving you of a good life.   And the more I thought about it the more I could see that your future was so much brighter with them than it was if I kept you with me.   I knew that I had no future that would let you be in a secure home.   I knew that Ida did not work.   I thought it was the ideal situation. A mother, father in a safe, loving home.

I did not know Ida very well.   I am sorry now that I did not spend more time getting to know her.   Maybe it would have changed my decision, I don't know.

One day, Harrison said that he had a question for me.   He wanted me to take my time giving him an answer. I knew what he would ask before he asked me.   I had already been thinking about it.   But I took a week.   At the end of the week I could not think of one reason except being selfish about it. I had the opportunity to give you a life with this wonderful man that so clearly loved you and you loved him. I could think of many reasons that I should. They had a beautiful home in the foothills, I knew that you would have the best care, go to the best schools and have everything that I had not had growing up and could never give you.

To this day, I don't know if I did the right or the wrong thing.   I don't even think you can know this either. Maybe someday when you have children of your own you will be able to say if it was a good thing or if it was a bad decision.

I see the relationship that the two of you have and how you have turned out. You are thriving. And you will do wonderful things in your future.   You have strength, courage, and you have emotional resourses that I have never had.   I know you judge me now. But I hope in the future you can understand that I did what I did because I tried to do what was right for you.   I will never be able to tell you how much it ripped out my heart. I have not spent a day, agonizing over that decision. Someday, when you are older, have children of your own, I hope we can talk about this again. There is so much more, but the rest will have to wait.

Sharon ended her story here.

I did not press her for more information because I really had a lot to think about as it was.   I really do not know if she gave me away for what was best for me or for what was best for her. I hope I can figure it out in the future.   But I do know I am glad she did. I think I would be much different if I had not had Harrison in my life.

I am glad that I went to New York. I am glad that I had that time to get to know Sharon a little more and to hear more of the story. Writing it all down has been a big help too.

Mrs. Mason said something the other day that really caused me to think about the situation.   She is really good at seeing things clearly.   She said "Rox, you do not realize it but Ida has made you stronger and for the rest of your life you will have an appreciation for other people's problems that many, maybe even most, people do not possess.

So for now, I am glad that things have worked out the way they have.

July 27

Mary Jane and I had planned to start working on getting ready for the summer rodeos.   But El Con is favoring his right foreleg. So right now all my time and concern are for El Con. Joe said that he had been "walking on egg shells". So of course that meant that he was having some sort of hoof or leg problem.

Joe called Dr. Fedders, the vet that Brownie uses too.

Doc said that El Con has a hoof problem.   I had also been worried because El Con had started limping and when I was checking him I saw a tiny hoof lesion. Doc took some scrapings and said he will know more by tomorrow or the next day.

Aug 1

El Con is not acting like himself. He seems to have no energy and now it is very clear that he is favoring that leg.

Aug 2

218

Been in the barn with El. Doc has been coming and going. He has diagnosed El's problem as laminitis. Now El is shifting his weight off his front legs and extending them.

I had heard about laminitis but I really did not know much about it. So Doc gave me a very quick crash course. Turns out this is pretty nasty stuff. I actually had to write down what he said because most of the terms that he used were new to me.

Doc said that laminitis is a vascular disease that goes with ischemia or hemostasis and has to do with the laminae of the hoof. This laminae is what secures the coffin bone to the hoof wall. If it gets inflamed and cannot be fixed, the coffin bone could become detached from the horny wall. It could sink or "founder".

This will sound really silly of me, but I have just never thought of El Con being sick. He has been one of those outrageously healthy beasts and has never had any of the normal problems even. I am scared out of my mind. But Doc said that because he has such a strong constitution he should be able to be treated successfully.

So please, let this be true. I just can't handle being without him. He is so much a part of me and what keeps me grounded and gives me solace and I guess I could go on forever about that but for now I will just use all the resources for "making things better" that I can think of.

Joe helped me make a bed with two bedrolls and he scrounged up three pillows. Brownie sent down some clean blankets so I am all set. It should only be for a couple of more days anyway.

Aug 3

Sometime during the night El woke me up by going down in a thump. It was as if he just felt that his legs could no longer hold him up. And when I felt him, he had a fever. The hoof had been very hot last night and Doc F. said that was from the infection.

Now I see this is beyond what I had hoped would be the outcome. He has really gotten much worse in such a short space of time. Doc said he is doing everything he can. I believe him. Unfortunately I am questioning everything else in life. Right now I would bargain to be the best, most perfect person just to put this right.

Aug 4

Doc F. was here just after 6 AM. Thank goodness. He has started El on some very strong medicine mix to control the fever.

Dad was questioning how this could happen so fast and what could have caused it. Doc said that it can even be caused by a difference in diet and that El may have found something different that he had eaten when he was out of the barn and by himself.

Dad had brought out doughnuts, biscuits and sausage and strawberries in cream. I know he is trying so hard to help.

"Rox, Honey bun, you have to eat. It is not going to help El if you make yourself sick. If you are going to stay out here I have to know that you are eating."

And he kept talking about the coming school year and other stuff but I finally said, "Dad, I don't want to talk. Just let me spend this time with him" He gave me a long, sad look, "I will be up at the house with Brownie."

Dad had barely left and Joe came into the stall. El did not move but just watched me with a look that clearly said he did not understand why this was happening to him. I have never felt so helpless. To love a creature so much who has loved you and yet not be able to take away the pain is horrible. Even worse, to know the inevitable. I have been around these animals too long not to know what can happen.

Joe sat down by me on the bedroll. "Roxie Girl, you need to get away for a few minutes. You have not left here for three days. You are even using the barn outhouse and we all know how you feel about that. Go up to the house and get a shower. You look horrible and you don't smell much better. Go take a walk, or better yet, take Topper out and get a quick ride. I promise I will stay until you get back."

I shook my head, talking just seemed to take too much effort. I gave him a light punch on his arm and he surprised my by grabbing me and giving me a big bear hug.

"OK, but let me go get you some clean clothes. How about I make you a soda bucket? I will get a block of ice in town when I go get you some clothes. I'll call Gretchen and she can get you some clean levis and a shirt."

Joe left and in minutes, Wade came in. It was turning into a parade.

"Gosh, Wade, is it your turn to babysit?"

Wade did not do a very good job of acting innocent. "Nah, I'm just using this for an excuse to get off ol' June Bug. I been ridin' fence for three days and my back side's askin' my legs to do some work.

"Oh, Wade, I'm so sorry, you are doing my job!"

"Rox, my girl, I ain't complainin'. We all do what needs doin'. I just want to know you are both gettin' on OK. Listen, my Junie got lame, you 'member? Everybody thought she was a goner. She went down, stayed down two days and alls the sudden, she stands up and she come back and now she nigh perfect. With horses, you never know what's going to happen. With cows its different. Cow goes down, its done for. But I seen horses get right fixed just one step away from the glue factory. Oh, Honey, I'm sorry, I shouldn't say that. But you know what I mean."

"Wade, I know. And I appreciate how much you all care. Now go tell the rest of the guys, I am fine. I'll yell if I am not."

Now Wade reached over and gave me a very quick hug. Boy, talk about mixed emotions, I loved that they cared so much, but their concern also told me that I was right that things were bad and getting worse.

Both El and I slept fitfully for a couple of hours. I woke up each time he had tried to move. I could feel him trying to make his body do what he wanted it to do. He couldn't.

Joe came back with my clothes, a bucket full of chopped ice and Cokes and Nehi orange sodas. He had a bag with two hamburgers and a mountain of fries. We had a nice lunch sitting side by side on little bedrolls. After we ate, Joe and I just sat there, I leaned my head on his shoulder and we did not talk, he just let me stay quiet and I knew both of us were remembering all the times with El over the years. Finally, I told him that I was fine, I knew he had stuff to do.

"Roxie, girl, tell me what you need before I get back to work."

I asked him to go get me two buckets of clean water, a bar of soap, and a couple towels.

When he brought them back I asked him to stand "guard" while I cleaned up. He went out and I cleaned up as well as I could, then put on the clean clothes. Then I stretched out by El and we took another short nap.

I pushed my makeshift bed over to El and I have spent the rest of the day laying next to him with my body stretched out along his back. James came out and we have taken turns trying to cool him down with wet cloths. But his temp has just kept climbing.

James went inside and talked to Dad who had not left Brownie's all day. He asked Dad if it was OK if he stayed in the Barn. Dad said he thought it was a good idea.

The vet came back out and said things were not getting better. Dad and Brownie came out and now we were all taking turns keeping El cool and trying to make him comfortable. Horrible sounds were coming from him and long deep shudders.

I wanted to stay tight against him but was afraid of making him too hot so I laid as close as I could. I knew that he could feel that it was my touch. I kept rubbing his neck in that special sweet spot that he always liked.

I just could not sleep. Joe had put bed rolls in the next stall for Dad and who ever else was holding vigil. Dad and Brownie had put up a makeshift table out of saw horses and boards in the stall and cook kept it loaded up and with food. Cook kept bringing out hot coffee and more food.

If the situation had not been so serious it would have been a perfect part. Good friends together, sharing food, stories and concern for each other. They all love both El Con and me. I felt so much love for them and love for El and fear for what could happen. I was just overwhelmed with emotion. I was afraid if I talked I would start crying and not be able to stop.

The hands were dropping by and checking in and sitting with us in what had now become a "waiting room" stall.

Eventually Dad fell asleep, Brownie went back up to the house. James bunked down on his bedroll a couple of feet away from my goofy bed and he would reach over and pat my hand every so often. He drifted off to sleep and I think El and I slept a patchy sleep. Every sound and move he made woke me up.

At 2:16 in the morning, El's breathing became "different". He was making such an effort. I wrapped myself as tightly to him as I could and told him that he did not have to fight anymore. He had fought like the warrior that he was.

He sighed, and shuddered and life left his magnificent body. I could not move. I laid there until the sun was just coming up before I called out to dad to tell him that it was over.

Both Dad and James got up. Dad said, "When did it happen?" I told him and he said, "OK, James, you go on home. She will call you later." I nodded. James held my hand for a minute, kissed me on the top of my head, and he walked slowly out of the barn.

Dad gently pulled me to my feet. "Roxie, you have to go inside. You have done everything you could. Now you have to let me take care of the rest of it. Brownie and I have been talking and we want you to look at a place for him but not until tomorrow. I am going to take care of everything out here. Joe, Wade and I are going to do it right. You don't have to worry."

Just then Joe came in and pulled me out of the barn and walked with me up to the house. Brownie met us at the door. He told Joe to take me into the front bedroom that was faced away from the barn. I didn't understand why I had not cried yet. I just felt hollow. I could not breathe and my head was splitting open.

Brownie's cook brought me a bowl of ice and she was soaking wash cloths in the ice water and telling me to put it on my face. Suddenly the door to the room opened and Doc Harlan was there.

"OK, girl who thinks she is Wonder Woman, I am going to help. He gave me a shot of something, and the rest of the day was a merciful blur.

And the next was almost the same. I slept for most of it. In the middle of the next night, I got up and went out to the barn. I don't know why, but it was almost to the minute when I had lost him.

I stood in the stall and now the tears came. Floods. I couldn't stop, I couldn't breathe, and then I was screaming. Joe got there first, then Wade, some of the other hands, and then there was Dad, Brownie and even Brownie's cook. Joe looked ashen. The rest did not look much better. Dad kept saying "It's OK, It's OK, Don't Cry." Joe pushed Dad away and spoke in a quiet but very firm voice, "Harrison, leave her alone. She needs this. Better this than keeping it all in." I sank down to El's spot. I could still smell his wonderful clean horse smell. Joe brought me his bridle and put it in my hands.

He said firmly, OK, let's all go outside. She is fine in here. And they all left. I don't know how long I stayed. Finally, still clutching his bridle, I walked out, Joe was leaned against the fence and he walked me back up to the house and did not say a word. Wonderful, understanding Joe. Always knowing just what I need.

Dad asked if I wanted to go home or stay at Brownies. I said "Let's go home."

James called daily. We chatted briefly but he got that I was not ready to see him or anybody else.

I never knew there could be grief like this. I alternated between gut deep pain and feeling as if there was a huge hollow hole in my chest and wanting to run screaming. But I did not know where I could run to. For so many of my growing up years, when I had a problem or was hurting or sad, I had been able to go to El Con, saddle up and he would put me back together piece by piece.

Who was going to put me back together now? I had thought I had been hurt by Ida with the name calling and what she had done when she hurt me or destroyed what belonged to me. Now I knew that was nothing. Nothing! This hurt did not go away. It just seemed to keep burning bigger.

I was not able to go with Dad and Brownie to pick out the place for him. I knew the place they were talking about and it would be fine. So they made all the plans and they buried him. It was nine days before I could go out to his resting place.

It is the highest spot on Brownie's ranch. It is a small mesa ridge but there must be some underground water because of the trees. It has lush walnut and fragrant peach trees. So there is shade. Joe and Wade had made a beautiful mesquite bench. Somebody had gone to Tucson and gotten grass. The kind that comes in squares and you put over dirt and it makes a beautiful, instant green lawn. And flowers. This will be a wonderful, peaceful place to come to visit him. Wade does great carvings and he has already started one of El Conquistador.

I know gut deep that this is a grief that will never leave me. Joe says that I have to turn all of these memories to positive ones. I have the feeling that he has had his own "griefs" and he has learned to do this. For the first time I also have a deeper understanding about the way that Dad feels about Ida. No matter what she has done or what has happened he really loves her. I hope that will make it easier for me to understand why he kept bringing her back home. I get that he is having such a hard time living without her. And he made the supreme sacrifice to have two homes to keep us separated most of the time.

Dad had gotten my Angel Crew together. Even Mary Jane and her mother. Everyone was there. A real funeral for El Con. I know it was for both of us. I carried his bridle that I had intertwined with white roses and babies breath. And Joe had left a little open hole that I put three of his favorite stall toys into. I sang an Irish lullaby to him, _Toura Lura,_ all of my wonderful people, joined in on the second chorus. El Con had always let me know he loved it when I sang to him and I know that somewhere he hears. Now there is another angel watching out for me.

I pulled the flowers off of the bridle and laid them on the grassy plot. His bridle will hang on my mirror so I see it every day before I even see me. His show bridle. His every day bridle is going to hang in the living room over the fireplace. Dad is going to ask Ted to do a portrait of El. But he might not. I know he has been asked before and has refused. But he knows other artists and we can get one of them to paint the portrait.

Everybody left except for James. We sat on El Con's bench until sunset, not talking, just being there. It was mid-August but there had been enough rain to keep down the worst of the heat. I don't think we really paid attention anyway.

As we walked back down what was now called El Con's Mesa, James asked me if I would let him make a wood and silver plaque for his resting place. I told him I thought that was a thoughtful, tender idea.

August 22

I told Dad I did not know how I would start school. We had a very long talk.

"My Baby Girl, I know you don't know how you will do it. But you will do it. It is what is best for you and what is best for the healing. If you let this take you down, you will never get up. You can remember what you had with him and have it be positive. Or you can let this determine how you are going to live your life, or not live it. Turn it around, how much do you think he loved you? What did he want from you?"

'You gave him the best life any horse could have. You were there at the minute that life left him. His last thought would have been of you. Of course you will never forget him. But you can't stop your life. I wish I could tell you that you will never have to go through this again. I wish I could wrap you up and shelter you from anything that could hurt you. I want to make your life better."

"I have let you down in the past. All I can tell you now is that I will make life as good for you as I can. And I will never let you be hurt again by by my failure if I have a choice. But I can not fix everything. It is all part of life. Humans understand life and death. And grief. But the living must keep living and making life better for themselves and for others.

"You will make mistakes. But you will pick yourself up. There is a song you sang at one of the school programs. *Pick your self up, dust your self off, start all over again.*

"I have always seen people fall into one of two groups. Those who pick themselves up and go on to make things better and those who do not. They let life beat them down."

"Learn from your mistakes and go on. Just as long as you remember that you are going to be a person who makes the world a better place you will be fine, even better than fine."

"And Roxie, guess what? I have left the best thing for now. Brownie and I have an idea. We have been cooking up a plan. While Doc F was here last, he told us about a round up of mustangs. Some ranchers have been shooting them and getting

225

rid of them in other ways.   So Brownie said, he could take a big
section of the west side of the ranch and we can see how many we
can rescue and they will   be safe and they can run free in a
protected area.   They won't be ridden or broken, they can still run
free They will   just have a little smaller space.   People can also
bring them to the sanctuary.   There are already hands from three
ranches who are going to donate time for the project.   The very
best part?   How do you like the name EL CON'S MUSTANGS
RUNNING FREE?   Or change the name if you want."

"Don't worry about it now.   We are still setting up the plan.   But
it is a start."

Dad was right.   It was a new beginning.   I was a ranch kid.   I
knew I would always have a connection to the land. To horses. To
the people who cared for everything connected caring for this land.
In a while I would be ready for a new horse to nurture and to
nurture me.   I didn't know how long it would be.   But that was OK.
I had all kinds of new beginnings going on.   Grief may not have an
ending but I know, even at my age, that it will get better.   El is there
still squeezing my shoulder or nudging my back and nobody or no
event can take away those memories and those feelings.   Another
Angel.

Sept 5, 1955

Dear Diary, I am going to start my school year at the University
of Arizona in a few days.

So I will start a new journal with the college years.   As I write
this, it occurs to me that our stories are all on going and that we do
not really finish a story.   We just continue on the journey bringing
the past with us.

So I have a plan.   I will do the very best that I can do.

Maybe Sharon and I will have a chance to make a new part of the
story.

I am going to finish school.   I am going to live with Dad and
commute back and forth to Tucson.   I just can't leave him to rattle
around in that big house alone.

James and I have a plan too.   But that is a long way away.   Dad
says we need a plan to achieve goals but that things happen and
sometimes we have to allow for life.

All I know for sure is that I am very fortunate to have all of my
Angel Crew.   They have enriched my life.   They have been there
for all of the times, good, bad and everything in between.

Thank you my angels.   You know who you are.

Epilogue

March 12, 2010

Well, Dear Diary, as you can see, a few years have passed. Quite a few! Fifty-five years to be exact.

My granddaughter came to me the other day and said, "Grandma Walker, Mom just told me that you kept a diary during high school. Is that true?

I grinned at this beautiful, sweet, chatty child who seemed to be my clone, "Yes, Roxanne, my little namesake, I did." "Why?

"Oh, because I want to read it, can I, can I? Mom said that you said I could when I was fifteen. And I am fifteen and two months. Is Grandpa in it? I want to read about all of that. Mom told me some but said the diaries explain a lot. You wrote two diaries didn't you? One for high school and one for college clear up until you became a judge. Didn't you?

"Well, Miss Smarty Pants, if you know so much why do you need to read them?"

"Oh, Grandmother, I soooooooo want to read them!"

"OK, Roxie Girl, I'll tell you what. I would like to read them myself. I will read the first one and I will give it to you on my birthday. This somehow seems like the perfect time."

My birthday arrived and I gave Roxanne the first of the diaries. This will explain much of the family history to her.

Over the past years, which have flown by in the blink of an eye, much has changed. But then, again, much has stayed the same.

My angel crew not only got me through my growing years, college, law school and more, they are still there. They guide and protect me every day.

My beloved father, was there and is there still. He is there every time I make a decision that involves the lives of the families who come before my court. His legacy is that of selfless devotion to all of those he cared about. His charities and good works are still reverberating to this day.

He bought a house in Tucson so that I would not have to commute while I was going to school. We lived in that house until

227

the day that I married James.   Dad moved into the house that James and I built, the house where we raised a family.   A very happy house that we live in to this day.

My beloved father died in 1966. A loss I feel to this day.

Pug continued her own brand of good works until she left us in 1982.   She continued many of Dad's charities as well as her own personal ones.

Joe and Brownie died within months of each other.   Brownie left his ranch to a wonderful organization in Tucson, The Equine Friends. They work with children with disabilities. And many of the angel crew have continued to work with this group as well as recruiting new angels that keep this legacy going.   I know it will go on long after all of us are gone.

Mrs. Mason just left us in 2001.   Mr. Bertram went on to teach for the organization for International Exchange Teachers and became a director. I had not realized that when we were in high school, he had only been in his early twenties. We were his first students. His influence is still being felt in all of the new teachers and programs that he inspired.

One of the important pieces for me has been the knowledge that each child in the world does not just go from infancy to a full grown adult without many influences. Sometimes we do not know what kind of impact this will be.   It does take a village to raise a child.   I had a wonderful village.

Each child reacts and grows and will thrive with nurturing. For some children, something is not nurtured or cared for and another human being slips through the cracks in the societal fabric.

I am even grateful to Ida.   Yes, I have forgiven her and I have even been able to understand and feel incredible sorrow that she was one of the ones who really did not get what she needed. What could have been different and helped her I do not know.

Because of Ida, I have much more under-standing of many of the diverse issues that come before me as a judge.   She was as much a victim as I was, possibly more. It has taken society and the judicial system many years to understand mental illness.   Sadly, I think we are still a long way from understanding and treatment.

Ida was never able to leave the mental hospital in Tucson. Dad cared for her and was with her as much as her situation would allow until her death in 1964.

James went on to become a football coach for the U of A.   I earned my law degree in 1958. We married in 1960. And we are still as much enamored of each other as we were so very long ago.

I think we have outlasted so many of the other couples because we did take our time. We were friends who fell in love. That makes all the difference.

I have been in family court for twenty-six years. I am trying to carry on the legacy that was given to me by Dad, Joe, Pug, Brownie, Mrs. Mason, Mr. Bertram, and so many more.

I think about El Con, Pudgy and Fala every day. I have had other horses, other pets, but these were the ones who nurtured me into adulthood. I know they are in that pet heaven watching over me and mine.

Stories about the children and the grandchildren will have to be in the next diary. Another constant my life has been my diaries. Now there are eleven of them. Wait until Roxie hears that!

Writing in the diaries has been my private time, my way of reviewing my world, my ideas and my feelings. James has read them. My daughters have read them. And now a new generation will begin to read them. Life goes on. My children had their own angel crew as do their children.

And my circle of angels

are dancing on sun split clouds........

Made in the USA
Lexington, KY
05 July 2011